# HIGH PRAISE FOR L. J. McDONALD

## *THE BATTLE SYLPH*

"Lovers of *Stardust* and *The Princess Bride* rejoice! A must for every Fantasy library."
—Barbara Vey, blogger, *Publishers Weekly*

"Refreshingly different, with an almost classic fantasy flavor . . . an exceptional literary debut."
—John Charles, reviewer, *Chicago Tribune* and *Booklist*

"A fresh new voice in fantasy romance . . . I loved the characters and mythology!"
—A~~~~~~~~~~~~~~~~~~~~~~~~~~~~uthor of
~~~~~~~~~~~~~~~~~~~~~~~~~rkness

"An exciting n~~~~~~~~~~~~~~~~~~~~~~~~~~guchi, Borders
~~~~~~~~ce expert and bookseller

"A fabulous read, cover to cover."
—C. L. Wilson, *New York Times* bestselling author

"Unlike anything I've ever read. A brilliant adventure with tremendous heart. You'll love this book."
—Marjorie Liu, *New York Times* bestselling author

"A remarkable new voice and a stunningly original world. . . . An amazing start to what promises to be a truly engaging series!"
—Jill M. Smith, reviewer, *RT Book Reviews*

# ABDUCTED!

"Are you a virgin? Girl!" Lizzy's eyes opened after a sudden slap. "Are you a virgin?"

"Y-yes."

"At least they'll like that." The woman sighed. "If Eighty-nine goes for her first, though, just pull her out. I don't want him killing another girl."

"You can't do this!" Lizzy gasped. They started to haul her forward and she balked, trying to brace her bare feet on the slippery floor. "I won't go!"

"Shut it, girl!" the woman snapped. "The only reason you keep your tongue in there is because some of the battlers like the screaming."

Other *Leisure* Books by L. J. McDonald:

**THE BATTLE SYLPH**

# L. J. McDONALD

## THE SHATTERED SYLPH

LEISURE BOOKS　　　NEW YORK CITY

*To Oliver, for encouraging me in writing this book,
and for Chris, for making it better.*

*Also for, and he knows why:
The Bad Man*

A LEISURE BOOK®

April 2010

Published by

Dorchester Publishing Co., Inc.
200 Madison Avenue
New York, NY 10016

Copyright © 2010 by L. J. McDonald

Cover art by Anne Cain.

ISBN 10: 0-8439-6323-9
ISBN 13: 978-0-8439-6323-6
E-ISBN: 978-1-4285-0837-8

Printed in the United States of America.

10 9 8 7 6 5 4 3 2 1

Visit us online at www.dorchesterpub.com.

# THE SHATTERED SYLPH

# Prologue

A man known for crudity and violence, Cherod Mash came to Sylph Valley looking for a drink, a fight, and a tickle, in any order he could get them. Mostly, however, he came as one of the drovers of a trade caravan willing to give the new kingdom a try.

The place was said to have money—gems and metals dug from the heart of the world by sylphs. But no sylph could make those things into anything useful. For that, artisans were needed, and Cherod drove a wagon piled high with woven carpets and other crafted commodities from the southern kingdom of Yed. These had been commissioned for a good weight of those gems he'd heard about, and once the trade was complete, the caravan would continue through the mountains to Para Dubh and see if maybe they could buy some even more valuable goods brought across the sea from Meridal, which they'd take home and sell for tremendous profit.

Not that the logistics really mattered to Cherod. He left that kind of thinking to his employer and focused on driving his oxen—at least until they reached a town where there was beer to drink, fights to start, and women to bed. He'd never been to Sylph Valley, but from what he'd heard it was chock full of whores. He'd even heard they slept with the sylphs, which made no sense to him. Those damn things weren't even solid most of the time.

The convoy arrived in the Valley in late afternoon, the oxen blowing and men shouting over the creaking of the wagons. Yelling at his own beasts, Cherod guided them through the streets in the direction a local had pointed the boss, to a huge building towering over everything else at the end of the street. It didn't look like any warehouse Cherod had ever seen before, though. It was made from a solid piece of stone, veins of metal running through it like some sort of disease. It loomed before them, its front a massive door that stood open.

The buildings they passed to get there were exactly the same in that they were all totally unique. Cherod saw shops where the walls were transparent or where the roof reached into the sky a dozen or more stories. The roads were smooth stone, the sidewalks raised, and every block had a stairwell leading underground. To see people going in and out by way of those stairs was bizarre. What kind of man lived underground, or in a building that looked like the wind could knock down? All of the buildings seemed almost sickeningly fragile. The whole place might fall on you! Better was a proper house made of wood or stone, with a real thatched roof.

Still, he thought, this place mightn't be so bad. He watched a trio of women cross the street, darting past his wagon while the way was clear. They were laughing over something, their faces bright with smiles. One of them even wore pants like a man, and Cherod appreciatively regarded the place where her legs met her body. They had to be whores to dress like that.

An earth sylph trundled past, looking like a little mud-shaped girl. Cherod gave it a quick look, but otherwise kept his eyes on the women. He whistled at them. They looked back but kept walking, giggling. He grinned. This would be a good night.

Ahead, the wagons turned to pass through a wide door-way leading into the warehouse. Standing by the door, a fat man with sweat on his face gestured them all inside, shouting for them to pull to the right, for the gods' sake, pull to the right or there'd be no room for them to get their wagons out.

Cherod turned his wagon with the others, still thinking of those women, and nearly ran into the wall. The fat foreman screeched and Cherod swore, yanking the reins hard to the side to steer his oxen. They bellowed in protest and turned, the wagon wheels scraping the wall but finding clearance. That made Cherod forget about women; the boss would have his hide if he scratched the paint on those damned wheels.

Just inside the warehouse, a dark-haired man stood with his arms crossed, watching. He was dressed in blue trousers and a long blue coat edged with gold trim. Cherod's first thought was that he was a lord, but the boss had said this place didn't *have* lords. His second instinct was that the man was the law.

As the wagon rolled past him, the blue-coated man looked up but didn't say anything. Cherod kept staring forward. He'd spent far too many nights in lockup, and the boss had warned he'd be fired if it happened again. Cherod instead drove the wagon to the rear of the warehouse, where the first was already stopped. Another door loomed beyond, one for them to drive out of once they unloaded, and the entire ceiling was made of glass, letting in more than enough sunlight to see. It was a nice setup, if a bit unnerving. Usually he'd have to unload his damn cargo outside, no matter what the wind or rain.

What was even nicer was that air sylphs were doing the unpacking. Cherod couldn't see them, but carpets and other goods were flying off the wagons, vanishing among huge shelves while Cherod's boss screamed at the foreman over how much was there and in what condition.

Stretching his back, Cherod climbed down and walked over to the next wagon. There, Frem was watching the sylphs with his mouth hanging open. Cherod grinned. "Not bad, eh?"

"Yeah," Frem agreed, his mouth still agape. "Wish we got this everywhere. Damn, this place is different."

"Yep. Can't wait to see what the women are like."

"I think I'm afraid to know," Frem admitted.

In all, it only took ten minutes to unload everything, which to Cherod's mind made it a record. Even better, it was still too late to start off again before morning. While the boss was too much the skinflint to pay for rooms—he was of the opinion that his men could sleep just as well under their wagons—this meant they'd have the evening to themselves. They just had to make sure they were back before the convoy left.

They'd also been paid since the last stop. Cherod had coin in his pocket and a powerful urge to drink.

"Want to go find a tavern?" he asked Frem. It was always good to have a buddy along, mostly on the theory that he could be convinced to buy a few rounds.

Frem shook his head. "Sorry, I'm gonna get a bath and some sleep."

Coward. He just didn't like Cherod's reputation. Cherod himself didn't really mind, though. He was more interested in a different kind of company tonight. "Your loss," he grunted.

The boss waved them all over. A huge man who'd been a drover for thirty years, Thul Cramdon was one of the few men Cherod respected; Thul had nearly broken his hand for throwing a drunken punch. The boss was fairly open-minded, though, willing to have a drink himself and not caring what Cherod did, so long as he wasn't late and didn't cost Thul any money.

"There's a place we can store the wagons and oxen for tonight," Thul told them. "We get paid on the morrow, then we're out of here." He scratched his hairy chin. "Foreman here says there's a hotel of sorts down the road with a bar. Y' can stay there if you want, but it's right expensive." There were groans at that. "Otherwise, the blacksmith lets men sleep in the loft of his barn for a penny." That sounded better, though Cherod didn't really like picking hay out of his clothes. "Only other thing he said was, 'Leave the sylphs alone, leave the women alone, 'less they say otherwise, and stay the hell away from the men in blue and gold.' That's it. Settle yer animals and be back at dawn."

The men obeyed, discussing what they'd do while they drove their wagons out of the warehouse, following the boss to the empty lot provided for storage. A large paddock nearby was good for the animals. Cherod didn't join their conversation. He was going to find that bar—and as for a place to stay, women had rooms, didn't they? He'd just sack out with whoever took him home.

Waving at the others, he headed out and down the street, passing other warehouses and places to buy or repair farming equipment. All of the buildings had the same oddly organic look. More, everything seemed to be laid out according to some master plan . . . and it didn't take him long to realize that most of the buildings were going unused. It seemed crazy to build a bunch of places before you needed them, but he supposed if you had a whole bunch of sylphs to do the work, there was no harm done.

It didn't take him long to find the tavern the boss mentioned. The rooms above were overpriced, but the drinks were plentiful and cheap. The beer was made by a water sylph, the barman told him proudly—which explained the weird aftertaste. It was still pretty good beer, but unnatural.

The whole place was. Cherod had never seen so many sylphs as he had on the walk over. There were three in the bar itself, with the owner's water sylph washing glasses when she wasn't mixing hops, malt and water in midair. She looked like some sort of freaking kid, except kids weren't see-through.

Cherod didn't much care for her. More interesting was how there were two barmaids, one of whom was fat and middle-aged, while the other was much younger and pretty. They both carried drinks and bowls of stew to customers, chattering with the men as much as serving them. This meant Cherod had to get his first beer from the barman, but he took this time to watch, downing the mug and gesturing for another.

"Might want to slow down a bit," the barman laughed. "Pond puts more oomph in her beer than most folks. It's stronger than it looks."

"Just pour," Cherod growled. He drank half the results in a single gulp and gestured toward the younger woman with the stein. "She available?"

The barman blinked. "Cherry? Nah, she don't date customers."

Why not, with a name like that? Cherod smirked and drained his beer, slamming it down in front of the barman, who shrugged and filled it again, but with the warning, "I'd leave her alone. She's quick to yell for help."

That sounded even more interesting. After Thul nearly broke his hand, Cherod hadn't got into any fights with his fellow drovers, and fighting was his favorite hobby, next to drinking and whoring. "I'll take that under advisement," he told the barman, and lurched off his stool, swaying for a moment. "Shit, this stuff *is* strong."

"Told you."

Cherod ignored him, lurching across the floor toward

Cherry. She had her back to him, chatting with some stupid customer who'd brought his wife to the bar and was ordering dinner. The barman, realizing what Cherod intended, shouted for him to stop, but Cherod flung an arm around the maid, his hand latching onto her breast.

"Hey, girl," he slurred. "Let's go find someplace we can get naked."

Cherry screamed, trying to pull away, but Cherod just laughed, tightening his grip and taking another swallow from his mug. The barman was shouting for him to let go, rushing around the side of the bar, but he was a skinny little nothing, and everyone else was staring in shock. As if none of them would ever grab a whore for a tickle!

"You wanna try something?" he sneered at the barman, his grip tightening on the girl's breast until she started to cry. "Stop yer bitchin'," he snapped at her. "You know you want it."

The door crashed open. Immediately, all of the patrons turned white, scrambling out of their chairs and shoving each other as they fled to the back of the establishment. The barman went with them, while his water sylph gave a bizarre shriek and vanished, leaving her half-made beer to splash on the floor. The other sylphs who'd been wandering around vanished as well, or stood between their masters and the door.

Surprised, Cherod turned, Cherry swinging around with him. She saw who was there and started sobbing, reaching out.

The man in the blue and gold from the warehouse was entering the bar, his face so devoid of expression that Cherod hesitated before he started to laugh. From the look of it, he outweighed the newcomer by a hundred pounds or more, and the blue-coated fool didn't have a weapon.

"You have to be joking," he laughed.

A second man came in, then a third and fourth. In all, seven men in blue and gold entered, none of them speaking as they spread out to fill the bar. They advanced.

These weren't odds Cherod liked, but from experience, the worst he would get was a lump on the head and a night in jail. He glared, though, seeing his job leaving in the morning without him. Thul wouldn't wait for him again.

"What the hell's wrong with you?" he shouted. "Who gives a shit about some slut barmaid?" Somewhere behind him, someone groaned.

The men didn't seem to care. "The hive's in danger," one of them said in a soft voice.

"Yes," several more answered.

"The queen gave her permission."

"Oh, yessss."

They all hissed it, the sound continuing after they should have run out of breath, and Cherod looked around at them, suddenly nervous. "Look," he said. "I'm letting her go. See? I'm letting go."

He released Cherry and immediately she ran to the men, still crying. Half of their number converged around her, holding her and actually cooing. The rest kept advancing.

"Look," Cherod said. "I—"

He didn't get to finish. A blast of emotion hit him all at once, focused and deliberate, and he felt his bladder release as his tankard fell to the ground. His eyes widened and he screamed in terror. Hatred that wasn't his filled him, crippling his courage, leaving him shaking and helpless and his heart threatening to burst in his chest. But this didn't last long. The men's focus narrowed and something else came at him, something invisible and very deliberately aimed.

Cherod's right arm blew off at the shoulder. It was the one he'd grabbed the girl with, intending nothing but some harmless fun, though if she felt bad about it in the morning, oh well. He drew breath to scream again, and his left burst off as well. He did scream then, his voice so high-pitched he couldn't recognize it—and then the blue-coated battle sylphs he'd been warned about took off his head.

# Chapter One

The Ceremony of Bringing, as it was called in the jungle kingdom of Yed, was held in a great domed building with spectator seats rising in tiers. For most of the summonings there were only a handful of people watching, but this was a call for a battler and everyone was curious to see the woman die. The seats were full. Another reason for their attraction was the fact that the sacrifice was a voluptuous, soft-eyed blonde, her gaze stupid and uncomprehending even as she was carried in and strapped to the blood-stained altar, the crowd cheering at the sight of her nudity.

The man who'd been chosen to bond the battler she would draw stood at the foot of the altar, waving with a smirk at the crowd. He was dressed in the finest of clothes, a red cloak of silk around his neck despite the heat. He wore sandals on his feet and a thin golden crown on his forehead. He didn't look much brighter than the sacrifice.

Leon stood in the shadow of a servants' passage off the summoning floor. Dressed in a plain linen shift, he carried a covered tray and waited with the rest of the domestics. Once the ceremony was complete, wine and cheese would be served in celebration, though only to the participants. The audience would have to be content with merely watching government-sanctioned murder.

Murder. That was all it was, and it was a type of murder Leon had once engaged in himself, to his eternal sorrow. There were six types of sylph: water, earth, air, fire, healing, and battle. Most were lured through the gate from their own world with simple objects that appealed to their natures. They bonded to the men who called them, forced to forever obey their master's orders and feed from their energy, many even being passed down through generations of a family. The sylphs actually liked the arrangement, being single-minded creatures starved for attention. They received that attention from their masters, along with their binding gifts.

Battlers were different. What appealed to their natures was women, but when *they* came through, the women were killed, leaving the battlers bound unwillingly to murderers who would name them and force them into a lifetime of servitude they couldn't escape until their masters died. Leon had done exactly that, accepting a command to kill a girl in order to gain a battler. In time, he'd learned how wrong that was and what he'd really done to the creature he bound. He'd also learned what the battlers actually wanted, what in Sylph Valley they now got: willing women to be both their masters and their lovers.

In the rest of the world, battle sylphs were rare creatures, hard to control and feared by the populace for their violence and unending hatred. In the Valley, having what they truly desired, they didn't feel hate at all. When Leon had left for this mission, there had been nearly fifty of them—which horrified every other kingdom. Battlers were incredibly destructive, a single sylph able to wipe out entire armies. Not knowing how the Valley did it, their neighbors struggled to increase their own supply of battlers in the traditional, bloody way. The rumors of that happening in Yed were why Leon was here now.

Spread around a summoning circle, priests chanted and swayed, building up the energy needed to open the gate. The circle was already starting to glow, and the low-level prince, who probably never would have received a battler if it weren't for the Valley, raised his arms in triumph. He was almost dancing on the dais, grinning for the crowd the same way he'd been smiling all week, announcing in every bar and marketplace that he was the next chosen, as though there were still anyone who didn't know.

"Don't overdo it," Leon murmured, watching through a lowered brow. He couldn't go out there, though. A single servant would be noticed immediately on the shiny floor, and there were also guards inside, lined up against the back wall.

Above the circle on the dais, a second disk appeared in midair, a portal shining with different colors while the crowd sighed. On the altar, the girl simply blinked up at it, and Leon wondered if she was drugged. She barely re-acted at all as the prince loomed over her, raising his dag-ger high in anticipation.

The chanting grew louder, the disklike gate changing from red to green to blue to black. From there it shifted to a noncolor, and the crowd roared its approval. The prince stared upward, as did his sacrifice.

Everyone held their breath: on the other side of the cir-cle was another world, and something was peering through. An air sylph would be drawn by music, a fire sylph by art, an earth sylph by something being built, and a water sylph by something growing. A healer, the rarest sylph of all, would be drawn by someone needing true healing. But a battler? He would be drawn only by the promise of love—a promise betrayed in the first instant by a killer. Leon burned with the old shame.

It was pure luck whether what you offered would appeal to the sylph on the other side of the gate. Only another sylph could tell what lurked there, and with the exception of those in the Valley, all were bound to silence. Leon had no idea if the right kind of sylph was looking through at all, or if this gift of a woman would be rejected and the summoners would have to try again another day. It could take months or even years to find a battler, no matter what the priests promised. But Leon didn't dare take the chance. The girl hadn't been his mission when he first arrived in Yed, but she was now. Even if this attempt was a failure, he had to get her out.

The prince was yelling in triumph, pumping his arms above his head, and the crowd was cheering again. Something came through the gate, and Leon inhaled as he felt it, for no other sylph radiated this kind of aura. Huge and incorporeal, the battler looked like a black cloud laced with lightning, eyes glowing red, while black wings made of smoke arced out to either side. He came through the gate, cooing lustfully at the girl as she squirmed, staring back up at him. Purring, he reached for her.

"Now!" the lead priest called. "Do it now! Kill her and bind him!"

That's how it was done, how it had always been done. This time, though, the prince threw down the knife and turned. He looked out at the priests, the idiotic happiness gone from his face, and started to change.

"Don't do it," Leon breathed, knowing his partner could hear him.

His words went unheeded, which was no surprise. From face to feet the prince changed, growing taller, his hair lightening to blond, his eyes paling to gray. Anger twisted his expression and hate flared out, the loathing of a battler in a full rage. The priests gaped in momentary shock, the crowds screaming, and then the man thrust out both arms.

A wall of destructive energy flashed forward, slamming into the line of priests with vicious force and turning them into chunks of quivering meat, passing through and slamming into the guards who'd been lining the walls, blowing them backward as well, though by then much of its strength had been spent. In the stands, the crowds screamed in terror, scrambling over each other in their drive to escape. Chaos took control of everything, while on the altar the new battler cooed and tried to figure out how to mount the sacrifice.

Leon yanked the cloth off his tray to show the short sword replacing the cheeses he was supposed to be carrying. The servants with whom he'd been standing had already fled, which was good; he wouldn't have let any of them stop him from running out into the hall, racing on sandaled feet toward the altar.

He was in fantastic shape, but was still forty-seven years old and no match for all those guards that his battler hadn't killed. A few of them looked as though they'd only been stunned, and more would come in response to the fleeing spectators. Ril had managed to kill all of the priests, though. Without them, no more sylphs could be drawn, which meant no more battlers for the kingdom of Yed— which wasn't their mission, but Leon had always been an opportunist, and Solie had admitted that she didn't want them to be a threat anymore.

He reached the dais and altar. On it, the new battler was trying to gnaw through the blonde girl's ropes without hurting her, and Leon had a moment to wonder just how idiotic the thing was. Apparently, shape-shifting into a human form hadn't occurred to him. He was still smoke and lightning, unable to make physical contact.

For now, Leon ignored him. His own battler lay sprawled on the stone at the foot of the dais, one hand trailing on the floor.

"Ril," Leon gasped, kneeling beside him. "Get up."

Ril just groaned. He was a battler, but he'd been injured badly in a fight six years before, only surviving thanks to the efforts of a healer sylph named Luck. His ability to use his own powers was severely restricted as a result. His recognition of those limitations was even more incomplete. Leon never would have brought him, but even if the battler hadn't needed to stay close enough to feed from his energy, Ril had given him no choice, and for the sake of his pride, Leon agreed. Besides, Ril was the only Valley battle sylph with a man for his master except the queen's battler Heyou, who also had a male master, though one even older than Leon and in no way interested in intrigue. To bring a healthy battler along would have meant bringing a female, most of whom were middle-aged widows, and none of whom was prepared for the kind of danger this mission entailed.

But neither was Ril. Leon breathed his sylph's name, shaking his shoulder. "Come on, wake up." He wanted to push his energy at the battler but didn't know how. Half the time he couldn't even feel Ril draining him unless Ril took too much, and for the last six years the sylph hadn't needed much at all.

Up on the altar the new battler screamed in growing disappointment and more than a little desperation. Ril shifted, groaning and opening his eyes. He processed Leon's smile in a daze and pushed himself up onto his hands. "I guess that took a bit much out of me," he admitted.

Leon didn't reply. Just changing shape took nearly everything Ril had, and was excruciatingly painful as well. Leon would have forbade him to do it again if he hadn't sworn never to give the battler another command, and if they hadn't needed him to become the prince to get close to the priests and the girl.

As the only ones in the Valley with any experience at

the job, the two of them had come to gather intelligence on Yed and determine the kingdom's actual threat. They'd already done the same in Para Dubh, and even in their original home of Eferem, where Leon had needed to be very careful while setting up a small spy network, just in case someone recognized him. That had left Ril to do most of the work. They'd spent months at a time away from home on these jobs, but it was necessary. Sylph Valley was a new kingdom with no real allies; they needed all the information they could glean. Battle sylphs were a tremendous equalizer, but there were ways to cripple a kingdom despite them. Ril had just done so, after all.

Their mission had now changed. They had to save that girl, and because she had a battler, she and her sylph had to be taken back to the queen.

Carefully, Leon pulled Ril to his feet. He turned to the altar, very watchful that he made no threatening moves. Battlers didn't generally like men, and if this one felt threatened . . . Then again, the sylph hadn't felt threatened by Ril committing mass murder three feet away.

The girl was staring up at the battler, her chest heaving. She was a gorgeous thing, but from the look in her eyes was either drugged or not terribly smart. Given he was still trying to bite through her bonds, neither was her battler. He could shape-shift into anything he wanted, but all he'd done so far was try to turn into a solid version of himself. That gave him real teeth and a mouth, but he couldn't use them effectively, as he was flopped off the edge of the altar and had no legs.

Slowly, Leon reached out and put his hand on the girl's gag. "Name him," he whispered. That would complete the bond and make her the battler's master. She blinked at him, and he pulled out the gag.

"What?" she gasped.

"Wat," the battler purred.

"Oh, that's just perfect," Ril groused. "And I thought Heyou was a stupid name."

"I gather your kind has its morons, too," Leon commented. Ril just shrugged, watching a few of the guards, who were stirring by the wall.

"Who are you?" the girl whimpered.

"Wat!" Wat said.

"My name is Leon Petrule," Leon told her, cutting her wrists and ankles free from their bonds. Grabbing Ril's cloak, he handed it to her so she could cover herself. "This is Ril. We need to get you out of here."

"Why?" she asked. Her lip was quivering and tears shone in her eyes.

Ril looked over his shoulder at her. "They want to stab a knife in your heart and turn him into a slave." He jutted his chin out at Wat. "Now tell him to make himself look like a human, and both of you come with us."

"We'll take you somewhere safe," Leon added. "You have to trust us."

The girl looked at him uncertainly, and then at Wat. "You can do what they said?"

Wat thought about it. "Yes," he said slowly.

Her eyes lit up. "Oh! Can you look like my first boyfriend?" Ril rolled his eyes, and Leon had to resist the urge to slap a hand over his face.

"He can't look like someone he hasn't seen, girl. Just tell him to look human."

"Oh, okay. Look human."

Wat blinked and shimmered, condensing into an average-looking man, much like one of the bodies lying nearby. Like her, he was completely naked.

"Wow," the girl breathed. "What's your name?"

"Wat."

"What?"

"Yes."

"But what's your name?"

"Wat!"

"Huh?"

"We don't have time for this!" Leon shouted. The stunned guards were starting to push themselves upright. Ril didn't have the power anymore that he used to. Once, he would have been able to wipe out the entire hall, but now he didn't have much left for a second shot, and Leon didn't dare ask Wat to do anything. Not if it required actual thought.

"Like calls to like, I suppose," he muttered, helping the girl down before grabbing her by the arm and towing her across the floor. Wat followed docilely.

"And what does that say about you and me?" Ril groused, bringing up the rear.

"You want something?" Wat asked.

They went through the servants passage in which Leon had waited, the girl whining fearfully the entire way. Leon was careful not to let go of her, or to let Ril fall too far behind. He wasn't entirely sure if human weapons could kill a battler, and he had no desire to find out. Wat stayed close to the girl, nearly tripping over her, and Leon had to bite down the urge to tell him to back off. This did not look to be an easy trip home. At least the battler didn't seem threatened by any of them. Leon suspected he was too stupid for that—which was actually a lucky break for them, at least for now.

As a group, they ran down the corridor into the building's kitchens, Ril locking the door behind them. The subsequent corridor led past pantries and cold-storage rooms filled with ice, now seemingly deserted. Leon was pretty sure there were still a few servants in hiding, but so long as they stayed that way, he didn't care. He kept his sword ready though, just in case. He couldn't be positive there wouldn't be more guards, either. There had been very little time to plan this mission. Their biggest advantage was that no one was expecting it. Leon already had ideas for changing the Valley's summoning ceremonies as a result. They only had a handful of priests themselves, and none of them were ever guarded.

For now, he focused on escape. He wasn't an expert on the layout of the building, but he did know the corridor they were in would bring them outside and behind. But while the door had been left open during the ceremony, now he sucked in a breath as he saw that someone had locked it behind them when they fled. Leon cursed. The girl only stared dumbly, while Wat started rubbing himself up against her. Distressingly, she didn't seem to mind much.

Ril stepped forward. "Move," he growled, pushing his master back.

"Don't," Leon started, but Ril aimed a palm at the door. Leon felt the blast wave, and the heavy door blew off its hinges, crashing noisily to the ground. He barely caught Ril before the battler hit the floor. Swearing, Leon handed his sword to the girl.

"Hold that," he told her. "And for the sake of all the gods, don't have sex now!"

She blushed prettily and stepped away from Wat, who looked deeply disappointed. Leon didn't really care. Shifting Ril around, he heaved and managed to get his sylph up across his shoulders. Unconscious, the battler wasn't light.

Praying there weren't any guards outside, or else he and Ril were probably dead—Wat would protect the girl, if no one else—Leon headed outside. There was no one in sight. Giving a quick glance, he led the way across an empty, garbage-strewn lot. From there, Leon plunged down one of the alleys he'd mapped out during the previous day, while Ril was busy pretending to be a prince. Their belongings were only a few blocks over, hidden under a pile of old lumber behind a shop. In the hope of everything going right, Leon had stashed extra clothes for all of them, as well as travel gear. Their horses were in a stable a few blocks farther. Again, just in case, Leon had procured four.

Ril came awake with a bit of water splashed in his face, and Leon left him to slowly dress in travel clothes as he got both the girl and Wat ready.

"What's your name?" he asked the blonde, and held up Ril's cloak for privacy while she dressed. Behind them, Wat struggled with his pants.

"Gabralina," she told him. "Can I go home now?"

"I'm afraid not. Not with him, and he won't ever leave you. We do have a place for you, though. You'll be safe there."

She regarded him with eyes that were wholly innocent, sweet, and empty-headed. "Is it beautiful?" she asked.

"Absolutely," he promised. That at least was no lie. "It's a long journey, however—nearly a month by horseback.

"We have no choice. You'll be hunted down here," he added, when she looked stunned. He shot a look at Wat, who had both feet in the same leg of his pants and was falling over. Ril simply watched, eyebrows raised. "This is very important, Gabralina. You need to listen to me." She nodded. "Do you know what Wat is?"

"No."

"He's a battle sylph—a *good* one," he added, at her frightened look. "He loves you and he wants very much to make love to you." His gaze hardened. "You mustn't let him. If you do, horrible things will happen."

"What sort of things?" the blonde whispered.

"Really terrible things," he replied, trying to think.

Every instinct Wat had would be telling him to mate with her. If he did so before he was taken to the queen and subsumed into her hive, it really would be a terrible thing. The greatest secret of the Valley was that any battler without a queen who mated with a female master would make her a queen herself, able to sense and control every sylph close enough to be drawn into their broadcast energy pattern. That was how Solie had become queen, and she was a good ruler. But given these two, it would be a nightmare.

"While you're travelling with us, I want you and Wat to be like a brother and sister. Don't let him touch you, got it?" he said.

Gabralina frowned and stepped out from behind the cloak, clad in a simple riding dress of cotton with brown shoes. Her hair shone like gold over the top of it, and her curves were obvious even through the loose material. The woman was gorgeous, making Leon wonder why she'd ever been picked as a sacrifice. She looked more like she should be some nobleman's mistress.

She didn't seem to notice Leon's appraisal, instead looking down at Wat, who was on his back, trying to pull his pants on by way of his head. Ril looked as if he wanted to kill the other sylph. "How about Wat and I just have sex then?" she suggested instead.

# Chapter Two

Para Dubh was a kingdom with a land mass ten times the size of Sylph Valley, comprising dozens of little hamlets and villages scattered through the mountains that made up most of its geographical territory. The center of its power and its greatest architectural achievement, however, was a massive city of the same name, built on the sloping shores of a wide ocean bay.

Though she had memories of living in another city when she was a child, Lizzy Petrule had never before had the freedom to simply explore—and the city of Para Dubh was much larger than Eferem's capital ever hoped to be. Lizzy was sure she would have been impressed with Eferem anyway, if she'd been allowed to wander, but her mother had always been around, or one of her three sisters with whom—as the eldest—Lizzy had always been expected to help, even though the family had servants. She hadn't minded most of the time, but she'd always wanted the freedom to do as she pleased just once.

Now, though it took her weeks of begging her mother, there were no parents in sight and she was almost on her own. Giggling, she and her friend Loren hurried down the sidewalk that led to the docks, Loren's water sylph, Shore, hurrying at her side and holding her mistress's hand. Shore was getting good at mimicking human shape, and she looked like a pretty realistic little girl, if a bit wetter than normal. Three blocks behind, the rest of the group that had come to the city with the two girls were still unloading wagons.

"They're going to be so mad at us," Loren sniggered. "Did you see Daton's face when we ran off?"

"He was furious!" Lizzy agreed. She was a little nervous of what their ostensible chaperon would say when they returned, and she truly didn't want her mother to find out, after all of her promises to behave, but mostly she was too giddy to care. She was eighteen and legally an equal to any man in Sylph Valley, if not here. And even if Daton reported this to her parents, her mother would only yell at her for so long. Her father had left months ago with Ril. Lizzy was still angry at that. She'd begged to go along, but Leon and his sylph weren't as easy to wear down as her mother, and they'd refused. She'd argued until she was almost blue in the face, but neither her father nor Ril would budge. So, she'd had to stay behind. She hadn't forgiven either one of them yet.

Well, she was having an adventure now. With Loren at her side, Lizzy ran through the strange city, marveling at the sights and the sloping roads. Para Dubh had been built on a hill by *human* hands, unlike how things were built by sylphs in the Valley, and the roads zigzagged down to the ocean.

Neither had seen the ocean before, and after Shore's reaction, both girls immediately chose the docks as their first destination. The little water sylph had been struck dumb by the sight of all that salt water, and it was their duty to take her to see everything up close, they decided. The others could unload the wagon. It was just a single load of iron ore, sent as a gift to the ruling family of Para Dubh as part of a trade agreement—and to test the people bringing it. Except for Daton, everyone who'd come was under the age of twenty.

Loren had the only sylph. Usually, responsible adults were the only ones allowed to have sylphs, but Loren had been chosen after her water sylph's first master died. Loren had been fourteen at the time and was almost twenty now, making her close to two years older than Lizzy, but the girl was so immature that Lizzy doubted she would ever have been selected for a sylph if the decision hadn't been left up to Shore.

Ahead of them the road zigged, the side that faced the ocean fronted by a waist-high wall of cobbled stone. For a moment the two girls leaned on it and looked out over the beautiful old city, the rooftops covered in gardens and the spaces in between filled with walls, statues, and strips of park. Neither had ever seen anything like it, and they stopped to regain their wind, confident that they were far enough away from Daton that he couldn't just call them back.

"I love it here," Loren breathed, turning her face into the salty breeze that blew over them even this high up. It brought the scent of flowers, as well as salt and fish. Beside her, Shore turned in the same direction, smiling. She didn't say anything—not so that Lizzy could hear—but Loren smiled down at her.

"We'll start moving again in a minute. It's not going anywhere."

"I wish I could hear her," Lizzy said.

"You have to be her master," Loren replied smugly, which was an attitude Lizzy always hated. Loren thought she was better than other girls because she had a sylph. It made Lizzy want to point out the fact that her father's battler Ril had told her he loved her and that she was his queen. He'd said it many times.

But that wouldn't help any. "Solie's the queen," Loren would taunt, and though battlers were crudely known for their single-minded ability to both fight and fuck, Ril was not. The joke around the Valley—told only where her father could never hear—was that Ril had been turned into a eunuch by his injury. He certainly hadn't looked at her since he was hurt, Lizzy thought bitterly. Except once.

"We should get going," Lizzy told her friend instead. "It looks like it's a ways off."

Loren made a face, but both of them were used to a lot of walking: to school and back, to the fields and back . . . Sylph Valley had more sylphs than any other kingdom in the world, but they weren't slaves. Humans had to carry their own weight, and both girls had picked more corn and fruit and planted more seeds than they ever would have liked. This on top of tending the family garden, chickens, and horses. Lizzy's father told her it was good for her. Not that he ever joined in, though she'd sometimes seen him help with the heavier work.

Of course, this year he and Ril had missed the entire planting. Lizzy herself got to miss half, thanks to this trip.

The two girls ran down the steep road, Shore keeping up easily and all of them laughing as they darted around street musicians and performers, groups of old women dressed in black and men carrying heavy baskets on their shoulders. There was nothing like this back home, and they reveled at the sights, smells, and sounds. If either of the pair had had any money, they would have spent it tasting everything.

But they didn't. Instead, they just stuck to the road, following it down along switchbacks that passed homes hidden behind tall stone walls with wrought-iron gates, and then past shops filled with myriad objects neither girl had ever imagined. And the buildings only grew more common, spaced closer together on the level ground before the water, homes and other shops replaced by markets specializing in fish. The girls clasped hands, hoping not to lose each other in the suddenly thick crowd, and Lizzy looked behind her for a landmark along the road they'd taken down. They could just follow it back up to where they'd left the others.

She found a marker easily enough: a statue of a man on a rearing horse, beneath a streetlight with a glass bowl over an oil lamp. Trotting under it, however, already seeing her and waving madly, was a tall, lanky boy barely older than herself, his jaggedly cut hair hanging in his eyes.

"Justin?" Lizzy gasped.

Loren turned. "What is *he* doing here?"

Looking for her, no doubt, Lizzy realized with a little flutter she couldn't decide was excitement or irritation. Justin was the son of Cal Porter, one of the Valley's original drovers and—as he liked to keep reminding everyone—the one who'd first brought Solie and Heyou to the Community. Cal was also very vocal about the idea that his nineteen-year-old son would make the perfect husband for Lizzy Petrule, ever since Lizzy was caught giving him a kiss at the harvest dance when she was sixteen. It was the only time he'd kissed her, however, and it had probably only happened thanks to lots of hard apple cider and her own frustrations—and it wasn't the only kiss she'd received that long night.

He'd been wooing her ever since, in his awkward, shy way. For her part, Lizzy wasn't sure what to think. She liked Justin. He was honest and friendly, completely incompetent at lying to anyone, and he never gave up on her, even when she snubbed him or joked about him to her friends, or when she skipped out on dates their mothers arranged, laughing at him when he looked crestfallen. He just kept trying, and in the last year she'd stopped laughing at him and skipping out on their dates. She was even wondering when he might have the nerve to try and kiss her again . . . and if she'd let him.

Part of the reason she'd come on this trip, though, was to get away from most everyone she knew. She'd thought it would help her decide what she wanted to do with her life. Her dreams from when she was twelve and thirteen hadn't come true, and she wanted to go somewhere she could reflect on life and maybe learn to look at Justin with fresh eyes. Only he'd come along, and now here he was again. Part of her was glad to see him, but the other part was terribly angry.

"What are you doing?" she shouted when he got close.

Justin, who had been grinning, skidded to a nervous halt, his Adam's apple bobbing. "I followed you. Daton said no one was supposed to be alone here."

"Do I look like I'm alone?" she groused, facing away from him with her hands on her hips.

She was tall, but Justin still towered over her. "But you're both girls," he protested, and winced as he realized what he'd said. Lizzy and Loren both glared at him. Even Shore frowned, her eyebrows drawn together. She was dripping on the ground, Lizzy noticed absently.

"Don't call me a girl," Loren snapped, and made a face at Lizzy. "I'm not staying with him." Turning, she headed for the closest dock, which stretched out over the water, small ships and longboats pulled up to either side. Men were frantically busy loading and unloading gear and fish and shouting at each other. Loren made her way through this, leading Shore.

Lizzy eyed Justin. He seemed miserable. He hadn't meant to offend anyone, she knew, but sometimes he just blurted out the worst things possible. Usually it was only when someone else was nearby. When he was alone with her, he was much more confident.

"You're lucky a battler didn't hear you say that," she complained, still a bit angry at him for following. He sagged even more. Most of the world still considered women second-class citizens, but the battlers in the Valley got very cranky at such treatment. No one had died yet for anything they'd said, but everyone had learned to keep sexist opinions to themselves.

Still, Lizzy couldn't hold on to her anger for long. Justin meant well, and she and Loren running off hadn't been terribly smart, even if Loren was supposed to be old enough to be responsible. Of course, if Loren were, Lizzy thought, she wouldn't still be hanging out with girls in their teens.

"I'm sorry," Justin said.

She sighed, turning and slowly heading down the dock after Loren and Shore. "It's okay, but I told you that I wanted some time to myself."

"I know. It's not really safe here, though," he replied. "Daton told me to come after you."

She should have known. There was always someone around to make sure she was being a good girl. If it wasn't her father, it was Daton, or Justin in Daton's place. Lizzy had to bite down on her anger before she started yelling again. It wasn't really Justin's fault. She supposed she should be glad they trusted her alone with him—though really, that was just one more thing to be annoyed about: they weren't afraid of her being alone with Justin at all.

In her mother's mind, Lizzy suspected, the marriage was already fixed. It would have been, she was sure, if Queen Solie hadn't banned arranged marriages entirely. At least no one could *make* her marry someone she didn't want, though they'd hint endlessly. She shot a sideways look at Justin where he flanked her, looking around with the same wonder she herself had been feeling until now.

She just wasn't sure if she wanted to be married to anyone. Not yet.

Marriage. Loren would tell her to haul Justin out behind the barn and get any itches scratched and then not worry about it, but Loren was the sort to haul nearly anyone out behind the barn. She'd even told Lizzy that she'd seduced battlers. Lizzy wasn't so sure of that. Loren had never actually named any battler she'd been with, and for all their reputation, they were supposedly loyal to their masters. And from what Lizzy had heard about their appetites, they might be more than even Loren could handle. Of course, Lizzy didn't expect to ever know what they were *truly* like.

"Have you seen the ocean before?" she asked Justin, by way of apology.

Justin shook his head emphatically. "It's unbelievable. And it smells!"

Her anger gone, Lizzy laughed at that, and she daringly reached out to take his hand. Justin squeezed hers and beamed. Perhaps his following them wouldn't turn out to be so bad after all.

They walked down the long dock, their boots making a clomping sound on the wood. It was wide, but still they had to step around stacks of goods or men trying to unload the boats. There was shouting and curses, and Lizzy stared about her, seeing skins of a dozen different colors and clothes she never would have imagined, even as she had to nearly dance out of the workers' paths. She saw tall men, short men, dark-skinned men, and pale men. She saw men with tattoos over all or parts of their bodies, and some with more jewelry than the vainest woman. Others were completely hairless. She giggled and clutched Justin's hand tighter, dragging him along as she hurried to catch Loren and Shore.

The older girl stood at the very end of the dock, Shore crouched nearby, as though she was contemplating a leap into the water, while her master flirted with a man in loose, flowing clothes. He was bare chested and had tattoos curling around his torso and up his arms to encircle his neck. He grinned down at Loren in a way that made the hair on Lizzy's neck rise, and she stopped a few feet away, not sure what to do.

"Maybe I did come here to find someone like you," Loren was telling him, tapping his chest flirtatiously with a finger. Behind her, Shore got ready to jump, but her master grabbed her shoulder without even looking. "We certainly don't have anyone quite like you back home."

"And where's home then?" he leered, his intentions as obvious as a battler's. The way he pronounced his words was strange to Lizzy's ears.

"Sylph Valley," she told him. "Just over the mountains. *That* way." She made a vague gesture, still smiling.

"Really?" the man asked. His eyebrows rose, and his shipmates, who'd been unloading a longboat nearly twenty feet in length while he flirted, looked over curiously at her announcement. Lizzy felt the tension in the air change from sexual to something else.

Shore glanced up, her mouth hanging open. Loren didn't sense it at all and fluttered her eyelashes at the sailor. "Of course. Why would I lie to you?"

"Sylph Valley," he repeated. "The place with all the battlers?" He frowned. "You didn't bring one, did you?" He looked over at Lizzy and Justin, his eyes cold.

Lizzy's hand tightened on Justin's, which was getting clammy. She'd been hoping for help, but he simply stepped back, pulling her arm to its full extension when she didn't retreat with him. She couldn't move. Something was horribly wrong, and Loren couldn't see it.

"Of course not," she told the sailor smugly. "I prefer real men."

He grinned. "Good."

Of all of them, Shore moved first. Squealing, the little sylph grabbed her mistress, shedding her fake human form as she wrapped watery tendrils around Loren and then threw them both backward over the edge of the dock. Lizzy saw the surprise on Loren's face before they went underwater with a tremendous splash. The man with the tattoos closed his arms on the empty air where she'd been and then rounded on Lizzy and Justin in a rage.

"Grab them!" he shouted. "You know what they're worth!"

Justin fled. Dropping Lizzy's hand, he turned and ran up the dock, screaming hysterically. Surprised fishermen watched him go, unintentionally blocking his pursuers and even Lizzy's own escape. Furious, she kicked one of the tattooed man's cronies in the knee when he lunged at her, and darted in the other direction. She had no idea if she could swim, but she planned to find out.

She wasn't fast enough. A step shy of the dock edge, the man with whom Loren had been flirting caught her around the waist, pulling her back against his wide chest. Lizzy screamed, kicking and bucking madly, but her father had never taught her how to fight. In Sylph Valley, there were so many battlers, there was no need. None of those could hear her screams this far away, though, and the nearby fishermen just stared at her uncertainly. A few looked as if they wanted to say something, but the tattooed man and his crew pulled knives, grinning at them dangerously.

The sailor carried Lizzy to his boat, ignoring her struggles. She managed to get an arm free and punched him in the ear, but he only glared at her and threw her into the longboat. She fell across a seat, all the breath rushing out of her, and the craft rocked from her impact and that of the men piling into it. One of them sat right beside her, a hand gripping the back of her neck painfully and holding her down across the board while their leader shouted for them to push off and forget the rest of the cargo—she was more valuable. Lizzy had no idea what for.

In pain and terrified, she started to sob, crying for someone to come and save her, but there was no one to hear and no one to come, and the longboat pulled away from the dock, heading out into the open ocean, where the great ships of a dozen different kingdoms were anchored. The men who'd captured her started to laugh, and all she could do was stare at the curved floor of the boat, unable even to look up and see if anyone was watching her abduction.

# Chapter Three

For six years, ever since the first day she ran away from home to avoid an arranged marriage, Solie had lived a life apart. The adventure had led her into the arms of a battle sylph and away from everything she'd ever known, in order to become a queen. She recognized how lucky she was, though, and how easily everything could have been so much different. Worse.

Her battle sylph, Heyou, felt that renewed realization in her, and also her horror and outrage as she sensed that he was ready to attack the messengers standing before her simply because of the message they'd brought and how it made her feel.

She reached out and grabbed his arm, holding him beside her until he made himself relax. "Do you know where they took her?" she asked, leaning forward on the great stone chair the earth sylphs had made for her throne. They'd carved it intricately, turning it into a shape as delicately lacy as a snowflake, and she'd piled pillows on top to make it comfortable. One of these tumbled to the ground, but she didn't notice, staring at the group who stood at the foot of the throne's small dais. Solie didn't want anyone bowing to her.

The oldest of the three was a man whom Heyou didn't know very well and whom he watched carefully as the human shook his head, his expression miserable. He was upset—Heyou could feel that—but he was also a strange male. Heyou had learned to like men, but it was still on a case-by-case basis, and he didn't really want any of them getting too close to his queen. Neither did any of the other battlers who waited in the room.

Daton felt them all watching him and shuddered before he answered. "No, my lady. Justin says he saw them rowing to a large ship with three sails, but by the time I got there, the ship had put out to sea. We don't even know where they came from. We decided to come back here as fast as we could."

"The docks don't keep records?" Solie asked.

"No, my lady. At least, none they'd admit to."

Solie closed her eyes for a moment. "There has to be someone who saw her. Did you ask around?" She was sounding more exasperated by the moment, and Heyou hissed. Daton started in terror, and the boy beside him gasped.

Only the girl was able to look Solie in the eye. "You think it's our fault or something?" she snapped. All the battlers growled, but she ignored them. Everyone knew that women were safe from battle sylphs. "What were we supposed to do—go looking for her and end up getting kidnapped ourselves?"

"Try telling that to her father," Solie said dryly.

The girl flushed. Her name was Loren, Heyou remembered belatedly, and she was actually a friend of the queen. He knew her sylph much better. Shore cowered next to her master, staring at the ground.

*You saw what happened?* he sent. The little sylph looked up at him, her emotions miserable. She'd run from the danger; that much was obvious. But why shouldn't she? She was never made for fighting.

*They wanted my master. I took her and ran. I could only carry one.* Shore sent Heyou the emotions she'd felt at the time, the feelings she'd picked up from the men, and Heyou sighed. There wasn't much there. Most of the battlers knew Lizzy quite well, but they could only track their own masters or the queen. Had it been Solie who'd been grabbed . . .

Well, if it had been Solie, all of the kidnappers would already be dead.

"I want her found," Solie was saying. "I want everyone on that dock questioned and the harbormaster to give some answers. Someone has to know where that ship is going!"

"You want us to go back?" Daton asked uncertainly. Beside him, the boy swallowed, staring at the floor in fear. Loren just sniffed.

"No," Solie replied flatly. "I don't plan to send you at all."

They crested the peaks of the mountains against which the city of Para Dubh sat, making no attempt to hide their presence. Sixteen strong, they swooped down over the buildings, a flock of lightning-streaked black clouds with red eyes, and teeth formed of electricity. They kept their auras tightly contained, but those who saw them still screamed in terror. Most didn't know what they were—most had never seen a battler in his natural shape—but given their speed and the fact that the smallest was nevertheless larger than a peasant's cottage, fear was a natural reaction.

Mace felt no surprise. Humans were always afraid of his kind—not that it mattered to him. He was created to protect the hive and his queen. Added to his responsibility were the human friends he'd made, and Lily, his master and lover, who bossed him around in front of everyone else but smiled at him in private. She'd been very much in agreement when he told her of Solie's command: if Lizzy was to be found, he was to find her.

As with the other battlers, it was an easy order for him to accept. He *liked* Lizzy. While most of the humans in the Valley had grown used to his kind, only a few non-masters didn't retain a small undercurrent of fear in their presence, and Lizzy was one of them. She even entered the chamber the battlers shared to relax, visiting regularly to play and talk. The thought of someone having taken her angered them all.

The city sped by below, buildings dotting the slopes of the mountains almost like the combs of a beehive. Mace rather liked the look, but he didn't slow. Instead, he angled out toward the wharf, the others flanking him and falling back to form a huge V. They rocketed over the docks, spreading out to cover them all, and Mace changed shape, landing heavily only a few feet shy of one end. This was the dock across from a statue of a man on a rearing horse, just as Loren and the boy had described.

Mace straightened and turned, looking at the white-faced fishermen who'd been unloading their catch. "A girl was taken from this dock three days ago by men with tattoos. Tell me where they took her."

The fishermen glanced at each other and then went diving in a panic off the side of the dock.

Face twisting in annoyance, Mace changed form and went to retrieve them.

The battlers landed everywhere, demanding answers of Para Dubh's terrified dockworkers. The responses they received were mostly useless, the men pleading for their lives instead, terrified of these shape-changing inquisitors. Finally, many of the battlers lost their tempers and lashed out with their hate—which made things even worse. They found no one on the docks who remembered a blonde girl being grabbed by a group of tattooed sailors.

Mace ordered his fellows next to inquire of the nearby women, but none of these had been present, and most were just as terrified of the battlers as the men. Which made the trip a failure. Angry and frustrated, Mace stood on the dock and stared out over the ocean. Whoever had taken Lizzy, they were far away now. There were ships close by. His battlers were flying around them, demanding to know if the crews knew anything, but none was the craft they wanted. Mace had little doubt that even if his contingent spread out and tried to find the boat, they wouldn't. The ocean was a big place, and they had no way to track her. If only it had been *Loren* they grabbed, they could have followed Shore to her.

He'd been harboring wonderful ideas of what he was going to do to the kidnappers, and his fist clenched briefly. From now on, no woman would leave the Valley without an escort—Mace didn't care what they said. But Solie would never stand for it. *Lily* would never stand for it . . . He blew out a breath. Battlers couldn't guard every single woman in the Valley, just as they couldn't guard every single sylph. "Dammit," he muttered.

Behind him, he felt hate. It wasn't from one of his fellows. Mace knew all their energy patterns well. These were bound battlers, driven nearly insane and hating all the time, punishing their male masters even while they served.

Mace turned, calmly watching the creatures approach. Unlike the battlers of the Valley, who took human forms that would appeal to their female masters, these wore twisted shapes. Designed to frighten, they boasted oversized teeth and claws, vile and hideous. Mace just snorted, unimpressed. He'd been trapped like that himself, forced to look like a suit of armor at the whim of a sadistic dandy. He would free these creatures if he could, but to do that, they'd have to be subsumed into his hive, their energy patterns changed to match his queen's, and that could only be done in Solie's presence.

Their masters walked well behind the battlers, of which there were four. Mace looked at the men directly, not terribly interested in talking to anyone who'd trap one of his kind, but Solie had given her orders. They couldn't be at war with the entire world.

"We're from Sylph Valley," he told the men loudly. "A girl was kidnapped from a delegation sent to this city and taken away on a ship with three sails. We're looking for anyone who knows where she might have been taken."

The four battlers stopped, snarling and frothing like misshapen dogs. Their masters looked at each other uncertainly, and in that time the other battlers Mace had brought landed around him, taking on human shape or floating overhead in their natural form. The bound ones glared at them, their envy obvious.

Their masters saw immediately how bad the odds were. One battler was enough to destroy the city. The entire kingdom of Para Dubh had eight. Sixteen had to be beyond their comprehension.

Sylph Valley hadn't done anything about their most immediate neighbor, preferring to set up trade agreements with Para Dubh, though they had no formal alliance and were watching very carefully to be sure Para Dubh's battler population didn't suddenly increase. Solie felt that forcing any sylph into slavery was evil, and that what was done to bind battlers was an abomination. Mace agreed with that assessment, though he had no urge to do anything for these. As Solie said, they couldn't be at war with the entire world. Of course, by sending Leon and Ril to get information on Yed, fully intending them to do sabotage if they could, she was walking a fine line that would eventually erupt in conflict. Especially considering the attack by Eferem six years ago. But a smart general picked his own battles in his own time.

Mace watched the men confer. They were afraid. He could tell that even without his kind's natural empathy. The men knew they couldn't fight off this contingent, outnumbered as they were, but they had to save face—hopefully without turning the city into a crater.

"We had nothing to do with a girl being kidnapped," one of them said.

"We know," Mace replied. "She was taken by men wearing loose clothes and tattoos, men from a boat. We came here only in order to start looking."

Two of the battler masters continued to watch him carefully, but the one who'd spoken nodded. "Men with tattoos and a three-sailed ship?" he mused. "They could be from Meridal. A lot of the sailors from there have tattoos, and a lot of Meridal merchants use triple-sailed schooners. They're just about on the other side of the world, though." He frowned. "To be honest, it makes sense. They kidnap and sell girls, the bastards. They agreed not to do it here, though. They want our trade more than our women."

The battler master was clearly horrified by the idea of slavery, though Mace reflected with disgust that the man's attitude did not extend to his sylph. Mace waited, hoping to hear more, digesting the idea of Lizzy being sold and the massive amounts of violence in which he'd like to engage. "Where would they go?" he asked at last.

"South," was the answer. "If they are from Meridal, if they grabbed a girl, they'd head out to sea and sail straight there to sell her. They have air sylphs to help push their ships. They would be hundreds of miles away by now, and once they got there they could sell her in a dozen different cities." The man's frown deepened. "If they grabbed one girl, they might have grabbed a dozen. You going after yours only?"

Mace shrugged. "We'll bring back any women we find."

The battler master nodded. He obviously didn't want them there, but he was diplomatic and grateful for help against slavers. "Good luck in your search," he told them, then turned and walked off, his battler heeling. Acting as though sixteen foreign battlers on their docks was nothing to be worried about, he headed back the way he'd come, leaving the fishermen and merchants to gape and stare, afraid to return to their work but even more afraid to protest. The other battler masters regarded him with surprise for a moment before hurrying after him.

Mace looked at his flight, sixteen strong. He looked out at the ocean, huge and inscrutable. He'd never seen so much water. "Spread out," he told them. "Find her." The battlers roared, flashing up into the air and away, spreading out across the waves and racing the winds above, hunting for any ship that had three sails and a crew of men with loose pants and tattoos.

Mace watched them go, shifted to smoke and lightning, and then rose into the air himself. He soared straight south, shooting over the whitecaps as quickly as he dared. Battlers were powerful and they were angry, but they weren't limitless. The ocean was huge and heavy, and the only energy they could feed from in this world came from their women. Without Lily at his side, Mace could only go so far, and he was already tired from flying so quickly over those mountains. Push too far, and he wouldn't have the strength to get back. If that ship was hundreds of miles away, driven by winds harnessed by air sylphs, they might never find it at all. They might search a hundred years and never even see a glimpse.

In the end, he was right.

# Chapter Four

Ever since his injury, when he'd been torn in two by another battler in defense of the hive, Ril had needed to sleep. Before that, in fifteen years of slavery he'd slept no more than a dozen times, each briefly. Now he slept as humans did, lying insensate and feeble as a corpse every night. Useless.

He'd never been much of a dreamer, even with his increased need for slumber, but now he woke from nightmares he couldn't understand or remember, shuddering from confusion as images of a small, confined space shivered out of his mind, replaced by a woman shrieking. Every instinct told him to get up, to shift to his natural form and attack whatever threatened, but as he went to do so, he gasped in pain, his entire body rebelling. Agony like a thousand burrowing maggots shot through him, and he fell back against his bedroll, shaking. He could shift shape, if he accepted the pain, but to return to his true form was beyond him now. With his mantle tattered, he couldn't hold his natural shape anymore, not without help and not without even greater pain. He'd fall apart into nothingness if he tried.

Ril sat up, staring around him as a mix of different emotions flooded in from the others. It was past dawn, past breakfast, and his companions were awake. Leon was standing over a small campfire and waving his arms wildly, cursing and yelling at Gabralina to calm down. The blonde was dancing around madly, screaming.

"A bee!" she shrieked. "It's a bee! Kill it! Kill it!" She flapped at a tiny, buzzing form and leaped back. Still swearing, Leon waved it away, his emotions frustrated and angry.

Awake now, Ril lunged out of bed, tossing his blanket back as he bolted across the clearing. Leon saw him coming just as Ril launched himself. He hit the taller man hard, knocking them both to the ground. Rolling, Ril forced his master underneath him and threw up a solid wall of force, ignoring the pain it caused.

The clearing exploded. Ordered to hold in his hate aura, Wat had still moved to defend his master. The full power of his blast slammed into Ril's shield, washing over it and past, vaporizing trees and bushes, obliterating their camp and the horses that had been tethered beyond. An instant later it was gone, and Ril had a moment to wonder if the idiotic battler had destroyed his own master in the attack, thereby banishing himself back to their original world.

Apparently he hadn't. Ril heard her crying as he rolled off Leon, shivering in reaction. Once, he could have held that blast back easily. Now he was useless.

Leon pushed himself upright, checking on his battler first before looking over at Wat with raging eyes. The sylph stood with Gabralina in the center of a circle of destruction nearly five hundred feet across, cooing. Except for a patch of grass right under her feet, everything around them was simply gone, blasted right down to the bedrock. The girl stared around in amazement, absently stroking her battler's arm while he held her. Taking that as an invite, he started to lick her neck.

"Wow," she managed. "You really killed the bee."

"And everything else, too!" Leon shouted, his face red. Wat glanced over, glaring, and Leon visibly forced himself to calm down. "That wasn't necessary, Wat."

"She was under attack," Wat protested.

"It was a *bee*," Ril said, staring up at the sky that had been half-obscured by trees until now. It felt good to just lie still for a minute. He could get up later. "That was overkill."

"What's overkill?"

"When you obliterate everything within five hundred feet to protect your master from an insect the size of a thumbnail." Leon shook his head and looked down at Ril. *Thank you*, he mouthed. Ril just shrugged and closed his eyes, dozing.

"I don't like bees," Gabralina said innocently, smiling at her battler. "You're so smart!"

A moment later, Leon had to go over and pull them apart.

The day was almost lost. They were two and a half weeks out of the kingdom of Yed but still more than a week and a half from home. Worse, to Leon's intense discomfort, they were within the borders of the kingdom of Eferem, whose king he had once served. Alcor was still on the throne, but with his priesthood nearly destroyed and six of his battlers lost—three subsumed and three destroyed in the conflicts six years ago—he was afraid of challenging Sylph Valley. Instead he cowered in his castle, his battler Thrall always at his side. Leon knew the man was power hungry and paranoid, but his fear controlled him more than anything else and he wouldn't risk another attack. Not unless circumstances changed. That wouldn't stop him from wanting to see Leon's head on a pike, though.

They were still at the southern end of the kingdom, well away from the main city, but Leon didn't want to stay there any longer than necessary. Especially not after

Wat's little episode. They'd moved a few miles farther, but that blast zone was right by a well-traveled road. It couldn't help but be noticed, and Alcor did still have battlers. Leon wouldn't trust Wat against one, and he wouldn't risk Ril. They had to wait before they made a run for it, though, at least long enough for Ril to rest.

The battler lay on his side at one end of the clearing, wearing the shape of a lean roan horse, his rusty red coat sleek and smooth. He was breathing regularly. Changing form was horrible for him, but he was fine once the work was done. Leon had suggested he sleep for a while, and Ril hadn't protested. He was tired after holding off that blast and changing forms. Leon was unsurprised. Once he got Ril home, they were both going to take a very long break.

He was looking forward to that—and more especially to being rid of Gabralina and her moronic battler. Leon knew the girl had undergone a terrible shock and was still nervous, but she'd been whining about the loss of their supplies all afternoon until he'd finally threatened to paddle her if she didn't stop. That had shut her up, but now her feelings were hurt and she looked almost ready to cry. Wat stood nearby, staring at Leon blankly.

"Wat, will you please turn into a horse?"

"A horse?"

Leon prayed for patience. "An animal like the one Gabralina was riding. The black horse with the white nose. Turn into that animal."

"Why?"

"Because she needs a horse to ride. I'll be riding Ril. See him? He's already like a horse."

"He's not black with a white nose."

Leon clenched his hands. "It doesn't matter what color you are."

"Then why'd you ask me to be a black horse with a white nose?"

"What's wrong with Ril?" Gabralina spoke up, apparently distracted from her sulk. "Is he sick?"

Leon took a deep breath. "No. Changing shape is hard for him. He's sleeping."

She frowned. "Wat doesn't sleep."

"Wat doesn't need to," he explained. "He's a very healthy battler. Ril isn't. He doesn't like that pointed out, though," he added.

"Oh. So Wat is stronger?"

"Yes." He sighed. "Which means he should have no trouble turning into a horse, no matter what the color."

"Why?" Wat asked again.

"Because you turned our horses into dust, and it's too far for Gabralina and me to walk!"

"How come Ril is weaker than Wat?" Gabralina asked.

The girl asked more questions than a child, but that was probably just another sign of her fear. She didn't seem to know how to relate to Leon at all, except by whining and questioning. After two and a half weeks of her company, however, Leon knew that failing to provide some form of answer would just make her ask more questions as she started fearing he didn't like her. The people of Yed had likely picked her for a sacrifice just to shut her up, he'd decided. Ril was in full agreement with that assessment: he loathed the girl. Leon didn't feel *quite* that strongly, but if he wanted to answer an endless round of questions, he only had to go see his three-year-old daughter Mia. She asked so many questions that his wife Betha had sworn off having any more children. And Mia at least could be put down for a nap.

"He was hurt once," Leon answered, hoping that would be enough. "Wat, please, just turn into a horse."

"How?" Gabralina asked, and eyed Wat worriedly. "I thought they couldn't get hurt."

Leon sighed. His head was starting to throb. "He was torn through his body in his natural form by another battler. They're very vulnerable in that form. He would have died if a healer sylph hadn't saved him."

"That's terrible," Gabralina whispered, teary eyed. "Won't he get better?"

"No," Leon said. "Can we get back on topic now? Please?"

She shook herself. "Okay. Wat, I'd love it if you were a horsie."

He gazed at her adoringly. "Anything you want." An instant later he was a chubby black horse, only without a white nose. Gabralina squealed in delight and started to direct him in how to perfect his form.

Leon left them and trudged over to Ril. He didn't know if his battler had heard his name, but Ril was awake, rolled onto his belly with his legs tucked under him. Seeing Leon, he lunged to his feet.

Leon put a hand on the sylph's warm neck. "That girl is going to be the death of me," he muttered, pressing his face against soft hide. Ril whickered gently, and Leon looped an arm around his neck and relaxed, leaning against him.

When he was calm and paying attention, he could tell when Ril was drinking his energy. He could feel that sensation now: a faint pulling deep inside him that made his heart start to beat faster but otherwise wasn't entirely uncomfortable. Ril didn't take much. He couldn't absorb as much as he used to, and even that had never been particularly noticeable. Leon didn't know how the battlers could draw so little and do so much with it, but they did. What was just spare strength in him was everything for Ril, and so he stood there patiently, letting the contact be as easy as possible.

Eventually, Ril stepped away, his eyes brighter as he tossed his mane. He looked back at Leon and pawed at the dirt, clearly eager to be off.

"You and me both," Leon said.

He stepped around to the left. Grabbing Ril's mane with one hand, he levered himself onto the sylph's back. Ril snorted but otherwise stood steady. "Tell me if this starts to bother you," Leon cautioned him. They'd never tried this before, but neither of them had seen any horses for sale along their journey. Nor did they want to risk taking Wat and Gabralina into a town.

With hands on his neck, Leon turned Ril with gentle nudges of his knees. Ril obeyed willingly enough, though his tail flicked up periodically to smack his master. Leon had to smile. "Just imagine how sore my ass is going to be from sitting on your spine by the end of the day," he assured the battler. Ril gave a horsey laugh.

They'd have to stick to back trails, he realized. Horses being ridden without bridles would be noticed. But as he looked up, he blanched. Gabralina was now proudly sitting sidesaddle on a tall, elegant, magnificently white horse that glowed from his silver hooves to his silken, ground-length mane—and to the point of the pearlescent spiral horn rising out of his forehead.

"Oh, for the love of the gods!" he snapped. His headache was back.

Lizzy huddled in a tiny cage in the bowels of the ship to which she'd been brought, seasick and terrified. Goats bleated in other cages while chickens clucked, all of them protesting the up-and-down motion of the ship, and also the darkness. Her abductors hadn't even left a single lamp for her to see by. Crouched in a corner, she kept her arms wrapped around her knees and sobbed, unable to help it.

She'd never been so frightened in her life, not even when the battler that nearly killed Ril broke into the chamber where she and everyone else were hiding. She'd seen his mad eyes glaring right at her before Heyou tackled him, saving her life. She'd had nightmares of that moment for six years, afraid of the battler coming back. Whenever they became especially bad, she'd sneak out of her bed and across town to the chamber where the battle sylphs rested. They didn't usually sleep, but they'd socialize in there, floating together in a great mass of intertwined clouds and light. Lizzy went there and slept in a corner, feeling safe under the weight of their silent protection. She wanted to be there now, wanted it so badly that it was an ache inside her.

"Ril," she whimpered, wanting him to come to her rescue, but Ril was her father's battler, not hers. "Daddy," she whispered instead. "Oh, Daddy."

The ship surged, riding up onto a wave, and Lizzy's stomach heaved, though she had no food or water to bring up. Her captors fed her, but only once a day, and the water they brought her three times a day was already drunk. She'd tried not to swallow it all, but she'd been so thirsty that she hadn't been able to help herself.

On the deck above, she distantly heard sailors hurrying back and forth, shouting to each other as they worked. Part of her wanted one of them to come down, just so she could see another person, but another part of her dreaded it. The men had been ordered not to rape her—an intact woman brought a better price on the block—but a few had looked as though they were willing to reimburse the captain for a shot at her.

Lizzy buried her face against her knees. She was going to be sold, turned into a slave for her blonde hair and her virginity, but most important, for her knowledge of the battlers in Sylph Valley. The ship's captain knew about them and how Solie had frightened the leaders of the world, and he was sure he could get a good price selling her for information. He wouldn't have bothered otherwise, he'd told her grimly. He wouldn't be able to revisit Para Dubh for a long time, thanks to their views on slavery, but it would be worth it for the coin she'd bring. A thousand gold pieces he'd ask for the secret of the battlers!

She wept, wishing she were home. Worst was, she knew the secret. She knew why the battlers in the Valley were so common and willing. No one was supposed to talk about it . . . but how could she expect to hide it if they tortured her?

The bars of her cage were cold. Finally, she knew how Ril had felt when she was a child, trapped as he'd been in the shape of a bird, not allowed to speak, not allowed to act, only able to communicate with her by pushing lettered blocks together to form words. He'd told her he loved her!

Lizzy wept, wishing he were there—and that, sometime over the years, he hadn't changed his mind.

# Chapter Five

The road led around the edge of the wasteland, hugging the mountains that separated Sylph Valley from the kingdom of Para Dubh, but there was still nothing alive on either side, save gray scrub plants or the occasional lizard. Plodding interminably onward, the group reached Sylph Valley after dark, while the moon was still climbing in the sky. The town itself was at the other end, near the small lake the basin boasted. Other than that, there were only a few crofters dotted through the rest of the landscape, set close to the herds or the fields their owners tended.

Gabralina had wanted to stop at dusk, but with them so close to home Ril had refused and just kept trudging, though his head hung low with fatigue. The blonde girl—now mounted on a Wat who at least looked like a normal horse—had been given no choice but to follow, jabbering nervously all the way about what she was going to do if no one there liked her.

"Quiet up and you'll be sleeping in a real bed tonight," Leon told her sharply. His butt was just as sore as he'd predicted, but he kept that to himself. He could almost smell home and his family. His need to see them was overwhelming. He'd be *home*. It had been months.

"Really?" Gabralina asked, perking up. "You promise?"

"Yes. Now hurry. Just another few miles and we'll be in town." Leon lifted his head into the breeze, imagining that he could almost smell the wheat and corn growing in the fields and hear the lowing of the cattle, and he tightened his knees against Ril's ribs, conveying his eagerness to be home. The battler's ear flicked and he broke into an easy canter, moving quickly down the wide road that earth sylphs had molded out of the broken rock of the plains.

Behind them, Gabralina yelped and called for Wat to catch up. Hooves sounded on stone, and the white horse reappeared. The blonde girl had swung her leg over his back, riding him astride, and her face was lit up as her hair streamed out behind her.

She'd never done anything before but sit placidly on Wat's back, or on the back of the gelding before that, but Leon could tell she'd ridden at some point in her past by the way she held his mane like reins, urging him forward. Wat cantered past Leon and Ril, his nostrils flaring with excitement. In response, Ril's ear twitched again and he snorted.

Recognizing what was going on, Leon sank his hands into his battler's mane, getting a solid grip there and with his knees. "Don't overdo it," he whispered, already knowing he'd be ignored. Ril broke into a gallop, racing furiously after the other two. He passed them in an instant and galloped ahead, his hooves like thunder upon the ground.

Leon had to laugh at the look of surprise on the girl's face. "That's not fair!" she wailed, and Wat screamed, immediately doubling his pace.

The two battlers charged forward, galloping neck and neck across the stone. Leon leaned close to Ril, chuckling in his ear. "I didn't know you could run so fast!" The battler just snorted and redoubled his efforts, pulling ahead of Wat by a few feet.

Gabralina was wildly kicking her heels, and her sylph roared and pulled abreast of Leon and Ril again, then passed them a second time. Ril forced himself to make up the distance, and the two once more ran neck and neck.

Faster than any living horses, the pair flew down the road. It curved and bent, and then dipped tremendously down. Deep and huge, the valley proper stretched farther than Leon could see in the moonlight, but he could spot the lights of the town on the far side, single glows from lone farm dwellings shining closer. The two battlers hit the crest and leaped, landing on the sloping road, their bodies stretching out as they raced toward their destination, their hoofbeats echoing through the night. The moonlight was nearly gone in the shadow of the Valley, but Leon didn't worry about either mount losing his footing. Not these two.

Leaning close to Ril's neck, he looked over at Gabralina. For the first time her face was alive and unafraid, her eyes gleaming and her smile huge. He hadn't realized she could be anything but a chattering mouse. He didn't mind the discovery. Her love of such sport was perhaps the only thing they shared.

Ril won at the last moment. Familiar with the layout of the town, he jigged off the road, hurtled a fence (and the man behind it, who'd been heading to the outhouse), took two strides, leaped the fence on the other side of the yard, and came out into the town square a full ten feet ahead of Gabralina. The look she gave him was thunderous. Leon would have laughed if she hadn't also looked confused. Instead, he just gave her a smile and she blushed, turning her face away from him.

"You two cheated," she decided.

"I wasn't aware there were any rules," Leon told her mildly, less concerned with her reaction than with what his battler had done to himself during that crazed run. He stroked Ril's neck and hummed to him comfortingly, aware from the tingling along his arms that his battle sylph was already drawing from his energy.

Alerted by their noisy arrival, or more likely aware of the group from the moment they entered the Valley, three battlers in blue and gold dropped down into the street, eyeing them warily. Wat just stood there like an idiot. Behind him, men and a few women stepped curiously out of the tavern that doubled as the inn.

"Claw," Leon called to one of the battlers. "Please get the queen. I'll need to see her in her audience chamber as soon as Ril is settled." The bizarrely blue-haired battler shivered and disappeared, flowing as smoke toward one of the air vents that fed into the underground section of the city and disappearing down it.

That finally got Wat's attention. He stared after the vanished battler, his ears pricked up.

"Gabralina," Leon called. She looked at him. "Welcome to Sylph Valley. I'd like you to take Wat to the queen's audience chamber. She'll be thrilled to meet you." He nodded at one of the tavern serving girls. "Cherry, please take her there."

"Where are you going?" Gabralina asked, clearly nervous all over again. She slid down from Wat's back, and he shifted immediately back to human form. The battlers all tensed. Anywhere but here, they'd have attacked him already.

"I'll be right back," Leon assured her. "Promise."

He could feel Ril trembling under him, but he nudged the sylph with his knees as though there was nothing wrong and trotted him around the corner. The instant they were out of sight, he was off the battler's back and braced against him, helping to hold him up. "You *ass*," he said. "Are you trying to run yourself into the ground?" When Ril shot him a venomous look, Leon shook his head. "Come on."

He led the battler to a door set in a wall between two

buildings. On the other side, steps descended into the complex that stretched under the town. It was a place where the entire population could retreat in harsh storms or if they were attacked. The way was lit by oil lamps that were always kept full, and Leon helped Ril down the stairway, which was wide enough for them both, though really too steep for either a human or a horse. In the corridor at the bottom he saw an earth sylph stomping toward them.

"Please get Luck," he told the small creature, nodding at her. She regarded him from a genderless face made of mud and hurried off, not much faster than they.

Leon took Ril to a chamber that was right next to the queen's throne room. He hadn't wanted Gabralina to see it, or to bring Wat there. At any time, ten or more battle sylphs floated in the huge chamber, intertwined, and the arrival of an unfamiliar sylph in the heart of their home would likely have gone badly. He had no idea how many battlers were there now.

The chamber was a hundred feet across, the ceiling made of clear glass that actually reached aboveground and into the air, but which was currently obscured by a cloud of smoke and lightning. Myriad minds looked down on them, and a few battlers drifted free, detaching to swarm Ril. He stepped away from Leon and walked farther into the chamber, enveloped by swirling energy.

Something shimmered behind him. Leon turned and saw a vaguely human shape enter the room, floating directly to Ril: Luck. She was the only healer they had, and she was Ril's savior. She put her hands on him, and he changed painlessly, shifting to smoke and lightning.

He didn't look complete somehow—his form seemed less substantial than the others, less *there*—but Luck soothed the transformation while the other battlers surrounded him, holding him within their mantles as they apparently would their own newborns. It was the only way Ril could take his own shape, and Leon felt his battler's relief. Some of the other sylphs would stay with him while he slept, and when he woke Luck would change him back. It had been this way for the last six years, and would continue for as long as his battler lived.

"Sleep well, Ril," Leon murmured and went to deal with his other responsibility.

Gabralina glanced around fearfully, holding one of Wat's arms with both hands. The sylph had ignored Ril the entire trip, she supposed not recognizing either him or Leon as a threat, but he now watched the dozen battlers who stood around him, lip curled hatefully back from his teeth. It was the longest he'd gone without trying to feel her up, she realized, and tried to process the underground chamber to which she'd been brought. It was well lit by a fire sylph, had tables and chairs along the walls, and an ornate stone chair rose in the back. Gabralina had never seen anything so delicately beautiful.

"What is this place?" she whimpered.

Her guide, a far less attractive woman wearing an apron, shrugged. Her name was Cherry. "The queen's throne room and audience chamber."

"Do all these battlers have to be here?" They made her nervous.

The woman shrugged again. "They protect the queen. They're kind of crazy that way. At least they obey her. She's the only woman here to have one who isn't ancient." Cherry regarded Gabralina with vague disgruntlement. "Except for you. It's not fair, you know."

Gabralina blinked, not really marking the other woman's jealousy. She was too used to it. "They obey her? Don't they have to obey their masters?"

"Sure. But all the sylphs obey the queen first. It's just the way it is."

On the other side of the chamber, a door opened, and in came a young woman with long red tresses. She wore rumpled clothes and her hair was a bit mussed, as though she'd just got out of bed, but she was pretty. A battler in the shape of a beautiful young man followed, his gaze finding Wat and not looking happy.

Seeing the redhead, the battlers in the room all bowed, and Gabralina realized something. "*That's* the queen?" she gasped. "How did she get to be so important?"

"Uh, she had sex with her battler, from what I heard."

"Huh?"

Leon's hand closed around her arm, and Gabralina's startled yelp echoed through the room. "Quiet," he soothed. "We're short on formality here, but this place echoes badly." He led her forward, Wat following them across the floor.

"I thought you told me bad things would happen if I had sex with Wat," she whispered.

"Bad things *would* have happened," he assured her. "You would have become a queen like Solie. More than one hive is too many, though. Don't worry, it'll be safe in a moment."

"Safe for what? How?"

Leon stepped up to the queen, who was waiting beside her battler, and nodded to a huge, heavily tanned man standing a few feet to her left. "He's all yours, Mace."

"What?" Gabralina squealed. Wat glanced over, picking up on her fright and the cry that was unintentionally similar to his name. She was suddenly intensely afraid for him. Leon hadn't warned her about any of this.

There was no more time to think. Mace lifted his hand and Wat stiffened, eyes widening. Gabralina cried out, feeling his sudden immobility and fear, but Leon held her back. Something inside Wat was changing, shifting, and though she never lost her connection to him, she felt his attention become divided, the essence of what he was re-forming itself. He shuddered once, and then it was over. Blinking, he vigorously shook his head. Many of the battlers wandered out of the chamber, including the huge one called Mace. Those who remained didn't look inter-ested in guarding against him at all, not anymore.

"Wat?" she whispered. "What happened?"

"He's a member of the hive now," Leon explained. "He'll be accepted by the others." Shrugging, his expression a bit amused, he added, "The warning about not sleeping with him? It's okay now. Nothing bad will happen."

Nothing? Nothing. Except now she had a lover and a home in a place where no one would have any reason to ask her about her past. All of the tension flowed out of her as easily as it had from her battle sylph, and Gabralina smiled beatifically as she turned to greet the queen.

Even as introductions were made, Solie stared past the new girl at Leon, who stood with arms crossed, looking tired and hungry but willing to wait until all the protocols were finished. He'd taught her everything she knew about diplomacy and running this kingdom, and he'd probably even make sure Gabralina was settled in and comfortable before he went home—which meant he obviously had no idea about his oldest daughter. Solie's heart sank. She didn't want to tell him, but he had to be apprised of what had happened before some well-meaning idiot blurted it out.

Despite sharing the girl's experience of nearly being sacrificed, and fearing she was being rude, Solie smiled at the blonde who was the newest citizen of Sylph Valley and cut her short. "It's so good to have you here! Still, you must be exhausted. I'll have Devon take you to a room so you can rest." She crooked a finger, and Devon stepped forward, looking surprised. "We have a lot dug, just in case. Most of them aren't used most of the time . . ."

The blonde girl just blinked at her stupidly, and Solie realized she was starting to babble. Determined to end things, she waved a good-bye and moved to address Leon. She took his arm. He had both eyebrows raised. "Leon, come with me."

Without a word of disagreement, he fell in beside her. She led him out of the chamber and into a private room farther down the hall, one near the battler chamber where she'd learned Ril was resting. Heyou shadowed her, wearing a worried expression. He was concerned about how Lizzy's father would react, Solie knew. So was she.

"What's wrong?" Leon asked in an undertone once they were alone. Solie just shook her head and closed the door. The room they were in had a narrow bed and a chair, as well as a bucket and a mop. Leon stepped away from her and spun, his arms crossed. "Okay, tell me."

Solie took a deep breath. Heyou moved close, his hand caressing her shoulder, and she forced herself to remain calm. This was, of all men, the one for whom she had the most respect. The Community wouldn't have survived its retreat to the cliff hive six years ago without him.

"Leon, I'm so sorry, but I have bad news. It's Lizzy." She was forced to swallow and took a deep breath. "She's gone. She went to Para Dubh and was kidnapped. I sent sixteen battlers to try and get her back, but they couldn't find her. We . . . we don't know where she is."

Leon froze, his face draining of all color. So close to him, Solie couldn't help but share his emotions through Heyou. She felt his pain like a knife. "Wh-what?" he managed.

"Leon, I'm so sorry," she begged. "I sent them there but

I never thought anything like this would happen. Please forgive me."

She had no idea if he did. Leon turned, fumbling for the doorknob, and was out in the hallway a moment later, rushing toward his home and family. Solie hung her head, and Heyou put his arms around her.

Leon hardly felt his boots touch the ground as he ran, or heard his own panicked gasps. Someone had his baby, and he couldn't think beyond that. Someone had his Lizzy.

He ran up the same stairs he'd brought Ril down, stumbling and falling to one knee. He didn't acknowledge the pain, instead leaping up again, crashing through the door at the top and off down the street, his sheathed sword slapping against his leg and his arms pumping at his sides. He might have passed people who stopped and stared, but he wasn't sure. Someone might have called out to him, but he didn't hear.

His house lay a few streets over from the main thoroughfare, close enough to the main market to make Betha happy but far enough that they didn't feel as though the entire town was on their doorstep. Their dwelling wasn't as large as their old manor in Eferem, but they didn't have any servants, either. They maintained everything themselves, the girls keeping the interior clean and the clothes and linens washed, and he and Ril seeing to the repairs and upkeep. Everyone took care of the garden in the back and the chicken coop, along with the small barn for their few horses and single cow. Lizzy's wardrobe door had been squeaking, he remembered. He'd intended to fix it when he got back. She'd told him it drove her crazy, but he'd never got around to it. He should have fixed it!

The top floor of the house was dark, only a single light shining in the sitting room below. Leon clattered up the porch steps and through the front door they never bothered to lock. The hall inside was dark, the light he'd seen from outside shining off to his right.

"*Betha!*" he screamed.

There was a startled exclamation from the sitting room, and his wife of twenty-five years appeared, clad in a rumpled dress with her hair half-fallen out of its bun, eyes red-rimmed and glassy. They saw each other and crashed together, both of them crying and hugging each other until it was painful. Footsteps sounded from the second floor, and the other girls came racing downstairs in their nightgowns, calling for their father.

Cara was twelve, her curly hair down from its usual pigtails. Behind her scrambled nine-year-old Nali, with dark hair like her mother's, her eyes filled with tears. Behind her and leading the three-year-old Mia came seven-year-old Ralad, already weeping but determined to be responsible. Hanging on to her hand, Mia babbled questions Leon didn't know how to answer.

Still holding his wife, Leon sank to his knees, pulling her down with him and reaching out an arm for his girls. They crowded against him, bawling, and Leon wept, too, wishing he'd never been so foolish as to leave home.

Underneath the town, wrapped by the energy of another battler and floating within him like some sort of unborn child, Ril maintained his natural shape and slept.

And sleeping, he dreamed.

# Chapter Six

Feeling both rested and hungry, Ril came awake as Luck shifted him back into his human form. He sat on the floor while she scanned him intently and then, satisfied with what she saw, patted him on the head and left. Glancing up at the battler who'd held him all night, Ril nodded his thanks. Dillon's reply came back, a wordless welcome.

His hunger not unlike a man's for food, Ril stood and walked out of the room, yawning. Nearby, battlers wandered in and out of the queen's audience hall, all of them dressed in blue and gold, and Ril looked down at his travel-stained clothing before ducking into the next chamber, one layered with dozens of cubbies. His own space was near the door, specifically chosen at a level easy for him to reach.

He retrieved and put on his blue and gold pants and white shirt, the blue and gold coat over top. This uniform had been Solie's idea, so that anyone who didn't know their faces would be aware whenever they were dealing with a battler—there had been a few accidents early on. The clothes felt stiff and formal, but he'd never intentionally have been seen in town without them. He was a battler, no matter what anyone might think or whisper.

Ril straightened proudly as he did up the buttons on the coat, and then he made his way to the surface, his thoughts not much farther-reaching than finding breakfast—or perhaps lunch, he realized as he saw the sun already high in the sky. Some people found it odd that sylphs used such terms for feeding from their masters, but what other words were they supposed to use for it?

Walking down the sidewalk, humans parting to let him pass, he headed to Leon's house. He could tell where his master was at all times, though he didn't always bother to focus on what the man was feeling. But right now—Ril frowned—Leon felt upset. *Very* upset. Almost hysterical.

Ril sped up, and before he even realized it, he was running, nervous humans ducking frantically out of the way. Above, other battlers roared, picking up on the distress that was being fed to him via his master, and every sylph outside vanished, many of them taking their masters with them. Not that Ril noticed. He soon took Leon's porch stairs with a single bound and crashed through the house's front door. It flew off its hinges, slamming into the wall as Leon appeared in the doorway at the end of the hall, a knife in hand. He was bare chested and unshaven, his eyes wild and bloodshot. Ril hadn't seen him look so bad since the day he was nearly hanged, and he skidded to a halt before his master, staring. Behind Leon, Betha and the youngest girls sat around the kitchen table, all of them still in their nightclothes.

Ril stared. "What's wrong?"

Leon swallowed heavily, choked, and let the knife fall to his side. "We lost Lizzy."

That didn't make any sense. Ril tilted his head to one side. "What?"

"She's gone," Leon said miserably. "She was kidnapped. No one can find her. We don't even know if she's alive." At the table, Lizzy's sisters started weeping.

That *really* didn't make any sense. His head still tilted, Ril kept staring at Leon, though he didn't really see him. He was hungry for the man's energy, but he didn't think to take it. Lizzy? His Lizzy? He'd seen her birth, guarded her childhood, even promised her she would be his queen, until Solie got to him first and subsumed him into her hive. He'd promised Lizzy everything—until Yanda the battler tore him in two and left him broken and unworthy.

"Ril?" Leon said.

Ril turned, moved unsteadily down the hall and back out onto the porch. The neighbors, who hadn't known Leon was home but had seen Ril go inside, were gathering to give their condolences. Ril ignored them and closed his eyes. His Lizzy, his beautiful Lizzy! He'd loved her, wanted her to be his queen, had even begged for her love, and in her innocent granting of it, he'd taken her pattern into him, beneath Leon's and Solie's. He'd ignored it for years now, knowing that he wasn't good enough for her anymore and that she lived in a town surrounded by *whole* battlers. They would protect her, he'd told himself. They'd kill for her, and she could find a life for herself. Marry, have children. Forget him.

Ril focused on that years-old pattern, let it fill him. Then, while the humans all watched, he lifted his arm, pointing, reaching and slowly turning, angling more and more to the south, pointing off toward the edge of the valley.

"There," he said at last. "She's there."

Behind him, Leon's shock nearly broke his trance. "What are you saying?"

"She's there," Ril breathed. "I can track her."

Leon shoved clothes furiously into a travel pack, not caring that they got rumpled or perhaps even torn. Clothes, money . . . He'd need money to hire a ship and to buy horses on the other side. An ablution kit. Would he need that? Of course he would, what was he thinking? Something of Lizzy's? Some clothes for her? He had to stop for a minute and put a shaking hand over his watering eyes. He'd thought she was lost to him, only Ril could track her. How the hell could he track her? Leon didn't care. They'd hunt her abductors down and kill them and get his baby back. Just him, forty-seven years old and starting to feel it on cold nights, and a crippled battler. None of the other battlers would come along and risk their precious masters.

He sobbed hard but swallowed it, shoving more gear he couldn't focus on into his bag. Ril was changing in the next room. Mace had said he'd take them to Para Dubh, and Solie had given them as much money as she could, including several gems now hidden in the fake heel of his boot. Lizzy was probably going to be sold. Maybe they could buy her back.

They were going to sell his little girl? Leon had to put both hands over his face.

He heard his name and looked up to see his wife standing in the doorway. She'd never yelled at him for all the times he'd deserted the family to go on one of his damn missions, or for how he spent more time with Ril than with her. She had to be aching to get him going this time, but she walked forward instead and put her arms around him.

"Make sure you come home," she whispered. "All of you. You got it? Don't you come back without her!"

"I won't," Leon promised, hugging her tight. "I'll bring her back."

"Then we'll never let her out of our sight again," Betha added viciously.

Leon started to weep. He couldn't help it, and his wife wept, too, her fingernails digging into his back as she held him.

"Papa!" Cara shouted. "Papa, come down here!"

Leon separated from Betha, wiping his eyes. "I better

get down there," he said, managing a smile. His wife matched it, her eyes shining with tears.

"You do that. I'll finish packing for you, silly man." She turned him to the door and patted his bottom to send him on his way.

Leon went out into the hall and down the stairs to the front porch. Outside, Mace was sitting on the swing beside the Widow Blackwell, his master. Leon didn't have the faintest idea what the woman's first name was, but she looked at him sympathetically. Of all the others, he knew she was the most likely to go with them, but she was the dorm mother of every urchin and orphan in town. She was the last one who could leave—which meant Mace couldn't go, either. Not farther than Para Dubh.

He considered her for only a moment before turning to the front yard. Most of the neighbors were still there, standing in groups and conversing, all of them shooting looks at the young man waiting nervously at the foot of the stairs, a heavy travel pack by his feet. Justin Porter. He looked up at Leon, twisting his hat nervously between his hands.

"Um," he stammered. "I'm coming with you."

Leon blinked. "What?"

The boy took a deep breath, and Leon wondered distantly where his father was. Cal Porter would have a heart attack if he knew what his son was suggesting. Either that, or he'd talk them all to death.

"I was with Lizzy when she was kidnapped. I should have protected her, and I let her down. I need to make up for that."

"We're not going out there to salvage your pride, boy," Leon responded coldly.

"That's not it!"

"I don't have time to care," Leon replied, turning to go back into the house.

"I love her!" Justin shouted. Leon stopped, every muscle tense. "I love her," the boy repeated. "I want to marry her." Leon turned and saw how miserable Justin looked as he added, "I *have* to go. If you don't take me, I'll just follow you anyway. I don't care what it costs, I'm going to get her back."

Leon studied the youth, really studied him, wishing for once he had Ril's talent for empathy. Not that Ril cared what others thought. Right now, Leon envied the battler that as well.

"Fine," he said, vaguely aware that he would never agree if he weren't already emotionally drained. "But you have to keep up." When Justin beamed, grin huge and innocent, Leon sighed and said, "Get inside." The boy ran past, carrying his pack, and Leon rubbed his forehead and looked at Mace. The big battler stared quietly forward, one of the widow's hands held in his own. She was smiling.

Leon headed back inside, stepping over Mia and around Ralad. He could hear Cara and Nali in the kitchen yelling at each other. As he walked down the hall, both girls turned from Justin to him.

"I wanna come, too!" Cara demanded.

"Don't you start with me," he told her, and looked at Justin. "Show me what you brought." The boy nodded frantically and started to dump the contents of his pack onto the table.

Ril entered the kitchen. Mia hung on his leg while he tried to fasten his cloak. Seeing Justin, he stopped, one eyebrow raised. Justin saw him, too and froze, swallowing repeatedly. Ril eyed Leon.

"He's coming," Leon declared. Stomping out of the room, he went to see what his wife had collected. Behind him, Ril looked at the frightened boy and growled. Justin flinched.

For the second time in the same number of weeks, Mace flew over the mountains toward Para Dubh. This time the only battler to accompany him rode within his mantle, along with two men.

They were awkward to carry, as he needed to remain incorporeal enough to fly quickly but solid enough to keep them aloft. He was careful not to jostle the trio, but he was also glad when he finally dropped down yet again at the docks and let them loose. Ril shook himself, staring out at the water while Justin pulled his pack onto his back and waited nervously.

Leon turned toward Mace, nodding. "Thank you."

Mace shifted his energy in a nod of his own. He'd have to project his thoughts to speak in this form, and he couldn't do that to a human other than Solie or Lily. He certainly didn't want to do it with any *man*, though Leon was different. He had to be, for Ril to have forgiven him. Mace never would have stayed with his original master, even if Jasar hadn't been a sadistic, back-stabbing woman killer.

*Good luck,* he sent to Ril instead. The younger battler turned and raised his hand in a wave.

Mace couldn't imagine living as damaged as Ril was. Back in the home hive, Ril wouldn't have been allowed to survive his wounds, since they made him next to useless in a fight. Still, Solie's word on that was law, and Ril was a brother. *Come back to us,* he added, and he lifted off the ground again, rising up into the air to return to the Valley. His tarrying would only make it harder for them to hire a ship.

*Don't I always?* Ril sent faintly. *Guard the queen.*

That was something else Mace couldn't understand.

To actually leave the queen . . . ? Ril was a very strange battler indeed. Mace flickered and soared high, eager to get back to Lily and Solie, where life wasn't so complex.

Below, Ril watched the battler who had been his first real friend in this world head for home. He knew Mace's thoughts and his opinions. Battlers didn't have secrets from each other, which was something that the humans didn't really understand. *They* lied to each other all the time without even meaning to. Battlers didn't.

He acknowledged what Mace felt and turned again to look at the sea, the dark blue expanse across which Lizzy had been taken. It felt as deep as the world and wider than the universe.

He didn't look back.

# Chapter Seven

Lizzy didn't see it when the ship docked, but she felt the side shudder against the wharf and heard the men shouting in renewed excitement. Everything lurched in a way that was different from progress through waves, and stopped. Then there came only an idle up-and-down motion as the ship bobbed.

It was hours before they came for her. Lizzy huddled in the corner of her cage, one hand over her eyes as the light threatened to blind her. The door rattled as the chain was unlocked, and she cringed back farther into the corner, her heart pounding. She should be brave, she knew. She should fight them. That's what her father would do. But all she could do was whimper as they grabbed her arm and dragged her out of her confinement, laughing harshly at her. She was pinched and grabbed in places no one had ever touched her, made to shriek and cry as they put her in irons, shackling her feet and wrists with a long chain hanging between. Their weight pulled at her wrists. Her father would swing that chain and brain his captors; Lizzy was dragged by it across the floor and up some wooden steps.

It was the first time she'd seen the sun since she was kidnapped. She kept her head down, her eyes squeezed shut as they led her across the deck. She heard the sailors calling to each other, but they didn't speak to her at all—she was just cargo to them. Lizzy kept her eyes closed. The light was painful and she was afraid to see anything anyway. The heat of this place was near to overwhelming, like a wall that pushed on her chest, stealing her breath, and she could smell strange things over the salt water, the reek of unwashed men and her own dirt.

"She's filthy," a voice said, sounding unimpressed. "And scrawny. Did you even bother to feed her?"

Lizzy forced herself to look up, her eyes shielded by her trembling hands. Before her on the dock stood the man with whom Loren had been so stupid as to flirt. He was ignoring Lizzy, instead looking uncertainly at someone else: a fat, heavily tanned man with what looked like a sheet wrapped around him and more jewelry than Lizzy had ever seen. He reeked of cloying perfume.

"She's from that valley with the free battlers," her kidnapper said. Lizzy still didn't know what his name was, but he looked at the newcomer with grudging respect. Lizzy had a guess that if he didn't convince the robed man of her value, he was out a lot of money. The thought of what he'd do then was terrifying. "She knows how they do it."

"Oh." The perfumed man sniffed. "I don't buy fairy tales. Do you think me stupid? Free battlers. Hmph. You sailors believe anything." He looked Lizzy up and down while her kidnapper sputtered apoplectically. "Skinny, next to breastless. Too pale to put in the fields. She'd die from the heat. Too blonde for service. No one wants a girl with hair like straw." He sniffed again. "Too *northern*. I'd have to sell her far inland to keep their diplomats from seeing her and screaming that we're breaking the treaties. Barely worth the effort."

"You can't be serious!" the kidnapper whined. "Do you know what I gave up to bring her here?"

"That's not my fault. I never told you to." The perfumed man stepped forward, eyeing Lizzy critically. She felt like an insect. "Twelve gold," he decided.

"Twelve!" the sailor wailed.

"All I can use her for is a battler sacrifice." The buyer turned away. "No negotiations. I don't need her."

He headed down the gangway, back toward the pier. Lizzy's abductor shot a hateful look at her, his fist trembling as though he were about to lash out, but he hurried after the robed man instead. "Fine! Twelve! But it's an unfair price!"

"It's twice what you'd get selling her to a brothel, and you know it." The robed man turned to give Lizzy a final glance before setting again on his way. "Bring her," he ordered, waving negligently at a small group of henchmen.

Two men and a woman came on board the boat, all of them dressed in short blue tunics made of extremely light fabric. Their legs were bare, even the woman's, and their skin was a deeply tanned brown. One of them handed the sailor a dozen coins while the others removed the heavy shackles Lizzy wore, replacing these with lighter ones, including a length of chain that rose to a collar they placed around her neck. Her abductor ignored her completely as he studied his gold, testing each piece with his teeth while Lizzy was led away. She never did find out what his name was, or even the name of his ship.

Her new captors tugged her along behind them as they walked, likely following the man who'd bought her. Lizzy let them drag her, stumbling on the hot ground in her bare feet in the abbreviated steps her chains allowed. Tears poured down her cheeks. She knew what a battler sacrifice was. They were going to kill her.

*Daddy!* she wailed silently. *Ril!* She also cried for her mother, or Loren, or anyone who could save her. No one answered. There was no way anyone would come for her here. She was going to die in this place, murdered to trap a battler.

Lizzy sobbed silently at the end of her chain, towed

along a pier that stretched more than a mile out into the ocean. Once, she would have marveled at that, and at the floating city that hovered directly overhead, but now she felt like she were already half dead and all that remained was taking the final blow.

# Chapter Eight

*Southern Dancer* moved steadily south. Built to carry passengers instead of cargo, she had no sails. Instead, three water sylphs swam under her, bearing the ship onward and leaving her deck clear of masts and lines. Most of her passengers were wealthy merchants or nobility heading down to warm cities in the south for business or leisure. These seemed accustomed to soft lives, where a walk around the railing on the ship was an unnecessary amount of exercise. Thus, the activities of those on the front deck were truly alien, if entertaining to watch.

Leon ignored this audience, used to being stared at when he worked as the head of security in the king's castle in Eferem. Of course, back then the spectators were students eager to learn, not a group of effeminate weaklings without the common sense of a dog. To go on a pleasure cruise along the coast . . . ? Didn't they know there were pirates in these waters? Or that Meridal wasn't the only kingdom to practice slavery, no matter how they all promised they wouldn't take anyone from the continents to the north? King Alcor hadn't liked to deal with them, no matter how wealthy the southerners were. That was one piece of paranoia with which Leon agreed. The south used sylphs in ways the northern kingdoms never dreamed.

Across from him, Justin was less relaxed at the idea of being watched. He glanced nervously around at the spectators, his hands shifting on the long stick he was using for a practice sword.

"Ignore them," Leon said. "Attack me."

The boy swallowed and lunged, nearly stumbling over his own feet as he tried to jab the end of his stick into Leon's stomach. Leon stepped neatly out of the way and brought his own weapon down on Justin's, knocking it out of his hands. The youth stumbled and landed face-first on the polished deck.

Leon was about to tell him all the things he'd done wrong, when the faint boredom tickling the back of his mind turned to sharp intent. Gasping, Leon spun and brought up his fake sword, catching Ril's before it could break his shoulder or perhaps his head. The battler's eyes widened with surprise, not realizing how he'd given himself away, and Leon looped his sword around, forcing Ril's arm up and away, and swinging for the back of Ril's knees. His legs taken out from under him, the battler crashed onto his back and found Leon's weapon at his throat.

"Much better," Leon gasped, his heart pounding. His entire arm threatened to go numb from where he'd caught Ril's swing. Stick or not, the battler could have taken off his head. "Don't strike so hard next time, though. This is supposed to be practice."

Ril glared, and Leon could feel his humiliation. Six years he had been trying to convince the battler to learn swordplay. Ril couldn't rely on his powers anymore, even if he didn't want to believe it. The sylph had ignored the suggestions and near orders for too long, but now the threat to Lizzy had finally changed his mind. He wasn't terribly good yet, though.

Six weeks it would take them in total to get to Meridal at this boat's speed. Every day, Leon drilled both Ril and Justin in combat. Justin was clumsy and nervous, while Ril was just as bad for other reasons: besides being a reluctant student, he relied too much on power and speed and very little on technique. Essentially, he still fought like a battle sylph. Still, Leon was glad he was trying. He didn't want to order his battler to do anything ever again—had in fact sworn to him that he wouldn't—but to save his daughter he was prepared to do anything. Ril had to learn to live and fight as a human. If they were ever forced to reveal he was a sylph, they would likely have only one chance.

"You did really well," Leon told him, but the compliment fell on deaf ears. The battler shoved himself to his feet and stalked off, pushing his way through the murmuring crowd. Leon sighed.

"I didn't think you'd be able to beat him," Justin said, standing up.

"Keep thinking that," Leon replied, turning around and dropping back into an attack position. "Now defend yourself."

The boy yelped and dropped his fake sword at the first hit. Silently groaning, Leon gave him a few seconds to pick it up before going at him again. They only had a few more weeks before they reached Meridal. Before that, he had to turn Justin into someone who wouldn't get them all killed.

He stepped out of the way of the same uncoordinated lunge as before and swung his sword, smacking the boy across the buttocks as punishment. Justin screeched and went rolling, and the audience roared with delighted laughter.

Ril stalked down to the room they'd been given in the belly of the ship. He didn't know how much it cost, though he'd seen how the negotiations made Leon cringe. They hadn't got much for their money. Theirs was a windowless room with a narrow bed against three of the walls. His own was on the wall across from the door.

Ril dropped into bed with a groan. He hadn't even

wanted to fight the stupid man, but what other choice did he have but to learn? He'd ridden Leon's shoulder in the enslaved form of a hawk when he first learned about Meridal, and he knew as well as his master about the battlers there: they patrolled the cities, attacking anyone who broke the law. If Ril used his powers, they'd sense him, and he couldn't defend himself from even *one* of them. He would have to hide his aura like a hatchling from an attacking hive, and that meant learning the sword if he was to kill whoever had Lizzy. He hated swords. They felt weak.

Throwing his arm over his head, he closed his eyes, feeling again the rocking motion of the ship as the water sylphs pushed it through the ocean waves. He could feel them as well, and hear them as they chattered to each other. Silence hadn't been demanded of these as it was of the sylphs summoned both farther north and to the south, and they never shut up. Ril hadn't slept well since they set sail, and he suspected that if he could actually eat food, he'd be vomiting it up on a regular basis.

Still, he was tired now, and even if those idiot sylphs were babbling, at least he didn't have to listen to the idiot boy snore on top of that—or feel the edge of Leon's dreams. Ril had never before had any idea he was in danger of falling into them, not until he'd started needing to sleep every bloody night like some kind of human. So far, he hadn't gone far enough to join in any of his master's dreams, and he had no intention of ever doing so.

Relaxing, the arm over his eyes slid down above his head. His eyes stayed closed, his lashes fluttering as his breathing deepened. Ril slept and dreamed, and even as he drifted off, telling himself that he wouldn't wander, he did.

Lizzy, after weeks spent in a cage that usually held goats, now found herself in a cell with walls of pale adobe. The front of the cell was barred, which at least meant that the chains were gone from her wrists and ankles. The collar remained, though, heavy around her neck. The entire room was barely six feet across, though that was worlds more room than she'd had before.

She didn't explore. Instead, she lay curled in a ball on her tiny bed, clenched fists held up to her face. So much had happened, she'd gone numb. She'd had to—only if that were true, how could she still be feeling such terror? She shuddered, exhausted, still filthy and frightened. No one would explain anything to her, and the wing she was in was otherwise empty.

When she was brought here, she'd seen dozens of floors where catwalks wound through hundreds of stacked cages with humans inside: tired, tongueless people who gaped at her silently while sylphs flitted everywhere, dropping down and drinking their energy. She'd recognized what was happening, having seen her father feed Ril enough times. The battler would just stand there with his eyes half-closed, seemingly doing nothing for a few minutes while Leon waited patiently. These sylphs did that, too, but *their* masters screamed soundlessly in protest. Although how could a slave be a master? And why would the sylph then go to the next cell, and the next, drinking from three or four inmates before flitting out again?

She didn't care. Lizzy curled up even tighter, trying to become as small as possible. She tried to think only of her parents and her sisters and Ril, even of Justin, who'd abandoned her, and Loren, whose stupidity had caused all of this. She had to keep them in mind or she'd go mad, she just knew it.

"Ril," she whispered, falling asleep to the memory of those half-closed eyes and the feeling that he was draining something from her father, taking something that she herself could nearly feel, as though he were taking it from her as well.

Dreaming, she found herself walking across the grass that grew beyond the town in the Valley, the sky above a rich blue and boasting massive white clouds stacking up to the size of mountains. The breeze was cool on her skin, streaming her hair out behind her. Ril was walking toward her, stripping off his blue and gold coat and dumping it in the grass behind him.

Lizzy moved eagerly forward, her fingers fumbling with the buttons of her blouse, forcing them out of the holes and the garment off over her shoulders, leaving her breasts and stomach bare. Ril pulled off his shirt and unbuttoned his pants, still walking, his eyes locked on hers. Lizzy pulled down her skirt and stepped out of it, naked, and then suddenly his arms came around her. She pressed herself against his warm body, her hands reaching up to cup his face and comb through that blond hair he wore long in front, shorter in the back. He gasped at her touch, his mouth open, and ducked down, pressing against her lips.

Lizzy cried out at the feel of him. At that sound, Ril bucked back in pain, his horrified eyes staring down at her, and he began to break apart under her hands, his face fracturing into a thousand pieces. She screamed, but he fell away from her, dissolving into smoke and lightning— only there wasn't enough of him left to hold his shape. He blew away in the wind, scattering as motes of dust across the meadow.

Ril started awake, gasping. For the first moment, he didn't know where he was and tried to change shape. Sudden pain shocked him back into awareness, and he sat up slowly, wincing. Now he could feel the rocking of the boat and hear the endless gossip of the water sylphs. He put a hand to his head, barely aware that his hand was shaking, and he closed his eyes, just focused on breathing. He had to breathe.

It wasn't fair, he decided. On top of everything else, why was he now getting nightmares?

Shalatar Misharol walked down the passage in the holding cells, checking the feeders. It was important that their health remain high, and he'd earned the accolades of the emperor by instituting a weekly exercise regimen and change of diet that made them the healthiest feeders possible. This was reflected in the work of the sylphs who lived off their energy.

It was a good system. Every sylph summoned here had a primary master who gave the orders, but after that, each was bonded to five submasters, men and women who'd had their tongues cut out to prevent them from giving orders. To help ensure that, the sylphs were under strict orders to ignore any attempt to communicate by a feeder, no matter what it was, and to report such to the nearest handler. The feeders learned quickly that any of them who tried were put to death. They existed only to provide energy for their sylphs, and with access to that kind of power, even the youngest, weakest sylph could manage miracles a northern sylph would need twice the age to accomplish with only a single master.

Shalatar took his responsibility seriously. The sylphs here were the backbone of the empire, and their work was hard. The emperor's city was entirely airborne, and it took nearly a hundred air sylphs alone to manage that. And of course, there were other elementals who served different functions. Ninety percent of Meridal was city and the remaining ten had to produce the food required to feed the population, no matter how poor the desert soil. Five thousand sylphs in all meant twenty-five thousand feeders. This stable alone serviced two thousand sylphs, and Shalatar was in charge of the health and happiness of each.

He had been one of the first to recognize that the health of the feeders made a difference. Their happiness was another matter. Each was in his own cell, and the cells were kept scrupulously clean, but other than weekly walks in a guarded courtyard, they never left the prison. These men and women stared at him dully as he passed or, more often, didn't pay him any attention at all. Their cells were nearly silent as well, save for the shuffling of feet or the sounds of the sylphs coming in at regular intervals to replenish their energy.

While he could only spot-check the stable for quality, for the most part he found nothing but good results. Clean feeders, clean water, clean cages. He saw one man scratching at lice and made a note for him to be shaved. Another was twitching spastically, drool coming out of his mouth. That wasn't good. A crazed feeder might pass bad energy on to a sylph. An ensuing note listed the feeder to be destroyed. He was easier to replace than a well-trained sylph.

Beyond the feeder cells—all located deep underneath the city, where it was easy to keep them cool—were the cells for the sacrifices. Shalatar had nothing to do with that element of the business, not having any truck with battlers beyond feeding them, but his twin sister did. He had come here to find her.

His tablet tucked under his arm, Shalatar walked down rows of cages holding women. All were beautiful but flawed in some way—they were good enough to lure a battler but not quite right to be assigned to the harem. Either that, or they'd already spent time in the harem and were now being liquidated. This happened when either the battlers ignored them or one took a particular interest. Once any battler started to mate exclusively with a woman, it was time to get her out of there, before he started focusing more on her than his duties. The harems were to keep the sylphs happy, not lazy.

As Shalatar passed, the women stared at him in fear or pleaded for him to either let them go or return them to the harem. He ignored them all. If the women didn't end as sacrifices, they would be sold somewhere else in the city—if anyone would actually want to buy a woman who'd been used by battlers—or made into feeders with removed tongues. That was all they were good for and was their most likely fate. Once a woman had been bred to a battler, she couldn't reliably be used as a sacrifice to draw a new one. Somehow, battlers knew and would rarely come for ex-concubines. And of course no battler was allowed to feed from a woman, only to fuck her. Once, these women had found their throats cut when they were deemed useless for the harems, but that had upset some battlers. Nor could the women be used for sport in the gladiator arena. That drove the battlers mad. No, they could only be used as feeders for the elementals . . . which meant a loss of revenue for the battler section. It was a logistical headache that he didn't envy his sister.

She handled it well, of course, the same as she handled the battlers. While their masters were male, to go into the harems and direct a battler took a very delicate female sensibility, for which Rashala was renowned. She could calm the most outraged battler with a touch and a word.

Shalatar found his sister in the quarantine section for new women. The cages were kept tremendously clean, but there was always some chance of disease, and the idea of using a healer for slaves was outrageous. They did have access to one, for use in the arena in case a fighter was especially valiant and earned the praise of the emperor, or if a sylph was injured somehow, which happened sometimes, if rarely. Once or twice, Shalatar had used her to deal with his own stomach pain, though it always returned when he became stressed. Still, he couldn't imagine calling on her when a simple standard quarantine would remove all issues.

Rashala was standing on a walkway above the pens, looking down. Like him, Shalatar's sister was shaved hairless to show her status as a bonded serf, risen from the status of slave due to the excellence of her work. Her quality had given Shalatar the chance to show his own, as her brother, which was a boon he'd never been able to repay. She wore berry juice on her lips, staining them a harsh purple, and her robes were a similar color to his own.

Shalatar walked up beside her and put a hand on her shoulder. "What are you doing, my sister?" he asked. "We were supposed to have lunch."

"Bakl bought a new slave," she said, and pointed. Shalatar looked down at a skinny, dirty girl with hair like straw and raised an eyebrow. "I'm trying to decide if she's worth putting in the harem."

He made a face. The girl was nearly white, with no golden tone to her skin at all. "Eighty-nine might like her. You told me he goes for the unique ones."

"True, but then he obsesses over them. That girl with the tattoos over her entire body . . . ?" Rashala shook her head ruefully. "We barely got him off her, and then we had to sell her to another kingdom when he kept trying to get to her. He killed the previous three. I don't want a repeat of that."

"So sacrifice her."

"I'll have to. But Bakl paid twelve gold for her. The idiot

thought he made a good deal because of her yellow hair. The sellers wanted ten times as much."

"The sellers always do." Shalatar turned away. "Leave it for now. I'm hungry. You can tell me about it over lunch."

His sister was reasonable, and so they left, but not before Rashala made a note on her tablet: the yellow-haired girl would be killed on the altar at the next sacrifice. Better that than putting her in the harem and having Eighty-nine decide she was the love of his life. That was far more trouble than it was worth.

Exiting the pens beneath the floating city, they took a shortcut through the cells holding the slaves and criminals intended for the gladiatorial arena. Most of these seemed glum, though they all still had their tongues and at least some chance at glory. Not that any of them had ever found it. Not when their opponent in the arena would be a battler.

# Chapter Nine

Propelled by its trio of water sylphs, *Southern Dancer* made its way down the coast, stopping at seven progressively warmer cities before turning at last into deeper waters, pushing against the current toward a far more distant shore. Just to be sure they were right to continue, at each stop Ril stood at the front of the ship, focusing, and each time he shook his head no. When the ship lost sight of land completely, Justin was afraid they were heading away from her entirely, but the battler was not. Wherever Lizzy was, he swore they were headed in the right direction.

"How does he know?" Justin asked Leon one day. They were all gathered at the above-deck passenger tables for lunch, Ril there simply to maintain the illusion. He stood at the prow of the ship, ostensibly eating while he watched waves break against the ship, but he was really throwing spoonfuls of food down to the fish below.

"Know what?" Leon asked.

"Where Lizzy is."

Leon shrugged and took a swallow of wine. "I don't know."

"Why don't you ask him?" Justin asked, a little bemused. If it were him, he'd have demanded the answer right away.

"Because if he'd wanted me to know, he would have told me."

"But he's your b—" Justin broke off and flushed at the

older man's expression. "He's yours. Doesn't he *have* to tell you?"

"No. He's not a slave. If he can find my daughter, I don't care how he does it."

Justin sighed, returning to his meal. He wanted to know everything the battler did, but Ril frightened him. So did all battlers, but he could avoid the rest. Not Ril. Every time he came to Lizzy's house, the sylph seemed to be there, watching. He didn't say anything—Justin didn't even think he'd ever exchanged a greeting with the battler—but he knew the creature didn't like him. Sometimes that made Justin mad. He was tired of dealing with someone who could make him want to wet himself with just a look, and he'd always wished Ril would just go away. He'd even had a few daydreams about challenging the battler to a fight and beating him, with Lizzy watching in adoration. Such thoughts would be suicide with most battlers, but Ril was a cripple. A good fighter could beat him, which Leon had proven by knocking him right on his ass. Justin had needed to bite his tongue to keep from cheering about that.

Leon was staring at him, and Justin flushed, staring down at his plate. He wanted this man to be his father-in-law. It would be mortifying for him to learn how Justin wanted to humiliate his battler.

The older man regarded him and then Ril, who had finished emptying his plate and now leaned against the railing, staring out at the empty horizon. He turned back to Justin. "Leave him alone."

"Sir?"

"Just leave him alone." Leon finished his wine. "Don't make the mistake of thinking he's weak."

Justin went red. "I'd never—"

"You were. I can tell. So can he. You say you want to marry my daughter? Before I give you any blessing, you better prove yourself man enough for her." Then Leon stood and walked away, carrying his plate and glass.

Ril turned, watching Justin, but he finally followed his master. When he passed the table, he gazed down at Justin and his lip curled up in a silent snarl. Justin's cheeks burned. He'd do what Leon said. He'd try. But that wouldn't stop him from hating the battler as much as he feared him.

Leon had registered both Justin and Ril as his sons in the ship's books. Justin was young enough and Ril certainly looked young enough, even if he was actually centuries old. None of them really resembled the others, but at least Ril had Leon's sandy blond hair and Justin a somewhat similar nose. Nonetheless, twice a day Leon took Ril to his room, and he wondered how much of the lie the passengers believed and what they really thought was going on. He doubted they had any idea of the truth.

He now stood in his cabin, his back against the door. Ril fronted him, one arm braced against the wall behind Leon's head, his other hand resting against the side of his master's neck. It wasn't often that the battler touched him. He didn't touch anyone if he could avoid it, save Leon's girls, but his hand was warm and relaxed now. His eyes were half-closed and unfocused, his breathing slow, and he fed, drawing in the energy Leon released just as a natural by-product of living. Leon had never really asked, but Ril once remarked that his energy felt like a thick warm mist coming off his master's skin. After twenty-one years, Leon could feel the drain. Most masters couldn't—not even Solie—but Leon had always been fascinated by the intimacy he shared with Ril, this proof that there was one being in the world who would always need him.

Standing there, Leon let himself relax. Ril's feeding felt like a light brush against the hair on his arm, barely there but undeniable. Except for Solie's, it was the only energy Ril could digest, or absorb, or whatever term it was he wanted to use. The rest of the world was poison to him unless he took the pattern of another human within himself. That was why before they left the Valley, Leon had suggested Ril be impressed with Justin's pattern as a precaution. Mace could have arranged it through the queen easily enough; even Petr's priests could do it. If Leon died—and he didn't discount that possibility—Ril would quickly die of starvation. Ril had simply growled. It wasn't just the energy, Leon knew. Easy though the bond was to make, it was also permanent and sylphs obeyed the humans to whom they were patterned. They had no choice. Ril despised Justin, and from the look the boy had just given him on deck, granting him the power to command the battler would be a mistake.

Leon assessed his seemingly human battler. Even if he were killed, he suspected Ril wouldn't take a new master. He'd let himself die first. Which was just another reason to stay alive, he told himself—for his daughter and for his pretend son. And for Justin as well, whom he'd only brought out of guilt. Was his daughter in love with the boy? He hoped so. For her happiness, he truly hoped so.

Ril took a deep breath, draining one last draft that tingled along the length of Leon's arms. A moment later the sylph fully opened his eyes, gazing at his master. His irises were pale gray, like ice chips under a cloudy sky, and they were unguarded, as they always were right after he fed. Leon had seen his battler's soul this way even when Ril was trapped in the body of a bird and hating him for it. He'd never told Ril, though, for fear the sylph would never look at him during that moment again.

His battler's eyes were troubled, even frightened, and he was desperate to act, though this was all covered by helplessness. There was despair there, deep and nearly overwhelming. It was heartbreaking to see.

"What's wrong?" Leon whispered.

Despite himself, Ril was most likely to answer him when he'd just fed. Now was no different. "Lizzy. I could feel her. She was so terrified, I could sense her even from here. She thought she was going to die."

Leon went cold. "She's not . . ."

"No." Ril pushed away from the wall and went to sit on his bed, staring at the hard pillow. "Her fear is less. At least, I can't feel it anymore. Whatever happened, she survived."

Leon felt his terror ease, replaced by both relief and curiosity. Justin had already asked the question, how was it that Ril could track her? He shouldn't be able to. None of the other battlers could, but Ril had pinpointed her immediately. If anything, given his injury, he should have been even less able to find her. Unless . . .

Lizzy couldn't be his master, could she? She *couldn't*. He'd know, wouldn't he? Ril didn't treat Lizzy any different from any of Leon's other daughters. In fact, he focused more on the younger ones. Lizzy was the last one he paid attention to. That wouldn't happen if Lizzy were his master. In fact, given how every other battler reacted to a female master . . .

Leon narrowed his eyes, thinking. One thing he could be sure of was that Ril wasn't sleeping with his daughter, or with anyone else. He'd heard the jokes, and he knew they were true: Ril had lost all interest in women after he was hurt. Leon ached for him, but that didn't mean he wanted his Lizzy involved with the battle sylph. She deserved children, a family, and a husband who could think and feel the way she did. Much as Leon personally loved Ril, his sylph couldn't provide any of those things. She deserved a human.

So his ability to track her had to have something to do with how Lizzy was Leon's daughter. Perhaps Ril could track all of his children through his bloodline.

The sylph jerked and looked up at him, his eyes again guarded. Leon nodded. That's what it was: a link through the blood. There was still so little he and the others knew about sylphs. Even the sylphs themselves didn't seem to know. They just accepted and acted on instinct. Humans needed a reason.

"You don't know what happened to her?" he asked.

"No," Ril said. "Just that she expected to die and didn't."

Leon sighed. "At least she's alive. Can you feel what's happening now?"

"No."

Leon stepped close, reaching out to run a hand through his battler's soft hair. Ril gazed up, silent. "Try," Leon said, his emotions roiling. He meant to comfort and encourage, so he didn't realize that he'd inadvertently given an order instead.

Lizzy's terror had been real—real and overwhelming. She'd lain nude and spread-eagled on a stone table dark with blood, a gag in her mouth and her limbs tied down. A man had towered over her with a hand sickle sharp enough to cleave off her head. A gate shone above.

They'd known there was a battler sniffing around on the other side, were told so by a healer sylph who didn't look the slightest bit inclined to save Lizzy even if her head did come off. She'd been so terrified, she'd been screaming inside her mind, wailing for her mother, for her father, for Ril, for Justin, for anyone. She'd soiled herself as well, and her heart pounded until she thought it would just burst and spare her all of this.

Despite that, nothing had happened. The battler circled the gate and she felt him looking at her, but he didn't come through. He watched her for a while and finally vanished, leaving the man who was supposed to bind him screaming at the priests who'd set up the ceremony. Apparently, this wasn't supposed to happen.

Eventually, the man left, still swearing, as did the priests. Finally Lizzy was untied and returned to a cell, tossed a simple cotton shift to wear, and left alone. There she'd collapsed in a daze, shaking. She might have fainted for a while, as she lost track of time, and when she woke, a woman with neither head hair nor eyebrows was standing outside her cell, staring in and talking to a muscular woman at her side.

"There's no point in putting her up as a sacrifice again." The hairless woman frowned, regarding Lizzy as though she was a terrible inconvenience.

"Do you want to send her to the feeder pens?" the second woman asked.

The first frowned even more. "She's completely useless to me then. I still want my twelve gold out of her." The bald woman turned away. "Put her in the harem."

"Yes, mistress."

While the second woman groveled, bowing deeply, the bald woman looked in at Lizzy one last time before she left. Lizzy shrank into the corner, wondering what was going to happen to her now.

They cleaned her. Lizzy had been washed for her aborted death sentence, but now she was bathed in scented water, her hair shampooed and combed before being curled into ringlets all around her head. The servants who did this tutted about her skin tones and spent hours scrambling for light enough makeup for her to wear. Then she was dressed in a gown made of she didn't know what kind of material, which was pale green and completely translucent.

They hadn't needed any makeup, she decided. She was too red in the face for any of it to show.

"You can't be serious," she gasped, seeing a mirror on the wall. She tried to cover herself, but she wore fine chains on her wrists and the guards kept pulling her hands away from her body.

"She's too thin," decided the woman who'd directed her transformation. The other women who held her chains, and therefore her hands away from herself, sniggered in agreement. Lizzy closed her eyes, not wanting to see them laughing at her.

"Are you a virgin? Girl!" Lizzy's eyes opened after a sudden slap. "Are you a virgin?"

"Y-yes."

"At least they'll like that." The woman sighed. "If Eighty-nine goes for her first, though, just pull her out. I don't want him killing another girl."

"You can't do this!" Lizzy gasped. They started to haul her forward and she balked, trying to brace her bare feet on the slippery floor. "I won't go!"

"Shut it, girl!" the woman snapped. "The only reason you keep your tongue in there is because some of the battlers like the screaming."

Lizzy fought them all the way down the hall and up a short flight of stairs. There were no windows, but there was light coming from somewhere, shining down through vents in the ceiling. The floor and walls were the same pale, adobe color, but the door ahead was pure ebony wood and heavily carved. Two women with spears guarded it. Any hope Lizzy might have had about getting away were dashed. Any one of the five women looked stronger than she, and there was nowhere to go but back the way she'd come.

Only one of them needed to hold her, despite her struggles, while the others opened the door. Perfume and screams wafted out. "Oh gods," Lizzy whispered, just before they yanked her inside.

Within was a massive room, well lit and soft, the ceiling held up by columns that were draped with gauzy silk. The floor was covered with pillows, and on many of them lounged women dressed no better than Lizzy, providing they were dressed at all. Others were dancing or playing music. The room was fifty feet wide but hundreds of feet long, stretching away from them. A smaller door could be seen distantly at the other end.

The long walls held dozens of small archways covered by gauzy curtains. From many of them came moans, and right in the middle of the floor, she saw with her first startled glimpse, a man had a woman on her hands and knees, backside hiked high as he pumped furiously into her. Lizzy went even redder than before and made a strangled sound.

"Welcome to the battler sex pit," one of the female guards laughed, undoing her chains. Putting a hand on Lizzy's back, she pushed. Lizzy went sprawling into the room. The door shut behind her.

Immediately, the battler in the middle of the room looked up at her, even as he continued to— Lizzy couldn't even think of a term crude enough for what he was doing. He was big and bulky, his skin an olive shade and his legs bending backward at the knee, his feet and hands long and clawed. His eyes and nose were normal, but his chin was absurdly long and he had no mouth. Bare skin stretched over where it should have been. On his chest, the number 408 had been tattooed.

Four-oh-eight looked at her speculatively, then down at the woman he was with. Then back at her, as if trying to make up his mind whether to finish with his current lover or switch immediately.

Lizzy scrambled to her feet and bolted for the closest wall, right through one of the doorways and into an alcove . . . where she found a different battler with a woman underneath him. He snatched at Lizzy halfheartedly, not really interested, and she backed out, retreating and instead moving up the length of the main room.

The chamber was nearly three times the size of the market back home, large enough that the hundred or more women she guessed were here had room to stretch out, or to retreat into a corner with whichever battler expressed an interest. There didn't seem to be anywhere to retreat *from* the battlers to, though, other than several bathrooms. These were placed after every tenth alcove, and Lizzy quickly locked herself into one.

A knock came at the door. "Are you going to come out?" a female voice asked.

"No," Lizzy gasped. She knew how battlers felt about sex. There was no way she was going out there.

The female voice sighed. "Look, if you stay in there, the guards will take you away, and it's much worse to be a feeder. Besides, that's the only bathroom where the shower gets really hot. The rest of them are lukewarm."

"I don't want to come out," Lizzy said.

"They'll make you a feeder instead."

"What's a feeder?"

"Tongueless slaves who spend their lives getting their energy sucked out by sylphs. At least here you can talk."

Lizzy shuddered and slowly reached to open the door. Outside, a woman older than herself with long black hair and tan skin looked at her curiously. She was dressed in a translucent silk gown even sheerer than Lizzy's. "What bizarre hair," she said.

"Is it safe?" Lizzy whispered, looking around. A group of women were playing cards nearby, acknowledging her quizzically, but the curtains around an alcove close by were shaking and she could hear a woman screaming hysterically from the other side. "Is—is she okay?"

The black-haired woman glanced over her shoulder. "Who, Ap? Sure. She always screams like that. They love it. She's been here nearly longer than anyone." She regarded Lizzy again. "My name is Eapha. What's yours?"

"Lizzy. Is there any way out of here?"

"No. There's only the one door out, and the battlers come in through passages in the ceiling. A human can't fit through. I know a couple of girls who tried." Eapha ran a hand through her hair. "Look, you may as well make the best of it. Battlers are fantastic lovers."

So Lizzy had been hearing for the last six years of her life. She didn't care. "I don't want to!" she wailed, and the other women clucked sympathetically, though a few laughed.

"It doesn't matter," Eapha told her. "Even if you want to say no, they pour so much lust into you, you lose control. Trust me. It sinks into your bones. After the first time, you'll wonder what you were ever frightened of."

Lizzy shook her head, backing away. This was insane. She did *not* want to spend the rest of her life as some sort of sex toy to keep a bunch of battlers happy.

Behind Eapha, Ap's screams finally died out in a sated moan. The curtains moved and another battler exited. He was shaped exactly like the first two, with the olive skin and backward legs. Strangest of all was his mouthless face. He padded out, his erection bobbing in front of him. The number 391 was tattooed on his chest. He looked in their direction briefly, then went wandering up the length of the room until a plump woman beckoned lovingly and wandered into an alcove. Three-ninety-one followed.

"He's usually good for two or three goes," Eapha told Lizzy. "You wouldn't know it from Ap, but he's very gentle. Most of them are."

Lizzy noticed the way she'd stressed the word *most*. "Is this all they do?" she asked miserably.

"Sure. This is where they come to relax. Our job's to keep them happy." Eapha sighed and took Lizzy's hand. "Come on." When Lizzy balked again, afraid of where she'd take her, the woman smiled. "I'm not going to throw you at one of them."

Reluctantly, Lizzy let her lead. Eapha took her past the alcove Three-ninety-one had gone into and down to the far end of the room, passing more distracted battlers watching a trio of women dance. To her horror, Lizzy counted fifteen of the creatures.

"How many are there?"

"Battlers? Hundreds. You saw the numbers on their chests. I think the highest number I ever saw was seven hundred and two."

"And how many women?"

"Lots. We have about a hundred in here, and there are two or three other harems I've never been in. The battlers are only allowed in one specific harem so that there are enough to go around. They share us, but they don't much like it."

"So I might not have to sleep with any of them, if there are a hundred of us to pick from." Lizzy sagged in relief.

Eapha looked at her sympathetically. "Don't get your hopes up. The average is five women a visit. I've even seen a few who'll cycle through twenty or more." Lizzy felt ill again.

"Here we are." Eapha opened a normal-looking door at

the back of the chamber and led Lizzy into a spartan room lined with bunk beds stacked three high. There were at least fifty. "The guards check that no one is hiding in here, but the battlers usually stay out. This is where we sleep, though if someone isn't outside all the time, the battlers come looking for us. There aren't enough bunks for all of us at one time anyway. Why don't you try and get some sleep?"

Lizzy headed for one of the unoccupied beds, shaking with nervous exhaustion. She didn't even manage to say thank you before she crawled in, pulling the scratchy blanket up around her and putting her head on the pillow. She was asleep in seconds.

Eapha shook her head and headed back out. She knew how Lizzy felt. It wasn't so long since she'd been the terrified newcomer. She'd got over it soon enough, though. Surely the new girl would be the same.

# Chapter Ten

Sylph Valley had observed the Harvest Festival since the town was established. The first few celebrations were sparse, the harvests small. The Community wasn't starving then, not quite, but everyone's belt was tight. Then the harvests became good, and the dancing and celebrating went on long into the night. Lizzy loved each and every festival as much as she was able. As the oldest, she had to take care of her sisters, staying home to care for them in the evening while other girls went to the late-night dance.

At sixteen, she was horrified to discover her parents' expectations hadn't changed. "That's not fair!" she wailed at the breakfast table, trying to show in her eyes the torment through which were putting her. It didn't help. Her father sipped his cofi, looking unimpressed, while her mother regarded her with annoyance.

"Life isn't fair," was Betha's response. "It's your job to take care of the little ones."

"Yeah," Cara added. Her father tapped her on the head and she went back to drinking her milk.

Lizzy ignored her sister. "What about after they go to bed? That's when the dance starts. I want to go to the dance."

"I'm not letting you go on your own to a dance where there are boys."

Lizzy stared in desperation at her mother. It was the best dance of the year, and everyone her age went. To not go would be horrific.

"Maybe I can chaperon her," Leon suggested. When his wife shot him a look, he shrugged.

Such a solution was worse than horrific. No one would pay any attention to her with her father there! Lizzy looked at the chair next to her, where Ril sat, the one-year-old Mia in his lap. He was patiently feeding her some mashed turnips, ignoring the family conversation.

Impulsively, Lizzy threw her arms around his neck and he flinched, nearly dropping both the spoon and the baby. "Ril can take me!" she begged. "He'll protect me." She pressed her cheek against his, her arms tightening around his neck. He smelled like the wind in tall grass. "Please, Ril," she whispered, and he shivered. The feel of it made her heart start to pound. He was very warm, she realized. He also seemed to have stopped breathing.

"What do you say, Ril?" Leon asked.

The battler hesitated.

"Please," Lizzy begged again, pressing herself against him as she tightened the hug. "Please!"

"Okay," he mumbled.

"Get off the poor man," her mother snapped. "You'll smother him."

Lizzy let go of the sylph, beaming at him, a flush on her face. Ril in turn gazed back, seemingly uncertain, and she couldn't help but wonder if it was because of her that his eyes were so wide.

Ril had been her father's battler for longer than Lizzy was alive. For most of that time he'd been a bird, communicating with her by spelling out words on a set of blocks. She'd lost those blocks when they left Eferem's capital, along with all of her toys, but she hadn't noticed in the wonder of seeing Ril as a man. She'd loved him as a bird. She'd loved him even more as a human, with all the passion of her twelve-year-old heart. He hadn't returned that love, though. He did cherish her, she knew, but he cherished Cara, Nali, Ralad, and Mia, too. When she was thirteen, he'd broken her heart completely. By sixteen, she was over him.

Yet when she went with him to the dance, she in her best dress and Ril in his blue and gold uniform, she wondered if some of that passion was coming back. At sixteen she knew she was too old for silly crushes, but it felt good to pretend she'd come with him. So she hung on his arm, giggling and waving at her friends and dragging the battler wherever she went. Ril let her, saying nothing as they headed around the tables set up in the harvested field, Lizzy laughing, tasting the food, and smiling tauntingly at the boys. She had no idea how he felt about any of it, and didn't ask.

The battler on her arm, she discovered, brought her more attention from the boys than she ever would have received on her own. Pumped up on sugared punch and youthful hormones, they challenged the battler by talking to Lizzy, pretending he didn't frighten them at all. That excited her even more.

"Don't you scare them off," Lizzy warned Ril, watching as a group of boys sauntered toward her, Trel Mils and Justin Porter among them. They were both a year older. The attention made her heart pound.

Ril sighed. "Leon doesn't want you to do anything."

"Did he order you to stop me?" she snapped. "He didn't, did he?" Her father never gave Ril orders. "Just because you don't like girls doesn't mean no one else does."

"Lizzy . . ."

"Nothing's going to happen," she assured him. "I just want to have some fun. And don't you dare tell Father!"

Ril didn't answer.

The boys came up then, and she forgot him along with

her long-ago crush. Giggling, she let Trel and Justin bring her a glass of punch and some snacks, reveling in the envy of the other girls as much as in the direct attention. She was a pretty girl, she knew that, and for once she wasn't saddled with three little sisters who liked to cause her trouble. When the band started to play—enthusiastically if not well—she let herself be led again and again out onto the patch of earth they were using as their dance floor. It seemed all of the boys wanted to take turns.

Ril stood on the sidelines, watching without expression . . . which bothered her, oddly, even while she had what was surely the best time of her life. He was a battler—an asexual, broken one as well. He'd rejected her! No, he'd done less than that. He'd ignored her until she gave up hope. Why did she feel guilty?

Almost, Lizzy heard his voice in her mind. He seemed to be telling her that the boys only wanted to dance with her to show bravado. They wanted to tell their friends that they'd danced with her despite her guardian—but she rejected this furiously. The boys liked her. She glared at Ril and turned her back on him, turning her attention on the boy with whom she was currently dancing.

Justin Porter seemed almost afraid of his hand on her hip as he led her stumblingly through the steps of the dance. He was tall and skinny, his Adam's apple jiggling up and down. He had acne on his face, and his hair needed to be cut. His shirtsleeves were also too short. Lizzy regarded him seriously, appraising. He was someone she knew only a little bit, but he'd always been nice, and he was older. For her, older was better. He wasn't as bloody old as Ril, though, who had no idea how many centuries he'd been alive.

The battler was still watching her, she knew, disapproving. On impulse, Lizzy lifted onto her toes and pressed her lips to Justin's.

It was her first kiss. Justin's mouth was wet, his lips thin, and he started in shock at the touch. Physically, it felt a little like kissing a slab of warm meat, but the moment she acted, she heard shouts and clapping. Everyone had seen and was cheering. Lizzy flushed red.

An instant later, Ril had her by the arm. He snarled at Justin, who barely even realized the battler was there. The boy just stared at Lizzy with a look of sudden love on his face. Then her father's battler yanked Lizzy off the dance floor, dragging her despite her protests through the crowd and away.

"Stop it!" Lizzy shouted as he hauled her through a dark and barren cornfield back toward town. "Let me go!"

Ril did so, turning to eye her in the darkness. She could barely see his face, but she could feel his anger.

"What's wrong with you?" she yelled.

"What's wrong with you?" he retorted. "I could feel those boys. All they wanted was to show how brave they were, dancing with the battler's girl." He pointed at her. "They didn't love you!"

Her cheeks burned, and she was glad he couldn't see them in the darkness. "Maybe I don't care! Did you think of that?"

"You kissed him!"

"So?" she shrieked. She advanced on Ril, forcing him back a step. "It's none of your business!"

"What did you think I came out here for? Your father—"

"Leave my father out of this!" She slapped a hand against his hard chest. "I don't care what my father thinks! If I want to kiss someone, I will!"

"I won't let you!"

He sounded so outraged, his gaze burning behind those long blond bangs. She'd always wanted to brush that hair out of his eyes, ever since the first time she saw him. They made him look like one of the characters in her favorite childhood storybook, which her father had read to her at bedtime while Ril nested on the pillow next to her head, more often than not preening her hair while she fell asleep.

She laughed. This was ludicrous. What was she expecting out of him, a human reaction? "What are you going to do about it?" she asked. "Guard me the rest of my life?"

"If I have to!"

The thought of Ril following her around and chasing boys away for the rest of her life made her laugh harder, and her anger was gone just like that. "Well, don't bother. It was a horrible kiss anyway." It had been. She rubbed her mouth, wishing she hadn't done it, that she hadn't tried to make Ril angry or ended up in a fight with him. "That was my first kiss, too. Are they all that bad?"

"I don't know," he answered. "Let's find out." He leaned down and kissed her.

Lizzy's breath caught, her heart nearly stopping. Where kissing Justin had been like kissing a slab of warm meat, Ril's lips were dry and full, and so warm they sent a shock through her that made her body tingle from her lips all the way down to her toes, which she actually felt curl up in her shoes. Her eyes fluttered shut and she just stood there, her mouth pressed to his and not knowing what to do other than feel. It felt good—so good—and in an instant she fell in love with him all over again.

Then Ril was pulling back, his breathing heavy as he backed away into the darkness. Lizzy stumbled, caught herself, and stared at him.

"Ril?" she said.

But he'd left, telling her it never happened, that they hadn't happened, and he'd never brought it up again, or touched or even looked at her. That's what had happened.

Lizzy remembered, even as she realized that she was dreaming about something that had occurred two years earlier. But this time, Ril didn't desert her. He stepped forward instead. His uniform was gone, replaced by plain brown traveling clothes, and his face was exhausted and lined by strain.

"Lizzy!" he shouted, though his voice was barely audible. He reached for her, and his form wavered. This reminded her of the other dream she'd had, where he'd kissed her and suddenly blew away into nothingness.

"Ril!" she shouted back, "I'm here!" She ran toward him, but she couldn't get closer. No matter how fast she ran, he was still a half dozen feet away, reaching helplessly for her. "Ril!"

"Lizzy! We're coming for you. Don't give up. We'll find you!"

Lizzy's eyes widened and tears poured down her cheeks. "W-we . . . ?"

"Your father and I. Leon . . ." Abruptly, Ril put his hands to his forehead, wincing, and the scene changed from the nighttime fields of that long ago dance to the kitchen of her parents' house. Ril shuddered and looked past her. "Leon."

Lizzy turned. Standing in the doorway, dressed in the soft cotton pants and shirt he always slept in, her father stared at her, his hair disheveled and his eyes wide.

"Lizzy?" he gasped. "Baby?"

"Daddy!" Lizzy threw herself forward, sobbing. "Save me, Daddy!"

"Wait—," Ril started.

Lizzy fell into her father's arms, but instead of feeling his embrace, she tumbled into nothingness, shrieking in terror as the dream dissolved. Ril screamed and vanished with it. A moment later she started awake, blinking. Her heart raced. She was back in the bunk where she'd fallen asleep, in the room off the main harem.

She buried her face in the pillow and groaned.

Leon awoke, gasping. He'd dreamed he was back in his house getting ready to go upstairs to—for whatever reason—take a potted plant to his wife. Something had changed, though, and the dream, if that's what it was, morphed. Suddenly, both Ril and Lizzy were present, the battler's image wavering but his daughter seemingly solid and real. The dream *had* been real, only when she touched him, he'd woken up. He stared up at the ceiling of the room for a moment, breathing heavily. That dream had been real, but how . . . ?

A soft cry sounded in his ear, right near his head, and something hit the wall. Leon rolled over and reached for the oil lamp, turning the light to full. In the bed across from him, Justin groaned. Ril lay shuddering in a bed closer by, and he convulsed, slamming against the wall. He shimmered, trying to change into smoke and lightning. If the battler succeeded in changing without Luck there to hold him together, he'd die.

"Ril!" Leon shouted, scrambling out of bed, while Justin sat up, looking scared. Leon grabbed the battler, his fingers sinking deep into the sylph's arms—*through* his arms—and shook him. "Ril, wake up!"

For a second he thought the battler was going to disobey, that Ril would keep dissolving until there was nothing left. The sylph gasped in air, though, choking, and his eyes opened, frightened and pale.

"What's going on?" Justin whimpered.

Leon ignored him, staring straight into Ril's eyes while he drew a finger back and forth between their noses, forming a sightline on which Ril could focus. "Ril, don't change shape. Go back to being a human. That's a direct order: go back to human."

Ril shuddered, unable to think but incapable of disobeying. His shape solidified, his skin becoming solid again under Leon's hands. He drew in a deep breath and started coughing, his eyes squeezed closed. Someone in the adjacent cabin banged on the wall, shouting for them to shut up.

"Will you tell me what's going on?" Justin asked.

"Not now." Leon sat down on his bed, wiping his mouth with a shaking hand. All of his attention was on his battler as Ril shuddered again and slowly sat up. Trembling, the sylph shifted over onto his knees, looking at him, then lunged forward, his arms encircling his master's neck. As Ril's weight came down on him, Leon felt the battler start to draw energy, desperately replenishing himself.

"What's he doing?"

"Be quiet, Justin," Leon snapped. Ril's draw was so strong he didn't need to relax to feel it. The last time that happened was when the sylph carried his entire family from Eferem to the Community, outrunning an air sylph a thousand years older than himself. He'd exhausted himself so thoroughly that he'd been afraid he'd kill both Leon and Solie, drawing from them. Mace had made sure that didn't happen.

"That was you, wasn't it?" he whispered so Justin couldn't hear. "You connected our dreams, didn't you?"

Still shivering, Ril nodded. "I don't know how," he whispered back. "I just did it."

"Why?" Leon asked. To see his daughter again, even so briefly, had been wonderful, but Ril had nearly killed himself doing it.

"You told me to," Ril said.

Leon stiffened. "I never meant—"

"I know." Ril pulled away and wiped his mouth. "Never mind." He looked across the room at Justin, who was sitting on his bed staring at them, and he snarled.

Justin cowered. "Hey! What did I do?"

"You looked at me."

"Easy." Leon put a hand on his battler's shoulder. "Be calm, both of you. We have a long way to go still."

Ril shrugged, settling down as though nothing had happened, his back to them both. Leon didn't know if he was all right, but he couldn't ask. He wanted too much for Ril to connect their dreams again, to find his daughter and make sure she was all right. He rose and pulled on his clothes, finding his boots before heading outside to clear his head.

"What's going on?" Justin asked, following him up to the ship's deck.

"Nothing you need to worry about," Leon told him. They were still three ports away from Meridal. When they arrived, they'd be docking just long enough for the ship to drop off and take on new passengers, and to renew their stores; then it would continue south. It was up to Ril whether they stayed on the ship at that point. Leon hoped not. He wanted to be doing something. He wanted Lizzy to be in that city, preferably on the dock waiting for him.

"I need to know," Justin said behind him. Leon sighed and turned. Justin was a man, he reminded himself, and he cared about Lizzy as much as any of them. He was also risking his life.

"I don't know what happened," Leon admitted. "I think Ril connected his dreams to mine and Lizzy's."

"I didn't know battlers could do that," Justin gasped.

Neither had Leon. Then again, Ril was the only battler to sleep on a regular basis, let alone dream. "Don't call him by that word," he said instead. "Not here."

Justin hunched his shoulders. "Can he do that to me? See into my head?"

"I don't know."

Justin glanced uncertainly toward the cabin, probably wishing they didn't need Ril at all, but finally he sighed and turned back. "Lizzy's okay?"

"She seems to be." That at least was a relief.

Justin smiled, his shoulders relaxing and dropping away from his ears. "I've been thinking. Of after. I'd like to have my father's earth sylph Stria build a house for us near the lake, where all the blackberry bushes are. My father promised me half his herd when I marry, so we'll have money. It's not a big herd, but I can be a drover as well." The shoulders went up again. "If you don't have any objections."

Leon managed a smile. Justin wasn't the first person he'd choose for a son-in-law, but he couldn't fault the boy's courage. No one else had been volunteering for this trip. "Don't you think you need to ask Lizzy?"

"Yeah, but, well, I need your blessing first, don't I? Can I have your blessing? To marry your daughter?"

His daughter, married. Grandchildren. Leon's smile softened. "If she'll have you, yes, you have my blessing."

Justin beamed.

# Chapter Eleven

When breakfast didn't seem imminent, Lizzy poked her head out of the room where she'd slept and peered around nervously, just in case someone was waiting to grab her. Eapha was outside, giggling madly along with a half dozen other women who ran around the main room, dodging a battler with the number 200 tattooed on his chest. He wore a breechcloth and seemed to be having a glorious time trying to grab them. The sylph snatched Eapha around the waist, pulling her against his chest and nuzzling her neck while she shrieked. Letting her go, he lunged after another woman, his clawed feet digging into the marble floor as he chased the dark-haired girl down the hall. Lizzy had to giggle. She knew how fast battlers were. This one was playing.

Eapha trotted over. "Good morning, sleepyhead. You slept all night."

Had she? Lizzy remembered her dream and smiled. "I guess I was tired. Do they ever feed us?"

"Of course. They leave the food at the other end. Most of it will probably have been eaten by now, but there'll be some left."

So the girls were forced to walk the entire gauntlet if they wanted to eat, Lizzy realized. She shuddered but made herself step out of the sleeping chamber. Her belly was rumbling and she couldn't stay hidden forever. Eapha just laughed and took her hand, leading as she had when first showing Lizzy where to rest. Lizzy followed, tugging her gauzy gown closer around her, for all the good it did, and trying to comb out her sleep-tousled hair with her fingers.

Even though she was watching for just such a thing, she didn't see Two-hundred pad up behind her—not until he put his arms around her, his hands on her breasts, and pulled her back against him. Lizzy screamed.

Eapha spun around, her eyes wide. "Lizzy," she gasped. "It's okay! Don't hurt him!"

Hurt him? How was she supposed to do that? Lizzy wondered, even as Two-hundred sniffed her neck, inhaling deeply. He froze, and a moment later released her. Lizzy looked up to see him staring at her with confusion. He leaned close and sniffed again. Then he glanced to Eapha and back. Silent, he nonetheless made a discrete series of motions with his hands and straightened.

"W-what?" Lizzy managed.

Eapha looked equally confused. "No one's going to want her?" Fear crossed the dark-haired woman's face. "They have to!" She shot a look at Lizzy and back at the battler. Then she looked past him, up at where the walls joined the ceiling. Before Lizzy could turn to see what she was looking at, with a forced gale of laughter Eapha grabbed both of them by the hands and dragged them into the nearest alcove.

The place was small, wreathed in silk with a soft mattress sunken into the floor. Eapha stumbled on it, pulling the battler with her, and turned to face Lizzy. "If no one wants you, they'll turn you into a feeder."

"What?"

Eapha looked at Two-hundred. "They have to sleep with her!"

"No, they don't!" Lizzy squealed.

Eapha grabbed the battler's arm. "They'll cut her tongue out, Tooie! They have to!"

Tooie looked at Lizzy again, and back at Eapha. Silently he shook his head.

"Well . . . pretend!"

Tooie considered that and finally nodded, his eyes sparkling. Wandering over onto the mattress, he started to hop up and down. The mattress squeaked loudly. He looked amused.

Lizzy stared at Eapha, baffled. "What's going on?"

The woman sagged. "I told you. They only keep girls who the battlers will have sex with. Tooie says no one will want you, though. That's nearly a death sentence in this place."

"Um. It's not like I want to, but . . . why not?"

Eapha shrugged and turned, making a series of hand motions at Tooie. To Lizzy's surprise, he returned them. Eapha made more and finally finished. "He says you smell mated already. I don't really understand. He'll pretend, though—he already does with a lot of the women. The handlers think Tooie's a lot more active than he is. They won't care about one more."

"I don't understand," Lizzy said.

Eapha blushed prettily. "I shouldn't tell you this. I hardly know you . . . but I'd feel awful if you got turned into a feeder, and Tooie wants me to ask you about that mate. When he wants something, well . . ." She grabbed at her hair, tugging it with a groan. "I hate this! You better not be a spy. No, you can't be a spy. Tooie would know."

Tooie made more gestures at her while he bounced, and finally Eapha sighed and clasped her hands. "It's the handlers. They're evil. I've known Tooie for years. He loves me and he doesn't want to be with anyone but me, but the handlers don't want the battlers to love. If they knew he loved me, they'd turn me into a feeder right away. So he pretends to sleep with a whole bunch of women to hide it."

Lizzy gaped, even though she'd had six years of experience interacting with battlers. Given a choice, they all preferred monogamy. "He does?"

Eapha regarded Tooie again, and her expression made Lizzy's throat thick. "Yes. There are a bunch of us with battlers who want to be exclusive. Tooie pretends he's sleeping with all of them. So do the other battlers. There's only about a dozen of them that are that organized, though, who talk to each other to plan out who's going to be with who. Believe me, most battlers won't talk to each other at all. They just jump anyone who interests them."

Lizzy noticed Eapha didn't say whether any of those battlers had ever shown an interest in her. "How do you talk to him?" she asked instead.

"Gestures." Eapha made a few motions with her hand. Tooie returned them. "They all mean something. One of the women who was in here a few years ago had a deaf brother. She taught the gestures to a few of the girls and a couple of the battlers. There aren't many of us who know how to do it, though, and we have to keep it a secret." Her face hardened. "I'll teach you how to sign, but please, don't do it outside the alcoves if you can avoid it, and be careful who sees you. Tooie never should have done it out there, but you surprised him. Me, too. The handlers watch us through vents at the base of the ceiling. If they knew we did this, they'd take us all for feeders. It might be even worse for Tooie and the others. They're not supposed to talk at all. The handlers have no idea, though. They can't see what's happening in the alcoves, and we usually only talk in here. Still, please be careful. There are some girls we think spy for the handlers, and there are a lot of battlers I'd never trust."

Behind them, Tooie kept bouncing on the bed, slapping the ceiling with his hands on every bounce. Lizzy watched him for a moment before looking again at Eapha. That they were friends she didn't allow herself to doubt. In this place, she needed friends. Now she had two.

"Has anyone ever escaped?" she asked.

"No. I know women who've tried, but the only way out is the door, and that's locked and guarded." Eapha saw Lizzy glance at Tooie and gave a bitter laugh. "He can't help either. He's under orders not to help us get free. Battlers can't disobey their masters—did you know that?"

Lizzy nodded. Back home, no one took advantage of their bondage. She'd seen one man abuse his fire sylph, driving the poor creature to distraction, but the battlers had sensed her distress and told Solie. She'd had the sylph transferred to a new master and the abuser banished. He'd been lucky the battlers hadn't killed him. They'd wanted to. Also, her father was always careful never to order Ril around, knowing Ril had no choice but to obey.

Thinking of the blond battler and the warmth of his lips, Lizzy blushed. They were coming for her, Ril and her father. He'd told her so in her dreams. But was that even possible? Lizzy wanted to believe with every bit of hope left in her, but there was so little remaining after weeks caged in the dark, and now in this place, with its soft fabrics and interminable lust.

She could feel it now that she was rested and calmer: the need of the battlers broadcast through the harem in order to turn the women's own inhibitions into uncontrollable desires. If a woman wasn't willing, they'd make her willing, and the space between Lizzy's legs tingled even as she wrapped her arms around herself, still trying to hide the sight of her near nudity from Eapha and Tooie. Not that either of them cared. In this place, how could anyone even pretend at modesty? She couldn't let her arms drop, though. Not yet. Hopefully not ever. She never wanted to become so used to this place.

Please, Ril, she thought. Don't let that have been a dream.

"Now what?" she whispered.

Eapha shrugged. "Breakfast?"

# Chapter Twelve

Life for Lizzy formed a pattern that she knew would eventually drive her as crazy as a wild bird trapped inside a house. She'd beat her wings against the walls until they broke, would end up like the women she saw sitting in corners of the harem, women who just sat there, not speaking or reacting to anything. Eventually, even the battlers avoided them. Then came the handlers.

Lizzy quickly learned to hate those tall female guards as much as the other women did. She especially learned to hate Rashala Misharol, the official who led them. The bald woman was vicious as a snake, and as cold. In the middle of her second week in the harem, Lizzy watched Rashala order one of the women taken to the feeder cages, her tongue cut out before she was moved. Lizzy was afraid they'd do it right there, but the handlers dragged her off first. Rashala strolled away without even a quelling glance. She hadn't needed one, Lizzy realized later—none of the others had tried to do anything. A hundred women against three. Not one of them moved.

Still, for now at least she was safe, though safety was a tenuous concept in the harem. She was also still a virgin. Tooie and eleven other battlers like him would take her into the alcoves, usually just picking her up and carrying her there, and they'd stay with her for an hour or more, pretending to do things that Lizzy found less and less frightening, surrounded by it as she was. She didn't want to sleep with any of them, even if they'd been interested in her, but the idea of it wasn't so strange anymore. A girl who'd only had two kisses herself, now Lizzy walked unblinkingly past women having sex with battlers right in the middle of the harem. The only result was a subtle arousal inside her that never went away.

"Where's Tooie?" she murmured to Eapha one morning as they sat eating a plain but edible breakfast of cheeses and breads. Most of the cheeses were unfamiliar to her, some of them strange colors and a few rank smelling, but all were delicious. Once a week they also received meat and fish to eat, cut into small pieces as the women had no utensils in the harem, and certainly no knives. Tooie usually showed up shortly after they woke in what she couldn't quite be sure was morning. He stayed for half the day, amusing himself with different women and somehow always including time with Eapha. Then he would vanish, turning to smoke and lightning and rising up through one of the openings in the ceiling. He spent the remainder of his day working, she knew, but he usually didn't start so early.

Eapha put a small fruit in her mouth and chewed. "He told me he's fighting in the arena for the emperor this week."

"Isn't that dangerous?" Lizzy asked. She liked Tooie. He was really very sweet, and he'd been teaching her their sign language whenever they were alone in the alcove. Not that she'd managed to learn much yet—certainly not enough to answer his questions about her being mated.

Eapha smiled. "He's not fighting other battlers. Nobody's that stupid. He only fights criminals. Executes them, actually. There's no danger for him."

It sounded as though there was a lot of danger for the criminals. Lizzy didn't ask what sort of offenses people committed in order to be given such a sentence. Instead, she reached for one of the last pieces of bread.

A bell sounded. It was one of those in the shafts that the battlers used to get into the harem. Their passage would sound the chimes, alerting the women inside and, more important, the handlers who watched from without. Lizzy wasn't sure how many handlers there were, or how often they actually watched, but she'd learned to spot their peepholes: tiny gaps high on the wall and placed at regular intervals. These couldn't observe into the alcoves in the walls beneath them, but they viewed nearly everything else. There were even peepholes in the sleeping chambers and bathrooms! Lizzy had never thought she'd get used to observers, but she had. She never forgot them, though. According to Eapha, those who did wound up as feeders.

In the center of the ceiling about thirty feet away, a smoky shape laced with lightning flowed out and down to the floor. A battler in his natural form resembled almost any other battler, but Lizzy had learned to identify most of those here. She'd been able to do it for years back home. She'd never seen Ril in his natural form, but she'd always been able to recognize Mace or Heyou and the others. The lightning moved differently inside each of them. This one she didn't recognize at all, and the lightning within him flickered like fractured ice.

He flowed down and solidified into the same olive-hued form they were all ordered into when relaxing. Lizzy didn't know what the other permitted shapes were, but apparently the battlers in this country took on specific, sanctioned figures for different jobs. In the harem, however, they were always the mouthless, backward-legged creatures she'd first seen, distinguishable from each other only by the tattooed number they wore.

This one was numbered 89.

"Oh no," Eapha whispered. "Tooie must have taken his place in the arena!" She scrambled backward, suddenly finding something fascinating amongst the stacks of used plates they'd put by the door for retrieval.

The other women who'd been eating started backing up as well, one even going so far as to dart into an occupied alcove. Lizzy heard a startled squeak from whoever was already inside. At the same time, another battler—one numbered 417 and one of the dozen who'd been pretending to sleep around the way Tooie did—abandoned all pretense of boredom. He snatched up the woman whose hair he'd been fondling while she ate, took two steps, and grabbed a woman named Kiala, who was his actual lover. Four-seventeen carried both into an alcove.

Eighty-nine didn't seem to mark the reactions, though he did flare his hate at another battler who was glaring at him. The two bristled but didn't take the confrontation farther—battlers were as forbidden to fight amongst themselves as they were to talk. Eighty-nine jerked his head at the other insultingly and went back to examining those women who hadn't managed to hide.

It didn't take him long to spot Lizzy, with her long blonde hair. She saw his eyes widen, and suddenly he was running toward her, blindingly fast. Eapha moaned, a world of pain in her voice.

Lizzy didn't have time to react. Eighty-nine grabbed her, his claws painfully close to tearing through her skin, and hauled her up. He didn't even bother to take her to an alcove, instead slamming her down on her back in the middle of the floor. His eyes gleamed with undeniable excitement as the breath woofed out of her. He filled her with his lust, with his undeniable need to push her legs apart and spear himself into her, pumping again and again until she tore apart. The power of that, the animal pleasure rushing into her, was overwhelming, and in that first second while her lungs were trying to inhale and her brain was struggling to catch up, Lizzy actually climaxed.

"Stay away from Eighty-nine," Eapha had cautioned her. Even the handlers had warned her in their round-about way. Battlers were empathic: they enjoyed their partners' pleasure at least as much as their own. Eighty-nine didn't. He gave pleasure—she'd just experienced that, and he still had his breechcloth on—but he wouldn't stop. He'd killed women with his lust. In three or four days he'd still be raping her, whether she was alive anymore or not.

Pleasure rocked through her, and her body quivered in expectation as he undid his breechcloth with one hand and ripped her gown off with the other. Yet that orgasm had nothing on Lizzy's feeling of violation. But no one would come to her rescue—the battlers were forbidden, and the women wouldn't dare. There was no sign of her father, and Ril was somewhere far away, only showing up in her dreams to whisper promises of salvation.

She was supposed to be safe, she recalled in a sudden rage. Something inside her made her unattractive to battlers—even the ones who weren't in the circle with Tooie and Eapha. He'd said she was mated already, something she'd had a lot of time to think about. All she'd had in her life were two kisses, one given in a moment of petulance at a dance, and the second taken in secret afterward. One had been wet and rather forgettable, if the boy involved hadn't insisted on not forgetting until he'd abandoned her on a dock to a bunch of slave traders. The other had made her toes curl and her nipples perk, and flashbound her heart with a fact that she'd made herself forget during the subsequent two years. Ril loved her. She'd made herself forget that in the face of how much he hated himself.

Eighty-nine got his breechcloth off with a gleam of joy in his eyes and what she was sure would have been a yell of triumph if he had a mouth. Now he was going to rape her in front of everyone, ignoring whatever etiquette made the other battlers turn away. And so . . .

Lizzy rejected him. Not physically, since her lust-soaked body was already dripping for him and her legs were wedged so far apart her joints ached. Even if she were strong enough, spread out that way she couldn't move to defend herself. She rejected him with her mind instead, knowing he was empathic. She thought of Ril, and hit Eighty-nine with the memory of him. Of Ril sitting on her arm as a bird. Of Ril spelling out his love for her with the blocks. Of him carrying her and her family to that cliff where the Community had fled, running himself nearly to death but still cradling her so softly, letting her ride above his mantle where she could see. Of him coming to her room at night when she had bad dreams and sitting there to watch over her, somehow always knowing her need. Of him kissing her in the field after she'd already betrayed him by kissing Justin. Of him coming to find her even after she'd decided he wasn't the man for her and had led Justin on with the idea that he might be. Justin, who'd left her. Ril, who loved her, and who had always loved her, and who had somehow marked her as his own even in this place where women were less than nothing and the battlers volatile property.

Eighty-nine hesitated, his alien eyes staring into hers as she glared and forced those images at him. And this one: *I. Do. Not. Want. You.* Eighty-nine howled silently, and his fist came down on the floor beside her, cracking the tile. Madness was in his eyes, but his erection was wilting even as he pressed against her, and Lizzy knew in that moment that she'd won. He might kill her in the next second, but she'd won.

The victory was a painful one. Eighty-nine howled and shoved against her, hard. It hurt, bruising her from the middle of her thighs right up through her crotch, but he was flaccid and couldn't penetrate. He shoved again and pushed himself off her, his hate flaring out wildly. This banished the last bits of lust he'd forced into Lizzy and set the rest of the battlers to flashing out their own hate. Women screamed, cowering, but Eighty-nine leaped into the air, shifting to erratic smoke and lightning. He vanished up one of the shafts, his hatred following.

Lizzy lay there for a moment, just gasping. Her crotch hurt terribly, as did her head, and in that pain she could hear Ril screaming. He knew her torment and was terrified. She hadn't known he could be terrified.

"I'm fine," she whispered, sending that thought to him. *I'm fine.* And *I love you.* She had no idea if he heard.

Eapha leaned over her. "Lizzy?" she gasped. "Are you all right?"

Lizzy eyed her wearily and sat up with terrible slowness. Her groin ached so badly that she dreaded the thought of what it would have felt like if she hadn't managed to get Eighty-nine to stop. Her dress was transparent and useless, but still she tried to rearrange it around herself, wanting at least a modicum of decency. "I think so . . . ," she started to say, still dazed and really wanting nothing more than to limp away and take a nap. She couldn't feel Ril anymore. All she could feel was her bruises, and they seemed to be deep.

The door to the harem opened only a dozen feet away from where they'd been having breakfast. Both Eapha and Lizzy froze, staring at it in horror. The handlers had been watching. They'd seen Eighty-nine go for her and retreat. Lizzy had a sudden, horrifying vision of them taking her away because of that, turning her into a feeder because Eighty-nine had shown an interest, just as they'd promised.

Eapha whimpered, leaping to her feet and running off into one of the alcoves. Lizzy felt her tongue and mouth dry up at being abandoned again, but she forced herself to her feet. She'd frozen when the sailors kidnapped her. She'd been useless when Rashala sent her to the sacrifice altar, and she hadn't fought hard enough when they put her in here. Finally, she *had* fought back and stopped Eighty-nine, but to what end?

Four guards stepped into the room, Rashala behind them. She stared at Lizzy with bemusement, obviously pondering exactly what had just happened. Lizzy backed up, not willing to just let them take her this time. Not again.

An arm came around her, a nose nuzzling against her neck. She stiffened, suddenly convinced that her defiance hadn't been enough and Eighty-nine had come back after all. Hauled off her feet and spun around, tucked under an arm and carried swiftly into an alcove before she could do more than muster breath to scream, she was set down on her feet before she could release it. And then Lizzy saw Eapha. The woman stood before her with the two others Four-seventeen had taken away. Sitting at her feet the battler just winked at her, and he started bouncing up and down on the bed.

Lizzy goggled at Eapha and started to cry, realizing what she'd done. The other woman moved to hug her and started crying as well.

Rashala frowned thoughtfully as she stepped out of the harem, unprepared to disturb a battler during coitus— especially not one who had no preference for any specific woman that she'd ever been able to see. Still, something odd had just occurred.

Down a doorway to the right was a gathering area for the women who worked with the battlers. One of these followed Rashala out of the harem: Melorta, the lead handler and a slave. Rashala had picked her up in the market ten years before, and now she relied on Melorta as much as herself. The woman had started out just as Rashala had, as a concubine in the harem, and like Rashala, Melorta had a truly uncanny knack for calming battlers. More important, she'd reported on any of her fellow concubines who were trying to break the rules, even uncovering a plan by several to escape that might actually have worked.

"Do you have any theories about what just happened?" Rashala asked.

Melorta shook her head, the hair that she wore in a plait down her back to show her slave status swaying. She shrugged. "Eighty-nine lost interest."

"Did he?" Rashala wondered aloud. She hadn't seen the actual attack, but had just been alerted to it by those who had. By the time she arrived, it had all been over.

Melorta shrugged again. A narrow nearby corridor shared a wall of the harem, and while these rooms were all at a level, every ten feet boasted wooden ladders with grates at the top so that handlers could peer in and observe. It was too dangerous to go into the harem on a regular basis, since the women might take it into their heads to attack, and both Rashala and Melorta were aware of that fact. Also, it was expensive to lose a good handler to a horny battle sylph, and a handler turned concubine didn't survive nearly so long as the reverse.

Climbing the closest ladder, she looked through the grate and sighed. "I want to see into the damn alcoves." But there were too many battlers who would be upset by that. They seemed to need their privacy every so often, just as any other creature, and so the alcoves remained inviolate. After peering through the grate for a time, she finally regarded her mistress and amended, "She drove him off."

Rashala nodded slowly. She hadn't seen it, but that's what she'd been thinking. Melorta *had* seen the attack, and from what she'd described . . . "She overpowered his will."

A woman who could force her dominance onto a battle sylph and make him do what she wanted, even without orders . . . ? That skill had brought them both out of the harem, but it didn't always work that way. A woman with that kind of will who didn't see the way they did could be a serious threat indeed. Melorta's promotion had come from uncovering one such woman, after all, before she could attack with the army she'd shaped out of a hundred ignorant and unarmed women. The whole episode had been an embarrassment and the entire harem was purged as a result. Four battlers were then put down, having gone mad from the slaughter.

"Watch her," Rashala decided. The girl hadn't earned back the money spent on her yet, and it was silly to be wasteful. The girl wouldn't be becoming a handler, though, not strange and foreign as she was. They could never trust her.

"Yes, ma'am," Melorta agreed, peering back through the grate. Their vigilance had to be never ending. Both of them knew that, but they also knew things could be much worse.

Eighty-nine had come through the gate for the same reason as the others. Hatched into a hive with thousands of battlers but only one queen, only a very lucky few gained her favor, and even fewer kept that for long. Like all of the rest, Eighty-nine had striven for her attention to no avail, and by the time he'd found the gate opening in the ether near his patrol, he was already going mad. He'd taken the bait of a fertile female without hesitation, only to see her killed and to become bonded to a man who saw him only to give orders: guard the streets, guard the walls, fight in the arena. A hundred different tasks he had, all shared with the other battle sylphs, just as it was back in the hive.

Only this time there were women, hundreds of women he could mate with as though they were queens, women with whom he could relieve his terrible tension—and it was terrible indeed, worse because he could only have their bodies. The bond with a queen was mental as well as physical, but he couldn't find any mental link with the women he fucked. Instead he had a mental link with male masters whom he couldn't touch, the bond a travesty that left him empty even after all these years. To forget, he turned to the women, pumping into them, searching for that elusive natural bond and getting angrier and angrier as it didn't come, forcing himself harder upon them until the women were either dead or broken under him, and still he couldn't find it.

Already long past insane and not recognizing it, he went for unique women, hoping that some strange new physical attribute would relinquish the mental link he desired. He found it at last in the yellow-haired girl, but to his horror, it wasn't a link to him. Instead, she pushed him away with her bond to another. Someone else's pattern was threaded through her mind and soul, undeniably a battler's touch overlaying her female essence—a battler who could touch her mind as well as her body when he made love to her, a battler who could make her into a queen if the circumstances were right. Eighty-nine wanted that, too, wanted it so badly he'd tear her to pieces and try and dig it out of her . . . but she only had room for one pattern. A sylph could take many patterns into them—Eighty-nine had six masters, one who gave him orders, five who had no tongues and could only feed him—but this girl could only be a master to one.

One! Why couldn't she be master to *him*? Eighty-nine howled in silence, his mind reeling at the absolute unfairness. He wanted a female master with a female's mind, a female's body. He wanted her to be linked to him. But he couldn't take a master himself. It had to be done to him by priests, and none of them would ever give him a female. He could live a thousand years and fuck a million women and he'd still never have a queen. Now another battler's master lay under him, telling him no, and he couldn't even pretend to have her.

Eighty-nine deserted the girl and fled for the vent that would take him to the surface, broadcasting his hatred and pain as he went. She should have been his. She should have been his! He twisted up the curving tunnel, around corners and through accesses that were barely a foot wide. Fifty feet it rose, from rooms deep beneath the ground through a building to finally open onto the roof.

He emerged in hot desert air, still screaming in silence. Below him, earthbound Meridal stretched out with its marketplaces and businesses, the homes of its merchant class at the center. The slaves and lower classes lived farther out, in slums that formed the majority of the land-based buildings before the sylph-maintained fields to the north that provided all the food that the sea didn't, but all felt the indifferent shadow of the huge island floating above, upon which lived the noble class. Up there, air sylphs labored to keep the island afloat while water and earth sylphs grew verdant swaths of green that otherwise could not exist in the dry, hot climate.

Eighty-nine ignored such considerations, as he ignored the massive wall that cut off the seaport from the rest of the city, keeping foreigners from treading on the sacred sand of the emperor. Not that the emperor would walk on that sand himself, keeping instead to his floating island at all times, except when he dallied at the coliseum.

That was where Eighty-nine went, raging across the sky toward it, his hate sparking the anger of hundreds of other battlers guarding against infractions of Meridal's many laws. Those who did defy the rules of the emperor were taken here, to the arena, thrown without trial into the sand to defend themselves against battlers. A good fighter might be spared at the whim of the emperor, allowed to live on as a slave—or perhaps even as a gladiator fighting other humans in the opening battles—but none had ever survived a fight against Eighty-nine, not before and certainly not today.

He swarmed down another tunnel in the roof of the building beside the arena and into the stables below. There, the stink of frightened men only fed his rage. Men like this were allowed to own him, but not women. No women except the untouched handlers were allowed in the stables for the arena, and none had ever stepped on the sand where these men might die. And die they would. Eighty-nine had finished his time in the arena for this month. He was supposed to have the freedom of the harem for a while, to calm and ready himself for more combat. He was good at it after all. He hadn't done patrolling guard duty for years, not since he became a favorite of the emperor. Eighty-nine had been looking forward to returning to the harem, but now he wanted to fight and kill.

He landed on the stone floor, the men who worked the pit to ready its various combatants staring in confusion as he changed shape. He didn't become the creature he'd been in the harem. For the arena he had a unique form, as did each battler. He swelled to become that, his jaws opening in a roar that could be heard through the cheers already sounding above. He heard the cheering stop for a moment and then grow even louder. The arena was the only place Eighty-nine could make any sort of sound with his voice, and the crowd all recognized it.

Ignoring the handlers as well as the other battlers, who growled and snapped at him, Eighty-nine turned and rushed for the arena ramp, his heavy legs churning at the ground. He went up quickly, barely fitting his bulk through the wide space, but found the gates down to keep the current competitors from trying to escape and dying where the emperor couldn't see. Eighty-nine shouldered through, the metal tearing with a shriek that sounded too much like a woman's.

He charged into the arena, the sand kicking up around him. In the encircling stands, thousands of spectators rose to their feet, screaming, while the emperor himself leaned speculatively back in his box seat.

Eighty-nine ignored them all, roaring again. All that mattered to him were the two men cowering in the middle of the arena, staring at him in horror. There had once been six, but the other four lay broken, killed by a battler in a hulking, ogrelike shape with the number 200 showing clearly on his chest. Two-hundred looked flatly at Eighty-nine, his emotions cautious. Two-hundred's arena shape was boring, barely twice the size of the men he was killing. Eighty-nine was as large as any battler could push himself, and his rage was absolute. Even on an ordinary day, Two-hundred didn't share his anger in the arena, and today, Eighty-nine felt crazy.

Eighty-nine lunged forward, his head low to the sand and jaws gaping. The humans screamed, trying to run, but only Two-hundred was fast enough to get out of the way. Eighty-nine scooped the first man up in his jaws and bit down, shaking his head. Half of the hapless criminal flew across the arena; the other was spat onto the sand. The crowd roared its approval.

The second human was running for the ramp up which Eighty-nine had come, weeping in terror. Eighty-nine swung his tail, sending him flying. Around the circular walls of the arena were free-standing walls. The prisoner crashed into one of these before hitting the ground, every bone in his body turned to shards jammed through pulp.

It wasn't enough. Eighty-nine turned, growling low in his throat as he looked at Two-hundred. The other battler dropped into a crouch, his own growl of warning an echo through the renewed silence. To Eighty-nine's mind, Two-hundred was laid-back and weak, but he was no fool. While neither could change their shape or hit the other with energy, Eighty-nine shielded himself. Against a simple human he wouldn't bother, but against a battler . . . ? It had been so long since he'd had such an opportunity.

Head low, he advanced, his feet shaking the ground, and his hiss was nearly laughter. Two-hundred crouched lower, his arms wide as he readied himself to move. The audience was nearly silent, but there were whispers now. Battlers weren't put into the arena with other battlers. Their orders were clear: they weren't to fight in the streets or the harems. No one had precisely said not to fight one here, though. Normally, Eighty-nine would never be put onto the sand with one. There were battlers who fought in teams, though not against each other. There were others who only pretended to fight each other, in carefully choreographed dances. Eighty-nine had never been one of them. When he killed, it was for real.

He'd kill Two-hundred, he decided, tear him apart and watch his energy drain into the sand. Maybe he'd roll in it or see if he could drink it. Perhaps that would still this screaming inside him. He couldn't kill the unknown battler who'd taken that blonde girl for his own, but he could kill this one. His snarl grew to a painful volume as he readied himself to lunge.

"Stop."

Both battlers stopped. Each had a half dozen masters, only one of whom had a tongue to give an order, but their commands were clear, and the first of them was to obey the emperor.

Neither of them wanted to, but still they turned, bowing low to the ground for the man in the gilded box towering high over the arena. A dozen battlers shaded him, and a healer sylph stood there in the shape of a woman far more beautiful than any human could ever be. The emperor was garbed in silk, and he gazed down at them, his expression bored, his emotions amused.

"Our Eighty-nine looks unhappy," he said, his voice soft but the acoustics fantastic. "We are displeased." He raised a hand. "Bring him more toys to play with, and return Two-hundred to his stall. Let sweet Eighty-nine have his fill, if he misses us so much."

Eighty-nine lifted his head and roared, drowning out the cheers of the crowd. Two-hundred turned and padded toward the ramp, clearly not minding being sent back to the harem. Just as Eighty-nine didn't mind staying. There were always prisoners to kill. Perhaps there might even be *enough*.

They forced his first panicked victims into the arena even as Two-hundred disappeared down the ramp. Eighty-nine turned on them, hissing, and he didn't wait for them to pass the inner walls before he attacked.

# Chapter Thirteen

Ril knew they were close even before the ship docked at the deep wharfs of Meridal. He told Leon, who'd already had his suspicions from how Ril had stood on the prow of the ship, staring without pause. This was the city that Lizzy had been brought to, Ril was confident. Every night now he dreamed of her, of journeying to her side. They didn't say much. He knew she was underground and that she was safe enough. In these dreams, which were often fleeting, they just sat or walked together. Unfortunately, the less stressed Ril was about her safety, the harder she was to reach. Disappointing as that might be, Leon finally decided it was a good sign they'd recently had less contact.

Arriving in Meridal, the trio of rescuers looked around, Leon and Ril to get the lay of the land, Justin because it was just so amazing. Leon didn't really know much about the place, although he was fairly sure he knew more than almost anyone else from his homeland, since that had once been part of his job. One of the few facts he recalled was that the people here were even more classist than those in Eferem, embracing slavery, while feeling that foreigners were almost worse than slaves, unclean. Meridal didn't allow foreigners into the heart of their city, so only the outer edges would be accessible to them. Leon already knew they'd have to go farther.

Right now they stood at the foot of *Southern Dancer*'s gangplank on a pier that was ten feet wide and bobbed up and down with the water even though it looked to be made of stone. It also jutted from the shore for almost a mile, and was hardly the only one. The trio had seen close to a hundred piers pointing out into the water, far enough to allow even the very deepest-hulled ships to moor. These weren't protected by any bays, so Leon expected there were air and water sylphs present to keep the ships safe. Para Dubh was famous in the northern continent of Arador for its large harbor. It had nothing on this place.

"It's huge," Justin gasped, looking around with wide eyes. Ahead, the piers all joined the land, upon which rose the city itself, climbing the slope to become many times the size of any city Leon had ever seen. Above that floated a huge circular plate, trees and more buildings showing on its edge. Beyond all of it, the white desert stretched.

Everything was unbelievably hot, so much so that it almost hurt to breathe. The men stripped down to their undershirts, Leon and Justin out of desperation, Ril to maintain the illusion. It wasn't perfect by any means. Leon hoped that no one would notice the battler wasn't sweating.

"It is huge," Leon agreed, refusing to let that get to him. Alone, he wouldn't have any chance of finding his daughter. But he had Ril.

The battler ignored his glance, peering ahead at the city. Barely waiting long enough for the other two to shoulder their travel bags, he started off, picking his way through the crowds along the jetty. Leon and Justin hurried in pursuit, afraid of losing him.

The pier was swarming with people and animals even here, so far out into the ocean. And they were loud. The cries of a hundred different types of beast were a constant assault, and the reek of the unwashed horrendous. Behind them, *Southern Dancer* was already being reloaded for the next leg of her journey, with more than half her passengers disembarked. A large group had cursed being forced to walk to shore through the lower classes, but they were in for a rude awakening, Leon knew everyone who wasn't a Meridalian was lower-class here. Or a slave.

He glanced again at the ship. *Southern Dancer* would sail in the morning, continuing her journey south before looping back. If they got Lizzy and returned in time, she could return them to Para Dubh. If not, he'd have to find another ship. He hoped there was one. They'd been very lucky with *Southern Dancer*. There was no guarantee that there would be another ship leaving anytime soon, and it might not be willing to carry a slave girl. Leon had no idea how the locals would react to what he planned, and no urge to find out. If they had to, they'd travel up the coast to the next city to find passage there, but the best solution was to go back the way they'd come.

Ril made his way along the wharf, leading them. It took twenty minutes to reach the end. From there the battler started upward through a marketplace. Though they didn't know the city's layout, he stayed fixated on Lizzy.

Sweating under his clothes and the heavy fabric strap of his travel bag, Leon followed, keeping only a few feet back. Justin hurried to keep up, wobbling a bit on legs that had grown used to the sea. "Does he know how far away she is?" the boy asked excitedly.

Leon shook his head. Close, was all he could guess. Closer, at least. Ril was nearly sniffing the air, leading them now through narrow streets between shabby buildings. People tanned dark from the sun passed in all directions, but there were enough pale-skinned people that they didn't stand out.

For all of Meridal's acclaimed wealth, this city was poor, the people obviously suffering. Leon passed a half dozen beggars, several with limbs and features rotted by disease. There was garbage everywhere, and the excrement of animals, some from humans. The island overhead cast its shadow across half the city, making temperatures more bearable but killing anything that might otherwise grow. The wealth was there, Leon saw, out of reach. Fortunately, Lizzy apparently wasn't.

Ril finally hesitated at one of the street corners, letting Leon catch up. "Battler," he murmured under his breath, turning away.

Leon stared ahead. Unmoving on the corner was a tall creature wearing a breechcloth. Obviously male, the thing had olive green skin and stood on hind legs that were like a dog's, bent backward at the knee and forward again at the hips. His hands and feet were clawed, and while his bald head was human enough in shape, he had no mouth and an absurdly long chin. The number 640 was either tattooed or burned into his chest. He was watching the crowds, and those who passed moved swiftly and obediently. There were no beggars nearby at all.

Ril clearly didn't like the look of him. Usually, Leon knew, battle sylphs didn't hide from each other. They made their presence obvious to foreign males as a way to protect their hives, showing their strength and numbers as a matter of course. All threatening sylphs were killed or subsumed after the death of their queen, their pattern changed by force, as Mace and Heyou had done to Ril with Solie. But Ril couldn't do that here. Battlers obeyed their masters, and the men of Meridal had surely put in some kind of order about dealing with invaders. Leon had been warned when they boarded *Southern Dancer* that no foreign sylphs were allowed here. Only the ones who worked on the ships were allowed to set foot on the docks, and they couldn't enter the city. Such an infraction was punishable by the death of every human involved.

And that was hardly the worst thing that could happen. Leon grimaced, thinking of Ril captured and subsumed, standing on a corner like that other battler, guarding it for the rest of eternity. But that probably wouldn't happen. Given Ril's damage he would likely be killed. He had very little energy to shield himself in a true fight.

If hiding bothered him, Ril didn't show it. He passed a few feet in front of his fellow battler, forced to do so by the crowded street. The sylph glanced up but a moment later looked away. Leon made himself feel nothing of either triumph or relief, knowing the battler would read that as easily as a man could hear words, and followed. Justin hurried a few feet behind, shaking in terror—but that wasn't odd at all. Most of the people who passed the battler felt the same.

"Was that a battle sylph?" the youth whispered in Leon's ear once they were rounding another corner, the road heading steadily uphill, though not at such an angle as in Para Dubh.

"Yes," Leon told him. "Hush now."

"But didn't he realize that Ril's—"

Leon elbowed him hard in the ribs. "I said be quiet!"

The boy winced but held his tongue. He didn't have much concept of intrigue, and for the first time Leon really regretted bringing him. If Justin wasn't very careful, he could get all of them killed.

"Look," Leon added, speaking in an undertone as they circumvented a bizarre creature with a hunched back and a face like a cow with exaggerated lips. Leon couldn't begin to guess what kind of sylph it was, or what reason it had for being in that shape. Justin stared as if afraid that it was another battler. "When we go in to get Lizzy, I want you to stay with the gear."

The youth gaped at him. "What? No! I want to go with you!" His voice rose, loud and shrill. "I *have* to!"

"Quiet!" Leon hissed. "Do you want to give us away?"

Justin shook his head, frightened but also desperate. "No! You can't make me stay behind! Lizzy's going to be my wife!"

Ahead, Ril stopped and looked back, incredulous. Usually Leon didn't feel too much emotion from him, though as his master he could. Ril didn't like to share, and Leon didn't pry. Now, though, he felt shock and surprise from his battler, and over it all a terrible, confusing pain.

"You?" the battler managed. "Marry Lizzy?"

Justin was pale, but he forced his chin up. "Yes. As soon as we're home."

Ril stared at the boy, and suddenly his emotions were gone, all of them. Leon felt emptiness so thorough that it was like the battler was dead. "Fine." He turned and kept walking no faster than before, even as a few seconds later he passed another battler. It never even glanced up.

Leon stared at Ril's back, wondering if he'd just missed something very important. There was something there, something he should recognize . . . something he couldn't see or didn't want to see, but that was close, just about—

Justin tugged on his shirt. "I'm going with you," the youth demanded. "I don't care what you say. I'm going to rescue Lizzy."

"Fine," Leon relented, echoing Ril. From the look in the boy's face, he'd follow them even if they did try to leave him behind. Given that, it would be safer for everyone to keep him close at hand. "But don't do anything unless I tell you."

While Justin beamed at that news, Leon wished he himself felt a little more confident. They had barely a day to find and rescue his daughter, with no idea even of how or where she was being held. Still, they'd found the city she was in and were traveling as fast as Ril could lead them to her. They had more advantages than he'd expected in the first few hours after learning of her kidnapping.

Ril walked ahead in the street, dodging people and garbage, his shoulders as relaxed as if he were strolling across the market square back home. But as he led them around another corner, he stopped. Ahead towered a wall, fifty feet or more in height and made of sheer stone. At the base, gates let through men and a few odd women with the dark tans and loose clothing of locals. Many of the men had tattoos over their chests and shoulders. A battler stood guard, watching all who passed.

Leon froze and swore under his breath. No one was paying attention to them now, but he had no doubt that would change the instant they tried to go through that gate. There were even signs posted that forbade entry to any nonnative, punishable by death. Obviously, Lizzy had entered, Leon thought bitterly. Apparently they had different rules for slaves.

Ril considered the gate for a long moment, and then glanced over his shoulder at Leon. Turning, he walked to the left, parallel with the wall. Leon followed silently, Justin next.

The battler led them for more than a mile, away from the bustle of the main gate and to a portcullis that was locked but unguarded. On the other side was an empty park filled with ornately arranged rocks and sands of different colors, a few strategically placed desert plants growing at the center of each design. It would have been beautiful if the plants weren't long dead from lack of sun, and if the park weren't strewn with garbage. Rats scurried past.

Justin put a hand on one of the bars and pulled. The portcullis was solid. "Can you break it?" he asked.

The battler gave him a scathing look. "And bring a

thousand of them down on us? Are you stupid?" Instead, as Justin flushed, Ril went up to the gate and stepped through.

His leg barely fit, and there was no way he could slip his head and shoulders through the bars—even a small child would have trouble. Nonetheless, Ril pressed his shoulder against the gap, and a moment later he changed just enough. His shoulder went first, then his hips, his clothes and body rippling as he squeezed himself through. Leon saw pain on the sylph's face, but Ril just kept going. His head raised as though he was trying to keep himself above water, Ril pushed his face through next, gasping once it was on the other side and back to its normal shape, and then he did the same with his chest. Lastly, he lifted his other leg through and stood on the other side.

"Wow," Justin breathed.

Ril didn't respond. He stood there for a moment, just breathing, and then stumbled forward. Standing up against the gate, Leon could barely see the edge of his objective: a crank-driven wheel and chain designed to be turned by several men. Ril grabbed it and started to pull. The chain went taut as the sylph threw his strength into it, enwrapping the teeth of the wheel and forcing the portcullis to rise on squeaky hinges.

"Hurry," Leon cautioned, hoping no one would hear that wretched squeal. It was terribly loud, echoing in the otherwise-quiet midafternoon.

Once the gate was high enough, Leon dropped to his belly and squirmed beneath, well aware of the sharp spikes just above his back. Once on the other side he scrambled to his feet and turned to Justin . . . who actually balked, staring fearfully at the gap below and the dead park beyond. Leon didn't pause. "Come now or we leave you there," he warned. There was no time for waiting.

The youth swallowed convulsively and scrambled

through, the gate now high enough that he could nearly crawl.

Ril reversed the wheel, letting it drop back with a further low squeal and a thud. He hurried back to them, wincing, which was a blessing in disguise—if he had been standing alone by the wheel, they might have realized he'd lifted it alone, which no human could do.

As it was, the guards still struck him first, in a fluke that Leon realized later likely saved the battler's life, and by extension his and Justin's, since their attackers would have killed them all immediately if they'd known what Ril was. The first green shape that dropped hit the battler across the back of the head. Ril's arms flew up as though he were trying to surrender, and he pitched forward, landing unconscious on the ground hard enough that he probably would have knocked out all of his teeth if he'd been a man. Twenty other battle sylphs landed, summoned by what, Leon didn't know—the squeal of the gate, the thud of its closure, the heartbeats of three men who weren't Meridalians in a place where they didn't belong? He didn't have time to think much more as they grabbed him by the throat and hauled him off the ground, shaking him. He heard Justin screaming, but then they threw him down beside Ril and that was the last he saw.

# Chapter Fourteen

The sand was fine and gritty underneath their feet, a pale tan color that darkened to black in many places. The arena around them was oval in shape and large enough that a man would have to take a thousand paces to cross the narrowest part. At the edges, removed from the main wall by at least two lengths of a man, five-foot-thick barriers rose twenty feet into the air and extended to either side for thirty, ostensibly to give a person something to hide behind. The main walls were fifty feet high, and tiers of seats ascended for a dozen rows on three sides. Every seat in the arena was filled, the spectators cheering. A quartet of gates led into the complexes underneath.

Leon took all of this in as he was led with the others up a ramp from the holding pens and out one of those gates. His wrists were chained and the men who watched them were armed. Leon eyed Ril. The battler was chained as well, his eyes narrowed.

*Wait*, Leon thought at him as hard as he could. *Wait*.

There had been battlers in the caged area where they woke, where they were told their sentence was to fight for their lives in the arena. There were also battlers floating overhead, gathered around an ornate spectator's box set high above the wall at one of the narrower ends of the oval. The opposite end of the arena was empty, probably so no one could look directly on the exalted presence in that box.

Whoever it was they were expected to fight, Leon and

his companions had to wait for an opening to escape. Perhaps they could go over the wall at the opposite end from that box, or maybe through it. Maybe through one of those gates. Maybe if they won they'd be granted their freedom, though Leon doubted it. He didn't have high expectations about their chances at all, but he refused to give up. He had to hope.

"What's going on?" Justin sobbed behind them. "Why are they doing this?" He stared at the guards. "Why are you doing this?" They didn't answer, and Leon couldn't. Not yet. Whomever they were fighting, they had to be ready. Rather, he and Ril had to be ready. Leon didn't expect any help from Justin in this.

The guards led them to the center of the arena, nearly dragging Justin. Ril walked easily at Leon's side, looking calmly around. He glanced down at the blood-soaked sand and back at his master. *Run when you get the chance,* he sent. *Lizzy is south, maybe three miles away and underground.*

Leon stared at his battler and shook his head.

*Do it. Listen to me for once. Run and save Lizzy.*

Leon shook his head again. They would all get out of here. Leon had been fighting with a sword since he was fifteen years old, and even weakened he knew that Ril could defeat any group of armed men. They would survive this.

*Leon,* Ril explained, *this place smells of battlers. That's what we have to fight.*

The guards unlocked their chains in the center of the arena and left the three prisoners there, tossing down a trio of swords as they trotted away. Frantically, Justin snatched one up, staring around fearfully as the crowd started to chant.

"Eighty-nine! Eighty-nine! Eighty-nine!"

Leon stared at Ril, ignoring the crowd. "What?"

*I'll try and distract him. Save Lizzy. Please.*

The chanting rose to a roar, the crowd on their feet and screaming. Across from them, on one of the longer walls of the oval, a gate like the one they'd been brought through rose. Justin took one look and ran screaming to hide behind one of the free-standing walls. Leon and Ril stood alone.

A horror came through the gate, shaking the ground as it walked. Colored a nearly ludicrous shade of pale blue, hairless and leathery, it was huge, the top of its head nearly as high as the arena walls. It stood on four legs, massive claws digging into the ground, and its body was round and bloated, its head rising up on a thick neck high above. Its tail was long as well, tapering to a point. The beast's eyes were tiny, its mouth filled with so many fangs it couldn't close completely. It stepped into the arena and roared, its tail lashing.

What kind of sick joke was this? Leon wondered. They were seriously supposed to fight this thing with swords?

Ignoring the weapons left in the sand, Ril rushed the massive thing. Leon swore and dove for the blades, grabbing one up in each hand as he chased his battler.

Ril was blindingly fast, moving across the sand so quickly that the roar of the crowd changed to amazement. The blue monstrosity growled, turning to face him, and lashed out. Its jaws came together with a tearing crash, but Ril dove out of the way, rolled to his feet—and was immediately hit by the thing's flailing tail. He soared backward and slammed into one of the solitary walls so hard that rubble exploded out around him.

"Ril!" Leon shouted. What was he thinking?

The monster roared and charged, mouth wide. Ignoring Leon, it went for Ril, looking to finish what it started, so Leon swore and ran wide of the thing. Ril wanted him to go down that ramp and seize the chance of escape, but Leon couldn't leave him. Even for Lizzy, he couldn't leave him. Not like this.

Half buried in the wall, Ril coughed in pain and watched Leon circle behind the big battler. Idiot! Why did he never listen? If the world were fair, masters would have to obey their battlers.

Wincing, he shoved himself free of the wall, dropping down to land on one knee in the sand. The crowd had thought him killed by the impact, and they roared at the sight of him moving. So did the battler. Its size and shape limited its speed, however, and Ril jumped to his feet, running at an angle away from the thing and Leon. His energy he still hid inside him. His opponent didn't realize what he was yet. Even if he didn't have only enough energy for one really good blast, the thing would only give him a single chance—if that. But the monstrous sylph was cocky, used to easy victories.

It turned with him, undeniably fast enough to snatch a sprinting human, and closing in, it moved to catch him in its jaws. Ril was faster, though, slipping free just as its mouth slammed shut behind him. And then Leon, who would never have been fast enough to escape the creature had it been after him, ran up behind and hamstrung it.

The battler screamed. Its right leg buckled, the tendon severed, and it threw its head back, shrieking until the entire arena echoed with its cries. It tried to turn and bite Leon in half, but its crippled hindquarters slowed it down. Leaving one sword transfixing the leg, Leon escaped under its huge belly.

The battler hit him with its hate, but Leon had carried Ril on his arm for fifteen years. A battle sylph's aura was one thing he'd long since learned to ignore. He didn't even slow. Chopping with the second sword, he sliced cleanly through the tendons on the back of the left leg. The thing's entire hindquarters collapsed, and the battler sat down hard, its now-frantic bite still missing the evasive human, who was continually diving over its tail and back.

To try and run away would only get his master killed. To continue staying close would mean death as well. Ril changed direction and ran straight for it, putting on as much speed as he could. The thing's attention was focused on Leon, so it didn't see him coming, but it did hear the crowd roar at his approach. Frantically, it tried to turn.

Ril put all his strength into a sprint and jump, arcing high over the thing's head. Well clear of its teeth, he was completely upside down for a moment and rotating almost thirty feet in the air. From the silence in the stands, he knew he'd revealed what he was—which meant that even if he did kill this thing, the dozen battlers hovering overhead would take him next. He had to survive, though. If both he and Leon died, Lizzy would never be free.

He twisted in midair over the battler, forcing himself around so that he came down on the thing's back, midway between the shoulders. Its head shot up, its roar of surprise and perhaps recognition rumbling in its throat. Ril didn't give the thing any chance to put up defenses; he didn't have the reserves to cut through a shield. Instead, he stabbed downward with his hands and struck with all his power, holding nothing back.

The battler screamed, a sound no longer arrogant or even afraid. This was a death shriek, for Ril's energy tore through it, ripping the creature's mantle apart. The sylph's physical form exploded, shedding chunks of flesh that vanished into nothingness before they could reach the ground. Its shriek fading to a wail and then a gurgle, the monster became energy that sputtered away into shimmering specks of light.

Ril rolled onto the sand, inhaling the ozone reek of his foe's disappearing body. His own form, so terribly weak, suffered a shuddering pain that beckoned with the very same darkness, urging him to let go of his flesh and disperse, become energy himself and forget thought, forget life. But he fought that death, forcing himself to his knees as he wondered if the roaring in his ears was the crowd, or if they'd gone silent at the death of their champion. He heard Leon, though, screaming at him. He couldn't make out what the man was saying. He supposed that was a good thing. It meant he didn't have to worry about being ordered to stop.

He raised his arms again, hands pointed at the narrow end of the arena without the tiered seats. He could feel that the wall there was thinner, with open space beyond. Everything he had left, Ril took and used, the pain of the subsequent blast beyond anything he'd thought to experience. But the wall exploded in a shower of rock.

Ril fell back, sand stirred by his collapse sprinkling down around him. It felt as though some of it got into his eyes. It felt as though some of it got into his skin, for his body started to fracture, lines appearing all over him as if he'd just fall apart, fall into nothingness. At least it didn't hurt anymore, he realized distantly. He wouldn't get to see Lizzy again, but this was a good way for a battler to die.

Hands grabbed him, pulling him up and against something warm, something with a heartbeat he recognized and a mental touch that he knew as well as his own. Shouldn't Leon have run? He'd opened a way for the man to escape. That had been the point.

*Drink,* he heard. Leon had sworn he'd never order Ril again, but of course the man kept doing it. His master had ordered him to find Lizzy in her dreams, though he hadn't realized he'd done so. He'd ordered Ril to return to his human form instead of killing himself in a dreamwalk-induced attempt to return to his original shape. Now Leon was ordering him to drink and save himself—only how could the man run if he was feeding Ril? What would happen to Lizzy? Ril felt so weak. He might take every bit of life Leon had and still die.

Not that his concerns mattered. He had no choice but to obey. *Drink.* Leon's energy was a mist around him, a warm, honeylike haze. Ril touched and absorbed it, drawing it deep. It started to fill the reservoirs inside him, flowing into the pattern Leon had formed in his soul so long ago, and then into those burning chasms he'd created in himself with his attack. But doing so brought back the pain, and he cried out even as he drew more of his master's energy, his form so starved that the lines continued to spread and deepen.

"You look like a jigsaw-puzzle man," Leon whispered. His face was streaked with dirt and sweat.

"Run," Ril whispered. "You can't save anyone if they take you."

"I won't leave you," Leon told him. "We'll both get out."

Not out of this. Not from here. Ril felt darkness rising behind the pain and didn't know if it was death or sleep. It didn't matter. He couldn't fight either, and once he went, Leon would have to go, too, out the passage he'd created for him.

"South," he reminded his master. "Three miles. Underground. Find her."

"Ril . . ."

Leon's energy was still pouring into him, flooding the body he'd pushed much too far. Ril closed his eyes, not wanting to feel the pain anymore or the weakness. Or Leon's energy, for that matter, since he'd only keep draining it until they both were dead. Useless. He was useless. He let the darkness flow over him, hoping as it did that Leon would give up and listen to him for once.

Leon felt his battler go limp in his arms, and the terrible, screaming draw stopped. Ril's head fell sideways, his eyelashes dark against his pale cheeks. The sylph's skin was covered by deeply grooved lines—lines that Leon somehow knew went all the way to his core.

*Save Lizzy.*

Leon heard the battler's final words and wanted to listen. He didn't want to leave, but it didn't seem there was much alternative. And it looked as though Ril might fall to pieces if he tried to carry him.

Around them, only seconds had passed. The flecks of light that were all that remained of the huge blue battler continued to drift down around them, and the crowd was on its feet, screaming. The guardian battlers still floated above, circling the ornate box where a man was announcing something Leon couldn't make out through the roaring in his ears and the pain in his heart. Only a few dozen feet away, a hole gaped in the wall of the arena, and he saw the street outside. No one was there to stop him.

But he couldn't leave Ril.

Then again, if he didn't escape, his sylph would have died for nothing. Only his battler wasn't dead—he would be flecks of light if he were. But that didn't mean Leon could save him. And he could still save his daughter.

Gently, Leon lowered his battler to the sand, brushing

the hair out of Ril's eyes and folding the sylph's hands on his chest. He wiped a bit of dirt off the battler's cheek and stood, grabbing up his sword. Gasping, nearly crying— *wanting* to cry—he turned and ran through the hole and a cloud of dust.

Outside, he found slums. In this square behind the arena, all of the buildings he could see were run-down, their walls gray with soot. There was garbage everywhere, and the air stank of trash and urine. Wretched people wandered, some standing at small stalls filled with withered fruit or fly-covered meat, others with pottery wares or textiles. It was a market, Leon realized, one for the desperately poor.

Everyone was gaping at the hole in the arena wall. As Leon appeared, a naked sword in his hand, his eyes wild and his blond hair sticking up everywhere, they screamed in terror and fled.

Leon ran down the street. No one leaped out at him or gave chase over the top of the arena wall, and he dove for the first stall with textiles. It was mostly stocked with carpets, but it did have some robes as well, loose, billowy things that would at least keep the sand off.

The garment would also hide him. Blond haired, bearded, and pale, he'd stand out too much otherwise. Quickly, Leon grabbed one and pulled it on. The robe was hot and clung to the sweat on his body, but he ignored that and trotted down the street, his sword hidden beneath. It wouldn't do him any good to carry it openly, not with so many battlers around.

*Three miles south and underground.* Leon focused again on his daughter, sticking to the shadows and trying to find a populated area again in order to blend in. He couldn't go looking for Lizzy until he was sure that no one was tracking him. He kept his thoughts schooled to things that wouldn't draw the battlers, his emotions calm and relaxed. It wasn't until very late that night, hidden in an alcove deep down a filth-covered alley, that he let himself grieve. Then, alone except for a feral cat that ignored him, he wept until well past dawn.

# Chapter Fifteen

The emperor was very pleased. Rashala wished she'd seen the fight. Apparently it had been amazing. Shaking her head, she made her way down an ornate corridor, her brother at her side. Battlers were her speciality, but feeders were his, and they would need feeders indeed.

They stepped through a doorway guarded by a battler numbered 52 and into a large room with a soft carpet and windows open wide to soft breezes. The battler that had defeated Eighty-nine lay on a padded couch, the emperor's personal healer bent over him. It was only due to her that he survived—or perhaps it was better to say that he survived at the emperor's pleasure. It amounted to the same thing.

Unconscious on the couch, the wounded battler's body was covered in deep lines, fading now as the healer drew her hands over him. The sylph regarded Rashala and her brother calmly and said, "Feeders?" It was strange to hear her speak, but she was allowed for the sake of her work.

Feeders. As none was bound to more than a single sylph, that meant new ones. No matter what the local populace thought, they weren't so cheap or easy to find. And for battlers, feeders had to be men. She didn't envy her brother the task. It had been barely an hour since they received the news.

She looked at Shalatar questioningly. "They're coming," he said. "They'll be here in a few minutes."

"Where did you find them so quickly?" Rashala asked.

"There wasn't time to buy any, so I had to grab some from the arena. They're not perfect, but they're available. Their tongues are being removed now."

She nodded, looking back at the comatose battler. "How is he doing?" she asked the healer.

Except for the lines, his sunlit form was flawlessly human, if pale and yellow, but he had a strange sort of transparency to him. Rashala could almost convince herself that she was seeing right through the creature. He'd been badly hurt in that fight, though Rashala had heard he'd taken only one hit. Granted, Eighty-nine had taken only one as well. It was a loss, but Rashala couldn't pretend she was unhappy to see the crazy, woman-wasting monster gone.

The healer bent over him again, working her magic. "He's damaged," she volunteered at last. "Very old damage. He's extremely limited in what he can do. To change shape would be an agony for him, and he can't take his natural form without dying." She glanced up. "He nearly killed himself."

Rashala frowned. He wouldn't be much use to them as a cripple, but he was the emperor's newest darling. "Can he be made whole again?"

"No."

Rashala shook her head, sighing. A foreign battler—she'd love to know how he got into the city without anyone knowing!—who was crippled as well. How had he even come here, and where was his master? Rashala had heard about him as well. Rumor held that he'd cut Eighty-nine's leg off, though she found that impossible to believe. She did believe that he was loose, though, and the battlers assigned to guard duty were all under orders to find him. So far they hadn't. It was almost frightening. Surely it wasn't the start of an invasion, though. No enemy would have sent an infiltrator who was so obviously broken. Rashala looked at his yellow hair and tapped her lip with a finger, thinking of a certain straw-haired concubine in the harem.

"Here they are," Shalatar said at last, looking contentedly toward the doorway, and Rashala turned to see five pairs of guards, each supporting a stunned man.

The feeders were still in the clothes they'd been wearing in the arena. Their eyes were wild with shock and pain, and they stank of sweat and dirt. Rashala wasn't surprised, given that each had just had his tongue cut out and the wound cauterized. But no feeder could be allowed to speak, not when they would otherwise control a battler. Even with an unconscious sylph like this they couldn't take the chance. Rashala was truly unhappy that his master had escaped.

Her brother stepped forward, taking over. The feeders were shoved to their knees in a line before the couch and its occupant. Two of them were older, white-haired. The other three men were younger, the youngest of all a boy that her brother confided had been captured with the battler. It was too bad no one had thought to question him before they cut his tongue out. The boy stared with eyes widened by horror, still trying to talk even though his tongue was gone. Tears poured down his face, and he reached for the battler as though wanting to wake him. The battler didn't move, though, his energy so low that only the healer was keeping him alive.

Shalatar started to chant, working on the ritual that would bind the men and the battler together. Rashala stood clear, watching him wind them together, putting the pattern of those men into the battler so that he could feed from their energy. It took time, but Shalatar was an expert. He made the bond without the sylph even stirring, then stepped back and wiped his brow.

"Nicely done," Rashala told him.

The healer beckoned to the first man, who was pulled forward by his guards. She laid her hands on both him and the battler. The energy flowed, and the man was nearly fainting before she gestured for the next. She repeated the process, leaving all the feeders drained, pale, and shaken. All except one. Then, though the lines on the battler's body had vanished and that odd translucency was gone, the healer touched the boy and took his energy as well. The youth stared at the battler throughout, tears still trailing down his cheeks and an expression on his face Rashala easily recognized as hatred. It didn't matter. Most of the feeders hated their charges.

Finally, it was done. The feeders were taken out again. Shalatar would see that they were fed and cared for, so they could continue to energize the battler. Not that Rashala knew what the creature would be good for. Perhaps the emperor planned to keep him as a pet. Already she could see issues, though, if he couldn't change shape. How was he even to get to his feeders? She couldn't bring them to the harem. That simply wasn't done.

Finished, the healer stepped back, regarded them placidly, and drifted out of the room. The brother and sister were left alone with the battler.

"What will you do with him?" Shalatar asked while Rashala studied the creature. He truly looked human, which was abominable, but at least he was easy to spot. She'd brand him anyway, while he slept.

She glanced at her brother. "Until they track his master down? Not much. Who knows what orders he has." They had to find the escaped man no matter what it took. Until he was dead, his commands would be primary over any other master's. The battler would have to be kept locked away, just in case. Rashala was afraid the emperor would send for him, though, and if he did, they'd have to take all kinds of risks.

"At least he's weaker than the rest of them."

"True," Rashala agreed. "He can't do much." She sighed. Until the situation was resolved, she'd just do with him what they always did with new battlers, to counter both their hatred and defiance: let them know that there was a place for them here, a happiness in this life. "I'll put him in the harem."

Four-seventeen padded slowly down the street, his claws ticking against the stone. He made his way directly along the center of the thoroughfare, not caring as animals and humans struggled frantically to get out of his way.

It wasn't supposed to be his turn on guard duty, not again. That was all he ever did, though, mostly on the docks and in the quarters of the city where foreigners were allowed. That made him special, his handlers said, attempting as always to soothe him. Also, he'd been one of the battle sylphs to bring in the foreign battler and his master. He'd be able to find that master again. So they'd dragged him away from Kiala and back to work, despite the respite he was supposed to have.

He was forced to silence and bound with so many rules he could barely function, but Four-seventeen wasn't made stupid by them: He knew he'd also been pulled out of the harem as punishment, for bringing in a battler without realizing it. All of the battlers involved that day were out searching now. But how was he supposed to have known the creature was a battle sylph? Only hatchlings and year-lings hid their patterns. This one hadn't seemed different from any other criminal in the half second it had taken to knock him out. None of them had been given the chance to explain, of course. They never were. Four-seventeen sighed silently and stalked in front of a pair of camels, who rolled their eyes and spat fearfully, though not at him.

Now he had to be away from Kiala again, and he hated that. He was hers, both of them members of the same circle as Eapha and Tooie. None of the other battlers sent out to search were, which meant he couldn't even commiserate with them through the sign language he'd learned. Not that he talked much to the other battlers in the circle. Not if he could avoid it. For now, he just had to follow orders: find the man who'd come with the captured battler. The sooner he did that, the sooner he would be back with Kiala.

He'd started at the gaping hole blown in the side of the arena, which the earth sylphs had left up for that very purpose—all the battlers had started there, glaring at each other as they split up. But with no idea which way the man went, Four-seventeen followed emotions. A foreign man lost in a city where he'd just had both his companions taken? Four-seventeen searched for fear just as much as he sought pale skin and yellow hair. Find the terror and he'd find the man. Perhaps there'd even be hatred.

The problem, Four-seventeen discovered with disgruntled certainty, was that there was already too much fear. Wherever he went there was dread. Only the lower classes walked here: the poor and the slaves, the untouchables and the diseased. And every one of them knew intimately that to disobey meant death in the arena or life in the feeder pens. Four-seventeen couldn't track anything through the background noise of their unrelenting fear.

He changed to malice—rage, hatred, determination, any of that. Surely those emotions would be present in the man. How could he not feel hatred when so much had been taken from him? This was how they always found the rule breakers. Either fear or anger. One or the other always gave them away.

Four-seventeen padded down the street and through an intersection, glancing from side to side. He was in a more affluent area now, most of the garbage gone. There were restaurants and markets here, hundreds of people making their way to and fro. Most were better than slaves but not rich enough to live on the island. They looked at Four-seventeen in fear but not terror. They still got out of his way.

Hate—he felt it from one of the stalls. Four-seventeen turned at once, glaring, and a dark-skinned man at a water seller's booth blanched in horror. Four-seventeen padded close, glaring and sniffing until the man backed into his booth and his bladder let go. Dropping to his knees, the merchant started babbling in terror.

A new anger rose behind him, so Four-seventeen turned, especially as it was accompanied by pain. Forgetting the water seller, he ran across the market to where a man struck his wife and was now shouting at her for being stupid, unaware he was being watched. Not that there was a rule against beating women. In Meridal, females had fewer rights than sylphs. But there *was* a rule against fighting, and more men who beat their wives had ended up in the arena for breaking that specific rule than any other.

While the woman, a pretty fat thing, was still cowering from her husband's anger, Four-seventeen darted in and grabbed him, his claws digging into the man's arms as he hauled him up off the ground. The husband howled in terror, trying to get away, but Four-seventeen just tucked him under his arm and trotted back toward the arena pens. The yellow-haired man wasn't here, so he'd ditch this one and keep looking. Even if he didn't find him, he knew that eventually they'd have to send him back to Kiala. No one wanted the battlers upset. He just had to put up with this for a while longer.

Behind the battler's retreating back, the beaten woman quailed, not understanding what had just happened. Seeing her husband being hauled off, she gasped, her hands flying to her mouth.

"Are you all right?" she heard.

She glanced up. Standing over her was a man in a plain brown robe, his hair dusty with soot and his skin dirty. The darkness almost seemed to be sweating off him.

"Are you all right?" he asked again.

She ducked her head. Women didn't talk to strangers— not if they wanted to be thought better of than the women in the battler harems. She hadn't loved her husband, but she was alone now with far fewer prospects than ever. Angry and afraid for her future, she scurried to her feet and away, not looking back. It wasn't until much later that she had cause to realize that the man who'd spoken to her had blue eyes.

Lizzy was learning to dance from Eapha and the other girls, giggling as she swung her hips first to one side and then the other to the beat of a small drum. Tooie watched with great interest, sitting cross-legged on a pillow. But as the main door opened, Lizzy looked up, no longer laughing; it was the wrong time of day for food. Two brown-garbed handlers came in carrying a body, one holding him under the legs and the other by his shoulders.

Lizzy stared in amazement when she saw those legs. They were definitely a man's, dressed in long pants and boots like the clothing back home. She backed up into Eapha, whose mouth was also hanging open, but there was no chance to speak, not as Rashala followed the handlers, directing them in the soft tones she always used near battlers. The pair carried their burden to the nearest alcove, moving him as gently as they could.

Lizzy saw a flash of blond hair, and she felt her legs go weak. She fell to her knees, one hand over her mouth. This caused Rashala to look right at her, but Lizzy was barely aware of the woman's scrutiny. She couldn't see the man's face clearly, but she knew who it was, the only man it could be. The man it *had* to be.

The guards carried him into the alcove, and Rashala followed, letting the curtains fall back into place behind her. The group was in there for several minutes, while all the concubines whispered and the battlers sniffed the air, shifting aggressively. Eapha dropped to her knees beside Lizzy, asking if she was all right, but Lizzy could only shake her head, afraid to speak. Finally, the handlers came out, headed for the door. Rashala emerged next, and she considered Lizzy for a long moment. However, she finally followed the others. The door shut behind her, locking.

Everyone surged for the alcove except Lizzy. Even the battlers went to peer in at the newcomer. "It's a man!" one woman shouted. "He's got hair like Lizzy's."

They all looked at her. Slowly, Lizzy rose to her feet and stumbled forward, her throat so thick she could barely breathe. Her head felt light, her fingers trembling as she clasped them together, and the women and battlers parted to let her through. She walked into the alcove, knowing full well that Rashala would be watching through a peephole, but she couldn't stop herself.

A man with short blonde hair and long bangs lay on the down-filled mattress, his head tilted to one side. His breathing was soft, but it was so quiet now in the harem that she could hear it easily. He was pale, but other than a red-puckered brand on his bare chest that showed the number 703, he was just as she remembered. Lizzy found she was crying again. She hadn't only been dreaming of him after all.

She whimpered, dropping to her knees on the bed beside him and saying his name. He turned toward her in sleep, moving in the direction of her voice, and she bent over, pressing her forehead against his while cupping his cheeks with her hands.

"Oh, Ril," she said again, and started to sob.

As the next day reached its hottest temperature, Leon felt confident at last that the Meridal battlers weren't going to be able to track him and returned to the alley he'd found the previous night, where he tried to sleep. The stress of reaching the city, their capture, his escape—it had all served to drain him, with Ril's feeding compounding his exhaustion. The intense heat only made that worse, until he was realistically afraid he would collapse. He couldn't help Lizzy in this condition.

He huddled in the uncomfortable alcove he'd staked out, his robe loosely wrapped around himself, and tried very hard not to think about leaving his battler lying on the ground in that arena, or of Justin, whom he'd also left behind. He tried not to think of anything, and to thereby keep his emotions controlled. There were still battlers out hunting him, he had no doubt about that.

Physically, he could hide himself with relative ease. After so many years outdoors, his skin was leathery and dry and tanned easily, and thanks to the weeks of sea voyage it was dark enough that a little dirt could help him pass for one of the locals. And while the same sun made his hair blonder, soot stolen from the back of a bakery would work until he found something better. It was only his blue eyes that he couldn't hide, so he kept his hood up and walked hunched over, pretending to be a much older, more subdued man, and no one paid him any attention, including the patrolling battle sylphs. He was careful to keep his emotions just as quiet.

Honestly, the latter task was easy. Leon was so numb he could barely feel or think. Only blind determination made him rise when the afternoon cooled, wrap the too-warm robe around him despite the continued heat, and walk back out into the streets, his eyes downcast. He thought nothing at all about his lost friend and missing daughter, or of how many battlers he passed, all seeking him. He thought only, South, three miles, underground. South, three miles, underground. There his daughter would be, and there he would go. It didn't matter how long it would take or what he would find. That was where he was going.

He crossed the city, slowly working his way through the crowds until he reached a square that was bare save for a tiny building no larger than a shed, capped by a small dome with gilded openings shaped to resemble mouths. As he stood there, a battler erupted from one of the mouths, rising on the wind as a shimmering cloud. Humans came in and out of the door of the small building, always female, and he settled in a corner out of the way, legs crossed, to watch. Still, he felt nothing. He just watched and waited to see if there would be an opportunity.

Lying in the arena and dying, Ril had never thought he'd wake again. He'd focused instead on saving his master's life, and also on Lizzy.

He'd loved her for so long—since the moment of her birth, in fact, though it hadn't been until she was seven that he'd figured out how to shift the energy patterns inside himself and match them permanently to hers. It hadn't been easy. She wasn't a queen, and he hadn't had any help. He'd had to do it himself, against all sanity, and he'd caused himself terrible pain in trying—enough that Leon became convinced that he was ill and deserted his duties so that he could rest. That had made it a little easier for Ril, as he'd nested in a bed of blankets Leon made for him in his daughter's room, at her insistence and Ril's own birdlike cries. He'd stayed by Lizzy's side for weeks, resting and focusing and fighting, always fighting, trying to shift his pattern in ways that should never have been possible.

He'd wanted it, though, wanted her to be his master instead of this man who'd always loved him so dearly and whom he couldn't admit he loved in return. Leon had stayed with him throughout, sleeping in his daughter's room as well, and he'd been there stroking Ril's head as Ril used the last of his strength, still trying to force the change. Both he and Lizzy had been there, petting him and expecting him to die.

"You should go," he had told his daughter, looking from her to the nest of blankets, but she shook her head vigorously. She had one hand down by Ril's feet, her fingers tucked in through his talons. He held her with his toes, afraid to let go. He felt too much like he were falling, even lying there.

At Leon's suggestion, his grip tightened. It was all he could do to move. He'd fallen over onto his side, his ragged wings spread loosely around him and his head lying crookedly on the nest. He breathed in rasps through his beak, and he could barely see through his half-closed eyes, but he forced himself to make a strangled sound of negation.

Lizzy bit her lip and stroked his feathered neck, head, and the ridges over his eyes. "I'm not leaving," she said.

"Lizzy . . ."

"I'm not leaving! He doesn't want me to leave!"

Ril made another groan of agreement, shuddering. He had focused on her with everything he was, and he felt as if he'd tear apart if she left him. He was about to tear apart anyway, even if she didn't. He was so close . . . He could feel her essence just beyond his grasp, but he could also feel Leon so much more clearly. The man was in pain, grieving for him, but he didn't want that. Ril wanted Lizzy, whom he tried to reach for one last time.

He fell short. Making a pale little hissing sound, as though the life was escaping him like steam from a kettle, he shivered again, broken. Leon swallowed, his hand across Ril's feathered back.

Lizzy started to cry. She leaned over his body, wrapping her arms around him and pulling him against her. "Don't go, don't go, *please* don't go!"

And that was the difference. Her tears soaked his feathers, but more, her mind touched his, her desperate need for him to live leaving her essence wide open. Ril felt her unrestricted love, and he reached for it in desperation, bringing it inside him. In that moment, he realized his previous mistake: he needed her help to make the bond, her willing surrender. And in realizing, he felt something deep inside himself changing, realigning . . . and suddenly they were tied together. She was his master, his love. Ril shuddered again and pressed his beak against her, cooing. Lizzy started to cry even harder, and her father hugged them both. The worst was past.

It took Ril weeks to fully recover, and he realized as he did that his connection to Leon was still intact. That one bond he could never break. But it didn't matter. He had Lizzy, and he could feel her, and when she was kidnapped, he could track her. Leon had never asked him why that was so, or asked about what happened in those months when he'd thought his battler would die. Leon had always let him keep his secrets, including his hidden self-loathing that had made him turn away from his link to Lizzy and pretend he'd never loved her at all. Still, despite how it all turned out, Ril had succeeded at something impossible before Yanda the battler shattered his mantle, leaving him less than whole. If never again, for one moment in his life he had chosen his own destiny.

Now he thought he'd chosen death—to save Leon and, through him, Lizzy. Instead he opened his eyes and looked upward at a gauze-covered ceiling. He could smell incense and hear women's laughter. He could sense battlers as well, all bound, all queenless, from a dozen or more different hives but somehow content with each other against all natural rules. Of course, he thought dimly, they were with women. They didn't need to fight each other with so many women around to make love to.

There was a weight against his left shoulder, a woman's breath tickling his neck. That had never happened before in all his long life, and Ril turned his head, still dazed by his near death and the feeling of more energy saturating his form than he'd ever experienced before. Beside him lay Lizzy, asleep, her hair tumbling in ringlets across her face.

It was the last thing he ever would have expected. He hadn't seen this even during his wildest dreams in the slumber to which he was now forced. He was broken, shattered, inferior—not good enough for any female, let alone this one, whom he loved so much. He shuddered, and to both his delight and horror, her eyes opened.

Slowly she lifted her head to stare at him. Ril stared right back. Tremulously, her lip started to curl, shaping into a smile, and then she was lying half across him, her arms tight around his neck.

"Oh, Ril! You came!"

Ril thought he'd lose his mind from the feel of her. Certainly he couldn't breathe, but his own arms came up and around, hugging her hard against him. She was all right! She was alive, and safe, and *here*. He'd found her when instead he'd been expecting death.

Lizzy giggled, embracing him tighter, and she pulled back to press her lips against his in a brief kiss that nearly turned out his insides. Then she pulled back again, still holding him but smiling.

Her emotions were overwhelmingly happy. This close, he couldn't help but feel them clearly. She was ecstatic, and he managed a trembling smile just for her. "You're all right?" he whispered.

She nodded. "I am. As well as I can be here. Are you? How did you get here?" A frown appeared on her face. "Where's my father?"

Ril hesitated, suddenly wondering that himself. Had Leon taken the escape route he'd made? He closed his eyes, focusing, and felt a flash—of pain, of regret, but also of freedom. He shook his head, still too stunned to interpret.

"He's alive," he told her. "And free. I'm not sure where, though. I . . . need a few minutes." Actually, he felt as if he needed days. Perhaps even years. This was all so surreal.

Lizzy just laughed, hugging him again, and she sat up, tucking her hair behind her ear as she considered him with delight. Ril studied her in near bemusement. She was healthy, well fed, her emotions happy and real. Her hair was shiny and her blue eyes sparkled. Her dress was a shimmering green, cascading down her body but sheer enough to hide absolutely nothing.

Ril's eyes widened. He'd been hatched as a cloud filled with lightning, but he'd spent a very long time indeed around human women. "What in the . . . ?"

Lizzy looked down at herself and turned bright red, suddenly covering her body with her arms and hunching over on the soft bedding. "It's not my fault!" she wailed. "This is all they give us to wear!"

Ril shook his head and sat up. A faint twinge made him look down at himself to see a number branded on his chest. He read 703 in amazement and not a small amount of anger. "What is this?"

"They do that to all the battlers," Lizzy told him mournfully.

"Not to me they don't," he snarled, and tried to change his chest. Just that part of him. He shimmered, and pain rushed through him, but to his horror, the mark didn't fade. It remained clear and red.

"Eapha says they use another battler to make the mark and it doesn't go away."

That meant they'd carved it right into his mantle, which made it permanent like all of his other injuries. Ril swore and forced himself to his feet. "Come on, we're not staying."

Lizzy rose willingly enough, but when he went to step outside the alcove, she grabbed his wrist with both hands and pulled him back. He eyed her again, puzzled.

"You have to know about this place," she told him. "There are rules we all follow, just to stay."

"You want to stay here?" he asked.

"No, but there are worse places," she explained, and with that she told him about the feeders and the concubines, and how they were all there to keep Meridal's battlers happy.

Ril's anger surged at that—at the thought of sweet little Lizzy in the arms of anyone. Suddenly furious, he went to rush out, his hate already flaring in challenge, but she yanked on his arm again, as hard as she could.

"None of them touched me!" she shouted. "They said I'm already mated, that I'm off limits!" Her voice dropped to a whisper. "Why would they think that, Ril?"

He stood frozen, his emotions so out of control he knew that she could feel them. He knew that Leon could feel them, too, wherever he was, and that the man was leaping to his feet, shouting in amazement, possibly giving himself away as he reached out for his battler with every paltry human sense he had.

*Leon!* he sent, even as he stared down at this girl for whom he was useless.

Not a girl, a woman. *Pure* woman. And she felt just as clearly what he did, clearer even than her father, for she was right here and she was his master, the one he'd made a conscious choice to obey. She reached out and put a hand on his chest below the scar. She was trembling, her relief at seeing him intense, her understanding of all the things he couldn't hide from her after crossing half a world wonderful. Ril trembled as well, especially as she slipped his loosened shirt back over his shoulders, down and off, and pushed him onto the soft bed.

"I didn't *ever* think you were useless," she whispered, and leaned down to kiss him.

# Chapter Sixteen

Ril and Lizzy made love in the small alcove in the battlers' harem. He couldn't stop her—didn't want to stop her—but he also needed her to instigate it and take control. He needed her to be the master.

She pushed him down and lay atop him, her soft breasts pressed into his chest through the gauze of her dress, her lips moving gently against his own. Ril returned the kiss, his tongue sliding against hers. Then he moved his lips along her cheek as she worked her own lips toward his ear. Her hands stroked his sides, and he felt a burst of her pleasure as his mouth closed on her ear, so he nibbled it.

Feeling her breath hitch as he touched her hips, he bunched her dress up enough to slip his hands underneath and place them on bare flesh. She sighed, exhaling gently against his ear. It was everything he'd ever dreamed of, everything he'd desired through hundreds of years of loneliness. It was every last thing for which he'd come through the gate and been denied. Now all of it was his in the form of this beautiful woman who was intent on giving herself to him.

Ril sat up and brought Lizzy with him, her legs straddling his fabric-clad lap. He pulled her dress up along her body, and she raised her arms above her head, no longer shy. He tossed the gauzy thing into a corner. Then he laved her bared breasts with his tongue, leaving her gasping and arching her back, her hands digging through his hair and holding him close, encouraging him even if he hadn't been empathic and known as a matter of course the very things that would please her.

Barely, he kept this from Leon. Her father didn't need to feel this. This was for the two of them alone, here in this place. Ril knew there were battlers outside, but they didn't matter any more than the other women. His warning went out, though. Here he was with his master, loving her, and woe on any who would intrude.

Lizzy drew Ril's head up and kissed him frantically, pressing her breasts into his searching hands, weeks of the low-grade lust that always filled the harem flowing through her, only now it felt right. She loved Ril, had always loved him, and could feel now how he'd loved her, too. The handlers could come at any time, could take her to be a feeder or him to be a slave, so she couldn't dare waste time being shy. Not after two wasted years she might have had, if only she hadn't been so foolish. In case she never got another chance, she would have him now . . . and it was glorious.

"I want to feel you," she whispered.

He shifted under her, his kisses never slowing as he pushed his pants down and off, kicking them away. The warmth of him drove her further down the path of insanity, but as she settled against his erection, as she felt the length of it so hard against her folds, she was suddenly blushing again despite her resolution.

Ril lay on the bed and stared up at her in amazement, his normally cold, gray eyes filled with wonder. That helped banish her fear. Lizzy smiled and slid herself along him, coating him with her moisture until he cried out, shuddering. She knew his pleasure, which was shivering through her as surely as her own.

"Why do I *feel* you like this?" she whispered, and stroked him again with her body. "You're my father's battler."

"I'm yours," he corrected. "Yours for all your life." He lifted up to kiss her. "You would have been my queen if Solie hadn't ascended first." He swallowed. "If I hadn't been broken."

She laid a finger on his lips. "Shh. Never say to me that you're broken, understand? Never even think it."

"Yes, Lizzy," he agreed.

She smiled, tracing the lines of his face and cheekbones. Ril closed his eyes, an unguarded smile on his lips, and so she reached down, watched his eyes fly wide as she grasped the proof of his devotion. She watched in fascination while he gasped, his mouth open and his head tilting back, but he didn't otherwise move, leaving that control to her.

His eyes never left hers. He needed her to take command, she guessed, to stop him from convincing himself that he wasn't worthy. This made her feel powerful, and she lifted him, bringing his sex up between her legs and against her core. Taking a deep breath, she sat down, letting gravity push him in.

For a brief moment it hurt, but then Ril was crying out and his pleasure was far more potent than her own swift pain. Lizzy arched back, wailing in joy to the ceiling no matter who might hear. He lifted against her, and a moment later they were moving in unison, flesh rubbing flesh, pleasure mingling with pleasure until neither was sure where one ended and the other began, whether in body or soul. Soon Ril held Lizzy to him, crying—only maybe it was her, or perhaps it was both of them—and they were grasping each other, moving, thrusting, dancing in a fire she hadn't known she could feel and never wanted to feel again with anyone else. Ril was *hers*. He was her battler, her lover, and she was his bond to this world and the reason he'd come to it . . . and she was also why he'd survived and continued to stay. All for her, always for her—and their celebration of that was exquisite. It exploded through them, carrying them to something higher and greater than either would ever have been able to feel alone.

Tooie observed Lizzy's alcove with far more interest than he usually showed toward another battle sylph having sex. But this battler, broken and limited though he might be, was patterned to that girl, bonded deeply to her soul, and Tooie's envy of them both was nearly a fury inside him. More enraging, the newcomer also carried a *queen's* pattern inside him.

He loved Eapha, Tooie did, had loved her since the moment he'd first taken her in boredom into an alcove and accidentally tickled her, making her giggle. He'd been so enchanted, he'd tickled her again. She'd hit him with a pillow. He'd known he was lost from that instant, and yet they shared no bond; the patterns within him belonged to men, and his worship of Eapha was limited to her body alone. This newcomer loved his lady straight through her soul—and so Tooie, like all of the battlers outside, watched with hunger and rage but also guarded the couple, if only that they might continue to feel the pair's pleasure and dream.

Elsewhere, Leon stood in the mouth of an alley, his cloak up over his head and soot-colored sweat dripping down into his eyes. He stared at nothing, a smile flickering around his lips.

His battler was still alive.

Rashala turned away from the peephole into the harem, frowning and rubbing her hands together. As she'd expected, the yellow-haired foreign slave had gone straight for the new battler.

Normally she would find that disturbing. Battlers could be dangerous even to their masters if they were too attached to a specific woman, and dozens had been put down during the kingdom's history for that very reason. But glancing toward Melorta, who was frowning and tapping her truncheon against her leg, Rashala shook her head. This time, she decided, the situation was to their advantage.

With his master still free, that battler was unpredictable. He was weak and unable to change shape, but he'd still managed to kill Eighty-nine and blow a very large hole in a stone wall three feet thick. He might bring this entire place down. Rashala didn't like that. If it weren't for the emperor's whim, she would have had the creature destroyed. Instead, the order had come: they were to bind him and take him to the emperor immediately, though his original master still roamed free.

Nothing like this had ever happened, so not even Rashala knew what it meant for a battler to hear commands from two separate men. Usually they only saw their masters once, after they were bound and before they were sent to the guilds from which they served. This was after they'd been thoroughly instructed to obey only certain people, such as the arena master or the emperor or possibly certain handlers, and given the hierarchy of whom they obeyed. This was very distinct, with only the emperor unlimited in what orders he could give. Handlers could never order a battler to attack, for example. No sylph had *ever* had two masters who could speak to them at the same time, however, as an entire class of rules had been created to prevent such a situation from happening.

No, no one could predict what would come of this.

Rashala hated the uncertainty, but she also knew it was not for her to question the emperor. She intended to keep Seven-oh-three as distracted as possible, though. For that reason, until his original master was dead, he could have the girl if he wanted her. If she kept him happy, that was all to the good. When the man who'd escaped the arena was found and killed, the blonde would probably have to be sold, but that was all right. Rashala had managed to get twelve gold out of her after all.

Lizzy lay on her side on the bed, gently stroking Ril's hair. It felt even softer than her own, and was somewhat darker and straighter. When the sylph's eyes opened, regarding her with renewed wonder before he shifted forward to kiss her, she sighed against his mouth.

"Why did we wait so long?" she asked.

He kissed the tip of her nose. "I was waiting for you to grow up," he admitted, "and I couldn't do anything as a bird, anyway. Then, when I was able to change shape, you were still too young and I . . . got hurt." He shrugged, not meeting her eyes.

He was ashamed—even if she hadn't been able to feel him, Lizzy would know. How long had he been hiding this, from her and her father both? Had her father suspected?

"Would you ever have touched me if I hadn't made you?" she asked instead. Ril's expression was answer enough. "Would you have let me live my entire life and never said anything?"

"If you were happy, yes."

She made a face. Right now, she couldn't imagine having any kind of life other than one with him, though that was why she'd gone on the aborted trip to Para Dubh in the first place: to decide what to do with her life.

"If it weren't for all of this, I probably would have married Justin," she admitted.

Ril's eyes flickered with something that might have been hatred. "He came with us. He asked Leon for his blessing to marry you."

Lizzy stared. "What? *Justin?* He left me on the docks with those men! I don't want to marry him!" Not after that, and especially not now. To marry a man who'd desert her when there was danger? She felt sick at the thought, even as her mind backed away from the fact that he'd come after her anyway with her father and Ril. "Did Daddy agree?"

"Yes," Ril said, "but I'll talk him out of it."

"How?"

Ril shrugged. "I'll just point out that if Justin ever tries to touch you, I'll tear his head off and feed his balls to the pigs." When she gaped at him and started to giggle, he smiled faintly and stroked her cheek, adding, "I'm yours, Lizzy. Nothing Leon says can change that, not even if he orders me. Battlers are possessive. I'd go mad if someone else touched you now."

He said it so matter-of-factly that Lizzy hugged him, thinking about the battlers here and how they had to pretend indifference just to keep their lovers from being dragged away and maimed. "We have to get out of this place," she whispered. "All of us. I can't bear the thought of Eapha and the others having to stay. It's awful what happens to them."

"I know," Ril soothed, though he didn't. He didn't even know who Eapha was. But he cared, she knew, and she nestled her head against his chest for a moment, thinking of something her father had said once: Sylphs weren't independent thinkers. They were born and bred to obey, and they wanted direction.

For all his intelligence, Ril wasn't much different. He was nearly always at her father's side, and it was her father who made the decisions. Sylphs could act on their own and sometimes did, but usually only when they were forced. Lizzy would likely have to be the one to figure out how to escape. The thought was fearful, and she wished her father were there.

"We should talk to Eapha," she announced. They hadn't exactly been working on escape plans, but now they had Ril, and he didn't have any stupid orders preventing him from helping them get out like the other battlers did. If he'd been whole, he could have exploded the doors and the roof and everything else and they'd already be free . . . but she steered away from that thought. Ril could do what he could do, her father always said. They didn't need anything more.

Ril nodded and rose, dressing himself. As she picked up the gauzy gown she had to wear, his lip twisted and he silently handed her his shirt. Lizzy smiled and pulled it on.

"Come on," she told him, leading him outside, trying hard not to look too much like she was *with* him. He'd have to pretend with the others, and she really hoped he'd be willing.

In the main room, many of the women were dancing, performing for a group of battlers. Lizzy saw Ril's eyebrow rise, but he followed her silently across the room, skirting the show while she sought out her friend. A few of the women turned as he passed, strange as he appeared, but it was the battlers who stared, shifting away from the dancers to gawk.

Ril hissed, pausing. Lizzy took a few more uncertain steps, glancing back over her shoulder. She could feel his hate, and theirs. Battlers back home belonged to the same hive, and here they all knew one another. She'd forgotten how much they normally loathed any foreign battlers.

"Ril?" she called. She'd never seen him so much as growl at another sylph.

Above, two more battlers came down through the access passages, shifting to their humanoid forms as they landed. Numbers 14 and 683. A few of the women called out to them, but they were ignored. Instead, the newcomers attacked.

Ril roared, his aura flaring and with it his power, but then they were on him, bowling him over. Lizzy screamed while the other women panicked, trying to run even as she pushed forward to go to Ril's aid. All the other battlers leaped to their feet as well, their auras flaring almost as if they were screaming, and their hate blew through every human mind. It was enough to make many of the women drop to their knees, shrieking and sobbing.

Lizzy felt the auras but tried to push through anyway, her heart beating madly and her stomach tightening until she thought she might vomit. She nearly stumbled into the currents of power surrounding the three battling sylphs, but Tooie grabbed her around her waist, pulling her back to safety.

The two newcomers had Ril in their grip, Fourteen holding one arm and Six-eighty-three the other. They pushed him down, forcing him roughly onto his back with his legs folded under him. Lizzy screamed, struggling against Tooie, but she was helpless in the face of his strength. Ril looked at her, his face hardening. He'd fight for her, she realized, no matter what the cost.

"No!" she screamed, even as his form shimmered in a change. Shape-shifting exhausted him, hurt him, and Fourteen and Six-eighty-three were both fresh and strong.

He'd have to become incorporeal to get free of their grip, and he'd never survive that. "Ril, don't!"

He shuddered and became solid again. "Lizzy!"

The door opened. Through it came Rashala, the woman all the concubines feared. Behind her were three more battlers, two handlers, and Melorta, their leader. Rashala looked at all of them, at the battlers who had been relaxing and at the two that held Ril.

"Bring Seven-oh-three," she ordered.

Fourteen and Six-eighty-three hauled Ril upright, dragging him between them to the door. Without another glance Rashala stepped outside, her prize right behind her. The other battlers followed, then the guards. Melorta paused at the threshold, glaring speculatively at Lizzy before pulling the door shut.

Tooie let Lizzy go. She stumbled forward a step and turned, hitting him. "Why didn't you help him?" she screamed, though of course there was no way he could have. A moment later Eapha was there, and Lizzy fell into her friend's arms, sobbing. There was nothing else to be done.

Ril was frog-marched down the corridor outside the harem, fighting every step of the way, but he'd lost so much of his original strength and there were too many guards. He screamed at them, though, and cursed . . . and it had no more effect than his attempts to wrench himself free.

Except it got Leon's attention. After more than twenty years together, the man's link to him was strong, and Ril felt Leon's concern in the back of his mind. There wasn't any more than that, he wasn't a telepath, but Ril drew fortitude from his master's concern even as he burned through the new energy with which he'd awoken.

Down the hall and through another room, then through

another corridor and other doors, finally he entered a massive chamber larger even than the harem. It was lined floor to ceiling with dozens of levels of cages, catwalks, and stairways, and Ril actually stopped his struggle for a moment to gawk. Men and women filled those cages, empty, miserable people who barely looked up as he was dragged by. There were thousands of them, their emotions oppressive, and even though the floors were scrubbed, the place still reeked of their sweat and despair.

There were sylphs here as well—all of the elemental breeds. They were flickering here and there, stopping outside certain cells to drink the energy of the people within. There were battlers, too. Ril saw them feeding from men who didn't look up and certainly didn't speak. No, the only voice was his, screaming in protest.

"What is this place?" he finally whispered.

He got no answer from the bald woman who led the way, and Ril had the sudden understanding that he never would. He wasn't an intelligent being to her. The only time she'd ever speak to him was if she needed to give an order. He screamed invective at that, trying to free himself even more, so he could fight her and the rest of them, but she was a woman. He couldn't quite get his mind around the idea of hurting her—and Lizzy's order had stopped him when he still had the chance. The battlers who held him had walls of power up now. Any energy he lashed out with wouldn't get past them.

They dragged him down aisles and through entire floors of cages. The human prisoners watched them pass, their bodies grown frail from lack of exercise, their hair long and tangled. They were clean but silent.

Beyond the pens was another door, this one leading into a smaller chamber that was still a hundred or more paces across. Ril saw the blood-stained altar at its center, and he stiffened, remembering another. He'd first seen it when he came through the gate into this world, drawn by the energy of a woman he didn't know was about to be killed. Leon had been the one to murder her, striking so fast she was dead before she knew it, before Ril even realized she was in danger. He'd forgiven his master for that at last, but they still never talked about it. Ril didn't want to, and neither, he suspected, did Leon.

To see an altar again, though, like this . . . He'd enjoyed going to Yed and rescuing Gabralina, enjoyed killing those priests who'd tried to use her to trap a battler. Now though, he screamed until his voice went shrill and inhuman, but still the battlers dragged him toward it.

"Can't you quiet him?" a man asked. He stood beside the altar, as bald as Rashala and sporting the same nose. He grimaced.

"You know I can't, brother. Still . . ." She turned and pulled a filmy scarf out of her pocket. "Gag him," she told one of Ril's captors.

The battler moved behind Ril. Ril tried to kick him, but the sylph avoided the blow and slipped the scarf around and into Ril's mouth like a bit, pulling it and his head back until Ril thought his neck might actually break. He stopped screaming, barely able to breathe.

"Better," Rashala approved. "Do you have a man for me, Shalatar? The emperor wants to see him within the hour."

"If His Excellency were willing to wait for two hours, then I would say yes. I'm afraid I'm going to have to do it."

Staring at the ceiling as he was, Ril couldn't see Rashala's expression, but he heard her gasp. "But Shalatar!"

"There's nothing for it. There's no one else available."

"But you won't be able to master anyone else."

"That's hardly a problem in my job. I don't need a sylph. You know the First actually commands them all anyway.

Seven-oh-three won't even need to see me after I set up his commands. Don't be sorry for me, Rashala. It's not important. Come now, hurry. Time is running away from us."

"All right, brother."

Forced to kneel on the floor, staring at the ceiling with the scarf pulled painfully across his open mouth, Ril heard the chanting start and gave a muffled scream. He could feel the ritual reaching inside and changing him.

They wove the spell with their strange human magic that so mockingly mimicked the bindings of a queen. They took him and everything he was, and they overlaid a pattern on the ones already there. Ril fought it as hard as he'd fought Leon's so long ago, but as with Leon, he was helpless. They took him and remade him, and when the battlers finally let him go, he didn't attack the way he so desperately wanted.

"Seven-oh-three," Shalatar told him firmly. "I am your master and you will heed my commands."

"Yes," Ril whispered. There was no choice but to obey.

# Chapter Seventeen

Leon grew terribly thirsty as he studied the dome that he suspected was the entrance to whatever place his daughter had been taken. It had been two days since their arrival and *Southern Dancer* had long since gone. The heat was growing unbearable again, even in the floating island's shadow, and finally he had to leave and search for water before he collapsed. Finding it took an unnaturally long time. Back home, he could take a dipper to anyone's rain barrel or borrow the bucket to their well with no more than a by-your-leave. In this dry country, water was a much more precious commodity. The day before he'd managed to drink from a water trough intended for horses, but the stableman had seen him and gone after him with a whip. Leon didn't dare draw attention to himself again that way and saw no wells or barrels. It didn't look as though there had been rain anytime in the last five hundred years.

He made his way to a restaurant instead. There was no inn above it—this was a place for locals, and Leon hoped he didn't stand out too much as he walked off the street and climbed a few steps onto a stone terrace with a roof held up by dozens of pillars engraved with scrollwork. Tables were arranged among these, many of them occupied, and the entrance to the restaurant's interior was on the other side. Leon certainly didn't know why anyone would want to sit outside. It was nearly as hot on the terrace as in the street, and he was starting to feel ill from both the clothes he was wearing and dehydration. He hadn't slept well, either.

Staring at the floor and attempting to assume the image of a weary local, Leon walked inside the building and suddenly saw why the terrace was full. It was even hotter inside, blisteringly so, and the only people there were employees. He smelled food cooking but couldn't even imagine what the kitchens would be like. His knees went weak and he gagged in the hot air.

A woman approached, bowing. She was young and wore the light fabric wrap of most Meridal women, her arms bare and her hair bound atop her head to keep it off her neck. Hairstyles seemed to indicate rank in this place. Braids meant someone was a slave. A shaved head showed a bound serf, which seemed to be a few steps up the hierarchy. Hair worn loose was reserved for whores. Hair up, as well as being practical, meant freedom.

The woman sweated, but she looked better than Leon felt. "May I help you, sir?" she asked.

He shouldn't have come inside, Leon realized; a local wouldn't in this heat. He'd just drawn attention to himself, and he saw her observing the heavier robe he wore over his cotton pants, and worse, his boots. The serving woman wore sandals like everyone else, and her toenails were painted bright blue.

"Sir?"

"Water," Leon croaked. He needed it too badly to try and leave, which would also seem strange. Battlers could be attracted by the curious as much as the violent. Back in the Valley, they thronged around anything new, and every child's game drew at least one. "Some water," he repeated. "I'll be outside."

"Yes, sir."

She bowed, and Leon left, briefly shocked by how cool

the air felt compared to inside. In the last two days, all the moisture seemed to have been sucked out of him. Even the slave pens before that disaster in the arena hadn't been so hot as this. Nor had the arena itself. There had been air sylphs keeping things cooler, though he suspected that wasn't for the fighters' comfort.

He settled down in a chair, pulling his robes around himself even though he longed to throw them off and just breathe. All of this was his fault. He couldn't have foreseen they'd be taken so quickly, but he was the one in charge. He hadn't planned well enough. Now both Ril and Justin were prisoners along with Lizzy, and those two were here because he'd brought them. Ril he'd had no choice about, and the battler was courage personified, but Justin . . . ? He never should have let the boy's guilt change his mind. To see him flee that battler in the arena . . . and now Leon couldn't even be sure if the youth was still alive.

The serving woman came out, turning her head into a slight breeze as she produced a clay carafe and a glass. Tired and parched, Leon stared up at her while asking the price, and saw her start. Damn. She'd probably never seen blue eyes before. Her own were dark as pitch.

"Five coppers," she said to him.

"Fine." He had to give her a piece of silver instead, having no copper, but she didn't say anything about it or about the strange denomination on the coin, nor did he. He just waited for her to go, trying not to gulp his water as he drank and trying even harder to calm his thoughts. She wasn't going to go running to the battlers. They weren't going to descend on him through the three open sides of the terrace. Nothing was going to happen, other than that he was going to get rid of this terrible thirst and find a new place to sleep. Then, when his mind was clear, he would figure out a way to rescue everyone he cared about.

The serving woman came back. Leon stared in surprise at the coppers she placed in his palm. He hadn't expected change. "Would the sir care for some food?" she asked.

"Yes," he replied, hoping that it wasn't a trap to keep him around so she could call the battlers, but knowing he didn't really have any other choice. He needed the water, and now that he'd had some, he could feel how badly he needed food. "Thank you."

"You're welcome, sir," she said, and vanished back into the sweltering kitchen.

Less than ten blocks away, knowing that Leon was alive and free but not where he was, Ril followed his new master out of the small domed building in the center of the square. Inside was really nothing more than a staircase, much like the one bored into the top of the cliff where the Community had toughed out its first winter—the place where he'd first met Solie and been granted his freedom.

Now he walked behind Shalatar, still in the same dusty pants and boots he'd been wearing when he was taken. Lizzy had his shirt, but he tried not to think of her. Not that he didn't want to, but he'd get lost in memories of her if he did and couldn't afford that now. Not if he was going to figure a way to get out of this.

He honestly didn't know how. Shalatar had him bound more deeply than he'd ever imagined possible. Ril followed behind the man, always three steps behind—as ordered. He didn't speak and couldn't. As ordered. A thousand commands saturated his mind, all given him in a rush by the brother and sister but without any mistakes. Leon had given him ten orders when he bound him and he'd felt trapped. These people had given him hundreds, and not a one contradicted the others. They'd had centuries to perfect their litany, and he would comply absolutely.

Though Shalatar was his master, Ril had an entire list of people he now had to obey: the emperor; the First, who controlled the sylphs; the Battle-Sylph First, who specifically commanded the battle sylphs; the matron of the harem, who was Rashala; all of the handlers and guards who watched over them; the Second of the feeder pens, where the battlers went to feed; and others with other needs. The timing of his meals, the timing of his matings, the rules of the harem, the rules of the pen, they all echoed through him. The rules of when he might obey a specific person and in which order he would obey, as well as at what times. He felt as if there was no way he could remember it all, but he knew the commands were there, indelibly a part of him.

Shalatar finished repeating the rules on the way up from the summoning room. Masters here weren't like back in Eferem. Ril would probably never see the man again. Instead, he'd bow to other people and obey them on Shalatar's earlier commands. He could feel the man's emotions, though, clearer than anyone else they passed, just as he could any of his masters. Right now, Shalatar felt . . . inconvenienced.

Ril would have screamed, but of course that wasn't permitted. Instead, he waited. The last time he'd been bound he'd gone mad, driven insane until he saw Lizzy's birth and found his way back through loving her. He couldn't afford that this time. He had Leon to worry about, and Lizzy—and whatever other orders his captors had given him, they'd given him permission to use the harem and the women in it as well. He would see her again and lose himself in her, and until then, all he had to do was survive.

Shalatar led him out into the square that circled the stairwell. Ril didn't feel the heat the way Leon did, but he blinked in the bright light and looked up at what descended toward them. It seemed like an ornate sled, only without runners. An invisible air sylph kept it aloft, her energies swirling around the thing as she dropped it lightly to the ground before them. The driver, a man as bald as Shalatar, bowed deeply and opened its door.

Shalatar stepped inside and sat. Ril followed, but he hunkered down on the floor by the man's feet. Not for the likes of him was the seat. Normally, he'd have followed in his natural form, but of course he couldn't do that anymore, and they'd had to make allowances. It was just lucky they thought he couldn't change shape at all. Ril had hopes of being able to use that against them, if only he could find a loophole in his litany of servitude.

For now he hunkered like an obedient if hateful dog at his master's feet, and the sled rose up into the air, floating smoothly and swiftly across the city. There were more sleds in the air, darting all around like multicolored honeybees, and Ril looked at their well-dressed occupants with contempt. They all saw him as less than nothing, just a commodity, the same as they saw Lizzy as someone who could be kidnapped and sold, then used like a whore against her will.

Thought of Lizzy brought back the memory of her soft skin and the smell of her, and he had to shove it away. He couldn't afford to get lost in thoughts of her, not if he ever wanted a reunion. The sound of her breathless gasp in his ear echoed through his mind, however, and he bit his lip, gripping the edge of the sled until the wood began to splinter.

"Calm yourself," Shalatar said, regarding him mildly. There was no fear in the man. Ril wanted to hit him with his aura of hate, but the rules were strict. He couldn't use his aura at all, unless he was in the arena. Ril closed his eyes and tried to relax. Without the hate aura to mask his emotions, Shalatar could feel them.

When he tried to calm the anger and the fear he felt, the man reached out to ruffle his hair, tousling it like a dog's. "Good boy," he said.

Lizzy was in one of the alcoves, hopping up and down on the bed and trying not to worry. Much as she'd loathed the idea, she'd forced herself to toss aside the shirt Ril gave her and return to her gauzy, useless dress. Her breasts bounced painfully in it, and she held them with her hands as she hopped.

Tooie bounced beside her, swinging his arms back and forth and watching. Lizzy had grown so used to his regard, and that of the other battlers, that she wasn't embarrassed. Besides, she could hardly call herself an innocent anymore. Not after having Ril's mouth on her breasts, his hands on her thighs, and the glorious silky length of him deep within . . . She shivered and caught Tooie eyeing her. He could feel what she did, she remembered, and blushed.

"Sorry."

One eyebrow rose, and his eyes twinkled with laughter. No longer bouncing, he made a few slow gestures with his hands and arms. Lizzy stopped as well, focusing. She'd been learning their gesture language as fast as she could, but there was a lot she still didn't understand.

Tooie kept it simple. "No. Good," she read. He repeated one of the gestures and added a second. "No. Sorry . . . Oh, 'Don't be sorry, it's good'?"

He nodded.

Lizzy laughed, still a little self-conscious after all. She bit her lip. "What do you think they're doing with him?" she asked.

He shrugged and gestured. "Don't. Know. Money."

She turned away. That was true. Ril was worth too much money for them to hurt him. She bit her lip, hating that as much as she hated being a slave herself. It was no wonder the Community split away and founded Sylph Valley. People could feel the emotions of their sylphs. How could anyone not understand that they were thinking, living beings with rights? Of course, she was from the same species, and they'd done this to her.

"People are horrible."

Tooie tilted his head to one side and lifted his arms, moving them around in a pattern she had to squint to understand. "Not. All. She. Good."

Lizzy smiled. "You really love Eapha, don't you?"

Tooie nodded. "Want. Her. Like. Him. You."

Lizzy wasn't quite sure what that meant. Eapha and Tooie had been together for years, and she and Ril had just found each other. Perhaps it was something lost in translation. "Well," she said with a forced smile. "Let's make sure that they don't have a reason to separate you." With that, she started to hop up and down again on the mattress, and after a moment he joined in.

Leon followed the young woman from the tavern, not because he felt any threat from her, and certainly not because he intended to harm her himself. Nor did she remind him of his wife or any of his plethora of daughters. He followed her on a hunch and because he needed more information on how this society worked.

She finished her shift well after dark and headed away from the restaurant down the dry stone streets, turning almost immediately into a long, narrow alleyway between buildings. The absence of the sun, which had been so blisteringly hot during the day, brought an icy chill to the air, and very few people were still outside. The young woman pulled a shawl around herself as she walked, moving as quickly as she could without running.

The route she took was one Leon would have hesitated suggesting to anyone who was unarmed, and he hurried after her partly now to lend a protective eye. But as she hurried deeper into the warren that stretched to the edge of the city, he soon followed her instead as his only way out. Darkened doorways loomed every few feet, each deep enough to hide a man, but no one sprang out at her, not in this place. It had to be because of the battlers, Leon decided. He could feel them floating overhead, watching and sensing, and knew they would descend in seconds if needed—probably to find new combatants for their arena, he thought uncharitably. But he had reason to be harsh. In the little time he'd spent in the pens, he'd spoken to four other victims. One had stolen some bread. One had escaped the feeder pens before his tongue could be cut out. The third had thrown sand at a nobleman, and the fourth didn't know why he was there.

The girl reached the outskirts of the city, where worn and battered walls held back the desert. Sand blew over the top, stinging one's eyes and getting easily into clothing. She made her way to and over the wall, heading outside the city itself. Silently Leon followed, seeing as he did that she wasn't alone. Other people headed out into the desert as well, wrapping scarves around their faces for protection.

While the city gleamed with light and life behind him, here he found a collection of hovels so vile that Leon didn't know how they survived. He also cringed at the thought of the likely resident diseases. Stretching as far as he could see in the darkness, there were dozens of dwellings made of stacked rocks and tattered fabric, many built against the lee of a massive boulder so that they at least were out of the main thrust of the wind. Fires were rising from open pits, and people gathered around these to cook and talk. There weren't many children, but Leon did see some, scurrying about and playing despite the late hour.

He hesitated at the edge of the light, watching as the woman he'd followed went up to others who, from the look of them, were family. Many people were living out here indeed, coming and going from the city proper. Leon watched the woman pool her tips with her family, then produce a flask of water that was passed around excitedly. Seeing Leon, one of the men waved for him to join them.

With a shrug, Leon did.


Ril lay as Shalatar did, prostrate, down on his knees, bent forward, forehead to floor and arms stretched out before him. The floor was made of glossy marble, polished well enough that he could see his own hateful expression as he glared at himself, not allowed to raise his head to glare at anyone else. He felt the emperor walk around him, and the skin between his shoulder blades itched.

The fact that Shalatar was in the same position gave little consolation. The man was content to be on his face like this, even honored. Ril thought he'd go mad if he stayed this way too long, and he took a deep breath, holding it and letting it go slowly. He wasn't prone to acts of rage, never had been. He deliberated slowly, planned things out, acted when he was sure. He'd find a way out of this, think of a way out. He had to.

"He's not terribly impressive to look at, is he?" the emperor said—to no one, since no one would ever dare answer. He was middle-aged, lean to the point of scrawniness, and as bald as Shalatar, though he had a fringe of hair above his ears. The robes he wore were much richer. It wasn't as though he needed to dress for the heat. The air in the palace to which Ril had been brought was as mild as a spring afternoon back home. At least a half dozen air sylphs would be needed to keep it cool. Ril had seen the place as he was brought in. It was huge, the ceilings a hundred feet overhead and everything constructed from marble and gold. The palace was ostentatious and ugly and a massive waste of space. He preferred Sylph Valley and its battler chamber, where he could sleep in his natural form, surrounded by his hive mates.

Don't think of that, he told himself. Don't think of them, don't think of Lizzy. Don't think of tearing this man's head off, because Shalatar would feel it and the emperor had been given control over him. The man could order any sylph in Meridal to do anything, a parallel to a sylph queen that made Ril want to laugh bitterly. The emperor's control was a joke—but it still kept Ril prostrate on the floor, pressed to the cold marble like the dog they thought he was.

"Still . . . ," the emperor went on, continuing his circuit around Ril. He stopped, and Ril actually felt the man's slipper on his back, pushing against him as if to see whether he'd fall apart. "He was beautiful to watch in the arena. I want to see him again. Not against the battlers, though. Put him up against gladiators and see how he does. Yes." He removed the slipper and circled Ril again before moving silkily back to his throne.

The edge of his robe brushed Ril's face, and Ril hissed under his breath. Not allowed to speak ever again, he could still make some sound, and he saw the emperor start in surprise. As victories went, this was paltry, but Ril still lapped it up vindictively, since he already knew it wouldn't last.

It didn't. The emperor made a gesture and a whip came

down across Ril's back. If it had been a normal whip, he never would have felt it, but this was formed of a battler and cut him deep, startling him into crying out. The lash descended again. He cried out again.

He was struck a dozen times before he realized the lesson they wanted to instill. Actually, he learned after the fourth hit, but he refused to acquiesce until the twelfth, when he felt his energy bleeding down his sides and started to fear he would die there, beaten to death for no reason at all. When the whip came down the twelfth time, Ril made no sound, nothing at all. There was a pause then, and still he made no sound, staring down at his own blank reflection.

"Good," said the emperor, and he returned to his throne. "You may leave."

Ril had to be dragged out.

# Chapter Eighteen

The people Leon met after following Zalia from the restaurant were among the poorest he'd ever seen. Living in their makeshift hovels, they existed in constant fear of sandstorms, as well as poisonous snakes and spiders. The heat baked them during the day, and the cold at night caused illness. They were filthy, sweaty, and stinking . . . and apparently the backbone of Meridal's human labor force. They were the forgotten servers and laborers, whom no one else saw.

Many were refugees from the floating city. A third of the men Leon met that first night had no tongues. At least a tenth of the women had been raped in the harems and then put up for sale as slaves, and when they weren't bought had been tossed into the desert to survive on their own. Like the other exiles, unwelcome in a city that was nearly a slum itself, they joined this collection camped on the outskirts that walked back inside each day to work or beg. However, by being outside the city walls, they avoided the notice of city magistrates and battlers. They probably had more freedom than the city's actual denizens.

The group reminded Leon of the men and women who'd founded Sylph Valley. Those originally had been the poor of Para Dubh, banding together and heading out into the Shale Plains to make a life of their own. They'd had the advantage of sylphs, however. Even leaderless and broken, driven deep into the lifeless Shale Plains at the start of a winter that promised to be utterly brutal, they'd had more than these people. Here Leon saw such sickness that noses were falling off, great sores spreading across people's skin to devour their features. Children looked like walking skeletons, and he saw very few elderly.

They welcomed him, though. Everyone who approached the hovels was welcome, so long as they didn't bring trouble, and Leon stood over one of the fires, warming his hands and glad now of his heavier clothing.

He eyed the woman he'd followed here. She was one of the few to have an actual job. "So, you work in the city to bring back money for everyone?"

She ducked her head, blushing, but the older man beside her answered. "She brings enough for water and a bit of food. She's a good girl." He beamed at her.

Leon wondered distantly how she stayed clean enough to be allowed in the restaurant each morning. "The battlers don't pay attention to you?"

"No, sir. They're not allowed outside the walls. No sylph comes here."

That was interesting. If he could get the others out this way, they could circle the city and head back to the ocean. Leon surveyed his surroundings, already making plans, then sighed. Plans would do no good if he couldn't get to his friends.

"Where are you from, sir?" Zalia asked. She was a pretty girl, which was probably why she found work, but not so pretty as to be taken for the harems.

"Far away," he told her. "From a place much to the north, where it snows in winter." He saw their expressions, but after he explained himself, he still wasn't sure if they were more baffled by the idea of snow or the concept of rain. They all used the same basic language, but not all words were universal. Leon was ruefully sure that they likely had a lot more words for sand than he'd ever heard before. "My daughter was kidnapped and brought here," he continued. "They put her in one of their harems."

Zalia's father grimaced in sorrow. "I'm so sorry to hear that. May you live to see her again." He made a complicated gesture that seemed intended to bestow luck.

Leon's face hardened. "I'll see her again, because I'm going to get her out." The people around him all stared in amazement. In their world, no one defied the emperor. Leon had no choice, though, not if he wanted to see his family again.

Perhaps these people could help. Not in infiltrating the harem for Ril and Lizzy—he wouldn't risk anyone else, even if he had thought they could make a difference—but they did know the city and could show him around. Also, they could explain to him some of how this place worked. Then perhaps he could beat the system.

Zalia and her father looked dubious when he began to ask questions, but that didn't matter. Just so long as they could provide information and be his guides. That was all he really needed for now. That, and a place to sleep. The dwellings here were awful, but he'd occasionally been in worse. And when he reminded himself of where his daughter was sleeping, his own fate didn't matter at all.

Lizzy lifted her head from the pillow as she heard the main door open and close far on the other side of the harem. Immediately she was out of the bed and running, though she forced herself to slow into an uninterested stroll as she exited the sleeping chamber to the harem proper. No matter what was out here, she had to act as though she didn't care.

It wasn't Ril. Lizzy saw the evening's meal being laid out, and she sighed, walking toward it with several other concubines. There were a lot of battlers visiting tonight, however, and many of the alcoves were occupied, the curtains shaking for real. One even was taking his conquest in the middle of the harem, uncaring of who watched—or perhaps preferring it.

Lizzy skirted the copulating couple, pretending as everyone else did that nothing was happening. Had it been her there, and she had no doubt it would have been, if not for Ril's strange protection, she wouldn't have wanted anyone looking, either.

She still didn't understand what he'd done to keep the other battlers away from her, though it had taken place before she ever reached this place. He'd called her his master when he made love to her, but how could that be? Her father was his master and always had been, and Ril had kept things that way even after being freed.

Though he couldn't exactly get rid of Leon. Masters were masters for life, no matter how many a battler had, and Leon would always be primary—though of course Solie trumped him as queen. But none of that made Lizzy a master, nor had his making love to her. It took spells to bind a sylph. She'd seen them, and they couldn't be cast by a sylph, save in the presence of a queen, and even then not upon themselves. Priests had to do it, otherwise, with all their elaborate circles and chanting. Lizzy had watched more than once, sometimes with Ril present, but he hadn't said or done anything distinctive. Yet somehow he'd made her his master. He'd made her safe here. Moreover, he made her *feel* safe. In fact, he made her feel wonderful.

Eapha appeared, smiling warmly. There was sweat on her lip and a faint odor on her skin that made Lizzy blush. Tooie had been with her for real, and she glowed.

"Do you know when Ril will be back?" Lizzy asked in an undertone.

Eapha walked to the table and helped herself to a bun

and several fruits. "No. He'll be back eventually, though. What else are they going to do with him?"

Lizzy took a bowl of porridge but didn't say anything more until they were safely away. None of the other women at the table were in the circle of enlightened battlers and their lovers, and it was foolish to risk having their secret discovered. No one had betrayed the circle yet, but Eapha had warned Lizzy of other women being betrayed for various freedoms. Melorta, the lead handler, was said to have been promoted that way.

They reached a corner of the back wall. Ap was screaming somewhere nearby, with whatever battler was making love to her. The woman honestly enjoyed sex. Lizzy was amazed that her voice never gave out.

"I was talking to Tooie," Eapha remarked. "He says that you're Ril's master. He was curious about it, but he can't talk to you, since your vocabulary is still so small." She smiled, dimples appearing high on her cheeks.

Lizzy laughed, blushing. "You mean you two find time to talk?"

Eapha lightly smacked her. "Be nice. I'm serious. He was really interested. I didn't think women could be masters of battlers."

"Oh, sure," Lizzy said, suddenly realizing that she'd never talked to Eapha about Sylph Valley. The woman hadn't asked, though. In this place, no one asked others about their pasts. Tooie must have been very excited indeed for Eapha to bring it up.

"Battlers prefer female masters," Lizzy explained. "Back home, that's all they have. Ril's the exception. He's my father's battler. He never says it, but we all know he loves Father." And me, she didn't add. "But everyone else has women. Well, the nonbattlers don't seem to care what they get, genderwise."

"How very strange," Eapha said.

"There aren't any harems, either. Battlers only sleep with their masters. Except Ril," she added as an afterthought.

Eapha laughed. "That would be very strange indeed. So, you're not Ril's master?"

"Not that I know of. But I can feel what Ril is feeling now, and you saw everyone. They don't want me. Ril does."

"Then what is Tooie going on about? He keeps complaining he doesn't have the words." Eapha huffed out a breath. "Silly boy. He spent half our time together asking about it. I could have yanked his ears off." Both she and Lizzy laughed. It felt good.

"I'm kind of curious about it myself," Lizzy admitted. About that, about the dreams . . . She had so many questions she hadn't let herself think about, given how worried she was for Ril's safety.

"Will you ask Ril about it when he gets back?"

Lizzy agreed eagerly enough, not realizing she wouldn't be able to after all.

Ril was taken to the healer after his audience with the emperor. They didn't scold him for his defiance. What, they were surely wondering, was the point of yelling at a dog? The healer laid her hands on his back, and he sighed as the pain went away.

Shalatar left sometime during that healing session, and with the distance he put between them, Ril's awareness of the man faded to a faint buzz that was easily ignored. Lizzy was easier to feel, given his love for her, and Leon was easy as well after twenty years of familiarity. Lizzy was amused and Leon determined, but while he could feel them, Ril couldn't speak to either. Not over such a great distance.

That was fine, actually. He didn't want them to know what he was doing as he got off the table he'd lain on. Wordless, he dropped to his knees and bent over, kowtowing to the battle-sylph First, the man put in charge of all the battlers.

The First snorted, amused by Ril's rage. "Bit slow at that," he said.

"The new ones often are," a second voice answered.

"Well, he's hardly new, is he? Anyone found his master yet?"

"No, my lord."

"Double the search teams. I want that man found and killed."

As the First walked around him, Ril screamed in silent protest of that order, shrieking in anger to his original master, trying to reach him with the sheer force of his rage. *Danger, hunters, run.*

"So, this one is for the arena, is he? Doesn't look like much."

*I know,* Leon's voice almost seemed to come back to him. His very calmness was soothing—which broke Ril's contact with him.

"Take this one to feed," the First continued. "Then put him in the harem. We'll try him in tomorrow's afternoon fights, after the other battlers are done with the latest convicts. Maybe before the battler-versus-battler choreographed rounds. Yes, that would make for a good opening for that new routine Eighteen and Fifty-two have been practicing. Make sure some of his feeders are ready for him immediately afterward, too. Damn. This one is going to be a logistical nightmare. I don't have the men to ferry him around if he can't fly."

"Yes, my lord."

The First left, and Ril looked up at the woman standing before him. She gazed back at him evenly, dressed in brown with an ornate pendant around her neck. According to Ril's orders, it gave her the authority to command him in a few very specific ways. The First had more control, but she had enough to do what was needed.

Ril focused on that necklace and stood. Sullen, he glared at the handler, who just studied him and shook her head, muttering something about colorless skin.

"Come," she ordered at last, and Ril followed.

They went to the feeder pens, Ril walking an inflexible three paces behind. His handler didn't speak, but she looked back periodically as she led the way to a specific set of cages arranged in a hexagon near the chamber entrance. Each held a man and Ril stared at all of them in surprise. He could feel them almost as clearly as Leon and Lizzy. They were masters to him that he hadn't even known about, and he shot a look at his handler in confusion.

"Feed," she ordered, sounding bored.

Ril hadn't considered this. He'd assumed he would feed off Shalatar, though he could feed from Lizzy if necessary. These six men, though . . . he could feel the various flavors of their energy rising off them, the vibrations echoing through his empty insides.

The wounding and subsequent healing had taken a lot out of him, so he stepped forward, hunkering down outside the first cage and reaching through to lay a hand against the feeder's cheek. He didn't know the man at all, so it was easier to draw with physical contact. He drank. The feeder looked at him with deadened eyes. His energy felt dead as well, and finally Ril pulled away, not full but not wanting to touch the man anymore. The feeder felt like nothing, as though every bit of life had been sucked out and only his body was left behind. It was like draining the dead, and Ril made a spitting motion before moving on.

The next was younger but no better. Ril sampled and gagged, wondering if this was his fate for the rest of his life—to drink lackluster energy from lackluster men in a place that treated them like dogs and cattle. He sipped from the third and kept going, nearly full but pretty sure he wouldn't be allowed to stop until he'd taken from them all.

The fourth was the oldest, his energy more flavorless than any of the others, and Ril wanted to retch at the thought of living off it. Leon had always tasted so creamy and warm, and Lizzy so fresh. He'd live off her instead, and damn these men. They made his skin crawl.

He moved around the cages, coming to the fifth, and there he stopped. From the other side of the bars, brown eyes stared back with equal recognition—and with loathing. Justin sat inside the cage, glaring out.

Ril was so surprised he just gaped, and both men were silent. Then Justin moved, rolling forward and shooting a fist out through the bars into Ril's nose. Shocked, Ril fell backward on his behind, and his handler swore, lunging forward. The woman was just fast enough as Ril rose back up, enraged, energy flaring painfully around him and about to blow Justin, his cage, and every other cage within reach to ashes.

*"Down!"* she screamed, lashing Ril across the back with the short crop she carried. It was as good as an order. His energy evaporated and Ril's forehead bounced off the floor, back in the same humiliating, prostrated position as with the emperor.

His handler twisted her crop in both hands and started screaming at Justin, calling him a thousand kinds of fool. The cage door opened and Ril heard her beating the boy, still yelling, and Justin screaming back as much as he could with no tongue. When the door finally slammed shut, Ril was grabbed by the hair and pulled upright. Justin cowered in the cage, his face puffy and bleeding. His hatred had been replaced by terror of Ril and the woman who'd struck him. But even seeing exactly what had been done to the boy, Ril felt no compassion. Regally, he let himself be stood up and directed out of the feeder pens, not once wanting to look back.

His handler led him up the stairway and down the corridors to where battlers were kept in their own well-stocked cages, into a guardroom before the doorway to the harem. The guards looked up curiously, and several moved to open the harem door. Ril went through immediately, and the handler closed it behind them, her emotions still feeling irritated. Not that Ril cared. He could smell women and sex—and the energy of a great many battlers, whom instinct told him to fight.

It took him a minute to spot Lizzy. She sat in a group playing a card game with three battlers that seemed to involve removing clothing for each lost hand, and she barely glanced at him. Her emotions didn't feel anything like indifference, though, and he stepped forward.

"Hi, gorgeous," a woman said, putting her arms around him and smiling seductively. Before Ril could absorb that, she propelled him into the nearest alcove, where she immediately released him. Her face was suddenly serious. "Lizzy said she didn't get a chance to tell you everything about how things work around here, so I'm going to, and if you don't want to lose her, you'd better listen."

Ril opened his mouth to ask what she was talking about, but nothing came out. He grabbed his throat, irritated.

The woman sighed. "So much for asking you about how

you managed to have a girl as your master. I figured they'd forbid you to speak. I just hope you're good at learning sign language." Crossing her arms she demanded, "Listen to me. My name is Eapha and I have a lot to tell you."

# Chapter Nineteen

He became the darling of the arena. During the day, Ril fought the human gladiators they sent against him, killing each to cheers from the crowd. At night one of the handlers would return him to the harem, where he spent his time with the women of Eapha's circle, women in on the secret that kept them all safe. Only once in a half dozen nights as the weeks passed did he take Lizzy to his bed, plucking her as nonchalantly out of a group as any of the other battlers might. He tried not to think how dangerous his actions were, just as he tried not to think of what her father would say if he found out.

But oh, how she felt beneath him! Lizzy would cry and weep, her thighs locked around his hips, drawing him deep as she kissed him, holding him against her with all the strength she had, neither of them wanting to let go, and oh, it was good. Silent, yes, so silent with him forbidden to speak, but so exquisite that he could forget the rest of his agonies for that time, just that short period that he knew they'd take away if they realized what it meant. A cheap lay? Yes, they would allow that. But love? Love would only distract him from his duty.

That duty now stood before him: three men in loincloths and helmets, ringed chain mail draped over their lean bodies to protect them. One carried a net and a spear, one a sword, and one a halberd.

Dressed in leather pants and boots, Ril was unarmed. The crowd cheered him, though. They screamed, and he could feel their excitement. It made the blood inside him boil, the crowd's excitement, and he didn't care for it at all. He just wanted Lizzy's soft body under his and her pleasured cries in his ear. A half dozen times over a month he'd had her, but he still hadn't found a way for them to escape. Lizzy was his darling and his master—but he had a dozen masters now and no way to disobey them.

The three gladiators spread out, circling. Ril watched, already knowing what they would do. They weren't afraid, well trained and experienced as they were, but their intentions were obvious to someone who could feel their emotions, who had been hatched and raised specifically for battle. They were hardly a threat to him, but his masters didn't care. The First had ordered Ril to kill them, and moreover, to take his time and strike only when he felt the crowd's excitement peak. Ril would rather have killed the men immediately and damn the rules, or better, ignore them completely. That wasn't an option, though, and he railed at the evil of being ordered to become a murderer. That's all it was, murder for no reason except someone else's sick desires, making a mockery of everything he truly was. Ril hated it, but he could no more disobey the First than he could Shalatar, though he hadn't seen the latter again after that first day.

The gladiators surrounded him, and Ril dropped into a ready stance, waiting. The man with the halberd charged, the jagged edge of his weapon stabbing toward Ril's chest. Ril stepped out of the way and brought down his fist, hitting the base of the blade hard enough to snap it off. The crowd roared in approval.

The man with the net spun and flung it, and Ril jumped clear. He landed close to the third gladiator, who thrust out his spear. Ril arched his back, the point missing just inches from his spine, and when the gladiator brought it around, trying to cut his legs with the spearhead's sharp edge, he flipped over briefly onto his hands and then again onto his feet. The crowd loved it.

Ril hated fighting like this. If everything were normal, he'd just blow the three apart with a blast wave, but he didn't know how many more matches they expected out of him today. He could have shape-shifted into a more efficient form or turned an arm into a weapon, but that hurt as much as the blasts would, and these people didn't know he could change shape. Convinced of that, they hadn't ordered him to hold his form as they did other battlers. Ril didn't know when he'd be able to use that advantage, but he didn't want to throw it away on a simple encounter in the arena.

Yet this particular fight reminded him of all those practice sessions with Leon on *Southern Dancer*, of how easily the man had dropped him onto his butt despite Ril's greater speed and strength. After all the easy victories he'd had when he first started fighting in the arena, his captors had upped the stakes. These men were nearly as good as Leon. Ril didn't feel any fear, though. That was saved for those he cared for, not for himself.

The halberd man came at him again, having reversed his weapon and now swinging the heavy metal ball at the end opposite the blade. At the same time, the spearman swung again at Ril's legs. Each weapon came from an opposite direction, and he leaped high, somersaulting over his opponents and landing clear while the crowd continued to roar its distracting approval.

It was the same trick he'd used against Eighty-nine, and a few times in earlier battles. Ril felt their confidence as he landed, so immediately he dove to the side. The net of the swordsman landed right where he'd been standing. He came to his feet again, snarling and backing away.

Keeping well clear of each other, though not clear enough that Ril could get through them, the gladiators advanced, herding him back toward one of the free-standing walls. Ril sensed that and growled, his lips pulling back from his too-human teeth as he flared his hatred. He projected his absolute loathing for them and heard the screams of those close enough to feel it in the stands, but the gladiators didn't pause. He could feel their calm and their focus, and the certainty that if they didn't defeat him they would die. Experienced as they were, his hatred meant nothing.

Ril shot a quick look up at the emperor's box. The man watched impassively. He wouldn't care at all if Ril died. He'd just find a new arena darling.

Ril hissed and darted behind the wall. Reaching the center, he hit it with his shoulder as hard as he could. The stone rumbled but didn't fall, so he slammed into it again, feeling something in his shoulder give as the heavy stone tumbled down. But even as it crashed into the sand with a deafening roar, through the resultant dust came the three gladiators, weapons thrusting. They'd had just enough time to get out of the way.

Ril jumped backward, and his back slammed into the outer wall of the arena. Howling, people above showered him with food and drink—which was too much. Ril roared in rage and focused. A wall of power erupted forth, bursting straight ahead like an invisible punch from a giant. It hit the man with the halberd and he disintegrated, scattering blood and entrails everywhere. His head, still in its helmet, bounced even farther, ending faceup in the sand, staring accusingly at the sky.

But the use of energy exhausted Ril. Even as the crowd went mad, he dropped to one knee in intense pain. The other two gladiators hesitated, but Ril could barely move and didn't have it in him for another shot. If only they hadn't spread out, he might have taken them all.

*Don't let them get close.*

Ril started at the faint voice in his head. Only one person knew him well enough and long enough to speak right into his mind without him starting the conversation, and he could only do so when he was in close proximity. Ril flashed his awareness back at the man, but no words. They were forbidden, even in his mind. Ril could only send emotions, and the one he sent was that of relief.

*Run,* the voice said.

Ril bolted. Abandoning pride, he sprinted off, the gladiator's net landing just behind him a second time and nearly catching his foot. He raced along the wall with blinding speed and no idea of where he was going.

*Fight them from a distance,* Leon ordered.

Ril sent back angry impressions. How was he supposed to do that? He didn't have the power to blast them, and this run was draining the last of his strength. The two surviving gladiators were returning to the main part of the arena, keeping clear of each other so that they wouldn't form a single target. Ril sprinted around the arena wall, on the far side from them now and already starting to flag. His shoulder hurt as though something in it had been ground up in a mortar.

*Throw rocks at them,* came Leon's suggestion.

Ril eyed the wall he'd knocked down. It lay broken in a dozen places, edges shattered into rubble that might indeed be small enough. He'd never fought anyone by throwing anything solid at them, but he could remember years before, when Mace had thrown a rock at *him* hard enough to spear through his wing. He'd managed to forget that. Leon apparently hadn't.

Curving away from the wall, he bolted across the center of the arena toward that shattered wall and the two gladiators. They readied themselves, the one with the net swinging it, but Ril chose to zig around the one with the spear. The gladiator lashed out with the sharp blade, and Ril hissed as he felt it cut along his ribs. Something that wasn't quite blood leaked down his side, but the wound wasn't deep and then he was past, skidding to a halt beside the wall. The crowd was roaring, all of them on their feet.

The wall hadn't broken up enough after all. Ril brought his fist down on a piece, shattering it into bits just the right size as the gladiators charged, perhaps figuring out what he was up to. Ril didn't care. He picked up a palm-sized shard, cocked his arm, and flung it as hard as he could. It hit the man with the sword and net so hard it went straight through his chest and out the back, throwing him right off his feet and into the sand.

The spearman kept charging, and Ril's second shot hit the sand at his feet. The man leaped high and lunged, roaring, but Ril threw himself out of the way and twisted. For a moment the two of them were side by side, Ril falling backward, his opponent lunging forward and extending his spear fully. Each saw the other out of the corner of his eye, and then Ril growled and slammed out his elbow, shattering the man's helmet and all the bones in his face. The bones splintered, driving into his brain and eyes, and the gladiator fell.

Ril stumbled to a halt, gasping. He felt awful, but he forced himself to look up at the cheering crowds. He didn't care about them, or about the emperor who was clapping slowly, still pleased with his darling. He searched for Leon instead, and finally saw him in the penny seats, robes pulled tightly around him. His emotions were relieved.

Ril stared at his master, sending his gratitude. He'd known Leon was alive—there was no way he couldn't—but he hadn't known more. Now, considering his fulfilled fantasies with this man's daughter . . . He blushed.

Leon didn't seem upset with him, though. *You did well. Are you all right?* the man sent, his voice much clearer now that Ril was focusing.

Ril shook his head. All he could convey was a feeling of weariness.

*I'm glad you're not hurt.*

The arena gates were opening, female handlers coming out to collect him. Melorta, the lead handler, came first, beaming in approval. Breathing heavily, Ril let the group surround him, all of them bowing to the emperor and making him prostrate himself on the ground before they led him toward the pens where he'd be fed and rested before his next fight, if there was to be one. Ril hoped not.

*I have a plan to get you out, Ril,* Leon sent. *I'm still working on getting Lizzy free as well. And Justin. I don't know if he's alive.*

His eyes narrowed, Ril sent as sharp an image as he could of Justin in a cage with his tongue torn out. He knew he'd succeeded, at least partially, as he felt Leon's horror. Then he was led underground into the cooler air of the pens, and the contact was lost.

The ramp sloped steeply, and he had to lean back to keep his balance. Then he was in the huge stable used to house the battlers. A few he recognized from the harems, but no one appeared the same here as they did there. Ril saw Tooie in the form of some sort of ogre, heavy and hideous, calmly lumbering past toward the ramp. Though that meant his fights were done for the day, he didn't let himself sag in relief. He wouldn't be able to do that until Leon came through and there were no more fights ever.

He was led to his stall, a glorified cell with walls made of heavy woods imported from across the ocean but only reaching halfway to the twenty-foot ceiling. He could have climbed out easily if he hadn't been ordered against it. The stall was thirty feet square, to make room for the larger shapes the battlers usually took in the arena. Tooie was considered small at ten feet. Ril was tiny. Eighty-nine, he supposed, had been cramped indeed within this place. The floor was marble but had straw scattered on it, as though he were some sort of horse.

As he was led inside, Ril ignored the three-headed battler in the next cell, who growled over the half wall at him. At least they'd brought him a bed since they'd learned he had to sleep after most of his fights. After heavy combat they would even leave him overnight. Of course, by the time he got to the harem the next day, Lizzy would be frantic. She didn't know where he went when he left her, and he didn't want her to know. He couldn't help needing the sleep, though. Even now he could barely keep his eyes open.

But there were other things first. Three feeder cages were grouped at one side of his cell, with a man crouched in each. Before he could go to them, however, the door opened and a slave came in bearing towels and clothing. She kept her gaze locked on the floor and was followed by a water sylph. All the elementals in this place took the shape of a pillar of whatever they were, without even a number branded on them to distinguish one from the other. They were forced to work without pause, and without even the illusory freedoms given to battlers in their harems.

This sylph's emotions were miserable and lonely as she

waited for the slave to strip off Ril's clothing, and then she flushed her water around him, heated just enough to cool him off without freezing his muscles. Ril closed his eyes and enjoyed it, lifting his arms and turning while the slave washed his body and hair with scented soap. She scrubbed his scalp sensuously.

Once he was clean, the sylph rinsed him off and the slave rubbed him down with scented oils. Ril yawned, already more than half asleep. All of the battlers got this treatment, and he didn't want to admit how much he liked it. He needed it as well, since he could no longer turn to smoke and lightning and return as clean and healed as if he'd never been in a fight.

Once he was oiled, the slave put balm over the cuts on Ril's side and shoulder and helped him step into fresh clothes, these smelling of desert flowers and falling looser than the leathers in which he'd fought. They were made of silk instead, bearing the emperor's sigil and showing his regard for his favorite. Bowing deeply, the slave retreated, the water sylph at her side. The straw-covered floor hadn't even got damp.

Ril shook himself, feeling more normal but still exhausted, and went to the feeder cages. Sometimes he'd hold out and wait for Lizzy, just pretending to feed on the men's energy, but now he was too tired to care how bland they tasted. Dropping down in front of the first, he reached a hand through the bars and laid it on the man's arm. He drank deep, skimming the energy off and into himself. Usually one was enough, but he'd worn himself out and his shoulder still hurt, so he went to the next, missing Leon's much richer energy even more after hearing the man's voice. His master would try to rescue him—he already knew that—but he honestly didn't know how Leon could succeed. He drank from the second feeder and then, though he usually didn't, this time he even advanced to the third.

Justin. Eyes red-rimmed and bitter, the boy glared at him hatefully. His energy was bitter as well, but Ril forced himself to drink it anyway, even as he forbade himself from growling. Justin was just as much a prisoner as he was, if not more so. Ril would even have explained about Leon if he could, but he couldn't and so went over to his bed. Falling across it, he was asleep immediately.

Ordered to leave him alone when he was sleeping, the handlers let him rest. Ril was unconscious the rest of that day and through the night.

At the back of his stall, a wide window had been cut. For a penny a visit, people could come down into the pits and see battlers close up. Crowds came to observe the strange new sylph, peering at him through the dirty glass, but while they'd enjoyed seeing his bath—especially the women—they didn't have much interest in a sleeping man. The other battlers were far more impressive.

And yet, one man stared at Ril for quite a while, a hood up over his dyed hair, his face calm. He studied the battler and the three feeders imprisoned nearby. Then, reaching out, he tapped the window. The sound echoed loudly through the cell.

The closest feeder looked up and his eyes widened. Quickly, Leon put a finger to his lips and motioned back toward his battler, intending to keep Justin hopeful. There wasn't much else he could do at the moment. Except . . . the passageway he'd come down had cleared, the spectators gone to watch Two-hundred kill the latest batch of prisoners. Their screams sounded in the passageway, echoing down air vents cut in the stone, so Leon took the chance to call "Ril!" several times, loudly.

His sylph didn't wake, but he moved, shifting closer in his sleep toward the calls. Ril still responded to him, despite whatever rules he had to be obeying now. Leon smiled grimly and left, eyes on the ground like any other lower-class person. He made his way out of the arena, right past battler guards who didn't pay any attention to his calm, relaxed thoughts. They let him go even while they searched for him, and he shuffled slowly along in his old, borrowed sandals, not in any rush at all.

Making his way to the city outskirts, he was soon back where the forgotten lived and the battlers never journeyed.

# Chapter Twenty

The sylph known as Two-hundred outside of the harem and as Tooie to the people he actually cared about didn't have guard duty. There were enough battlers who did only that, leaving his sole task to fight in the arena. Thus, his orders were a little different, and he'd never been told to watch for a blue-eyed, blond-haired man wandering the inner city. He could come and go as he pleased, save for the stipulation that he arrive at the arena and harem exactly at the times required, which left him a little leeway. Just a bit.

Deep in the middle of the night, Tooie lifted his head from the bed he was sharing with Kiala, one of the women in the circle and the lover of Four-seventeen. Four-seventeen was in a different alcove with Lizzy. Eapha was alone in the main sleeping chamber.

Tooie rose up silently and padded to the curtains. Careful not to wake Kiala, who just kept snoring, a trickle of drool running down her chin, he peered outside but saw no one. All the other battlers were occupied in alcoves, and the women were either with them or asleep. There was no real day or night in this place, but everyone seemed to slow down in the late hours anyway. That applied to the handlers as well, and Tooie couldn't sense any of them looking through peepholes.

He seized the opportunity. Taking his natural shape, a cloud of energy and red eyes with a huge mouth of teeth formed by lightning, he spread out long dark wings but didn't fly like any bird of this world. Instead, he floated upward, squeezing delicately into the vent that would release him from the harem. But he went with extreme care—there were bells rigged to ring the handlers and announce his departure.

The alarms stayed silent as he passed, Tooie having gone completely incorporeal. Hurrying on, he spiraled upward through the looping passage, squeezing through gaps a rat would have had trouble traversing, let alone a woman, though he knew some women who had tried. None had gotten past the bells. Eapha had suggested the same once, but he'd dissuaded her. She'd never make it out that way. Worse, if she tried, he was under orders to stop her.

Tooie rose through a half mile of tunnel, past the offshoot that would take him to the feeder pens, and instead went to the outside. That was his loophole: he had to be at the arena and at the harem at certain, specific times, but he was allowed to go to the feeder pens whenever he wished, without any restrictions on how long he stayed. Nor had he ever been ordered to go *directly* there. So long as he fed tonight, he wouldn't be disobeying orders.

He didn't know how many other battlers had figured out the same thing—and he didn't exactly care. Still, his one concern was that if even one of them gave the secret away, they would all have their orders tightened. It wouldn't do at all to have someone see him, so he rose up into the darkness, careful to present both the ground and sky with only his dark mantle. The great island citadel floated overhead, blocking out the stars in the same way it did the sun, and he flew through the shadow it cast, passing other sylphs on errands of their own. A few acknowledged him, shimmering, but none tried to stop him or speak. None were allowed. He could feel their misery, though. Even if he could have, he wouldn't have wanted to talk to them. He couldn't do anything to help.

After seventy years, he was used to not speaking. The sign language he'd learned was usually enough, but now he wished he could talk—or that Seven-oh-three could use the signs and tell him how he'd made Lizzy his master. Or who had done it for him. The humans here made masters out of the people they turned into feeders, after crippling them so they couldn't give a single order, but none of the feeders who served battlers were female. Nobody would tie a girl to one of them. That was law. So how had Seven-oh-three done it? And where had that queen pattern come from? They'd all lost such bonds when they crossed the gate, and Tooie couldn't imagine any queen crossing over herself.

He'd studied Seven-oh-three closely, trying to puzzle it out, had analyzed the other battler's patterns until he knew them as well as his own—and the one in Lizzy. He couldn't figure out how it was formed, which was driving him mad. If only he could make Seven-oh-three understand, force him to show how he'd done it, then Tooie could make Eapha his master. He couldn't talk to Seven-oh-three, though. Orders forbade it, and his natural loathing . . . Anytime two battlers came together, their natural hatred for each other got in the way. He flew across the city, angry with Seven-oh-three and angry with himself for his own limitations. There was so much he wanted and so little he could have. Such was the life of all battlers. At least he had love, he told himself. But it wasn't enough. He was so hungry, it could never be enough.

Descending through the night, he hovered at the edge of the city, just shy of the tumbling wall that marked the start of the desert. Farther out, lit by small fires and wandering through the darkness, he could see the energy patterns of the usual camp of the vagrants, as clear to him as if they walked in daylight. He couldn't go to them, but he didn't intend to. There were flowers growing along the wall and out in the sand, flowers Eapha loved. He got them for her whenever he could, and though she had to be careful with them, destroying them before anyone could see, collecting the blooms was always worth her looks of joy.

Tooie found three growing out of the wall. He plucked them with a tendril and carefully brought them back within his mantle, where he carried his breechcloth, but he wanted to give her a better bouquet. Thus he stretched out with his senses, scanning the life on the sand. He found scorpions and snakes, most sleeping. A lizard, also asleep. Children, women, men . . .

He sensed a flower almost at the edge of the camp and stretched out the tendril again, reaching for it. He couldn't leave the city, but he wasn't going to. He was just reaching out with the tiniest part of himself, and not even changing shape to do so, since that was forbidden. Reaching the flower, he wrapped the tendril around it, pulling it out of the sand and back. There, he broke the root off the stem and flower, which he added to the others.

Another would do it, he decided, and looked again, reaching out with his senses. There wasn't much. He'd plucked the area pretty clean already, and the children of the vagrant camps liked to pick the flowers themselves. They might have missed one, though, and he flooded his awareness over the camp itself.

That was when he felt *him*. Tooie started, thinking for a crazed moment that Seven-oh-three was in that camp, then that Lizzy was. But neither of those things made any sense. He focused his battler instincts closer, and only then did he feel the pattern clearly: a man, the same as he'd felt inside Seven-oh-three. The bond was stronger than the one to Lizzy and barely weaker than the bond to the queen. Certainly it was stronger than any of the feeder patterns inside Tooie. Tooie had never felt such a thing, and he suddenly wondered if this was the man who had bonded Seven-oh-three to Lizzy. If so, could the stranger do the same for him and Eapha?

Tooie quickly stretched out, reaching across the sand he wasn't allowed to cross for that pattern, lashing blindly through the darkness in attack.

Leon sat and sipped the cofi he'd bought, lost in thought. Across from him sat Zalia's father Xehm, mouth curved in an expression of bliss. Leon suspected it had been a very long time since Xehm had tasted cofi, or even the food he'd bought.

It wasn't much that he'd purchased. Leon had only the gems and coins Solie had given him, saved because they'd been hidden in his boots when he was taken. The guards had shortly expected to be peeling his clothes off his corpse, so they hadn't searched him. He had to hoard as many of them as he could to buy passage home, and yet he couldn't leave these people like this. Even with so many of them working, they were close to starvation. He didn't like the idea of leaving them in penury, but he had to be a realist. There wasn't much he could do. He had to focus on his own problems and hope that he found a solution.

To be fair, he thought he had, and thanks to Xehm's people he had more information on this empire than he would ever have uncovered on his own, including the fact that Ril spent most of every day in a place where he could be reached! Going to the arena had been a risk, but it had been a risk he'd had to take—both to see Ril for himself and to determine the battler's condition. He knew his sylph had been compromised. It was just a question of how badly.

Now Leon thought he knew the solution to his problems, but if he was wrong, he was dead. That was why Xehm and the others scouted the city, making the maps Leon needed on paper he'd bought, and watching the arena, learning the necessary schedules. It was for this that he'd bought them their food and cofi, though he suspected it wasn't necessary. They were good people, and they too had lost family to the slavers, feeder pens, and harems. They were desperate, though, and he wished he could do more.

"Good?" he asked Xehm.

"Oh, yes," the man breathed. "I haven't had cofi in twenty years." He inhaled deeply of the smell from the cup. "So good!"

Leon chuckled. The others who had stayed up swapping stories with him grinned.

Including Zalia, most of the women were asleep. They had to rise early. In this country, they were the most likely to be employed, serving as domestics and waitstaff. Most of the labors men normally did were performed by sylphs. There was some male employment, but only short-term and usually brutal. Xehm worked in the fall, butchering animals for market—that was one job elemental sylphs didn't do, though apparently there were some battlers who would—but it was Zalia who supported the family. Her mother was long since taken for the harem and her little sister dead of sickness. All of the people here had similar stories.

Leon shivered in the cold night air that Xehm didn't seem to notice. "All of you will stay away from the arena tomorrow?" he asked. If he was wrong in this, he didn't want any of them hurt.

The man's features danced in the flickering firelight as he stared enraptured into his tin cup. He nodded. "Yes, sir," he said. "The doors you need will be unlocked, though." Thanks to Zalia and a few of the other women and men.

"Thank you. Just be sure no one goes there."

"No, sir. We'll stay home." Xehm grinned toothlessly. "You can see us later."

Leon returned the smile, though he might not be back. Not if everything went according to plan. Of course, his plan included Ril visiting in dreams for orders. Leon had been waiting for that for days, and it hadn't happened. Now that Ril had seen him, he had high hopes that the sylph would come tonight. But Leon couldn't wait much longer; soon he would be forced to take a more direct approach. He'd already proven he could direct Ril in the arena, so he would risk going back there and telling him what to do, but . . . Ril wouldn't be happy about it.

"No one should bother you," Leon said to Xehm. "I can't swear to it, but there's no reason for them to suspect—"

A narrow black tendril swished almost silently through the sand. Pausing for a moment, it bulged and lengthened, became even thinner as it moved forward and up behind the rock Leon sat on to wrap around his leg. The thing tightened, squeezing hard, and pulled. Leon howled as he was yanked off his seat, nearly landing on his face in the fire, and dragged feetfirst into the darkness. Behind him, Xehm leaped to his feet, yelling in terror, and the other men rose as well, shrieking. More screams erupted from the hovels.

Leon clutched at sand that tore his clothes and skin as he was reeled in like a fish on a line. He bounced high over a ridge, gasping, and nearly lost his breath as he slammed down again and slewed through the sand, pulled inexorably toward a lightning-laced cloud hovering just over the city wall. It was glaring at him with red eyes and huge teeth.

"*Goddammit!*" Leon swore, somehow managing to draw the dagger he'd bought when he got the paper. Sitting up and feeling his pants tearing away beneath him, he slashed at the black rope around his leg. The thing fell away, and he skidded to a stop.

The battler bellowed in pain. Scrambling to his feet, Leon started to run.

A half dozen tendrils came this time, wrapping around his arms, legs, waist, and neck, and Leon saw Xehm's terrified face from the edge of the camp for only a moment before he was yanked off his feet and slammed onto his back. The horrible pull started again, dragging him even faster than before, and he had a frantic moment to imagine himself brained by the stone wall before he was lifted bodily into the air.

The ground simply dropped away. The battler was rising, Leon realized, flying who knew how high and taking him along. Leon saw a flash of the underside of the floating island of the emperor, and then the battler wrapped around him completely, bringing him inside his mantle. Warm and dark, it was just solid enough to keep Leon from falling.

Leon had ridden this way inside Ril previously, before Ril lost the ability to take the form. Though he'd seen no reason to tell his battler at the time, he had been able to tell from those trips how vulnerable it made battle sylphs to their passengers. He'd lost his dagger, but Leon now drew his sword, fully intending to drive it up and through the front portion of the battler's body, where the creature maintained its consciousness. He wasn't sure if he'd be able to kill the thing that way, just as he wasn't sure if he'd be killed himself when the battler vanished from around him, but the longer he waited, the higher they'd rise.

It was the smell that stopped him. Of all things, he could smell flowers inside the battler, and he reached down, feeling across the floor until he felt the stems and soft petals. Immediately the battler shifted, pulling them gently away as if afraid of having them damaged.

Leon put the hilt of his sword on his shoulder, its long point aimed at the battler's brain stem, if it had such a thing. "You're not kidnapping me, are you?" he asked.

There was no answer, but he could feel the creature's hesitation.

Leon pressed his free palm against the side of the mantle that enclosed him. "Press here once for yes, twice for no."

The battler pressed twice against his hand.

"No. No, you're not kidnapping me, or no, you *are* kidnapping me?"

Almost, Leon heard the battler sigh.

This was getting nowhere. Leon lowered his sword. "Are you kidnapping me?"

Two presses.

"Are you turning me in?"

Two presses.

What could a battle sylph want with him, if he wasn't turning him in? "Are you a friend of Ril?" he asked.

There was a pause, followed by two slow presses. A sort of no?

"Are you Lizzy's friend?" he asked dubiously.

One vehement press.

Leon's eyes widened, his sword forgotten. "Is she okay? Did she send you looking for me?"

One press, followed after a moment by two.

Leon forced himself to calm down. Whatever this

battler's reasoning, he wasn't free to speak about it, or free to speak at all. This was not going to be easy. "Please put me down," he requested.

The battler soared lower, shifting. Leon felt his legs drop out from under him and managed to land mostly upright on a stretch of road near the edge of the city, though away from where he had been. He couldn't see the campfires of the exiles at all. A flower fluttered down to the ground beside him, and he bent to get it. Straightening, he held it out to the battler. "Here."

A tendril looped down around the flower and pulled it back up inside the cloud.

Standing on the road, his body aching from where the sand had burned him, Leon eyed the battler. It was nearly the size of a small house, the shining red eyes staring back. Its mouth was closed, but he could see the lightning nonetheless. That sparking light moved quickly, a sign he'd learned to recognize as distress.

"You're not allowed to talk, are you?" Leon asked.

The cloud backed off a bit, extruding two tendrils as thick as arms. Quickly, he made a series of gestures.

"Whoa!" Leon said. "I don't understand." Was that some sort of sign language? If it was, he had no time to learn. "You're trying to speak to me, aren't you?"

The battler stretched out a tendril and tapped him against the collarbone hard enough to push him back a step.

Yes? Good. "Is this a sylph language?" Leon asked.

Two taps. Leon suspected he would be bruised in the morning.

"Does Lizzy understand this language?"

Two slow taps. Not really.

Leon eyed the creature, his thoughts already whirling.

"If Lizzy doesn't, is there someone who does? Someone who could tell Lizzy what you're saying?"

One very vehement tap. Leon winced and rubbed his shoulder, rotating his arm. "Try not to kill me, please." He looked around. "Follow me."

The battler trailing him like a sort of giant, demonic puppy, Leon walked along the inside of the city wall back toward the camp. It took nearly twenty minutes. He was lucky the battler hadn't headed straight across the city, he supposed—they could move terribly fast when they wanted, and he would likely have crossed the entire city. Any of a hundred battlers who were looking for him could have spotted him then. Leon suspected the battler had grabbed him on impulse, and it had been simply looking for somewhere quiet to talk. He just didn't know about what.

He returned to the camp, which was still in turmoil, stepping over Meridal's broken wall. "I'll be right back," he promised the battler, and headed across the sand, hoping the creature wouldn't become impatient. He was getting too old to be hauled bodily wherever the thing wanted.

As he trudged into the circle of firelight, Xehm's eyes widened in amazement and Zalia ran up with a shout. "You're alive!"

"Yes." Leon lifted his hands, tried to think of an explanation that wouldn't take an hour, and finally let them drop. "Give me a couple of minutes, okay? I have to do something." He went to his pack and dug out a sheet of the paper he'd purchased for making maps, along with a stick of charcoal. Taking both, he headed back toward the wall. Xehm and a few of the other men followed, but at the sight of the battle sylph retreated in panic. Leon really hoped they wouldn't shun him when he returned.

The battler watched as Leon climbed the wall and sat

down, putting the paper in his lap. "Move closer, will you?" he asked. When the creature did, the lightning glow was just enough for Leon to see the letter he wrote to his daughter, being sure to ask precisely what this battler wanted. He didn't tell her his plans, or sign the note, but she would know his handwriting.

Once he was done, he wrapped the parchment around the charcoal. "Take this to Lizzy," he told the battler. "She'll write whatever it is you want to ask me on the back. Return that to me. I'll be here tomorrow night. Understood?"

The battler nearly punched him over the wall in answer. Excitedly taking the paper, the thing flew off.

Leon sat up, definitely convinced he was bruised as well as abraded and full of sand. But Lizzy would be able to send him the creature's question. She'd be able to answer other things as well, things he still needed to know.

Ril would have to wait another day for his rescue, it seemed. Hopefully it wouldn't be one day too many. Leon sighed, stood stiffly, and made his way back to camp.

Tooie raced back to the harem, ablaze with hope. He hadn't been able to talk to the man—it had been a moment of madness to think they might communicate meaningfully—but the stranger had determined a way for them to do just that. Now he had to get Eapha to explain enough for Lizzy to write down his question. She never understood when he tried to explain, but maybe this man would. Maybe he was smart enough to interpret whatever was written. Tooie hoped so.

He reached the sylph building and flowed down the vent, careful even now not to set off the bells. The feeder pens came first, there being no choice if he was going to fulfil his orders, but he barely sipped from the sleeping men before returning to the harem. He hovered there at the lip of the pipe, waiting, and it was an agonizing amount of time before the last woman tottered to bed out of an alcove and the handler who'd been watching her went away. Then Tooie flowed down to his destination.

Four-seventeen lifted his head at Tooie's arrival in the alcove, and he growled, waking Lizzy, but Tooie ignored the other sylph's angry hissing. Shifting to humanoid form, he made his delivery to the girl, gesturing awkwardly for her to read the letter while holding Eapha's bouquet in his other hand. Four-seventeen gawked at both items, stunned. Paper wasn't something ever seen in the harems, not when most of the women couldn't even read or write. Plus, it could be used to write out plans for escape, but this letter was just asking about Lizzy's bond to Ril. There was nothing in it to trigger any order to prevent the women from trying to leave, or so Tooie believed, trying not to think about it too much. Four-seventeen looked dubious, but Tooie ignored him. He didn't like Four-seventeen on principle, but the other battler wasn't stupid. Once he knew what was happening, he'd be just as willing to help, if only to make the same sort of link to Kiala.

Blinking sleepily, Lizzy took the parchment and sat up, her eyes widening. Both battlers felt her sudden joy as she recognized the handwriting, and they watched in wonder as she started to cry.

# Chapter Twenty-one

Trembling, Lizzy read the letter. It wasn't signed, and it wasn't exactly addressed to her, but she knew it was her father's handwriting and meant for her eyes alone. She recognized the relaxed loops of each *l* and *s*, as well as his seeming inability to write in a straight line. His writing angled across the paper, slanting downward until he had to write very small at the bottom to fit everything.

> *The one who brings this to you has a question he wants answered, but he can't ask it of me himself. Find out what it is, and write it on the back. Also, tell me where you are and what it's like. How many people guard you. How many women are there. The rules the battlers are ordered to obey. Anything you can think of. Even the smallest detail could be important.*
>
> *Most critically, tell Ril to look for me in his dreams. I need to talk to him.*
>
> *Never forget that I love you, and I will not leave you there. Not ever.*

Lizzy wept. Her father had come for her.

Leaping up, she threw her arms around Tooie's neck and kissed him soundly on the stretch of skin where his mouth should have been. Immediately, Four-seventeen started waving his arms, indicating that he wanted a kiss as well, if kisses were being handed out, and so she kissed him, too. She'd kiss every battler there, she felt so good. She just wished Ril had come back tonight so that she could tell him.

"It's my father," she informed the two battlers while wiping tears out of her eyes. "He and Ril came all this way to find me. I'm so happy." They looked at each other, and Tooie poked the letter and made a series of gestures she didn't understand. Four-seventeen made a few as well, at Two-hundred. His movements were belligerent, and the two started making angry motions at each other next.

"Stop!" Lizzy said, before things could get out of hand. "I don't understand either of you. We need Eapha."

Tooie nodded, heading out of the alcove after waiting at the curtain for a few minutes with his head cocked. While he was gone, Lizzy reread the letter from her father while Four-seventeen looked over her shoulder.

"Can you read?" she asked him.

He shook his head.

"Ril can. I taught him when he wasn't allowed to talk. That's how we spoke to each other." She wiped her eyes again. "I'm so happy father's here." Four-seventeen patted her shoulder a little awkwardly, and she smiled at him.

Tooie slipped back into the alcove, leading Eapha. The woman was rubbing her eyes, and her hair was sleep tousled. "What is it?" she slurred.

"My father sent me a letter," Lizzy exclaimed. "Tooie brought it."

Eapha blinked and regarded the battler in surprise. He shrugged and made a long series of gestures, and at the end handed her a bouquet of flowers. Eapha's eyes misted over and she pressed her nose into them, inhaling. Tooie beamed happily, and Lizzy had to hide a smile.

Lifting her face, Eapha sat down in Tooie's lap, still holding her flowers, and he put his arms around her. Appearing a little put out, Four-seventeen settled behind Lizzy so she'd have someone to lean on, too, then Lizzy read the letter, her voice soft and full of wonder. Her father was here, as strong and undaunted as ever. She'd always been so in awe of him, loving his strength as much as his gentleness. He was capable of anything. She'd always thought that as a little girl, and the feeling came back now. Her father could save them all.

She didn't read the entire letter, though, remembering what Eapha had told her about battler orders when it came to women trying to escape. She left out everything her father said about wanting information on the harem and the guards. If she'd said that, both Two-hundred and Four-seventeen would have had to turn her in, no matter how much it would break their hearts. She only conveyed her father's love, and answered his first request.

"What's Tooie's question?" she asked at the end.

"I don't know." Eapha leaned back so that she could see Two-hundred's hands, and he signed for a long time, sometimes correcting himself and getting frustrated. Four-seventeen tried to interject at one point, but Tooie swiped at him.

Eapha put a hand on his arm and looked at Lizzy. "It's hard to explain. There aren't signs for it, but he tried to ask me this before, after Ril got here. I couldn't answer him."

"What is it?" Lizzy asked.

Eapha tapped her lip and looked down with a sigh, stroking the petals of her flowers. "He wants to know how you're Ril's master. I could figure that part out, but he wants to know how he has a . . . more-than-master? There isn't a word for it."

Lizzy blinked. "I'm not Ril's master." Except he'd said she was. But she'd thought he meant metaphorically.

Tooie made a series of angry gestures. "He says you

are," Eapha translated. "He says Ril makes love to you straight through to your soul."

Lizzy turned red. "You were listening?"

Tooie and Four-seventeen both gave her a look that didn't need any translation: they were empathic and sensualists, so of course they had. Lizzy put palms over her burning cheeks.

"I . . . if I'm Ril's master, I don't know it." But she could feel what he felt. And he could find her in her dreams and track her. "I don't know!"

Four-seventeen made gestures. "What about the more-than-master?" Eapha asked.

Lizzy didn't have the faintest idea what that was, but she tried to puzzle it out. Did they mean her father? Somehow, she didn't think so. He was just Ril's master, the same as the feeders were, even if they couldn't give orders.

"Maybe they mean the queen?" she said instead.

Both battlers stared at her, their eyes wide and every muscle in their bodies tight. Eapha glanced at them, obviously surprised. Slowly, Tooie nodded.

"That's just Solie," Lizzy explained. "Back home—I mean, where I come from—she's a girl about four years older than I am. She was supposed to be sacrificed to bind a battler, like you guys, but she managed to get free, and Heyou, that's her battler, he ended up bound to her instead. The first time he made love to her, all the sylphs nearby became part of this big hive. Ril got pulled into it later. She must be the more-than-master you felt in Ril. She controls all the sylphs in our valley."

"Are you serious?" Eapha gasped.

The two battlers were obviously upset. Tooie was even shaking, his hands clasped under his chin. Four-seventeen stared at the ceiling, not moving.

"Yes." Lizzy stared between the two, remembering how

crazed the battlers back home were for Solie. There was always one or more of them with her, and the rest kept checking if she was okay. For herself, Lizzy thought that would drive her crazy after a while. "She's really nice and all, but her commands are primary. The sylphs will obey her even over their own masters."

At that, Tooie lunged forward, almost dumping Eapha out of his lap. He grabbed Lizzy's arms for a moment and then let her go so he could make a bunch of gestures. One of them she recognized: How.

How do they do it? she realized. That's what he wanted to know. What he'd wanted to know from the beginning without being able to ask. How did one make a queen?

Lizzy gaped at him and then Eapha. The two battlers were shivering, their chests heaving, and other battlers were pulling the curtain back to stare into the alcove, drawn by their distress. Women were waking as well, as the battlers they'd been lying with rose and hurried away.

How many handlers were aware of this? How many were coming even now? "I don't know," Lizzy gasped. "Maybe Father does. He knows almost everything. Maybe Ril does, but he never told me. He can't talk, and I don't have any blocks to ask him." She buried her face in her hands. "I don't have any blocks."

Leon made his way slowly across the sand to the place in the exile camp he'd chosen for the times when they were happy to leave him alone, a place where he could let himself relax for a moment. He hurt everywhere. That battler had left bruises all up his leg and sides. His skin was abraded, and he'd bitten the inside of his cheek at some point. He'd been tasting blood in his mouth ever since.

He felt sand everywhere, so when he reached the little dip in the desert where he'd placed the rest of his purchased supplies, he stripped down carefully, wincing at the pain, and shook out his torn clothing. He next took a flask of water Xehm had given him and ripped a strip off his blanket. Wetting it, he used it to clean himself as best he could in the dim light. It was barely dawn, the sun rising up over the endless mounds of sand and the air still cold.

Leon hissed as the cloth scraped over his wounds, most of which were scratches. A few went deep, though. A stone was imbedded in his hip, which he had to use the tip of his sword to force out. Another cut on his ribcage felt bad and refused to stop bleeding. Hoping all the dirt was flushed out, Leon removed another long piece of blanket and bound it. He soon wasn't going to have much blanket left.

Finally as clean as he could make himself, he dressed again and lay down, slowly easing himself onto the sand. What was left of his blanket pillowed his head. The ridge of sand he lay next to would shield him from the sun for most of the morning, and once it didn't, he'd have to be up and about anyway.

His stomach rumbled, but he closed his eyes. That battler had cut and bruised him, and he still felt sick from the aftereffects of the adrenaline rushing through his system. He had been absolutely terrified for that first moment, even if he hadn't let it control him, and he was afraid even now. What did the creature want? Battlers preferred not to deal with men, unless it was a man they knew and trusted, or if they had no other choice. Only Heyou back home genuinely liked men, having deliberately taken the former trapper Galway to be his master along with Solie. And Ril, of course. Always Ril.

Leon took a deep breath and relaxed, sand blowing lightly off the ridge to dust over him. Thinking of his battler as he fell asleep, he dreamed of Ril and found himself standing on the crest that overlooked Sylph Valley, the mountains that separated them from Para Dubh rising purple and blue in the background.

Under his feet the earth was dead and rocky, broken only by bitter gray plants, but the Valley itself, which was actually a canyon dug into the bedrock of the Shale Plains, was lush and green. Its rolling grasslands and wheat and corn fields, stretched away from him. There were few trees, and they were all small and young, none older than six years. A lake even glistened near one end.

Once, this place had been as dead as the rest of the surrounding environs, obliterated centuries before in a battler fight that no one could remember, since no one had survived it. Elemental sylphs had brought back life, working together in ways masters in Eferem or Para Dubh would never have dreamed. Those masters had been taught that sylphs were just smart animals, only interested in serving humans and not forming any actual community. How wrong that was. They'd misjudged their slaves, denying them the right to think for themselves, always afraid of losing control. Leon himself had been afraid of losing control. He'd wanted his battler to serve him willingly, lovingly, and yet he'd kept Ril in hateful servitude.

He would have left you if you hadn't, his heart whispered. Ril would have left him, and Leon couldn't have borne that. To spend any great time as a master to a sylph was to feel their essence seep indelibly into your soul. Only the most heartless bastard could ignore that connection and abuse their sylph . . . though of course battlers were traditionally only ever given to heartless bastards. Leon had been exactly that, once, cold and brutal enough to earn the King of Eferem's respect and Ril's servitude. He would be one still if it weren't for Betha, whom he'd always loved, and his girls. And perhaps it was also due to

Ril himself, who'd sneaked into the parts of him that weren't swallowed by pride and ambition until Leon forgot what pride and ambition were and found himself to be an ordinary man after all.

A shrill cry sounded. Leon looked up and saw a bird with a shape nearly like a hawk circling above, floating on the warm air that rose from the valley. He cried out again and Leon raised his arm, whistling. Immediately, the bird swooped down, flaring his wings and reaching out with viciously sharp talons. He landed on Leon's bare forearm.

His weight was heavy, but Leon was used to that, and Ril folded his wings, eyeing him expectantly. There was no hate. Always before, Ril trapped as a bird had hit Leon with his hate, using it as did other battlers, not just to express contempt at his captivity but to hide his real emotions. Except sometimes Ril forgot—or so Leon assumed—and Leon would feel what Ril did for brief moments that he never let the bird realize, fearing they would end. He'd felt how Ril enjoyed clinging to his extended fist, the wind ruffling his feathers as Leon kicked his horse into a gallop. He'd felt how Ril loved his daughters as much as Leon did, and sometimes, how Ril enjoyed being touched until he remembered he shouldn't.

Leon reached out and stroked his battler's head, caressing the tiny feathers around the bird's skull, rubbing the ridges above the eyes. Ril let him, arching into the touch, and Leon stroked his neck, working his fingers under the feathers until he was scratching the bony skin beneath, his hand wrapped around his battler's throat. Ril let him, eyes closed and trusting.

Good boy, Leon wanted to say, but of course Ril wasn't some sort of pet. He was an individual, and this was a dream. Was it one of the dreams where Ril was really present, Leon wondered? How could he even know this was a dream, without waking?

Somehow he did, though, and he knew that somewhere Ril was sleeping just as he was, thinking of him, and this dream was for both of them. This was what he'd been awaiting.

"Talk to me," he said quietly, sure to make it an order in case Ril's rules extended even into this dream state.

Those cold predator's eyes opened, regarding Leon over his caressing hand. *What's there to say?* the sylph asked, his words echoing quietly in Leon's mind. Though most elemental sylphs only spoke mentally, Ril did so rarely. Leon suspected he was bothered by the intimacy of it.

*They made me into a slave again.*

Leon felt his heart tighten, and went to stroke Ril's head again. This time, the bird pulled out of the way, shifting down until he was balanced on Leon's fist.

"I will get you out of here, Ril. I promise. You, Lizzy, and Justin. I won't leave any of you."

*You're always full of promises. How will you get me out? I have a dozen masters now. I can't even free Lizzy.*

Ril's voice was full of bitterness. When Leon reached out again, the bird snapped at him. Undaunted, he kept reaching, and Ril's beak closed barely millimeters from his fingers, leaving Leon to wonder if he might wake up shy a few digits. But finally his hand touched feathers, and he stroked his battler.

"I'll get you out if you trust me, Ril." He lifted the bird up until they were eye to eye. "You have to surrender to me. Completely. You can't hold anything back this time. I gave you your freedom once. You need to trust I'll do it again. But until then, you can't resist me when I come for you."

Ril pulled away, alarmed, spreading his wings and rising

into the sky, beating heavily at the air beneath him. Around them, the landscape wavered. Ril was waking from sleep.

"Trust me, Ril!" Leon shouted after his sylph, but the world was swirling like a muddy cauldron stirred by some crazed witch. Ril escaped, rising above and away, but Leon was pulled down and under.

Their shared dream vanished. That morning he had no more dreams of any kind.

Jolted awake, Ril lay on the bed in his prison stall. In their individual cages, two of his feeders were still asleep, but Justin sat there glaring. Ril could feel the boy's hatred. He could feel every human's emotions, and tongueless or not, Justin was his master, which only made the boy's emotions sharper. Worse, however, Justin could feel Ril's.

Immediately he flared up his hatred to hide his fear. Handlers outside the stall shouted in alarm. This was part of why masters stayed away from their battlers, why feeders were usually kept separate, why the harem had been created in the first place. Ril's loathing filled the stable, and battlers there for the morning fights roared out their own rage, their own antipathy rising in challenge. Men screamed.

The other two feeders in Ril's stall awoke, shrieking in silent terror while Justin cowered, his hands held over his head and his emotions beating at Ril.

*Stop. Stop!*

Almost it was a word in Ril's mind, almost it was a connection such as Leon or Lizzy had to him, speaking to his soul, and he saw the order in it—the order he would have to obey, no matter how he fought, no matter how he hated. He could only avoid obeying if he surrendered and gave up all sense of self, all pretence of freedom. He couldn't surrender. Not even to Leon. Never to Leon. His abhorrence roared out, carrying defiance in this place where auras *were* allowed.

The heavy wood door to his stall opened and a woman hurried in. It was Rashala, the one Lizzy said ran the harems. She ran the stables as well, at least when it came to care of the battlers.

The woman hurried toward Ril where he lay on his side on the bed, propped up on one arm, and she slid out of her robe as she did, leaving herself nude. Ril was so startled that his rage faltered, and she dropped to her knees while reaching out for him. Her emotions were vivid: calm the battler, soothe and distract him. Ril started to snarl, but Rashala's arms went around his neck, pulling him down against her breast, and the distraction worked.

"Gently," she murmured, running the fingers of the hand not holding him through his hair, making little circles against his temples, then moving down the back of his head and along his neck to his back. It felt very good. "Gently, my beautiful one."

Ril's anger fumbled and crashed, his aura vanishing, and he heard calls of relief from outside his stall. Rashala just kept whispering to him, her mind calm, directing him to be calm as well, and to relax. She focused on him with all the strength of her will, overwhelming him, and before he knew it, he was asleep again, dozing with his head in her lap.

Rashala waited until the battle sylph was completely asleep before she slipped out from beneath him and stood, pulling her robe on again. Usually, soothing a battler resulted in them using her like a concubine, but this was good enough. She peered down at the battler impassively, sure to keep her thoughts and feelings steady. It had just been luck that she'd been checking on the stables this morning. If she found out he'd ever been this distressed before, she'd have the handlers here turned into feeders. Ten battlers he'd upset, as well as every servant, slave, and passing spectator. Possibly even the emperor or one of his staff! At least he wasn't so damaged that he hadn't responded.

She turned and looked at the three frightened feeders on the far side of the stall. She had no doubt they were what had upset the battler. She'd been doubtful about putting them here in the first place, but Seven-oh-three needed to feed after his fights and he could hardly fly to them. Yet feeders made battle sylphs angry. Keeping their contact limited made the battlers happy. Sending them to the harem right after they fed also did. She couldn't get rid of the feeders, and she couldn't send him to the harem after every single fight, so she'd use an alternate solution.

Rashala turned to the handlers who stood at the entrance to the stall, waiting on her patiently while she thought. "Go to the harem and pick a girl," she told them. "One he's had before. Bring her here for Seven-oh-three."

The women bowed and ran off, and Rashala went to see if the other battle sylphs were calmed as well. She'd have to move the ones in the stalls beside Seven-oh-three, she decided. Otherwise, they'd see the girl and all of them would want one.

Silly creatures.

The harem was having a bad morning. Few of the women knew what had happened the night before, but all of the battlers were alert. Some guessed at what was going on, others only picked up on the projected distress. Uncertain and restless, these padded around, swiping at each other or trying to distract themselves with multitudes of women.

Those who knew exactly what was happening, the dozen of the circle, tried to act normal even as they shivered with chained intent. Tooie sat on a pillow, watching Lizzy and Eapha dance, the girls chiming little bells with their fingers as they moved their hips. Lizzy was really very terrible at it, but Tooie wouldn't have noticed even were she expert. He only watched Eapha, imagining her as a queen. As *his* queen. He thought he'd go mad waiting for nightfall. He had half the paper in the letter to Lizzy's father asking his question. The rest Lizzy had kept to write her own letter to Ril. Either her father or Seven-oh-three would give him his answer, and Eapha would be his queen.

Down at the other end of the corridor, the door opened and Melorta led in a trio of handlers. They looked around and started up the length of the harem, the heavy door closing behind them. Everyone tensed, as they always did when the handlers arrived. Since they weren't escorting anyone, that meant someone was being removed. Except for Melorta, the handlers were edgy. It wasn't unheard of for a battler to decide to drag one off into an alcove. It also wasn't unheard of for Rashala to decide that woman would stay in the harem.

As the handlers approached, Eapha and Lizzy stopped dancing, looking up uncertainly. Tooie tensed, though there was nothing he could do to defend either of them. The handlers couldn't know, he assured himself. The letters were written already and hidden until tonight, and they couldn't know about them. They didn't know anything. He laced his fingers together and then pressed his palms against the muscles of his crossed legs, trying desperately to relax.

The handlers approached, Melorta murmuring to her followers and pointing. One took Eapha by the arm.

"No!" Lizzy cried. "Where are you taking her?"

Eapha was in a panic, her eyes wild. Two handlers had her by the arms now and pulled her along. A third pushed Lizzy away when she tried to stop them. Melorta followed, one hand on her riding crop.

Eapha. They were taking Eapha! They knew. Somehow they knew, and they were going to turn her into a feeder for the elemental sylphs. They'd cut out her tongue and lock her in a cage in a section of the pens where he wasn't allowed to go! Forgetting that he was supposed to pretend indifference, Tooie surged to his feet, his aura flashing out just as Ril's had earlier that morning. The handlers all spun, their eyes wide, and Eapha nearly got away as Tooie lunged forward, his toe claws digging into the marble floor. His hands were outstretched to—

"Stop!" Melorta shouted.

It was as though he'd run to the end of a chain wrapped around his soul. Tooie stumbled to a halt, shaking. He couldn't move. The handlers had limited abilities to order the battlers, just so they could protect themselves from an attack like this or order a battler away from a woman to whom he'd become too attached. A battler could take a handler for sex if he managed to overwhelm her enough with lust that she didn't give an order to stop, but there were too many and no desire for any of them in his heart. He could see the look in the handlers' eyes and feel their sudden certainty as they glanced at each other: he was in love with her, the one great sin. Tooie looked at Eapha and saw the horror in her face as well. Whatever reason they'd come for her, whether it was because they knew the circle's plans or something else, he'd given them both away.

Tooie clasped his hands together, wanting to beg, but

he couldn't. He shook, though, dropping to his knees as they dragged Eapha, ignoring her screams, across and out of the harem. The door thudded closed behind them. Lizzie dropped down beside him, sobbing, and he clutched her to him, wailing in silence for what he'd lost.

# Chapter Twenty-two

Ril woke again as the door to his stall opened. Blinking sleepily, he looked up to find a trio of handlers bringing with them a woman in a translucent blue dress. She had a collar around her neck, and he watched cautiously as they chained her to the foot of his bed. It was Eapha, he saw. Lizzy's friend.

"She's all yours, sweetheart," one of the handlers said, smiling. She went to stroke his hair but he bared his teeth at her. She yanked back her hand with sudden fright and straightened. When the other two women laughed, she flushed in anger.

"H-how long do I stay here?" Eapha asked. She was holding her chain with both hands and trembling.

"You better hope forever," snapped the woman Ril had frightened. "The way that battler reacted when we picked you, if Seven-oh-three doesn't want you, you're going straight to the feeder pens."

Eapha started crying, huddled at the foot of the bed. Ril watched the handlers leave, heading out of the stall and closing the door behind them. They stayed on the other side, though, watching.

Ril turned to the window cut for spectators. A few people stood there, staring at Eapha and murmuring to each other. Justin and the other two feeders were gaping at her as well. Ril sighed, hating this, hating them, but most of all hating himself. Standing up, he wrapped an arm around Eapha's neck. She eyed him with fright, but he pulled her against him, pressing his lips to hers.

Leon woke around noon, the sun high enough to roast him where he lay. Rising, he drank some water and stumbled out past Xehm, waving to the man blearily. He knew he looked terrible, but time was wasting and there were a lot of people around who looked worse.

Wrapping his robe around himself, he went into the city, his stomach rumbling. Breakfast could wait—or lunch, he supposed, given the time. It was broiling out, making him sweat under his robe. He didn't think he'd ever get used to the heat, though he hoped he wouldn't be around much longer to find out. Still, the temperature was the least of the things he loathed about this place.

As he walked, he kept his head down and didn't think about Lizzy or Ril. Instead, he imagined Betha and his four youngest daughters. Betha would be setting out lunch right now, Cara having helped her make it. Nali and Ralad would be sitting at the table, arguing with each other and drawing their mother's attention away from Mia's endless questions. These thoughts lightened his mood and filled his heart with a warmth that had nothing to do with the temperature.

Genuinely happy, Leon went past half a dozen battle-sylph guards, and at the arena paid his penny admittance down into the corridors beneath the structure. It was cool there, if bare and sandy. Narrow rectangular windows were set periodically along one wall, letting those who passed look into the stalls of the gladiator battlers. Leon strode past the first half dozen, glancing in just to see what was happening but not stopping. A few stalls were occu-pied, mostly by things that looked like creatures out of a nightmare, but the middle ones were empty, which they hadn't been on the last visit. No one was looking through any of those windows.

Ril's window was crowded. A group of people struggled to see inside, many giggling and pointing. A few held their children up for a better view. Leon paused, watching them. To leave now would be odd if anyone noticed. He glanced down for a moment, focusing, and tried to feel his battler. Ril felt . . . bored. Very bored. And a little annoyed.

Puzzled, Leon lifted his head and joined the crowd, carefully working his way close enough to see through the window. Ril was on a bed, a sheet tossed carelessly over his naked hips and legs. He had a woman under him and was moving against her, his upper body braced on his forearms above her.

Leon gaped for a moment in stunned amazement, a slow blush spreading over his face until he felt as though things might be cooler outside in the sun. He never would have expected this. Ril didn't even *look* at women, and he still felt bored . . .

Oh. Leon's eyes narrowed. Ril was faking.

*What are you doing?* he thought toward his sylph as hard as he could.

Ril's rhythm faltered, and the battler shot a startled look over his shoulder at the window. The assembled crowd giggled, but Leon just raised an eyebrow. His battler made a sort of embarrassed, apologetic shrug, and Leon had to hide a smile. *I'm not sure I want to know.*

Ril glared and went back to the woman, apparently finishing whatever he was doing and rolling off her to reach for his pants. She sat up more slowly and retrieved her dress. She had a collar around her neck, Leon saw, and was chained to the bed. He also saw three women in brown standing on the other side of the stall gate, watching. The feeders were staring as well. Justin's face held disgust.

Ril wandered into the center of his stall, ignoring the crowd, and he sat down, staring at nothing. The woman with whom he'd pretended to dally dressed and grabbed his bedsheet, wrapping it around herself toga-style. She was an attractive woman, probably around thirty, with full lips and a generous figure. She sat on the end of the bed, fingering the chain at her collar and watching Ril, who appeared determined to ignore everyone, though his emotions didn't correlate. Leon could feel Ril's boredom had turned into uncertainty—about him, he supposed, remembering that dream last night. He tried to send as much reassurance toward his battler as he could. He had no way of telling if he succeeded, though. Ril ignored him as much as he did everyone else.

The show was over. Still sniggering about it, the gawking men and women continued on. More important, the female handlers left. Leon waited until all had disappeared and the passageway was clear, then longer until he heard a fight start in the arena. Once it did, he tapped on the window.

Ril looked over his shoulder, seeing him, then down at his hands. Leon tapped again. Ril sighed and stood, approaching. It wasn't until he reached the viewing window that he lifted his head and met his master's gaze. Leon tapped the glass and stepped back. Ril slammed an elbow into it, shattering it.

Leon moved quickly forward. Above, he heard the screams of men being killed on the sand, and inside the pen he heard the other battlers moving and handlers calling to each other. Ril's three feeders stared at him. Justin was one of them. The youth shook the bars of his cage and screamed without coherence.

"Do you trust me?" Leon asked Ril. The battler closed his eyes for a long moment, then nodded.

It wasn't good enough. Leon could still feel his fear. "Do you *trust* me?" he asked again, even as he prayed inside that this was indeed the right thing to do. As far as he could tell, it was the only solution.

The woman with whom Ril had been pretending to make love sat on the bed, watching with wide eyes. Ril finally met Leon's gaze, studying him and probably his emotions, and after a long minute nodded again.

Leon took a deep breath and looked at Ril, really looked at him, focusing all his willpower onto the sylph. Ril's eyes widened, and Leon waited for him to relax again. It took a few minutes. Leon didn't let himself think of how someone could come along at any moment and see him standing before the broken window, or that the handlers could come back to check on Ril from the inside. He just focused on what he needed—absolute control of the being inside the stall.

Ril shuddered under that control even as he stared back. Did he trust him? Leon had asked him and meant it. He didn't know how many orders Ril had. He didn't know how strong were the wills of the people commanding him. Leon was primary after Solie, but that was never an absolute, not when the morass of masters and orders Ril did have could outweigh anything he said, through sheer numbers. Leon didn't dare just tell Ril to speak or rescue his daughter, or escape. There was too much chance of him being redirected or even driven mad by the contradiction of it all. Did Ril trust him enough to let him force his mastery far enough to overwhelm the hundreds of orders he'd received since he was taken? *Could* he trust him enough? Leon waited to see if Ril could.

Ril wondered exactly the same thing. No sylph had undergone what Leon was asking of him. They obeyed their queen and their masters. They were born to obey and reveled in it when the orders were kind. But what he wanted? Ril wasn't sure that Leon even understood it fully. Leon was asking him to give up himself, to give up all essence of individuality. He wouldn't be Ril anymore. He'd be an extension of Leon, a focus of Leon's will alone, and his own emotions and needs would cease to matter. It might even break his link to his queen, or drive him mad. He was already different from other battlers, strange and limited, but now he'd become something else entirely, something that wasn't a battler. He'd be rejecting his queen as well, which was a betrayal no true battle sylph would ever suffer!

If he did this, the orders of the Meridal masters wouldn't matter anymore, but neither would his love for Lizzy—not beyond how Leon himself loved her. To save Lizzy, Ril would have to give her up and accept a living death where he wouldn't even have enough of himself left to hope that Leon would put things right.

But . . . he'd have the chance to save Lizzy. For her, he'd be willing to do anything.

Leon waited as patiently as he could. Finally, the battle sylph's eyes dilated and went out of focus. The tension flowed out of him, and Leon felt his surrender. Ril was tired, he was afraid, and he didn't want any of this, but still he gave himself over to his master, letting Leon make the decisions instead. Once, Leon would have committed murder to have his battler do that. Now, he felt sick as he leaned close to the broken window. The circumstances precluded this choice being entirely made by free will.

"Ril," he called clearly, though he knew the woman and the feeders would hear. The handlers on the other side of the gate might as well, but he had to be absolutely sure that his battler understood him. "I am your master. I have been your master since you entered this world and I killed the woman who drew you. Her blood flowed over my hands and I chained you with your name. You are Ril. You are mine. You will always be mine. I am the first pattern on your soul, and I will always be primary."

Ril shuddered, and Leon ached for him. He'd never wanted to remind Ril of this. And yet he added, "I am your master. Say it."

Ril's mouth opened, his eyes blank. He tried to speak, but nothing came out.

"I am your master," Leon repeated. "I am primary. The commands given to you by others are nothing compared to mine. I am in your mind. I am in your soul. You will obey me. Obey me, Ril. Obey me. Tell me that I am your master."

"You are my master," Ril breathed, and the woman and the feeders both jumped. Justin's eyes narrowed.

"I am your master," Leon told him again. That was the most important point—and also the first thing he would rescind once they all escaped. Then he would pray that Ril forgave him. "You will pretend to obey the orders given to you by others, but you will only pretend. You will do what the others ask of you, but only until they contradict my commands. Then you will pretend. At all times, I will be your master. Your only master. You will obey only me. Say it."

"I will obey you."

"What will you do?"

"I will obey you. I will always obey you. The commands of others are nothing. I will obey you." Ril's face was pale, broken. Leon could feel the numbness spreading through him, could actually feel the core that was Ril retreating, and he wanted to stop, wanted to pull away and give Ril back to himself. Instead he kept his will firm, his intent absolute, and felt his battler fade.

"Free the feeders," Leon ordered him. "Be quiet about it."

Ril turned and walked numbly to the feeder cages. Grabbing the door of the first, he wrenched it off and the man stumbled out, staring wild-eyed at him while Ril went to the next. He freed all the men in the same way, Justin climbing out of his cage last to stand on unsteady feet.

"Free the girl," Leon ordered.

Ril went to the woman and, while she stared at him in amazement, snapped the chain confining her. Shivering, she wrapped the bedsheet tighter around her and went to join the men.

"Break the window completely."

Ril shattered the window, punching out the glass. Distantly, Leon heard men screaming in pain and a huge battler lumbering past, likely toward his stall. Shadows fell on the gate and Leon narrowed his eyes. "Hurry," he called to the freed men and the woman. "Come on."

Justin came first, scrambling out through the narrow window and into Leon's arms. Leon lowered him to the ground and grabbed the next. The woman was last, shivering against him. "Thank you," she whispered as he set her down.

Leon didn't answer, not while he had Ril to handle. "I want you to go to your bed and sleep," he told him. "When you wake, be confused by the missing people. Be upset. Be distracted and useless for the fights today. When you are returned to the harem, tell Lizzy what I have told you.

Then, come to me in your dreams. The orders I give you there will be orders that apply as much as these ones here." Provided he could think of what to say. He wished he could free Ril as well, though he knew he'd never then get to Lizzy. Ril was his only way in. "Tell me you understand."

"I understand," Ril said, already half dozing.

"Then sleep," Leon commanded. Ril returned to his bed and collapsed across it.

Gesturing to the freed slaves, Leon led them away from the window, Justin pressing against him. The men wore only shifts, but that wasn't so unusual in this place, and he'd brought worn leggings and sandals for them under his robes. The woman stood out a bit more. He hadn't been expecting her, and so had brought nothing, but she wasn't too strange, and more important, no one was expecting an escape. There weren't even guards at the door as they made their way outside.

He led the way across the road and into a building left unlocked by a woman from the outcast camp. Their biggest concern was battlers, but Leon hoped the four escapees' terror would actually act as emotional camouflage. They were still looking for Leon, but he was only one man. They wouldn't be looking for a group, and surely they wouldn't be interested in the terror coming from what appeared to be newly bought slaves. From under his robes Leon brought out a string of slave chains, bought for him by Xehm on the black market.

"Let me put these on you," he told the four. "When battlers see you, they'll think you're afraid because you're slaves. They'll leave us alone."

Two of the men stepped forward eagerly, their arms outstretched. Justin looked miserable but did the same. As Leon shackled them, the woman asked, "Are you sure this will work?"

"Yes," Leon promised. But this wouldn't work at all if the battlers recognized her. He studied her for a moment and grabbed a wide scarf, wrapping it around her head.

They took a moment to gather their courage, and then he led the group out the other side of the building and down the roads he'd memorized. They crossed the city, always moving, Leon trying not to think and draw attention from any battlers. The people with him drew none, and he brought them at last past the crumbling city wall, where Justin collapsed in his arms and sobbed in relief. Leon held the boy while Xehm and the others gathered in amazement.

One down. Two to go.

Rashala returned to the arena stables, furious despite her impassive expression. She'd been told personally by Melorta what happened, but she was still outraged.

All of the battlers had been moved, and those that weren't needed sent back to the harem. Seven-oh-three had been relocated to a new stall, one near the main entrance and very close to the handlers' picket so that he could be watched. She saw him in there, sitting on his bed and looking confused. One of the handlers was with him, massaging his shoulders and keeping him soothed. Rashala nodded in approval and kept going. The last thing they needed was a hysterical battler. If Seven-oh-three was as upset as she'd heard, that handler deserved a commendation for her efforts.

She went to his old stall, where three feeder cages had been broken, a concubine stolen, and the viewing window shattered. Thank all the gods that the thieves hadn't stolen the battler as well! But he'd been hard to wake when found. Something had been done to him, to the emperor's darling. She just hoped the emperor never heard about it.

She might lose her head because of this. Melorta likely already feared as much, but Rashala had work for her. The handler might save her own life if she did things right.

Rashala circled slowly, pondering the broken glass and shattered cages. The battler had been upset earlier. She'd attributed it to the feeders, but now she wondered. Had someone tried this assault before and the poor creature was upset because of that? Had he tried to warn them?

She swore under her breath and left the stall, directing one of the handlers to fetch her brother. He was still the primary rule giver for Seven-oh-three. She'd have him reassert his rules on the battler—all of them. She was taking no chances anymore. Afterward, he would be returned to the harem. From the way he was shooting looks around, as though expecting an attack, he'd be of no use in the arena at all. Luckily, the emperor wasn't watching today and his nephew preferred Three-ninety-nine. She'd recommend he be put in the fights instead.

Then she'd have to deal with Two-hundred. That had been a surprise. He'd always been one of the most easygoing battlers, and not really inclined to prefer any specific woman over another, but now he was hysterical about that woman being removed. There was no reason for it. She'd looked over the records, and Two-hundred gravitated toward a dozen different concubines, the same as a number of other battlers.

Rashala stopped, her mind suddenly making an empirical leap. There were a dozen women recorded as sleeping with Two-hundred. She reached into her satchel and pulled out a series of pages on Seven-oh-three. His preferred sleeping partners were listed as well, including the woman who'd been brought here and stolen, the one Two-hundred had been upset over.

She didn't have Two-hundred's records with her, but

her memory was excellent. Two-hundred wasn't sleeping with just the same number of women as Seven-oh-three. He was sleeping with *exactly* the same women.

Rashala cursed under her breath and turned, heading back out. She'd have to double-check, review all the records to be sure. But if she was right . . . She hadn't attributed that much intelligence to the battle sylphs, or to the women who serviced them. That was correctable, though. Quite easily, in fact.

Melorta walked swiftly down the corridor and into the guardroom before the harem. Several handlers glanced up but immediately returned to their duties. Given her mood, if any of them had dared to speak, she'd have ripped their heads off. Three feeders and a concubine gone, and it was her responsibility! She could find herself back in the harem as a concubine over this, and if that happened, she was as good as dead.

Those slaves had been stolen right under the nose of a battle sylph who'd been specifically ordered to prevent them from escaping. Melorta had considered this as she went to report to Rashala, and Rashala herself had come to the same conclusion: the battler's original master had done this. It was horrific to think the man was still alive, but there wasn't any other answer.

Melorta unlocked the main door to the harem and swung it wide, striding through with her crop in hand. She couldn't ask the battle sylph about the master. She'd heard of battlers being allowed to speak before, but the words they spilled were pure poison. There was no communicating with them. However, there was with concubines. And Melorta was interested in an interrogation.

With her yellow hair, the girl was easy to spot standing with a group of women partway down the harem, all of them cringing fearfully. They outnumbered her six to one, but Melorta wasn't afraid. The vast majority of concubines were cowards.

The foreign girl, however, seemed as though she might be an exception. Melorta walked up, glaring at the concubine's companions, who immediately fled. Left behind, the foreign girl glared right back, fists clenched. Melorta was unimpressed.

"Come with me," she said, grabbing an arm.

"No!" the girl shouted, trying to pull away.

Melorta smacked her across the side of the head with her crop. That quieted the bitch down enough to be dragged out of the harem and through the guardroom to a smaller, private chamber. Normally it was used for guards to catch short naps during long shifts, but it would serve this purpose as well.

Tossing the girl into the corner, she announced, "Seven-oh-three knows you. He knew you before. Don't lie to me, we all saw it." Melorta pointed and slapped her crop loudly against her thigh. "Tell me who his master is."

The girl gaped in shock, eyes wide with horror. "W-what?"

"Tell me who that thieving bastard is and where we can find him!"

The girl gawked a moment longer, and then her eyes filled with tears. "I don't know anything!" she wailed. "I don't!"

Melorta glowered, unconvinced. "Don't lie to me. You went straight for Seven-oh-three when we brought him in."

The girl covered her face with her hands. "His hair was so pretty, and he looked so normal. Not a f-freak like the others!" She began to cry.

Melorta sagged. It made far too much sense, and the concubine wouldn't dare lie to her. Not now. Melorta knew liars, and terrified women never did it well. Unfortunately, that left her responsible but with nothing to show regarding the theft.

Furious, and just wanting the bizarre-looking girl out of her sight, she grabbed the cringing concubine by the arm, hauled her upright and dragged her back to the harem. Seeing her coming, one of the handlers opened the door, and Melorta nearly threw the blonde inside, watching her trip and sprawl across the floor of the main chamber. Scanning the battlers, Melorta pointed at the closest.

"Four-seventeen! Come here."

He did, his claws clicking on the floor as he glared down the length of his nose at her.

"Easy, baby," Melorta soothed, reaching out to stroke his arm while she focused her will upon him. She wasn't as good at it as Rashala, but the battler settled, his eyes softening. No problem. "I have a job for you," she told him, leading him out of the harem and into the guardroom. Battlers didn't receive orders there very often, but there was a vent in the ceiling for them to use whenever they did. "I want you to go to the arena," she commanded. "The concubine Eapha was stolen from there. I know you've slept with her, so you can follow her scent. Find her and bring her back, but first, kill any men with her and bring me their heads. Do you understand?"

Four-seventeen nodded slowly.

"Good boy." She stood back. "Go now."

Four-seventeen changed into a cloud and flew up the vent. Melorta was left to wait for his return.

Back in the harem, Lizzy returned to Kiala and the others, shaken and frightened. Her fury was far stronger than her fear, though, and her focus was absolute. They wanted to kill her father. Still, they had to be getting desperate if they were asking *her* for information. Lizzy took a deep breath and forced herself to relax, managing a smile for the other women, none of whom had expected her to come back. For now, Father was safe.

Four-seventeen soared high over the city as he headed to the arena. He hated this. He hadn't known that Eapha was free, and he'd actually felt sorry for Tooie over her getting taken. The simple thought of Kiala being grabbed made him want to scream. Now they wanted him to track down Eapha, and once he brought her back, he knew what would happen to her. It would be worse than before. Still, Four-seventeen had no choice but to follow orders.

His *exact* orders. As he'd been commanded so long ago, he landed as soon as he could and assumed his greenish humanoid form, observing the arena and inhaling deeply. In his cloud form he could have moved quickly over the city and probably found Eapha in a few hours. He knew her pattern and would recognize it easily. Once he got close enough, it would serve as a beacon to him. But he wasn't allowed to hunt in cloud form, and Melorta had told him to follow her by scent. It was just too bad for her that patterns weren't sensed by scent, and in this form, he only had a human sense of smell.

Ril knelt prostrate on the marble floor, his arms stretched out before him and two battlers holding him down as his master repeated his commands, Shalatar being careful to make every rule clear and fully understood. Ril heard him, but the litany had no effect. Leon's voice echoed through his mind louder than anything Shalatar tried to say. *I am your master.* Those four words kept Ril safe, free of whatever anyone else wanted.

Freedom. He'd never felt so free, had never thought he'd find liberty through so strong a binding, but that was what had happened. He'd chosen his master with his eyes open this time. Not when he'd come to this world—no one would have wanted that. He'd chosen six years ago, when he'd had the chance to see Leon swing from a hangman's noose and decided to save him instead, knowing the bond between them would never be broken, that except for his queen, Leon would always come first as master. Leon was everything.

Now more than ever, Leon had full control. He'd promised to set Ril free once they were away, but right now, Ril didn't want that. It felt good, too good to be subordinate, too comfortable and freeing. He no longer had to worry or be afraid, because there was someone there to make the decisions for him. How could he give that up? Lizzy was a gentle soul. So was the queen. Leon, when he had to, ruled absolutely, and there wasn't any sylph who wouldn't exult in that, whether the master was a man or not. What did it matter that Leon couldn't be there for Ril the way he wanted physically? The love he'd felt for Lizzy was muted, there but not really that important. He'd been celibate for most of his existence anyway. More important was freeing Lizzy for his beloved master and seeing them both home to the Valley. Deep inside, something tickled him, saying he loved Lizzy, loved her dearly for himself . . . but it didn't matter. Both of them loved him, and they'd given him a greater freedom than he ever would have found without them. The two battlers who held him stared in amazement. They could feel that Shalatar was having no effect on him, master or not, that there was something stronger wrapped around and through him. They felt it and were envious.

Six years of freedom he'd had to make his own decisions and go his own way. He'd spent them following Leon anyway, working with him as closely as ever. Actually, they'd been even closer: Leon had treated him as an equal during those years. But he hadn't hesitated in this. Why had Ril ever been frightened? He had his place and his family, with Lizzy and Leon both. Love, and a purpose. He didn't need anything else. And nothing and no one could take that away from him.

Shalatar finished his recital of the rules and wiped his forehead. Rashala had been concerned, but it didn't look as though she needed to be. He didn't work directly with battlers, but sylphs were all essentially the same. The battler before him was in full submission. There hadn't even been a need for force.

He nodded to the handler who had brought the three battlers, the other pair acting as muscle in case Seven-oh-three was compromised after all. His master was still out there, Shalatar heard. That seemed impossible—the man had to be dead—but they couldn't afford to take chances.

The handler stepped forward, urging the three battlers upright, and they followed her docilely, headed for the feeder pens. Shalatar went to wash his face and return to his duties, forgetting in a moment a creature who should have meant everything to him.

# Chapter Twenty-three

Despite how blisteringly hot it was, Justin sat inside one of the stone huts that the exiles lived in, not daring to step outside where he might be seen. Not with battlers scouring the city. The sylphs still hadn't crossed the wall, but everyone was afraid that they might.

He sat in a corner, most of his clothing stripped off as he felt gingerly inside his mouth for the cauterized remains of his tongue. The flesh still hurt, but Leon had taken a quick look and assured him that Luck could restore it. He had to hope the man was right. The other two feeders hadn't seemed upset by their loss, just happy to be free. They were gone already, in search of their families. Justin prayed they wouldn't give the rest of them away if they were caught, but Leon had seemed to feel he had no right to stop them leaving.

Justin sighed silently. He'd cried for a long time after Leon freed him, sobbing in his future father-in-law's arms like a child. The man had held him throughout, murmuring reassurances that Justin wanted to hear but couldn't really believe. Leon didn't know what it was like to have his tongue cut out and burned. To feel himself twisted inside to become a feeder for Ril. He'd imagined the life was draining out of him every time that horrible creature fed, and he'd hated it and hated Ril—the battler, who was cheered in the arena; the sylph, who had women throwing themselves at him. If he'd had both his tongue and Ril right before him, he would have been tempted to order him into his natural form and watch him die.

Justin huddled in his corner and waited. The battlers were looking for them, but Leon had promised they were all safe here, so long as they didn't go outside. His bladder burned, but he didn't care. Nothing would tempt him outside, not and risk being taken back to that horrible place. This little hut wasn't much bigger than his cage, but he was free here, and that mattered more than anything.

A few feet away, Leon spoke with Eapha, feeling his horror grow as he got his first true account of what was going on in Meridal. He'd heard things from Xehm and Zalia, but both of them were on the outside. Eapha had lived right in the heart of the madness, seeing more even than Justin had, locked in his cage. There were so many things Leon hadn't known, so many things he hadn't thought to ask Ril. Eapha related all of it, including things of which he wished he'd stayed ignorant.

She told him about the harems most of all, the place where battlers went to slake themselves on women who had no choice but to be there. He knew from stories of Mace before he was freed that a battler could make a woman enjoy loving them, amplifying their lust much as they did hatred on men, but to him it still sounded like rape. He'd wanted to cry when he heard that was where Lizzy had been taken, tossed to battlers like some kind of toy. The women in the Valley were incredibly liberal, and he'd come to understand and accept that, but this was his little girl.

"They never touched her," Eapha assured him, to his relief. "Tooie said that she wasn't interesting to them, but they pretended just to keep her from being taken as a feeder."

Eapha had relayed that part as well, that the women who didn't perform were taken and maimed like poor Justin, as were the ones with whom the battlers dared fall in love. He'd had trouble believing that, even of these people. It was too impossibly cruel.

"Thank you for taking care of my daughter," he told Eapha. "All of you. It must have been a great risk for you to bring her into this circle of yours, seeing as you didn't know her."

Eapha shrugged, trying to work tangles out of her hair. She smiled faintly. "She's a good girl and with that yellow hair, she would have been gone immediately if we hadn't. But she played the game well enough for someone who didn't know what they were doing. I think it actually got easier for her once Seven-oh-three became her lover."

Leon felt his heart freeze inside him. "What?" he managed. Over in the corner, Justin stared, his eyes huge.

Eapha blinked, regarding him in puzzlement. "Seven-oh-three. You call him Ril, don't you?"

But Ril didn't even *like* women. "Are you sure?"

"Absolutely!" She laughed. "We brought him into the circle as well." The laughter faded. "Tooie said there's something more about them. He had a horrible time coming up with the words. When you sent that letter with him, he spent most of the night trying to get us to put down the right question."

"What is it?" Leon asked. He felt faint. Ril? With Lizzy? *His* battler? His *daughter*? Leon thought of Ril standing before him, taking in his orders, and had a sudden urge to wring his neck. Justin looked ill.

"Tooie said that none of the battlers wanted Lizzy in their beds because she was already bound to a battler. To Ril, actually. Even the craziest of them wouldn't touch her."

"She came in like this?"

"Yes."

Leon closed his eyes and shuddered.

Eapha eyed him uncertainly. "Are you all right?"

"Yes," he whispered. "Continue."

The woman settled back, still looking unsure, but at last she continued. "None of the battlers here have female masters. They're not even allowed female feeders— just us in the harem and the handlers. When Tooie saw Lizzy, though . . ." She shook her head. "He wants to know how Ril made her his master. That's his question. He wants to make me his master. Master of the harem, I suppose." She smiled faintly.

No, Leon thought. Not just master but queen of every sylph in this corrupt city. From female master to queen was only a single step after all, one that a woman from a harem wouldn't have any trouble taking. He paled, the implications hitting him all at once. Solie, becoming queen, had subsumed the fifty of so sylphs of the Community and those from her battler's original hive line, like Mace. Eapha would take in thousands. From the look on her face, Eapha had no idea. Lizzy must not have known, either, since she hadn't said anything.

Somehow, Ril had made Lizzy his master! He couldn't make her a queen, not with Solie's pattern already locked inside him. But he'd made her like what Leon was, and Leon had no idea how he'd managed it. It required the help of a trained priest, or a battler who knew how, such as Mace, who had to feed the pattern through the queen. Solie would have needed to be there when it was done, and she would have said something if Ril had come to her looking to bind himself to Lizzy. No, somehow his battler figured out how to do the impossible and had never told him.

And how would you have reacted if he had? he asked

himself. His battler had been keeping secrets from him. So had Lizzy. That hurt, but he put it aside. There was no time.

"I don't know the answer to your battler's question," he admitted, and saw the girl's face fall. She'd liked the idea of being master to Tooie, he realized, but only because she loved him. In many ways, binding a sylph was like marriage, and love was the best reason to do it. He hoped that love sustained her when Tooie turned her into a queen.

"I'll find out, though," he assured her.

She looked puzzled. "How?"

"Simple," he said. "I'm going to ask Ril."

The time for secrets had passed.


Tooie took the letter to Lizzy's father only because she begged him. It didn't matter to him anymore, not without Eapha. Without her, he thought in time that he would become as crazy as Eighty-nine—providing he could bring himself to even touch a woman again. It seemed easier to him not to. This kind of pain wasn't worth it, not when his love would only get another woman destroyed.

He went out after darkness fell, shimmered out and away, moving above the city as cautious as ever not to be seen. He didn't care for himself, but the letter inside him would result in Lizzy's death if it were found. Seven-oh-three's as well, though Tooie couldn't make himself care about a foreign battler, especially not now.

Tooie flowed through the darkness and down to the place where he'd picked the flowers for Eapha. Close by, he sensed Lizzy's father. Settling down at the edge of the city, right at the limit of his boundary, he gaped his mouth wide, letting the lightning that formed his teeth glow in the dark and show where he was. There weren't many campfires tonight, and all was quiet. The people there felt afraid.

All but one. Immediately, a shape disengaged from others around a campfire and made its way toward him. Tooie recognized him from his emotions: determination and calm. The man walked to the other side of the old broken wall and said the last thing the battler would ever have expected.

"Hello, Tooie."

Tooie started, his lightning ceasing for a moment in surprise. How did this man know his name?

"I have someone here who's been waiting for you," Leon explained, stepping aside.

A second black shape walked toward him—one he knew very well. For a moment he could only gape, and then she was running toward him and he screamed, a dozen tendrils lashing out to wrap around Eapha's sobbing form. He was forbidden to change out of his natural shape here, but he pulled her to him and wrapped his mantle around her, shaking. Eapha was safe! She was safe! How had she ever got here?

"Leon rescued me," she whispered. "And he's willing to help me become your master if we'll help him save Lizzy and Ril."

For giving him this, Tooie would do anything. The battler kept Eapha cradled by his heart and watched Leon, waiting for him to say whatever needed to be done. If he could do it despite all the rules laid on him, Tooie would.

As he learned in the next few minutes, it was something he could do very easily.

Freshly fed by the two feeders who still remained to him, Ril lay in one of the alcoves of the harem, his arms wrapped around Lizzy. She had her head resting against his chest, her breath still slowing from earlier. Eapha was gone, she'd told him, only to find out her friend had already been saved by her father. She'd wept in Ril's arms and then made love to him with near violence. In her relief, she hadn't felt his odd emotional distance.

Ril kissed her forehead, and she lifted her head to smile at him. "I guess I didn't need to write that letter. Eapha will tell him everything Tooie wants." Her eyes clouded for a moment. "Ril . . . am I your master?"

"Yes," he replied. "You were until Leon took me."

She stared at him and lifted herself up. He'd told her what her father had done and she didn't know what to feel about it. Did Ril still love her? He had to. He'd just *made love* to her. Any other thought was something she cringed away from in terror. When he tightened his grip, she settled back against him. "How is that possible for you to be mine?" she whispered. "You're father's battler."

"I was yours, too," he said. "I told you that. I was yours since the day you were born."

She made a face. "I can't have been too impressive as a baby."

"You were slimy and squalling and beautiful," he assured her. "I fell in love with you from the first moment I saw you." He saw and felt her puzzled look. "I made it official when you were seven."

"How?"

He stretched a hand up toward the ceiling, both of them watching as he turned it idly in the dim light—his perfect, human, inhuman hand.

"Do you remember when I was sick?" he asked. "I was sick from trying to take your pattern into myself. I *needed* it, but it wasn't until you reached for me that I was able to grasp it."

"I reached for you?" she said in amazement.

He nodded and brought his hand down to brush a stray hair from her face. "You wanted me to live so badly, you surrendered to me. That let me in. So, you became my master."

"I . . ." She swallowed and licked her lips. "Is that why I can feel you? But why couldn't I feel you before, if you did this when I was seven?"

He stroked her cheek and cupped it, moving her face around to where he could kiss her mouth. "I suppressed it," he explained. "You can only feel what I project to you, so I projected nothing."

Lizzy looked up into his pale gray eyes. She could feel his calm certainty and serenity. He was at peace with himself for what she suspected was the first time in his life, and no matter what her father had done, underneath it all, she could feel his love for her. "And now?" she whispered.

He regarded her for a moment, considering her, and then that love flowed out, turning to lust that soaked through her. She gasped softly and he rolled atop her, his arm under her head as he bent to plunder her mouth, his kisses as burning hot as a blacksmith's forge. She felt a little like steel being tempered or an instrument being strummed, and he filled her with his desire, blowing thought away as he pushed her legs apart and slipped inside.

Lizzy cried out, unable to hear herself as he filled her, body and soul. She could feel him, though, the ultimate depths of him, the inscrutable age and total loneliness that was now filled by her. He'd been taken by her father, but the heart of him that he himself likely couldn't feel right now loved her. He pretended, as Leon had ordered him to pretend with all his masters, but it was there, untouchable by him but understood by her. She was his life, his hope, his everything.

She wrapped her arms around Ril's neck and hung on, not able in her humanness to do more. She knew it was enough for him, though. It was more than enough, for he touched the essence of her and knew that he was loved.

Afterward, he slept. Lizzy left him there and went outside, to give him privacy and also so that the handlers wouldn't get suspicious. After the episode with Melorta, she should have avoided Ril entirely, but she hadn't been able to. For both their sakes though, she couldn't stay with him for long.

Besides, she didn't want to get pulled into his dream with her father. It was a little odd, but the next time she saw him, she wanted it to be real.

Lizzy was gone. It had been strange to make love to her, but she'd wanted it, and deep down underneath Leon's control, something in him had wanted it as well. He almost wanted to shy away from that feeling of want. All he needed was Leon, all he *was* was Leon. Yet still he'd held her and loved her, and deep inside he knew she loved him as well. It was hard to hold on to when she left his side, though, and Ril didn't try. Instead, he curled up in the alcove and tried to sleep. He'd slept a lot that day already, but he'd been through a great deal as well, between Leon and Shalatar, and it wasn't hard to relax and drop off.

He didn't really understand how he dreamwalked. He knew it was to his masters only, but he hardly did it every time he slept, and he definitely hadn't walked to Justin or any of the other feeders. It seemed to happen most when he was focused on his target as he fell asleep, so he thought in detail of Leon as he dozed off. Then he followed the pattern line of energy that linked the two of them, edging his way through the ether until he came to the sleeping mind of the man he sought.

Sliding up, he embraced it and slipped within.

The world brightened. Ril blinked several times and lifted his head, looking around. He was standing in the courtyard of the manor the Petrule family had lived in back in Eferem. The stark stone manor rose ahead, the moon shining high beyond. Leon stood on the steps that led to the front door, staring down at him.

"Leon," Ril started, walking forward.

Leon's forehead creased. "You slept with my daughter."

Ril froze, the tiny bit of him that was still himself suddenly so cold that he could almost believe this wasn't a dream. His mouth moved without sound, for he couldn't think what to say, not against this. Not against the anger he suddenly felt. Coming from the man currently saturating his soul, it was agony.

Leon sucked his lips into his mouth and wiped his palms on his pantlegs. He descended the stairs and stopped again, only a few feet away. "You slept with my daughter."

Ril hadn't been expecting this . . . but he had, hadn't he? He'd known Leon wouldn't approve. Leon wouldn't share. He wouldn't want his sweet Lizzy tainted. Ril felt his master's disappointment and anger, and the bond between them hurt. It hurt so much that he wailed aloud and dropped to his knees, shaking as he reached out to grasp his master's ankles. A single word, just one, and he'd never be able to touch Lizzy again. He'd go mad if that happened. He could feel it already, and he wanted it. Wanted the control to be absolute, wanted to be nothing more than this man's creature, with no will of his own, not even the will that screamed that he loved Lizzy. Would always love Lizzy with his heart, no matter who owned his soul.

"P-pleeaasee . . . ," he begged, sobbing, and he didn't even know what he was begging for.

Leon was furious when he saw Ril walking toward him across the stone as though he hadn't been doing anything wrong. To sleep with his daughter, to take advantage of her in this horrible place . . . ? Leon had never been so angry. Ril had given his trust over to Leon, but Leon had trusted his battler as well.

Even knowing they had no time for accusations, Leon made them, and saw the battler's eyes change, reflecting confusion and horror. This was never supposed to happen. Something greedy and hateful in the back of Leon's mind screamed that Ril was supposed to be his. He didn't want to share him with anyone else, and certainly not with someone that Ril could end up loving more.

Ril dropped to his knees, his entire soul bared to his master as he grabbed Leon's ankles, sobbing the word please, and he was more open than ever before, even just after a feeding. Everything he was he'd given to Leon, willingly, and yet under it all Lizzy remained. Ril loved her with everything that was still him. Yet, with a single word, Leon would be able to banish her from him forever. He'd have his battler all to himself, just as he'd always wanted.

Leon gasped and immediately dropped to his knees, drawing Ril up into his arms. The anger in him had whiplashed into horror, an instant of realization, and they both hugged the other hard. "No, don't beg," Leon told him. "Don't beg! It's all right, I won't take her from you. I promise I won't." He paused, and Ril felt the emotions in his master diminish, the man forcing them down and away, no matter what he might really feel. The pain eased. "It's all right. I'm sorry. It's all right, I'm sorry I scared you."

Ril leaned against him, shuddering. He couldn't even

raise his head as Leon stroked his back, whispering reassurances in his ear. He would have groveled, he would have done anything, and he was shocked at himself even as he closed his eyes in shame, wanting Leon's control back in full just so he wouldn't feel this tearing contradiction. He wasn't surprised. He was a battle sylph. He'd spent centuries begging already, for good or for ill.

"You had orders for me?" he whispered at last, still not looking up. Right now, he couldn't.

Leon sighed, sitting on the ground with Ril half in his lap, staring over his head at the nighttime skyline of a city neither of them expected to visit again in reality. "The woman I took from the arena—she says Lizzy's your master. Is that true?"

Ril tightened his grip. "Yes," he choked out, burying his face against Leon's shoulder.

Leon's emotions flickered for a moment, just a moment, and Ril felt the jealousy and then shame. He hurried to say, "You're still my master, too. I can't change that." He hesitated. "Even if you gave me myself back, I wouldn't." He couldn't imagine it. Now that the pain was fading, memory of Lizzy was, too, buried back under the strength of this man's presence in his soul. It was still there, though, deep down, which it hurt to know.

"Thank you," Leon said, and there was a lot of emotion in those words. "Ril, how did she become your master? We need to know."

Ril finally pulled back and sat up, surprised. Leon seemed tired and unhappy, but he managed a smile, whatever else he was thinking. His thoughts aside, the smile was real. "Ril?" he asked.

Ril swallowed. "I reached for her with the pattern inside myself. It wasn't enough, though, not until she reached for me. Until she surrendered to me." He looked down.

"That's basically it. It's not that easy, though. It took me months, and it nearly killed me."

"But Lizzy didn't know what you were doing, did she?"

Ril gazed at him. "No, she didn't."

Leon seemed grimly satisfied. He nodded and looked away again for a second. "Tell me one more thing. Do you love her?"

The battler swallowed. The pain rose again, the contradiction of caring for something more than this man. He had to answer, though, and do so with all the honesty in him. "More than anything."

"And you'll take care of her?"

"As much as she needs."

Leon nodded, took a deep breath, and put his arms around Ril's neck, pressing their foreheads together. "All right, son. So long as it's what Lizzy wants, I won't regret your being with her."

Ril closed his eyes and shuddered again, this time with relief. Leon gripped him tightly for a moment longer before finally letting him go.

# Chapter Twenty-four

Leon woke, blinking at the darkness that hid the ceiling of the hut in which he lay. There was a hole in the roof and through that he could see a couple of stars twinkling above. There weren't as many here as in the Valley, where there were fewer city lights to dim them out, but he could still see half a dozen twinkling like happy children with sparklers.

He lay quiet for a few minutes, watching and just breathing, calming himself as he'd been doing since he'd first come to this city. Serenity filled him, but it didn't go as deep as usual, and finally he sighed. Serenity wasn't what he needed. He needed to feel, and what he felt was guilt. He'd been angry with Ril; he admitted that now. Lizzy was his daughter. He had wanted to protect her and see her properly married, with children and grandchildren and an ordinary life. But the way Ril reacted to his anger had destroyed all of that. Despite all the ownership Leon forced on him, Ril had been terrified! Leon felt ill, and now his anger was directed at himself.

For fifteen years he'd held Ril as a bird, wanting the creature's trust and respect, believing as he'd been taught that the battler was nothing more than a clever animal. Upon learning the truth, he'd wanted him to be a friend, or even family, and he'd felt finally he succeeded in that. Now, to see Ril actually begging him . . . He didn't want to share, that was the heart of it, but that didn't mean he had the right to question. Lizzy and Ril were both adults. They didn't need his approval and they certainly didn't require his permission. Leon closed his eyes. He'd asked Ril to trust him with everything he was, and then he'd attacked the very core of his need. If he ever *expected* to be the most important person in Ril's life, then he didn't deserve to have him. The same went with Lizzy. It hurt, though. On a fundamentally selfish level, it hurt very much.

He also had no time for it. Leon had no idea how long he'd been sleeping, and Tooie could only wait so long before he needed to return to the harem. He might already be gone.

Scrubbing his hand through his hair, Leon rose and went out into the darkness. Xehm and Zalia sat by the fire along with a few other exiles. The majority had left hours before, preferring to find other places in the desert to set up their camps instead of running the risk of staying. Leon didn't blame them and was in fact glad they were gone. Battlers didn't leave the city, but that didn't mean they couldn't be drawn by the heightened emotions of this place.

One battler was present. Tooie floated at the edge of the desert by the wall, which Eapha sat atop, keeping him company. He was still made of smoke and lightning, due to his orders, and Leon could see the sylph's growing distress in the rate the lightning inside him flashed. Eapha was talking, but she couldn't stop him from going if Tooie reached the limits of his orders and had to feed. Worse, he'd been gone so long that his absence could have been noted, so if the battler vanished now, Leon had no guarantee that he would be able to return.

He strode forward, his jaw clenched. Red eyes turned to regard him, as did Eapha. "Did you find out anything?" she asked. She'd been dubious of Leon's talk of dreamwalking, but she hadn't been entirely disbelieving. He hoped she could keep that attitude.

"I did." He looked at the battler. "I hope you understand me, Tooie. I hope you understand what this means."

The sylph stared at him. He couldn't speak. Leon could tell he was listening, though.

"Ril told me that he made Lizzy his master by reaching for her with his pattern. He says he nearly killed himself trying, but it wasn't until Lizzy surrendered to him that it worked. She did it thinking he was dying. She didn't know." Leon turned to Eapha. "You do. Surrender yourself to Tooie, and he can make you his master."

Tooie surged, his lightning flaring throughout the cloud that formed him. Leon hissed for him to be quiet, even as Eapha regarded them both fearfully.

"Are you sure?" she whispered.

Immediately Tooie's energy was contained again, and he reached out with a dark tendril to stroke her cheek. She looked at him mournfully and laid her hand atop it.

"Your life won't necessarily be any easier," Leon told her. Ethically, he couldn't say anything less, knowing she would soon be a queen. He'd told her what a queen was, but she had no background to draw on to really understand. Only by experiencing it could she do that. "But it's the only way I can see for both of you to be free. You and him." He nodded at Tooie.

Eapha followed his gaze to her lover. Tooie stared back, his smoke swirling up around the wall and encircling her. Finally she smiled, ducking her head back down.

Leon nodded, stepping away. "If you can, be quick." Turning, he returned to the camp.

Tooie watched Eapha, the energy that was his heart vibrating on a thousand frequencies at once. What the man had said, how he claimed his battler had done the binding . . .

Tooie never would have thought of that! It wasn't that it was beyond him, but it wasn't something that should ever work. To reach out to a mind was one thing, but only the queen could take hold. Everyone knew that. It was a fundamental truth. Only the queen could grasp a pattern. Only the queen could accept a bond.

But sylphs bonded to humans every time one was made their master, didn't they? Humans could take their patterns, if not as powerfully as a queen, then nearly so. Enough to command them, enough to own them. Always before through ritual, but that was only to *force* the bond. All they really needed to do in their humanness was to take what was offered.

Tooie shrieked silently, ecstatic and overwhelmed. So much time wasted, by all of his kind. They'd had the ability to forge their destiny this entire time. Or at least to fall in love with those who could.

He regarded Eapha, able to see her energy pattern more easily than her body in his current form. Soon, that pattern would be inside him. It would be one of many, but she was female. Which meant . . . he could turn her into a queen. She didn't fully understand that, but he did.

Forming tendrils of his essence, he swept them in the signs Eapha had taught him. He wasn't quite so proficient in this shape, but he didn't need to say anything terribly complex. Trust me, he spelled out.

"I do," she whispered, though he could feel her fear as much as her love.

Tooie reached for her, stretching out his pattern the way he would have to a queen of his own kind, had his queen ever wanted him. Instead he sought Eapha and felt the essence of her just beyond reach, across a tiny distance that he could never bridge on his own. He reached out nonetheless, hoping, and slowly Eapha started to reach back.

Lizzy walked over to the food table, her stomach rumbling. There wasn't much left, and Kiala was picking over the last of the cheeses.

"Want some?" she asked, offering Lizzy the tray.

"Thanks," Lizzy said, taking a piece and popping it into her mouth. It smelled like feet, but the taste was divine. She chewed slowly and glanced around. The hour was late, and she and Kiala were the only two women in sight. "Eapha is free," she said after a moment. "She was taken to Ril at the arena, and my father broke her free."

Kiala's jaw dropped. "B-but . . . ," she gasped. "But how?"

"He's my father," Lizzy said. "He won't leave me."

Kiala's lips firmed. She'd heard about Lizzy's father before and never really believed. "No one's going to get you out of here."

"He will. He and Ril."

The woman shook her head, bitter and defeated. "No battler is going to save anyone. Not from this place."

The main door suddenly unlocked and opened. It was too late for the handlers to be coming for anything usual, Lizzy realized in terror, but three dozen of them filed in, armed with swords and clubs. Their faces were grimmer than she'd ever seen, and she shuddered upon seeing that Melorta accompanied them. The handler eyed her hatefully, as though she was remembering the interrogation as well. This was going to be much worse than earlier.

Lizzy and Kiala both started backing away. The handlers spread out, clubs at the ready. Behind them came Rashala. She looked serenely over the mostly empty harem, then at Lizzy and Kiala.

"Those two are on the list. Take them."

Kiala froze, gawking in terror. Lizzy screamed instead, and tried to run, but there were too many handlers and she couldn't escape all of them. They caught her after only a few steps and dragged her back by her hair. Frantic, she still tried to fight, but they pushed her down onto the ground and twisted her arm behind her back.

"Ril!" she screamed. *"Ril!"*

"Get the others," Rashala ordered, and the rest of the handlers obeyed, Melorta calling commands and breaking them into groups.

It was obvious that they knew just where they were going, where their targets were sleeping, for within minutes nine more women were dragged out of alcoves, crying and screaming. Four battlers trailed behind them, following the women, and their distress was obvious.

All of the women were from the circle. Lizzy gasped in horror, which drew Rashala's eyes. The woman's expression was worse than smug. "No," Lizzy whispered. How had they known? "Ril . . ."

Rashala cast her gaze over the frightened, assembled captives. "Take them to the feeder pens."

The concubines began screaming, struggling madly, and their battlers begged in silence, trying to come to their aid but ordered back by the handlers. Other women and battlers appeared at the openings to the alcoves and at the door in back, watching in terror but doing nothing. There was nothing they could do, nothing any of them could do.

"Ril!" Lizzy screamed again, shrieking with her mind as loudly as her voice. *"Ril!"*

His eyes snapped open as he heard Lizzy scream. Her panic beat at him, along with the terror of a great many other women, along with the rage and fear of countless battle sylphs, along with Leon's order to protect his daughter. Ril rolled over, swaying sleepily, but smacked himself across the face. The pain shocked him more fully awake, and he shook his head, forcing himself to his feet.

The intensity of his dream still had him, and he tried to change shape. The pain of that brought him all of the way awake, and a moment later Ril ran out into the harem. His boot heels thudding on the marble floor, he stumbled over a pillow, nearly falling, but he caught himself and looked up. Handlers occupied the harem in force, dragging nearly a dozen women toward the door. Rashala watched. Four battlers cowered and wailed in silence, their murderous wrath barely held back by orders. Ril recognized them as easily as he did the women.

Lizzy was closest to the door, and as he stood there she was pulled through, still screaming his name. Ril charged forward, his rage absolute, no matter if it was his or if it was her father's.

Seeing him approach, Melorta nodded at one of her handlers. The woman turned toward him, her palm uplifted. "Stop!" she ordered, her voice clear and firm.

*You are mine,* Leon's voice whispered in his mind.

Ril ran up to the handler and drove his fist into her face. It slammed through her nose and the bones of her skull, punched through the soft tissue of her brain and out the back. The woman's body convulsed, then dropped off his bloody arm to fall with a splat on the ground. Ril stared at the corpse in silence, realizing that he'd killed a female. It wasn't as though it was an impossible thing, but battlers normally never would. Females were female, not the enemy. He shuddered, aware that everyone was staring at him, the battlers shocked, the handlers and concubines terrified. Lizzy's fear stood out above them all.

Rashala passed a stunned Melorta and moved slowly toward him, her hands raised. "Seven-oh-three," she soothed. "Be calm. That's a good boy." Her will pushed forward onto him, dominating, overwhelming. "You're a good boy."

*You are mine,* Leon promised.

Ril smiled and spread his arms, one bloody and the other clean. Rashala took another step toward him, her will potent and focused . . . and Ril hit her with the full aura of his hatred.

His attack made the other battlers howl, but Ril didn't care. The women all screamed in panic. Many of the handlers lost their grip on the concubines, only a few of whom had the presence to run before Melorta yelled for her subordinates to master themselves. Few obeyed right away, but the concubines didn't need much controlling. The only directions they could run were either back past Ril into the harem or out the still-open doorway where Lizzy had disappeared. Most of them cowered instead, as frightened as the handlers.

Rashala stumbled backward, her eyes wide with horror, but she didn't give in to her fear. "Kill him!" she screamed instead. "*Kill* him!"

She cried out the order to the handlers, but Ril could tell that she meant it for the battlers as well. He laughed aloud. "You're not allowed to order battlers to fight, isn't that true?"

Rashala gasped and finally ran, spinning around and exiting the room in only a few steps. Melorta was on her heels. The door slammed shut, leaving Ril with nearly thirty handlers. Most were still frozen in terror, but close to a dozen started forward, swords drawn. They were afraid, shivering under the effect of his hatred, but determined.

Ril snarled, not liking the odds. Even if he had the energy to take them all in one energy blast, he'd kill Lizzy's friends as well. Fighting in the arena had taught him to use his power in a more focused manner, but he was still terribly outnumbered. Leon, though . . . Leon had forced him to learn to fight with a sword.

The handlers moved forward, even a few who had been paralyzed before. Ril glanced over his shoulder at the four battlers of Eapha's circle, creatures not of his hive to whom he would ordinarily never speak. Under normal circumstances, he would fight *them*, not these women. That was what was natural, what he was made for. Ultimately, though, the battlers were as useless in this struggle as the concubines.

The first handlers came for him, swords swinging. Ril lunged at each in turn, much faster than they, and buried a bloody fist in the gut of one as he ducked under the blade of another. Changing the shape of his left arm, hissing in pain as he did, Ril plunged what was now a jagged, multi-angled sword into his assailant's side. She gasped, vomiting blood as she fell into two pieces. The handler he'd punched curled over and fell to the floor, trying to breathe. Straightening, Ril fought to breathe himself.

His right arm he changed next, making it a blade slimmer but just as lethal as the first. The transformation was agonizing, but he had no choice. He didn't have enough energy to make any greater changes, and he couldn't hold them back with the hate aura. He couldn't even keep that up much longer.

He charged in amongst the handlers. Captive concubines dropped to the floor or ran, screaming, and he leaped over one woman with whom he'd pretended to be lovers to take a handler's head off right above the jaw. The woman beside her screamed and threw up her hands, dropping her sword. Ril drove his arm through both her and the handler cowering behind. He then pushed forward into a group of a half dozen more, including another of his fake lovers. When she shrieked, he booted her in the backside to get her moving toward safety.

The handlers kept attacking. Ril ripped his sword arm free, yanking it around just in time to block several blows before finding the gut of another assailant. The woman gagged on blood as he drew her upward, impaled, lifting her over his head and throwing her across the room into another half dozen handlers set upon killing him. Ril leaped after her, arms swinging.

Every impact ran up his arms, and he soon was slipping on blood, his body aching. A club thrown at him rebounded off his shoulder, and he cried out, nearly falling. A handler charged, hoping to get the better of him, but he felt her emotions as she approached and brought his arm up. She crashed against him, transfixed, and blood splattered his face and made it hard to see. Her emotions stopped with a crunch the same as a cockroach under a heavy boot.

Everyone was screaming and sliding on the bloody floor. The other battlers watched with interest as the women who'd tormented their beloveds died, over a dozen of them now gathered together. The women of the harem were in hiding, the last of Eapha's circle finally running for safety. Their battler lovers collected them but otherwise stayed still. Ril rather wished they'd help him.

He shook the dead woman off his sword and backed · away from the remaining handlers. They were determined to fight now, knowing they would perish if they didn't, and they called out to each other, the more senior among them issuing orders. He could still be beaten, they shouted. Ril wasn't sure they were wrong. He couldn't seem to catch his breath anymore, and he couldn't maintain his hatred. The aura faltered and fell, and he sagged, gasping and half blind from a face full of blood.

There were ten handlers still on their feet, several others stunned but trying to get up. Without his hate aura battering them, they quickly regained courage and determination. Distantly Ril could feel Lizzy, still terrified. He didn't have time for anyone else. He swung toward the main door to the harem.

His teeth gritted, he forced his arms to return to normal, trying to ignore the pain it caused. Facing the door, he focused. He'd learned a lot while fighting in the arena, given no choice but to use his blast wave in very controlled ways. Pressing his palms against the door lock, he used just enough energy to break the mechanism. Shoving the door open, he fell through and pushed it shut behind him, bracing his back against it, intending to keep in any handlers who tried to follow.

He nearly lost his head. He'd thought Melorta fled with her employer. Instead, the lead handler was waiting for him in the guardroom, and her sword stabbed viciously forward. Ril dropped purely by instinct. Landing in a crouch, he lunged and punched both fists toward her gut. Melorta threw herself backward in avoidance, tumbling onto her backside and somersaulting over onto her hands and knees. Ten feet apart, they glared at each other, Ril gasping for breath.

Melorta's will pressed against him, a definite force against his empathy. She wasn't as strong as Rashala, but he hadn't been so tired then.

"Seven-oh-three," she commanded, her voice remarkably calm.

"Don't," he snapped. "Your lies won't work on me anymore."

"How . . . ?"

Ril smirked. "My master has a much stronger voice than any of you. He set me free."

Melorta scoffed. "You'll never be free."

"And you'll never make Lizzy cry again."

Ril had his breath back. Bracing first against the floor, he lunged. Melorta tried to roll out of the way, her sword a flash of light. The blade carved a line of fire into his side, but at the same time Ril grabbed her jaw and yanked it around. Her neck shattered and the lead handler collapsed.

An alarm was going off somewhere far down the hall that led out of the guardroom, discordant and shrill. Ril ignored that, glancing around. He'd been here whenever he was taken to the arena or the feeders, so he knew the routes to at least those two places. Narrow corridors jutted out on either side, with peepholes for the handlers to spy into the harem. Across from the harem door was another, this one leading down into the maze of feeder pens. Lizzy was somewhere in that direction.

Stepping over Melorta's corpse, Ril approached the door, gasping and bloody. It didn't have a lock. Ril closed his eyes and focused, trying to sense what was on the other side. Nothing, at least not immediately. Melorta had been the only one brave enough to ambush him so far. He looked back at the door to the harem. With the lock broken, the remaining handlers could follow him once they worked up the nerve . . . but he sensed conflicting emotions from that direction. Some wanted to stay where they were.

Ril ran a hand through his hair, pushing it out of his eyes. Drawing the hand back, he saw it was bloody and shaking. He was tired and stressed, his body ablaze with pain. Lizzy was waiting, though. He opened the door and stepped through.

A crossbow bolt slammed into his chest, right where his heart would have been had he been human. He fell backward nonetheless, and broke the shaft off an inch above his skin. Fifty feet down the corridor, another handler glared at him, the butt of her crossbow braced against her belly as she pulled back the string to reload.

Shoving himself to his feet, Ril charged, sprinting forward at his fastest speed. Like Melorta, the handler didn't panic. She calmly locked the string and nocked a bolt. Not having enough time to bring the crossbow up to her shoulder, she fired from the hip. The bolt took Ril in the throat. He fell, rolled, and came up again, throwing himself at her. He and his assailant collided.

Ril still weighed more than she did, and she fell back, his body atop hers. The handler had dropped her crossbow and pulled her dagger, for which the two now struggled. Ril choked around the second crossbow bolt the whole time. It wasn't enough to kill him, but he did need air and wasn't getting much. Also, the pain was tremendous. He couldn't give up, though, not unless he wanted himself killed and Lizzy unprotected.

Instinct taking hold at last, he lashed out with energy. The woman underneath him turned into a smear of blood and shredded meat, and Ril slumped into that wet mess, groaning and drained. Even knowing Lizzy needed him, it took him a long moment to get moving again. Shuddering, he finally rolled over onto his back and withdrew the bolt from his throat. It was hard to get a grip, and when he did pull it free, he just lay there, shuddering.

His energy was leaking out as he closed his eyes, focusing

on trying to force the wounds to close, but only time and energy could heal them. Or Leon. It would help if Leon were there, so he could drink of the man's warm, comforting essence. But his master was somewhere else, unaware of what his battler attempted. Busy. Ril could feel that just as he could still feel Lizzy's fear.

Lizzy was so afraid that he couldn't calm down. Fear for herself, fear for him. He could tell where she was, though, and he forced himself to his feet yet again. He was covered head to foot in blood and gore, his eyes staring out through a mask of red. Staggering a bit, he continued down the corridor, passing doors that he knew led into offices and storage rooms as well as sleeping quarters for the handlers. They were really no different from the women they guarded; none of them were allowed to leave either. Ril also passed the staircase that would bring him to the surface, but Lizzy hadn't been taken in that direction. She was ahead, through the door that led into the feeder pens.

The door was locked. Ril tried the handle and returned to where Melorta lay. The key was in her pouch, and he took it.

The alarm he'd been hearing was much louder on the other side of the door, but no one was waiting in ambush this time. Everywhere, men and women shifted uncertainly in their cages, confused by what was happening and frightened. Sylphs did the same, around and above, most of them invisible from their own fright. They didn't know what the alarm was for, Ril realized. There was no specific alarm for an out-of-control-battler attack, or none that had ever been practiced. The people who ran this place were panicked themselves, most ignorant of the problem. Once they learned, though, he'd be in trouble—especially if they thought to bring in someone who *could* order the other battlers to attack.

A little bit more chaos would help delay that. Ril entered the first section of feeder pens, lurching drunkenly toward the closest cages. They were occupied by his own feeders, and the two men gaped at him in shock. Ril could feel it more clearly from them than the others. They were his masters after all, even if they couldn't speak and Leon's control made them impotent.

Ril gripped the cage bars and drank deep, the two men gasping as he drained their energy. For his part, the pain eased, and he felt their life flow into him, restoring his strength. Their energy wasn't as good as Leon's or Lizzy's, but it filled him and he drank heavily of them for the last time.

"Out the door I came through," he announced. "Turn right at the stairs and go up to get to the surface. I hope you make it," he added, and actually meant it. He never wanted to see anyone caged again.

He grabbed the front of one of the pens and pulled, hard, snapping the lock. The door opened and he went to the next. For a moment, the man he'd just freed stared in amazement. Then he stepped out of the cage, shivering, and ran for the exit.

Ril yanked the next cage open as well, and his second feeder fled after a grin of thanks and a bow. The alarm was still sounding all around, and sandals slapped on the catwalks linking the thousands of cages. Somewhere, people were beginning to get organized, but no one had come to find him here yet, and no one had called any battlers. One floated above him in his natural shape, watching gleefully. Still more floated beyond that. They couldn't fight, but they were allowed to come to the feeder pens whenever they wanted, and gloried in seeing someone who could. Ril wiped his mouth on his shoulder and headed down the catwalk after Lizzy, ripping cage doors open as he went and leading a useless army of battle sylphs behind him.

For whom they would fight was still a question.

# Chapter Twenty-five

Lizzy was hustled down the corridor she remembered from her first trip into the harem, her arms gripped so tightly by handlers that she sported bruises. Rashala hurried ahead, gasping. Their route lay through another door and the feeder pens, down the metal catwalks that formed the floor, Lizzy wincing as she crossed these in her bare feet. Whenever she stumbled, the handlers yanked her back up and made her keep running.

They fled along the first level, passing dozens of cages before Rashala turned down a flight of stairs and right into another section. Women filled some of the cages here, water and earth sylphs feeding from them. The sylphs moved out of the newcomers' way, and they kept going, finally reaching a central area with a real floor and walls, the room full of tables and cabinets. It also had a long rope descending from the ceiling, which Rashala ordered one of the handlers to pull. The frightened woman did so, leaving Lizzy with only one guard, and a bell started ringing somewhere out of sight.

Rashala turned. There were three other women from the circle with Lizzy, including Kiala. All of them were sobbing, held tightly by handlers who looked nearly as frightened. Lizzy didn't have any sympathy for them, even as she shivered at the memory of Ril's attack. She'd only seen the first few seconds, but that had been enough. The battlers back home didn't fight much, there being no need, but she'd seen them horse around. She just hoped he could keep up his strength and speed.

He was still alive—she could tell that. Now that she'd been with him, she could feel him as easily as she suspected her father could, not enough to tell what he was feeling unless he projected it, unfortunately, but enough to know he hadn't been killed.

"Keep that bell ringing," Rashala told the handler, who pulled the rope harder. She regarded the concubines, but she didn't ask them what was going on. Unlike Melorta, she didn't see them as people who might have answers, Lizzy thought—which was lucky for her. At least, she hoped it was lucky.

"What's going on, mistress?" one of the handlers begged. "How could it *do* that?"

"I don't know," Rashala murmured. Male guards from the feeder pens burst in, demanding explanations, and with them came a man dressed in the same type of robe as Rashala, his pate just as bare. Lizzy stood in the grip of her captor and eyed the way she'd come, hoping the confusion in this place lasted and that Ril was still safe.

Rashala turned to her brother, so frantic that she nearly fell into his arms and wept. Everything had gone so wrong so quickly. She'd confirmed the identities of the women the battlers were apparently sharing, and it had been easy enough to collect them. By morning, they all would have had their tongues removed and been caged for use as feeders with the next sylphs summoned. She'd already planned to visit the slave market after breakfast, in order to select women to take their place.

"What's wrong?" Shalatar asked.

"Seven-oh-three," Rashala whispered, aware of the

others listening. She led her brother into a corner. "He went mad, attacked the handlers. I've never seen anything like it." She shook her head. "He wouldn't obey our orders."

Shalatar gaped at her in horror. "I went over the commands with him again, thoroughly! He submitted to them. How could he disobey?"

Rashala shrugged. She didn't know. She'd been trying to think of a reason, but could only summon one possibility. "It's because of his original master."

"But no one ever found him. He must be dead!"

Either that, or he was better than the battlers who were looking for him. They should have killed Seven-oh-three the moment they took him. Rashala closed her eyes and ran her hands over her smooth head. Once, she'd had hair as long and dark as any of the women in the harem. She'd had to attain supreme confidence in herself to get out of there. Now, though, her confidence was shaken. For the first time in years, she didn't know what to do.

"Something got to that battler," she told her brother. "He's killing everyone. We need to stop him somehow. Turn other battlers on him." Only she couldn't give that order. Neither could Shalatar. No one except the Battle-Sylph First of the arena or the emperor himself.

The emperor was unreachable, but the First could be approached if they dared. He'd have them both put to death when he found out, but how could they keep him from knowing? How could they ever hide this debacle?

Rashala heard shouts outside and screams of pain. She heard metal tearing and the sound of running feet, most of them barefoot. The nearby handlers and concubines cowered in fear, except for the straw-haired girl. She looked toward the door, her stance relaxing, and Rashala made another empirical leap.

She understood at last what the battler was after.

\* \* \*

Leon stood by one of the exile's huts, looking toward where Tooie and Eapha stood. He could barely see the woman in the darkness, except as a silhouette before the flickering lightning that filled the cloud of the battler. There was a strange intimacy going on, a quiet that made him look away, not wanting to intrude on their privacy no matter how desperate he was for them to succeed.

Turning, he found Justin. The boy stood only a few feet away, obviously afraid to be too distant. Leon reached out and clapped a hand reassuringly on the youth's shoulder, feeling the tension in the muscles beneath his grip. Justin didn't flinch, quite, but he was clearly afraid. Leon worried that he would always be afraid.

"We'll be going home soon," he promised. When the youth nodded, Leon took a deep breath. "Justin, about Lizzy and you . . . I think . . . I think it's not going to happen."

The boy yanked away, his expression in the dim light that of one betrayed. Leon let his arm fall back to his side. "Justin . . ."

The youth shook his head again and pointed at himself, poking his chest furiously. Leon didn't have any doubt about what he was saying.

"Justin, Ril—"

The boy shook his head even harder, poked himself again before slamming his fists against Leon's chest. It didn't hurt, but the emotion was there, and Leon let him continue. He could understand the boy's fury, and felt his own guilt at bringing him and leaving him to be tortured, but he couldn't do what the boy wanted. Not without betraying his battler and—more important right now— his daughter. She'd made her choice and made it obvious: she wanted Ril, not Justin, and even if the rules of Sylph

Valley hadn't removed a father's right to choose his daughter's husband, he wouldn't force anyone on Lizzy. That would just mean a different kind of slavery than that from which he was trying to save her. And Justin could say it was unfair, but unfair would be to give him a spouse who didn't love him. Every person deserved more than that.

"Justin, I know I said I would give you my blessing, but I also said that was only if Lizzy wanted it as well. You and I both know what she's decided. I'm sorry."

Justin just kept shaking his head and hit Leon again, refusing to accept his words. The boy's mouth moved without making any sound, but Leon could read the words if not hear them.

*She's supposed to be mine.*

"She doesn't belong to anyone," Leon said. "Not even to me. I can't just give her to you. She's picked someone else. You need to accept that."

The frantic head shake came again, and Leon squinted to read the boy's lips. *No! I love her!*

Leon sighed. "She doesn't love you, Justin."

*I don't care! I'll make her!*

Leon made a gesture of dismissal, not wanting to talk about this anymore. Justin had gone through a lot, but that hadn't won him any special rights. He was going to have to go home alone. Leon hoped he wouldn't become bitter. He suspected the boy would, though, and that he'd blame Leon and Ril. Justin would probably blame Lizzy as well, for daring to love someone else.

Leon crossed his arms. Justin's emotions aside, he couldn't coddle the boy much more. They were still in a very dangerous position, and he honestly didn't know if Tooie could make Eapha into a queen or even what would happen in the near future. He didn't know Eapha well or Tooie at all.

He glanced at them—the woman standing in the contained storm that was her lover—and then back at Justin. "I'm sorry, son, I truly am, but you're going to have to accept this. You have no other choice." When Justin started to shake his head again, Leon raised a hand. "No. Let it go."

He turned away, intending to return to the campfire where Xehm and Zalia were sitting, neither exile knowing what was happening. He hoped that what came next would mean a better life for them, and for all the people in this place. But after taking a few steps, he stopped and glanced back over his shoulder. "One other thing, Justin. Once you get your tongue back, don't give Ril any orders." He let his voice harden, reflecting the dangerous man he truly was, and was both satisfied and sad to see the boy flinch. "I'll be watching."

With that, he went to the campfire, leaving Justin shivering in the cold night air.

Eapha stood in Tooie's embrace, trying to reach out for him as Leon directed. She'd seen Tooie in this form before, whenever he entered or left the harem, but she'd never really had the chance to study him. Not that she could see much now in the darkness, just the lightning that sparkled inside him, changing color to form his eyes and fangs. He looked to be half mouth, but she didn't feel threatened at all, and she plunged her hands into the depths of him, feeling the energy tickle around her and the hair stand up on her arms.

"You're really beautiful," she told him, meaning it. His tendrils enwrapped her, creating a rushing feel like furry little mice wherever he touched. The ball lightning that was his eyes was fixed upon her.

She couldn't feel him, though. Leon had explained

that once the bond was formed, she would be able to feel whatever he projected. She didn't quite understand what that meant, but she'd seen how much Lizzy loved Ril and how deep their bond was. She wanted that closeness with Tooie, wanted it even more with the knowledge that she could use it to free him. She'd be able to free *everyone*, Leon said—which was hard to understand. There were thousands of sylphs; she couldn't imagine them all listening to her. Instead, she just focused on how such a change meant she could be with Tooie.

He shuddered around her, his lightning flashing. He'd stayed nearly as long as he could already, and she buried her arms in his energy again as though that would help detain him.

"Don't go," she whispered, knowing that his leeway to stay was diminishing rapidly. Another few minutes and he'd be on his way back to the harem, and she didn't know if he'd ever be able to return. She'd wait for him forever if she had to, though, right here. She leaned farther into him, his energy tickling all over her body, and she loved him, giving herself completely to that feeling.

Something deep inside of her shifted, suddenly, twisting like a key inside a lock. She gasped, and at that instant she could feel . . . *him*. Tooie was ecstatic, his love for her as strong as hers for him. Eapha started to cry, leaning into him until he surrounded her, and she felt him shudder with his overwhelming emotion. He loved her, loved her so much, and she felt his happiness as well as his dread at going back and the increasing pull to obey his orders and return to the harem. There was desperation there, and a command he couldn't resist for much longer.

Leon had told her what to do, and he'd impressed upon her the importance of doing it right. She felt that need now as Tooie started to withdraw, no matter how badly he wanted to stay.

"Two-hundred," she said clearly, calling him by the name that bound him rather than the nickname they both preferred. "I am your master, and I order you to stay here."

He shivered, and she felt his sudden joy as he fully wrapped himself around her again. She couldn't see anything other than darkness, but she felt truly safe.

"Two-hundred," she continued, remembering Leon's other instructions. "I order you to speak when you wish. To change shape whenever you wish, into any form. To ignore every command given to you by another, should you so wish." But this was the question. Tooie had hundreds of orders he had to obey, all given to him by a master who was preeminent over Eapha and reinforced by other masters he'd been told to obey. That master had only given him the commands once, however. Tooie had spent years obeying others, and Leon hoped that the abrupt command of another true master would break through, at least enough for him to accept a direct order.

Tooie shuddered and pulled back, his form shimmering. He changed then, not into the green-skinned creature of the harem or the ogre he became in the arena. He became a tall, deeply tanned, black-haired man, staring down at her in wonder as she gasped.

"Eapha," he said, and she began to cry again. His voice was deep and rich and so very beautiful.

"Oh, Tooie!" she wailed, throwing her arms around him. His body was warm and firm, solid but without any sort of scent. His arms came around her, though, and she didn't care about that. Lifting her head, she kissed him, remembering what else Leon had instructed her to do. This part would be easy.

She'd never kissed Tooie before. Actually, she'd never kissed anyone since she was brought to the harem as a virgin. It wasn't Tooie who'd first had her, nor even throughout her first year of captivity. He felt like her first, though, as she moved her mouth against his, pleasure and happiness sinking deep into her belly along with his love. He was a clumsy kisser, but his hands moved gently on her body and she had to pull back for a moment, panting.

"Wait—come on," she told him, leading him to the closest hut. It was empty, and she led him inside. There was no bed, but she didn't care. Even if Leon hadn't told her she needed to consummate her relationship with Tooie, she'd have wanted to do just that, so she stripped off her thin dress the moment they were inside.

"I love you," he told her. His eyes were so soft, his emotions at last content. He just stood there, basking in her love while reflecting his own back to her.

"Make love to me," she said in a whisper.

Tooie came to her, his arms wrapping around her as she reached down to strip off his breechcloth. His size pleasantly hadn't changed, and he hooked one hand under her leg, pulling her knee up and against his hip as he angled himself into her ready depths. Eapha cried out and encircled his neck with her arms, holding on and kissing him as he pushed himself into her, crushing her against him as he moved.

It felt so different from any other time they'd been together. She could feel how much he cherished her, how much he gloried at the sensation of being inside her. They both felt her pleasure, and his, and the bond between them magnified everything, increasing her pleasure until her back arched and still Tooie thrust into her, his attention focused on her and the pattern of her soul. That he took into himself, flooding his spirit with her and filling the part of him that should have been filled by a queen and couldn't be touched by any normal master, not even her. Not until this moment. Now she flowed into that gaping hole, her pattern filling it and binding him even more deeply, her essence becoming primary over everything else.

Tooie groaned in relief. At the same time, he projected Eapha's pattern, sending it out as far as he could. Everywhere, sylphs stopped where they were, shuddering no matter what their masters said to them, none of them moving as they felt that queenly pattern and took it into the empty core of themselves, exchanging their original hive pattern that had been lost and useless for so long, all of them reforming into a new community governed by a single woman.

Not that Eapha understood this. She was simply enjoying Tooie making love to her, his ecstasy and fulfillment. Their shared pleasure overwhelmed her, and she cried out as the peak hit, sending her tumbling into absolute bliss, her exultation matched to his own as he buried himself inside her and finished, shuddering.

He laid her down on the sand, stretching out beside and still within her as he stroked her cheek with gentle fingers. "My queen," he whispered, testing it out. "Oh, my queen."

"My king!" She smiled, cuddling against him.

Shocked cries sounded from outside the hut, and suddenly she knew that sylphs were gathering along the crumbling city wall, all kinds of sylphs drawn by her ascension. She smiled up at her lover. "I guess we better go and give some orders," she said, though she preferred to stay just where she was.

Tooie wore a beatific expression. He really had a beautiful mouth, she thought. "Whatever you want." They rose and collected their clothes, dressed, and headed outside.

The wall that separated Meridal city from the desert was

covered in sylphs—hundreds of them, all looking hungrily toward her as she stepped out of the hut. The nearby exiles all stared at Eapha fearfully, but she shared none of their misgivings. Nor did Leon, who moved hurriedly toward her. She understood now what he'd meant, and waited to see what he wanted her to do next. She was queen, she understood, but knew as well that Leon was the only one who truly comprehended what that meant. At least, she hoped he did.

He did. Leon gave her several suggestions that made her laugh, and at last she turned to her new people. Everything was going to be so much better now, provided she didn't screw up. She'd have to meet this Solie that Leon told her about. That would help her to understand how to be a truly good queen. For now, though, she'd have to be a vengeful one.

"I have orders," she told the gathered host, able to feel their unanimous exhilaration as well as the joy of the rest of the sylphs in the city. All of them were linked now through her and Tooie, all of them listening to what she would say.

Soon the men who thought themselves masters would know that they had slaves no more.

# Chapter Twenty-six

Ril released more than a hundred prisoners, both male and female, before the handlers tried to stop him again. The freed slaves were everywhere, trying to find their way out or even to liberate others. Frightened sylphs flickered all around, some trying to follow their feeders and others trying to stop them.

The battlers all followed Ril, instinct making them want to attack—either Ril or the men he opposed—but their orders forced them only to watch. There were over thirty now, swirling in a storm that he would have liked to join if he weren't crippled and if they were all of the same hive. They were amused by what he did, though, and envious. The other breeds of sylph were just terrified.

Exhausted and trembling, Ril made his way along a metal catwalk, headed in pursuit of Lizzy. Her terror had eased, and he felt how badly she wanted him with her. He didn't need Leon's orders to want that as well, and readied himself to kill whoever threatened. He was already covered in the blood of the people he'd cut his way through, and his eyes stared out of a black and red mask of gore that had dried to itchiness on his skin.

The men and women he'd freed milled about like frightened sheep, staring in shock and horror even as he opened their cages. A few of the men kept their heads, though, and at last these tried to lead some of the others out. Ril hoped they made it. He had no idea what sort of force might be waiting for them. Still, it was possible they would prevail through sheer force of numbers—at least until someone appeared who could command a battler to attack. Ril hoped to have Lizzy well clear of this place before that happened.

At the other end of the catwalk, a male handler brandished an axe, screamed, and charged, dodging the freed feeders desperately trying to get out of his way, a few even running back into their cages in fear. Ril snarled and waited, letting his assailant get well within striking range before lunging forward in attack. The man's axe blade swung down, gouging his side, but then Ril was upon him, his hand closing around the handler's face. With a grunt, Ril yanked the head around, breaking the neck. There was a crunching sound and the handler collapsed. Picking up the axe, Ril tossed it to the closest feeder. The man looked down at the weapon in shock.

"Take that and get out of here," Ril told him. The feeder grinned before running off into the throng.

Ril continued onward, tearing doors off every cell he passed. It was tiring to do so, but all of the feeders were on their feet now, shaking the bars and screaming silently. He didn't much care for their feelings, but he couldn't leave them, either—not understanding slavery as he did. He tore every door off its hinges and made his way out of the feeder pens. Lizzy was out here. He could feel her easily.

His path led to the central office for the slave pens. Battlers still followed Ril, a swirling cloud framing him in smoke and lightning. He walked to the closed door at the end of the passage, his body soaked in blood. The door was locked, but Ril didn't even bother to check. He just kicked it once he was close enough, and it flew off its hinges, taking half of its frame with it. Swordsmen waiting on the other side were struck and mowed down.

Ril entered the chamber, stepping over the downed

men and regarding his assembled foes. Lizzy was with them. She stared at him in shock, clearly processing his bloody state with growing horror. Handlers, both male and female, stood in front of her, and Rashala and Shalatar behind.

"Seven-oh-three!" Shalatar shouted. "Stop where you are immediately!"

Ril eyed him coldly. "That's not my name, and you're not my master." The bald man blanched, and though he could feel him as clearly as Lizzy, Ril didn't care. Thanks to Leon, Shalatar had no hold over him. "Let her go."

"No," Rashala called out. She had a grip on Lizzy's arms and was using her as a shield. Her brother stood frozen, still reeling from the shock of his battler's disobedience.

Remembering an old promise he'd made while he was still a bird—that someday he would kill his master—Ril raised a weary hand. He'd eventually come to think that promise was no longer needed. How wrong he'd been. He fired a very contained burst of energy that slammed into Shalatar's middle and exploded, blowing the slaver off his feet and out of his sandals. Blood sprayed everywhere, over both his sister and Lizzy, before the man hit the back wall and crumpled to the floor. Ril felt the pattern of him snap and vanish from his mind. It was satisfying.

"Shalatar!" Rashala screamed, staring at her brother's corpse.

Ril pointed his hand again, aware that it was trembling. He was on the very edge of exhaustion and drew upon Lizzy's energy to fuel himself. He couldn't absorb much, though—she was too far away. He didn't have enough energy to fight much longer, not even with her there. He ached with weariness, and his eyelids were growing heavy. But his anger kept him going. He growled, the sound echoing through the small chamber. The handlers flinched but didn't retreat. There was nowhere left for them to go. Only Lizzy stared at him without being afraid of him. Instead, she was afraid *for* him.

There were twelve handlers, both male and female, with the men carrying longer swords than the women. Ril hissed, trying to shift his arms back into multibladed swords, but he winced in pain and they refused to change shape. Sensing weakness, and like a flock of birds deciding at the same time to take wing, all of the handlers charged.

Snarling, Ril leaped forward to meet them before they could force him out of the room. If they managed to get him back in the hallway, they could hold him off until he exhausted all his energy. Slamming a fist into one man's face, he twisted sideways to avoid the sword thrust of another—which brought Ril in line with a third, whose blade struck deep into his side.

Lizzy screamed, and Ril brought his elbow around in a deadly arc. The handler's nose shattered, leaving the man howling and falling back. The sword pulled painfully out of him, and Ril gasped for breath as he dropped into a one-legged crouch, his other leg sweeping around to trip the handlers closest. Three of them fell, nearly landing on him, while a fourth managed to evade. Ril rolled to avoid his counterattack, smashing into a different group. They all tumbled or crashed into each other.

He was much slower than he'd been in the harem, much more fatigued and getting worse. He was still faster than a human, but only barely, and there were so many foes. Another sword cut deeply into his shoulder, and he grabbed the blade, ignoring the pain as he yanked it out of the woman's hands and smashed the hilt across several other handlers. As they howled, he took it in his undamaged hand and pushed himself to his feet.

He tried to remember Leon's lessons back on the ship, about fighting like a human. This wasn't about strength—which was good, as he had hardly any left. His swiftness was nearly gone as well, but speed was less important than accuracy. Staring at the remaining fighters, he focused on them, on their fear and concern, and on the emotions that would give them away. He had to let go of his own rage. It was too distracting.

He sensed when they were going to attack, when each man would strike. He moved just a bit faster, anticipating, and the first fell with his guts sliced open before Ril retreated toward the wall. Two who were on his sides came next, and Ril cut them both down. Lizzy was only twenty feet or so away, but she might as well have been on the other side of the ocean.

Rashala glared at him with real hatred and grief. "Kill him!" she shouted.

"No!" Lizzy begged. "Ril!"

Ril felt the handlers' fear and anger, a chaotic emotional soup. There were so *many* of them. And they were preparing to attack again. But then, over it all, he suddenly felt something new, as did every other nearby sylph. For a moment Ril didn't understand, but then he did. Somewhere, a queen was ascending, her pattern overlaying all of the sylphs in the city.

All the sylphs were silent, frozen in joy and excitement as they listened. They let it take them. Ril felt it sweep through him as well, but he had such a pattern already. He hadn't lost his connection with her after all. Even with Leon's control, Solie was still there in the depths of his soul, an unassailable reality that blocked this new queen even as she distracted him with her arrival.

A handler dove forward, and Ril heard Lizzy scream. Looking down, he saw a sword blade sticking out of his chest. The man, dark-haired and bearded, sneered and twisted the blade before yanking it back out. Ril choked in agony and dropped to his knees, overwhelmed at last by his injuries—and by the anger of the battlers, all of whom were suddenly free to protect their hive. A foreign and therefore enemy battler right in the center of their hatred and loathing, Ril fell over onto his side and passed out.

Lizzy screamed as she watched Ril collapse. She tried to throw herself forward, but Rashala had too strong a grip on her arm. "No! You can't do this!"

The woman yanked her back. "Finish Seven-oh-three," she ordered the black-bearded handler. "And kill this one as well."

Lizzy felt herself shoved suddenly forward and released, and she fell to her knees. She kept staring at Ril, oblivious. He wasn't dead—he'd be nothing but flecks of light if he were—but he was hurt. She tried to crawl to him, not processing what Rashala had said. She was stopped as a handler grabbed her by the hair, yanking her head up and bringing a dagger to her throat.

Four-seventeen had watched Ril's progress with tremendous glee, happily following the other battler as he released feeders and killed everyone that Four-seventeen himself had been wanting to kill. The rampaging sylph even let Four-seventeen's feeders go, but that didn't bother Four-seventeen. He could find them again if he needed them, and he was actually glad to see them escape. Their energy had always tasted poor, and even seconds of freedom improved its flavor.

As the slaves ran for the exit, Four-seventeen followed Ril with the rest of the battlers who were lucky enough to witness this spectacle. They were all equally excited, flowing around each other in a storm of companionship they normally didn't share, and he didn't even realize what was happening for the first few seconds of Eapha's ascension, thought that the pleasure flowing into him was just more happiness at seeing his enemies obliterated. When he did figure it out, he froze, his senses stretched as far as possible. A queen? An actual *queen*? He felt her pattern being broadcast and absorbed it eagerly, letting it fill the deep cracks inside that had been empty ever since he'd crossed the gate.

Around him, the other battlers did the same. All of the sylphs were frozen in ecstasy, all of them suddenly aware of each other and changing internally, bonding, forming a hive larger even than all but the greatest back home—a beautiful new hive that needed protecting.

Faintly came the orders, broadcast by the lead battler as directed by his mate: *You are held by no commands but the queen's. You can speak, you can change shape. You will only obey the queen. You can go anywhere, do anything. You are free.* Finally, the last order came, fulfilling a promise made to the man who'd shown the queen her destiny. *Save the girl Lizzy and the battler Ril. Bring them to us.*

Freedom! Beautiful freedom!

Four-seventeen glanced at Kiala—his Kiala, his beloved Kiala, who secretly called him Yahe. She was standing fearfully in a handler's grip only a few feet from Lizzy, who was about to have her throat cut.

He shifted shape and attacked. He didn't take his old, strange-legged, mouthless humanoid form, but instead he became human, assuming a man's shape he knew would please Kiala. Lunging for her, he slammed through the surrounding handlers. He didn't use his energy blast, not when his beloved was so close, but he cut through them just as surely and slaughtered the handler who was about to kill Lizzy.

Saving her was satisfying. He liked the blonde girl, and orders from the queen were absolute. Of course, without them he'd have killed the battler he'd been cheering on just a minute before. He could feel how alien Ril now was, a foreign battler in his newly created hive—an impossibility, but one the queen had ordered.

Yahe—for he'd never answer to Four-seventeen again— stopped before Kiala. She stared at the branded number on his chest, then up into his face as her eyes filled with tears. Her handler let go and backed away, but Yahe killed her anyway. Then he took Kiala into his arms. She was stiff against him for only a moment, then embraced him and started to cry.

Behind him, the other battlers attacked. Even one was enough to massacre everyone in the room, and there were twenty. The struggle was brief.

Lizzy crawled forward, sobbing. Around her, battle sylphs were murdering the remaining handlers. Squeezing her eyes shut, she grabbed Ril's body, but he was unconscious and his form only partly solid. Her hands sank deeply into him.

"Ril! Wake up, Ril. Please!"

The battlers had finished the handlers. The only one left was Rashala, her face ashen. She stood with her back pressed to the wall, staring at the sylphs who coalesced before her. Some took human shape, others became more monstrous. A few even retained the green, odd-legged form they'd been ordered to use in the harems, but all wore the numbers Rashala and others like her had carved into their mantles.

"Stand back!" she shouted. "I'm ordering you to stand

back!" Her voice was forceful, her words strong, but she was no queen. Perhaps she could have been, had circumstances been different. Instead the battlers fell on her, and Lizzy looked away as they took their vengeance.

"Lizzy," Ril whispered.

Her heart missing a beat, she glanced down. He was soaked in blood, and his hair was so tacky that it stuck out at odd angles, but Ril's eyes were clear and fixed on her like chips of glossy pale stone. He took a deep breath, and she suddenly felt her energy flowing into him in great drafts, just as she felt his form grow more solid.

"Are you all right?" she whispered.

"I will be." He drank a bit more and relaxed, letting his eyes close for a moment before he reopened them and reached up to lay a bloody hand on her cheek. She leaned into it. Her dress was soaked with gore, ruining the translucency she hated but also making her skin crawl.

"What's happened, Ril?"

He surveyed their surroundings and sighed—almost regretfully, she thought. "A queen has ascended," he told her. "All of the sylphs here belong to her hive." His mouth twisted. "Except me."

Her eyes widened. "They wouldn't attack you for that, would they?"

"I would," he admitted.

The battlers surrounded them, staring, and Lizzy held Ril to her tightly, glowering up at them in fear. "Don't you hurt him!" she cried.

"The queen has forbidden it," said a battler numbered 32. "She said we were to bring you both to her unharmed."

"Who's the queen?" Lizzy asked, only a little relieved.

"Eapha," Ril said wearily. "Thanks to your father."

"What? Eapha? How?"

He didn't reply.

The battlers surrounded them, lifting both her and Ril and carrying them outside. Lizzy saw the entrance to her prison as she was carried past it. The door had been ripped out, along with most of the frame. Those from the circle returned to the harem and their women there, and more than a few concubines joined the procession that made its way to the surface.

It was still night, but the sky was nearly as bright as day, lit by fire sylphs celebrating their freedom. Air sylphs darted everywhere, dancing madly, while fountains made of water sylphs and mountains formed by earth sylphs exulted similarly. Lizzy had never seen so many sylphs! The sky was full of them, as were the streets, and there were people everywhere, too, staring in amazement or terror.

Battlers flew and roared among the crowds, bellowing from time to time and sweeping down to attack. People were everywhere, many of them freed slaves, others looking so poor that the feeders seemed rich by comparison. Anyone who'd ever been cruel to a sylph seemed to be paying for it now, and Lizzy could see the arena crumbling in the distance, the battlers tearing it apart, while earth sylphs swallowed the remains into the ground. Overhead, carried by hundreds of other battlers, the floating island she'd spotted on her first day here was moving toward the ocean, picking up speed as it went. The battlers carried the massive island out over deep water and dropped it, and Lizzy could nearly hear the screams as it fell. She jerked her head away, not wanting to see more.

Lizzy was encased in the mantle of one battler, Ril borne by another. Frightened, she sat inside the sylph who carried her, arms around her drawn-up knees, hoping they weren't about to cast her into the ocean as well. Instead she was carried toward the desert, stopping where a broken-down old wall marked the edge of the city. She was set upon the sand there, and found herself facing a small collection of ragged huts and campfires. Thousands of sylphs surrounded the huts, shimmering in the darkness.

Three huge battlers guarded the way. Lizzy was urged forward, though, Ril limping at her side. He was exhausted, but he looked at the battlers calmly and held her hand. Even so, she could tell he was afraid. He didn't belong here. He never had, but now he was in real danger.

People surrounded the nearest campfire, most of them eyeing the battlers in terror. Several disengaged, one running ahead of the others, and Lizzy recognized Eapha immediately, though she wore a man's linen shirt that fell to her knees. The brunette embraced her, crying and uncaring of all the blood, and Lizzy hugged her back, sharing the woman's joy and amazement.

"You're alive!" Eapha drew back and indicated the blood with concern. "Are you hurt? Healer!" she shouted, and a sylph in the shape of a beautiful woman stepped out of the crowd. She considered Lizzy critically, then Ril.

"Can you heal him?" Lizzy asked. The sylph consulted Eapha, who nodded, and so the healer laid her hand upon him. Ril sighed audibly, and Lizzy had to giggle at the sound of his relief.

"Lizzy . . ."

She turned at the voice, and Eapha stepped back with a smile. Her father stood only a few feet away, his fists clenched at his sides.

Lizzy's eyes filled with tears. "Daddy!" she screamed, and threw herself into his arms. He hugged her tightly, nearly breaking her ribs, and wept against her shoulder.

Ril stepped close, his eyes clearer now that he was healed but still somewhat nervous. Leon reached for him, pulling him into the embrace as well. For a long moment, Lizzy wanted nothing more.

# Chapter Twenty-seven

The hug seemed to go on forever, followed by exhaustion and finally slumber, in a building filled with silk and marble that was more opulent than anything she'd ever imagined. Lizzy now sat on the side of the bed, stroking Ril's hair as he continued to sleep, his face relaxed as he lay on his side, turned toward her. He'd drained himself beyond comprehension, nearly dying, all for her. Lizzy smiled as she ran her hand along his hair again, glad that he was safe.

Well, almost safe. She glared out the window at the shadow of yet another passing battler. The building was surrounded by them, and she had no doubt that they wanted very much to tear Ril to bits. If Eapha's orders hadn't held them back, Lizzy would have shielded him with her body.

She sighed, resting her hand against Ril's cheek. He turned slightly toward it, mumbling something unintelligible, and she wondered both what he was dreaming and if he was walking through someone else's dream. There wasn't any reason to assume so, she supposed, given that she and her father were both awake.

A faint knock sounded on the door, and it opened to admit her father. He moved quietly, seeing Ril was still asleep, and shut the door behind him without a sound.

Lizzy was suddenly nervous. Before, they'd all just been so hysterically happy to be reunited. She still couldn't imagine exactly what her father and Ril had gone through to save her, and gratitude made it tough for her to swallow. At the same time, she felt a wholly new shyness. When she left home, she'd been a naive little girl. Today, she was the confirmed lover of his battle sylph. She didn't know how her father felt about that. But if he disapproved, she wouldn't agree to stay away from Ril—she knew *that* much.

Her father approached, his newly gifted sandals making a soft sound upon the marble floor. He wasn't dressed in travel-stained clothes anymore, just as she had given up her translucent dress. Thin, expensive linen garbed them both, and she noted briefly that her father looked good in white. A moment later, she felt shy again and hated it because she loved him so much.

Leon gazed at his daughter and then at Ril. When Lizzy gulped audibly, he shot her what could have been an amused look and crooked his finger, moving to the window where they wouldn't disturb Ril. Feeling like a little girl about to be punished for eating too many sweets, she followed.

He stopped at the window, motioning to the clouds of battlers drifting angrily outside. "We'll have to leave as soon as we can," he said. "They're getting restless."

"Yes," Lizzy agreed. It would probably have been okay if Ril were any other kind of sylph, but as it was, he wanted to fight as much as they did.

"Yes," her father repeated with a sigh. He looked tired. While she was resting with Ril, he'd spent his time training Eapha in the myriad things she'd have to know as queen. From the look in his eyes, he hadn't been as successful as he'd hoped, though no one could expect much in a day. Lizzy just hoped that her friend had the innate character necessary to be a good leader. Certain qualities would never have been encouraged in a slave.

Another battler floated by, glaring. Leon and Lizzy watched him pass and then regarded each other.

"Daddy," Lizzy said. "I . . . Ril and I—"

He raised a hand. "Stop." He closed his eyes tightly for a second, clearly emotional, and Lizzy heard Ril stir behind her. Her father opened his eyes again, his expression sardonic. "I've had time to think. I didn't expect you to end up with Ril. If I'd thought of it, I probably would have ordered him never to touch you."

Lizzy's eyes widened, her heart pounding.

Leon sighed. "A father's prerogative . . . and it would have been wrong." His hand cupped her cheek with as much love as she'd earlier cupped Ril's. "I love you, and I love Ril. I always have, though it took a while longer to realize it with him, miserable bird that he was." Despite herself, Lizzy smiled. She didn't speak, though, afraid to ruin her father's confession.

"I loved you while you were still in your mother's womb," he continued, "from the moment she told me you were coming. And I know that Ril loves you. Even with everything I did to him, how I overwhelmed him with my orders, he still loved you despite it. I couldn't even touch that in him. So how can I think to stand in your way?" He smiled a little sadly before adding, "Just don't expect me to get in the way of your mother's reaction."

Lizzy giggled, feeling better even as she tried not to think what her mother would say. "Daddy, I really do love him."

"I know you do. I always knew that." He gripped her shoulder. "And you'll be good for him. Just never let yourself forget the power you have. He can't disobey even an unthinking order."

"I know," she whispered, though she wondered what he was getting at. She'd never abuse Ril. Lunging forward, she took her father in her arms. He hugged her back so tightly that her ribs creaked, and it felt wonderful. Her father had come for her, just as she'd believed.

"Hey." At the sound, Lizzy pulled back enough to see Ril sitting up in bed, his hair tousled. He rubbed his eyes with the edge of his palm and eyed them both. "What's going on?"

Lizzy's father didn't answer. His grip tightened on her for a moment and he said, "I have some work to do with Eapha still, until the ship is ready to take us home. But there's something more important I have to do first. Remember what I told you about the power you have."

"What . . . ?" Lizzy started, but her father pulled away and walked toward Ril, who was eyeing him dubiously. She was left by the window, cast in the shadow of another passing battler.

Ril gazed up at his master. He'd always been aware of the man, at first reluctantly, and later as a source of familiarity and comfort. Now that Leon had taken absolute control, giving him his freedom by removing it, Ril looked at him with complete surrender and it felt good. He didn't have to think or worry; Leon would take care of everything. He only had to fight when necessary, to protect both his master and his master's daughter Lizzy. Though he loved Lizzy for herself, too, didn't he?

Leon reached down, holding Ril's chin with a grip that was firm but not harsh. Those blue eyes drilled into him, grabbing his will far more tightly and holding it.

"Ril," Leon said. "I am your master. Say it."

"You are my master," Ril repeated with absolute conviction.

"I own you. You are mine, completely."

"I am yours." So good. It felt so good.

Leon breathed a little sigh—one so soft that even standing only a few feet away, Lizzy wouldn't hear. Ril felt a bit of selfish regret in him, a sorrow about having to share, and a determination to do so anyway, all gone in a heartbeat. "Ril, I release you."

Ril tried to jerk away. Normally strong enough to shatter stone, his movements now held no strength. He wanted to scream. No! He didn't want to go back to the way he'd been, vulnerable to the orders of anyone who'd imprinted him with their pattern. But Leon and Lizzy knew that of course. They knew how much at risk he was. They'd protect him from everyone else. And yet . . . wouldn't it be better to stay in this safe place where he could be a simple tool? That's all he was. That's all he was supposed to be, and it was easier, so very much easier. But even as something deep inside screamed yes, something else shrieked no, for there was no room for Lizzy. There was no room for himself.

Leon was relentless. "I give you your freedom, Ril," he said. Lizzy stepped forward, opening her mouth to say something, but he waved her into silence. "I give you the right to make your own choices."

The bonds wound through the pattern of Ril's soul loosened. They didn't go away completely. After all, Leon was still his master and always would be. Ril would always obey him, just as he would every master. To break that kind of bond entirely would destroy him, since it would destroy the most fundamental part of him, the very thing which made him a battler. Still, he felt his freedom return, and as it did, he welcomed it.

Exhaling loudly, he closed his eyes and he felt himself return. He hadn't realized how far he'd truly traveled away from himself, and he felt gratitude that Leon had. And despite all of the man's own feelings and need for Ril in his life, Leon had chosen to give him back control. It was a sacrifice.

*Thanks*, he sent.

The man smiled and let go of his chin, stepping to one side so that Lizzy could hurry up and make sure that he was all right. Not that it was necessary. He was. Ril was as happy as he'd ever been.

Eapha was staying in a mansion that had once belonged to a lesser noble not ranked highly enough to live on the emperor's floating island. His lack of status hadn't saved him, though. The entire male upper class of Meridal was gone—Leon didn't know where and he thought it best not to inquire. He didn't know either where the former lady of the house had gone, but she certainly wasn't protesting Eapha's presence.

He found the new queen in a gallery with huge windows that allowed in light and the view of a garden that would never have survived the desert without sylphs. Art that reached from the floor to the vaulted ceiling decorated the walls, scenes from a way of life now utterly destroyed. It was up to this woman to decide what kind of society would be the replacement.

Eapha was surrounded by her friends, the ten women who'd been part of the secret circle in the harem. All were dressed in sumptuous if thin fabrics and sat on pillows they'd gathered onto the floor despite the furniture. They were giggling madly. Leon watched them gossip and laugh, and he shook his head. These women were having a social gathering, not planning the future of a kingdom. A battler stood in the background, but Leon ignored him.

Upon seeing his arrival, Eapha rose and joined him, though the women immediately chorused for her not to go. She managed to shake them off nonetheless, and she paced beside him toward a quieter end of the gallery. The battler followed at a distance, his dislike of any man near his queen palpable.

"How are you doing?" Leon asked.

Eapha shrugged, trying to look casual. She bit her bottom lip, though, betraying her nervousness. Leon didn't blame her.

"I'm okay," she admitted. "I'm still trying to wrap my head around all of this. It's so . . . overwhelming."

"It will be," he agreed. "And it'll get worse. You have a lot to do."

She gazed at him desperately, her hands clasped together against her belly. The other women called out, shouting for her to come back and join the card game they were starting. Eapha eyed them, so Leon started to speak.

One last time, he told her what a leader needed to do—what to watch for, what to expect, how one couldn't expect everything, and how to handle uncertainty. He told her about economics, about warfare, about politics and choosing advisors. He told her about the weaknesses of humans and of sylphs. He told her about their strengths as well. She stared at him throughout, listening, and the sun passed overhead. The room never grew too hot, kept cool by air sylphs who hadn't given up their duties despite gaining their freedom.

It was a lot to throw at her, more than he'd given to Solie in a year when she first started to learn, but there was no other choice. Eapha had to become more than she'd ever dreamed. For the sake of her country, he hoped she succeeded.

The air ship that would take them home, a wind schooner named *Racing Dawn*, was ready to leave two days later. It had been a long wait, but the trip back would be faster than the journey here—and in most ways they were all quite ready to go. Even if they'd wanted to stay, the tension among Meridal's battlers forbade it. To have a strange battler in the confines of their hive, no matter how trusted by their queen, was too much of a strain on battler instinct. Both Eapha's hive and Ril himself felt the stress.

Leon regretted not having more time. He might have stayed for months, to help Eapha get her feet under her, to train her the way he had Solie, but he couldn't let his family leave without him. Not after everything he'd done to get them back. Besides, he'd promised Betha they would all return together. What he hadn't told Eapha, she would have to learn on her own. Still, with five thousand sylphs to do the work and over seven hundred battlers to protect her, he was pretty sure she'd survive any beginner's mistakes.

"I never imagined any of this happening," the ex-concubine confided to Lizzy as they stood on top of one of the tallest buildings in the city. Their air ship was moored there, manned by one of the oldest and strongest of Meridal's sylphs. Her newly chosen master traveled with her, the most sympathetic of the feeders she'd once fed from, his tongue restored by a healer.

Most of the sylphs had discovered that their feeders made much better masters than the men who'd first bound them. The majority of those masters had died, anyway, when the floating island plunged into the ocean. Where it was dropped, the waters had been deep enough that the entire thing sank, taking the majority of the miserable nobility with it and leaving a huge gap in power that Eapha now filled whether she wanted to or not.

"I don't think Solie did either," Lizzy admitted. She wore a silken dress, the material flowing softly around her body but thankfully not translucent. "She figured it out eventually."

Eapha sighed and looked over her shoulder at Tooie. Like most battlers, he'd assumed a truly attractive form, though Lizzy still preferred Ril. Tooie smiled at them both, giving them room even as he stood guard. He still didn't talk much, but that was normal for a sylph. Humans were much more chatty.

"Hopefully I'll be so lucky," the new queen said.

"You will," Lizzy assured her.

Her father thought there was fighting yet to come, probably against the other kingdoms in this part of the world. But surely he'd told Eapha that. Certainly he would have told Tooie. Either way, he'd made sure they would all stay in touch. The few days they waited for *Racing Dawn*, while Eapha was taking lessons and arranging the ship for their return, he'd spent a large amount of time drafting an alliance between Meridal and Sylph Valley. Lizzy hadn't seen the details, and she doubted Eapha fully understood what she'd signed, but Lizzy was sure the new queen hadn't been cheated. Even if Leon Petrule were the type, the fifty-three battlers of Sylph Valley would have no chance against Eapha's seven hundred, and he was smart enough to know they'd figure out any double-dealings.

But her father wasn't the type. In the time when he wasn't working on treaties or training Eapha, Leon had reacquainted himself with both Lizzy and Ril, learning to just enjoy their company with them as a couple. She had the best father in the whole world.

She smiled at her friend, the woman who'd taken her in and saved her life without any reason except kindness.

She couldn't think of anyone who more deserved to be queen. "You'll be fine," she assured Eapha again. "Father says we'll send someone from the Valley to show you how we do things. It'll all work out."

"I hope so," Eapha said. Leaning forward, she hugged Lizzy and smiled. "Take care of yourself."

"And you." Lizzy let her go and eyed Tooie. "Take care of her, you." He nodded.

Turning, Lizzy walked toward the air ship. Ril was standing by the gangplank, and he joined her as she ascended onto *Racing Dawn*'s smooth deck, headed toward where her father was talking with the captain. Justin stood only a few feet away. He hadn't spoken to her since his tongue was restored, but Lizzy knew he was always watching.

She stepped closer to Ril, who set a hand on her shoulder, his gaze never leaving the boy. Justin turned away, heading belowdecks. Lizzy felt bad for him in some ways, but she couldn't help remembering him leaving her on the dock. No matter what Justin had done or how he'd tried to make up for it, she'd made her choice and she had no regrets.

"My hero," she said, smiling up at her battler.

He raised an eyebrow. "If you say so." His lips twitched in a smile, though.

Her father finished his conversation and faced them. "We're ready to go. Have you said your good-byes?" When Lizzy nodded, he went down to cover a few last points with Eapha. She was certain he would never be entirely satisfied.

Within twenty minutes, though, the air ship was lifting off and racing north toward home. Lizzy stood with her father and her battler in the bow, leaning against her father's side while she watched the ocean pass beneath her. The sylph pushed the ship very fast, and her long, golden hair blew behind her as they went.

"Thank you for coming after me," she said. She didn't think she could ever say it enough.

Her father put an arm around her. "Anytime, sweetheart. Your mother will be glad to see you back."

"I miss her, too," Lizzy said. Her mother likely wasn't going to approve of her being with Ril, but she'd have to deal with it. Lizzy had some apologies to make, though. Her mother had been right in not wanting her to go to Para Dubh. Lizzy didn't regret going, not now, but she did regret the pain her mother must have felt. She owed her for that.

After a moment she glanced at Ril, who was staring at the horizon ahead, his face as inscrutable as always, but his emotions more joyous than ever. Her father could feel that as well, and Lizzy looked up to see him smiling.

Behind them, Meridal vanished in the distance, swallowed by the sea. There were endless waves ahead, but home would appear out of them eventually. And Lizzy could wait. She'd left unsure of who she was and what she wanted. Now she was with the two men she loved most in the world, both of whom loved her more than life itself. She didn't have any questions anymore. She knew exactly where she belonged.

# Gayle Ann Williams

## NO SAFE HARBOR

With her badass rain boots, her faithful dog, and the ability to predict the monster tsunamis that have reduced the US to a series of islands, Kathryn O'Malley isn't afraid of much. Cut off from all society, she takes to the airwaves as Tsunami Blue, hoping to save something of humanity as the world around her crumbles. But Blue should be afraid—because her message reaches the wrong ears.

Now she's the target of ruthless pirates known as Runners who want to use her special talents for their own profiteering—as soon as they can find her. Blue's only shot at survival lies with the naked stranger who washes up on her rocky beach. A man who might just be working for Runners himself. Torn between suspicion and attraction, the two will have to navigate a surging tide of danger and deceit if they hope to stay alive.

ISBN 13: 978-0-505-52821-6

# ELISABETH NAUGHTON

*THERON—Dark haired, duty bound and deceptively deadly. He's the leader of the Argonauts, an elite group of guardians that defends the immortal realm from threats of the Underworld.*

From the moment he walked into the club, Casey knew this guy was different. Men like that just didn't exist in real life—silky shoulder-length hair, chest impossibly broad, and a predatory manner that just screamed dark and dangerous. He was looking for something. Her.

She was the one. She had the mark. Casey had to die so his kind could live, and it was Theron's duty to bring her in. But even as a 200-year-old descendent of Hercules, he wasn't strong enough to resist the pull in her fathomless eyes, to tear himself away from the heat of her body.

As war with the Underworld nears, someone will have to make the ultimate sacrifice.

# MARKED

ISBN 13: 978-0-505-52822-3

# INTERACT WITH DORCHESTER ONLINE!

Want to learn more about your favorite books and authors?
Want to talk with other readers that like to read the same books as you?
Want to see up-to-the-minute Dorchester news?

## VISIT DORCHESTER AT:
DorchesterPub.com
Twitter.com/DorchesterPub
Facebook.com (Search Pages)

## DISCUSS DORCHESTER'S NOVELS AT:
Dorchester Forums at DorchesterPub.com
GoodReads.com
LibraryThing.com
Myspace.com/books
Shelfari.com
WeRead.com

# LEANNA RENEE HIEBER

With radiant, snow-white skin and hair, Percy Parker was a beacon for Fate. True love had found her, in the tempestuous form of Professor Alexi Rychman. But her mythic destiny was not complete. Accompanying the ghosts with which she alone could converse, new and terrifying omens loomed. A war was coming, a desperate ploy of a spectral host. Victorian London would be overrun.

Yet, Percy kept faith. Within the mighty bastion of Athens Academy, alongside The Guard whose magic shielded mortals from the agents of the Underworld, she counted herself among friends. Wreathed in hallowed fire, they would stand together, no matter what dreams—or nightmares—might come.

# *The Darkly Luminous Fight for Persephone Parker*

ISBN 13: 978-0-8439-6297-0

---

# ☐ **YES!**

Sign me up for the Love Spell Book Club and send my FREE BOOKS! If I choose to stay in the club, I will pay only $8.50* each month, a savings of $6.48!

NAME: _____

ADDRESS: _____

TELEPHONE: _____

EMAIL: _____

☐ I want to pay by credit card.

☐ **VISA**　　　☐ **MasterCard**　　　☐ **DISCOVER**

ACCOUNT #: _____

EXPIRATION DATE: _____

SIGNATURE: _____

Mail this page along with $2.00 shipping and handling to:
**Love Spell Book Club**
**PO Box 6640**
**Wayne, PA 19087**
Or fax (must include credit card information) to:
**610-995-9274**
You can also sign up online at **www.dorchesterpub.com**.

*Plus $2.00 for shipping. Offer open to residents of the U.S. and Canada only. Canadian residents please call 1-800-481-9191 for pricing information. If under 18, a parent or guardian must sign. Terms, prices and conditions subject to change. Subscription subject to acceptance. Dorchester Publishing reserves the right to reject any order or cancel any subscription.